Balancing Entropy

Written by: M. H. Cali   Art by: Laurie Ya

Content warning:

While what you'll discover within these pages is a cozy, steamy, mysterious and suspenseful tale full of feels, friends and family, we would like to issue a content warning out of an abundance of caution. Our diverse cast have equally layered lives and so you will stumble across some sexual content as well as mentions of gambling addiction, and drug use that could trigger certain audiences.

Additional Notes:

M.H. Cali would like to add the precision that no AI software was used at any step of the production of her books. The whole writing process from start to finish comes 100% from her own brain. Reading something by her means that you read something untouched by AI—even the proofreading and editing are conducted by real human beings. Cover art and interior illustrations (when applicable) of her novels also apply the same rule. They are made by real human artists.

In this case, Laurie drew traditionally on A4 90g/m^2 Fabriano art boards, using a mixed technique primarily consisting of graphite pencils. She loves to feel the grain of the paper and the pencils smudge on her hands when drawing, so this was her preferred way to create every single piece inside this book. Cover art was also realized traditionally by her with acrylics on Arches 300gsm paper.

To no one & everyone.
To every human who believes in creativity, inclusivity, and diversity
for creating a better world.
To those who think words are powerful, and art has to be nurtured.
To all those who impact our journeys through the universe.
May all find their anchor, and keep their wings.

Prologue

Any spot on Earth close enough to water is where Raven Collins thrives. She revels in the duality of the sea.

In its strength and calmness. Its soothing power and its endless provocations.

She loves to lose herself in it by watching the waves crash on the shore as much as she adores defying it by surfing its waves.

In that context, picking a travel destination after her graduation from *Harriers Law School* was done with the roll of a dice during one celebratory evening with her friends. The prestigious college and its vicinity had been the primary destination she visited the last few years. Too many spots on this planet were screaming at her to travel to. She let fate decide.

Turns out, ending up in Mykonos was one of the best decisions of her life so far.

The past week on this heavenly Greek island has been nothing but incredible.

She currently wouldn't want to be anywhere else than pressed against that limestone wall with Lucas' fingers combing through her ash brown hair as they make out. His short scruff is deliciously vitalizing on her lips, and his touch on her bare skin underneath her loose t-shirt is highly arousing.

The reverence with which he is tentatively dipping his fingertips under the hem of her denim shorts makes her arch into him, moaning against his tongue.

He smiles into the kiss as she rakes her digits into his messy medium length black locks. The second she sneaks her other hand beneath his shirt to scratch his abs gently, he groans.

She can hazily distinguish the soft moonlight mixing with the iridescent glow of the city lights behind her closed eyelids. The atmosphere is serene, and tainted with a definite sense of contentment.

She's always propelled into a peaceful sanctuary each time she finds herself with Lucas.

Meeting the recently graduated investment banker was unexpected, but the moments they shared in the last seven days have been magical. They hit it off immediately at that bar counter, and have been inseparable ever since.

Their shared thirst for justice in the financial world and beyond, their similar sense of humor, and the constant natural bantering made for an instant connection.

It led to lust-filled nights and sensual mornings. To pillow talk, and sleeping in out of elated exhaustion. Exploring the island with him, indulging in some training sessions, and spending hours roaming the streets have been spectacular experiences.

Through easy conversations and spontaneous laughs she had to come to the conclusion that they are a great pairing in more ways than one. If they had crossed paths back home, maybe something more could have stemmed from it.

They both agreed on not getting attached, and there's a couple of ground rules they came up with to not complicate things.

But if she's being honest, he might've left an imprint on her psyche already. It might be tricky to go back to—

He leans back, his emerald eyes peering into her aquamarine irises. "You want to go back inside?"

She hooks her index and middle fingers into the back pocket of his capris. "Do you?"

"Nah." He lets his thumb caress her jawline, smirking. "I like it here with you."

"Same." She admires the slight dimple at the corner of his mouth. "Although this nightclub is one of the best we've been at."

"Mhmm." He seemingly remembers their previous discussion from inside the venue. "You know, thinking about the future, I think my best friend Sa—"

She shushes him by placing a finger on his lips. "We said nothing too personal."

"Right." He kisses the pad of her index softly. "We are living in the moment, and chatting about general life topics."

"No strings attached." She pulled him closer. "And whatever happens here, stays here."

From the beginning, this has been their golden rule.

She has no idea what his last name is, nor does he know hers. She learned that he comes from Chicago, and he is aware she grew up in San Diego, but every serious subject related to any family member or friends has to be avoided. The one time something slipped up, she swiftly reoriented the exchange.

They are here to have fun. Not to build a meaningful relationship that will follow them State-side. That much was clear from the start between them.

"Suits me perfectly." He hums. "I still want to mention that my best friend has a brilliant life in front of her, and I hope to be able to achieve great things, too."

Both of them are at the commencement of their professional journeys. It's a constant underlying preoccupation of their discussions. They often circle back to their expectations and beliefs for the road ahead. How they would love to strive by staying true to their core principles.

The theme invited itself on the dancefloor as they were grinding to the upbeat remixes of the house DJ a few minutes ago. Their imminent return to reality is making those concerns creep into their discourse more and more lately.

"I'm convinced that you will." She glides her palm down his chest. "You're nothing but determined. You'll accomplish anything you set your mind to."

He smiles coyly. "You're so fearless that I don't see you failing either."

"Thank you for the vote of confidence." She toys with his unfastened top button. "Let's hope I manage turning into the lawyer I strive to be."

He traces the industrial piercing across the cartilage of her ear. "I'll be rooting for you from wherever I'll be."

She leans into his touch. "Me, too." She angles her head to kiss his wrist. "One thing is for sure: this break from our daily lives has been memorable."

He skims his nose along hers. "I can't believe we have to part ways tomorrow."

She sighs. "I can't believe our flights leave on the same day."

He smiles teasingly. "Maybe it's fate."

"You mean the fact that out of all the places in the world, we serendipitously met here?"

"Yeah." He inhales deeply. "On this phenomenal piece of paradise which is believed to be home to the giants slayed by Hercules."

She snorts. "I recall you being impressed at the explanation of the origins of the big rocks in the landscape here when the bartender told it to a customer the other day."

"How could I not? I like myths and legends. I didn't choose to come to Mykonos out of the blue."

She looks at him amusedly. "I thought it was for the parties, the beach, and the historical landscape."

He chuckles. "That, too."

She paints aimless patterns along his clavicle. "No matter what, coming here was a great escape from reality."

"Some people do tend to become other versions of themselves when they are away from home." He presses their foreheads together while dropping his tone to a murmur. "I don't do that. What you saw is all me."

She doesn't miss a beat. "Likewise."

"We could've been a phenomenal match, Rae."

A breath catches in her throat. His voice is laced with sincerity. It sends her mind spinning.

He dangerously feels as if he could fit in her routine. His personality is magnificently complex, and strangely both fits with and complements her own. She hasn't had that sentiment toward anyone in her life up to this point.

But she's only in her early twenties. She has her whole life in front of her. Her future is actively being written. Whatever happened between them here was definitely a fling.

A beautifully intense, and delightfully intoxicating fling.

She has to remember their pledge. This is insignificant.

She relishes in the cool seaside breeze and Lucas' applying entrancing pressure on her lower back vertebrae for a moment.

Existence is full of fleeting instants and inconsequential events while some others open doors to infinite possibilities. She willingly classified this hookup in the former category as soon as they first kissed.

They'll go back to their occupations, to their social circles, and to constructing their destinies. This ephemeral liaison will become a distant memory. It was solely a bridge between phases of their respective purposes.

This is what counts.

This is what she has to keep in mind.

However, she still can't shake the thought that they could've been legendary together totally out of her brain, so she offers him the closest truth she can think of.

"Maybe in another life, Luke," she whispers against his lips.

ONE

What's the Word?

N ew York.

The city that never sleeps.

The truth is that this town can either make or break anyone. It has a way to get under one's skin and overwhelm all senses.

It can bring out the best or the worst out of a person.

It's because of this duality that Lucas Blake feels at home here. This is where he thrives.

This is also why he accepted to work at *B.A. New Empire Group* directly when he got out of one of the most prestigious universities in the country; *Liberty Cove Business School*. He wanted to make a name for himself in a place that doesn't forgive failure.

If he was to succeed on Wall Street, nothing would be off limits moving forward.

He had first worked for the investment bank at ground level as part of an internship program through college. When they offered him a job after his graduation, they did so while praising his work ethics and risk assessment skills for their clients.

This opportunity undoubtedly gave him a head start compared to other young bankers in the field.

Within a little more than a decade, he made it to his current position: Managing Director of Mergers and Acquisitions. He might put in long hours, and be on call 24/7, he is now making a nice high six-figures salary, and works with powerful individuals.

All of it also means that he is wealthy enough to manage his life exactly as he wants to nowadays.

Which is exactly what he has always wanted.

Things can't get better than this.

That's what he keeps telling himself when everything gets too overwhelming for his own good, like this week has been.

As he navigates busy sidewalks along West 16th Street toward *The Nightly Disco Room* on this cool end of September evening, he sets on rolling up the sleeves of his gray shirt, and making sure it's tucked into his black jeans correctly.

He hums absentmindedly as the song playing through his earphones shifts from a blues melody to some folk.

He made sure his scruff was trimmed to perfection, and his quiff haircut gelled neatly before leaving his penthouse.

He remembers a time where he didn't bother putting any products in his black locks. That was before NYC.

Before he made it into the highest spheres of finance.

When his emerald gaze stared back at him in the oversized mirror of his smokey gray, black and white marble bathroom as he put the finishing touches on his look, he couldn't stop himself from curving a corner of his mouth upward.

He was pleased with the result.

As he looked closer, he couldn't help but notice the slight specks of gray that started appearing in his beard a couple months ago. He blames the incessant strain of his job for them. The stress is most than probably making him age faster by the second.

But by all standards, he still felt like he was looking good.

He nurtures his body by working out regularly and his mind by reading on all sorts of subjects to challenge himself. He likes to understand concepts that would otherwise be foreign to him while dealing with the finance world in his day-to-day job.

It's a point of pride for him to dig deeper and comprehend the world around him as much as he can.

When he was younger, he would spend complete evenings playing guitar and drawing to calm his nerves. He used to love the freedom that putting his thoughts on paper, and letting his imagination run loose, was granting him in those moments.

Back in university, his best friend Sabrina and her sister Brooke would tell him all about their latest findings from their respective studies in medicine and astrophysics, and he would create whole galaxies on paper trying to make sense of the cosmos and its potential inhabitants.

They would redo the world ten times over through those discussions.

However, he's also always been good at math and finances. He easily sees the world through complex equations. To him, numbers can help ground things in reality.

It's a concrete way to make sense of society, and everything that the system entails.

During those years at *Liberty Cove*, he also indulged in weekly poker games with his buddies. He always loved the challenges the game brought, and the constant opportunities to turn a well calculated risk into a win. It was an opportunity to display some of his strengths, and even refine his skills.

Unlike his best friend Felipe who thrive on adrenaline, intuition, and wanting to double the stakes more often than not when playing, to Lucas the selling factor of poker is that luck can be dissociated from logical thinking. He can look at his cards, come up with a plan, let his rationale shine, and take an informed decision to control the outcome as much as he can.

That's what he appreciates.

This pragmatic side of himself he constantly nurtures is also why he chose his investment banking career path: to build a life for himself.

It doesn't mean that he doesn't regret the days where he would let his originality shine like during those nights with his friends.

The last time he truly contented his daydreaming propensity was with a gorgeous brunette in Mykonos right after he graduated, and—

He shook his head.

All of it is in the past.

These days, the farthest he goes to quench his thirst for creativity is a small library in the West Village, and his guitar has not been used since he moved into his building eight years ago.

It's totally fine.

His path is fulfilling, he's the epitome of success, and lots of people would love to be in his shoes.

Not wanting to go too far down memory lane, he hastily tidied the counter near the rectangle vessel sink, padded into his bedroom to put on his high-top designer vegan leather sneakers, and rapidly strode out of his apartment.

Now crossing 9th Avenue, he's certain that he will be able to have an enjoyable evening with his friends, and potentially go home with someone.

He had his fair share of meaningless encounters as well as some relationships which lasted somewhat longer in the last decade. If he's being totally honest, he loves having no strings attached. It makes things easier.

Now approaching his mid-thirties, he might want to start thinking about settling down like his younger sister Lena keeps suggesting to him, but he greatly enjoys his life the way it is.

I only want to see you a little more carefree. You know, like you used to be. It seems like your work is the only thing that matters now, she keeps telling him.

I like what I'm doing. I'm happy. I don't need anyone to share it with, he always answers unfalteringly. *Plus, I'm always there for you guys. It's because of my work that I was able to buy mom a house, and that she's able to finally keep her head out of the water. I say that's a win.*

I'm just saying that you used to be way more fun, his sister usually concludes.

Even if he is only able to visit his family in Chicago on special occasions—and if time allows for it—he wants nothing but the very best for them.

He always does everything in his power to support the two most important women in his life.

Even from a distance.

Having been raised exclusively by his mother—who struggled to make ends meet after his father disappeared from them when Lucas was a teenager—convinced the man he became to never get attached.

Lucas vowed to himself a long time ago that he would only make an exception in the case where he would be absolutely sure to be able to commit fully to his partner with his entire being.

He doesn't want to recreate his father's pattern. No one has to live through such hardships if it can be avoided.

Which also means that Lucas kept a sure emotional distance with every one of his lovers.

He's way too busy to make space in his schedule for someone anyway.

His most recent long-term relationship that lasted more than a couple of weeks dates back from university. Stephanie and him were good together while it lasted. They had fun. Sadly, summer internships-induced distance got the best of them.

What Lucas is grateful for is that they were both adults about it, and broke up on good terms.

That was even if Stephanie had slept with someone else, and—

He furrows his eyebrows as he gets lost in thought while walking past a group of drunk people clamoring.

Once in a while—often when he's stressed and exhausted—it feels like his brain is bringing him flashes of all the directions he could've taken through his life so far.

But he chose the one he is currently on, and he's having trouble imagining anything else as a viable option.

He inhales deeply.

He reminds himself that he might've had a draining week closing deals, and meeting with potential future high-end patrons, that doesn't mean that he can't indulge in a night out to release some pressure.

He certainly needs it to keep his sanity in check.

Blowing off some steam with his buddies is exactly what he requires to balance things out right now.

He picks up the pace to get to his destination faster.

One of the sure advantages to having his office in the heart of the financial district, and his penthouse in Chelsea, is that he's constantly at the very center of all activities no matter the hour of the day or night.

The city is always bustling with frenzied energy. Everyone is set on living exactly the way they want to.

That's yet another benefit of being in NYC. There's no shortage of willing individuals who are totally fine with the concept of entertaining a no-strings attached romance.

Lucas certainly identifies himself as one of them, and tonight hopefully won't be any different.

He has to take his mind off his business for the span of a few hours. He'll get back to it all tomorrow.

As soon as he sees the neon sign of the nightclub in the distance, he pockets his earphones.

He walks assuredly past the people waiting in line on the loading dock to be admitted inside. As he approaches the entrance, he smiles and nods at the bouncer who reciprocates instantly.

The second the man opens the door for him, Lucas can't stop himself from smirking at the protests echoing behind him.

This club is very exclusive. No more than a hundred people are allowed inside at once. Getting in is clearly no easy feat.

It took him a couple of years to get this exclusive access.

He is now proud of all the special treatments he benefits from around town thanks to himself as well as his connections.

Whether it's in sought after renowned bars, at award-winning restaurants, for getting tickets at otherwise sold-out concerts or for getting access to the best medical care, Lucas gets treated like the successful and rich individual he is.

Thanks to his status, he is granted some of society's higher-end privileges.

It was dizzying at first. The power he holds. Now he is definitely set on surfing that wave until the end of his career.

He feels like he earned it.

He steadily carved his place in the highest spheres of finance with his hard work since he finished his studies.

He managed to let his natural charisma and wit shine to pique his potential clients' curiosity, and then individually gained their trust by working relentlessly to accommodate all their needs and demands.

Years later, he's still building one of the most flourishing elite rosters of any investment bank in America.

There's no door that closes to Lucas Blake these days. It's a token of how he played his cards right on a professional level.

He wears that achievement like the highest badge of honor.

Electronic music envelops him the moment he steps into the main room.

The beat delightfully thumps in his ears and resonates throughout his skeleton.

He smiles.

He adores this place. The luxurious decor that is paired with the neon spotlights is effortlessly making the whole venue cozy and chic at once.

He makes a beeline for the wooden bar counter and liquor wall to order an imported beer. As the barmaid fills in his request, he lets his eyes travel around the room.

The leather couches scattered around the floor are amongst the most comfortable in the city. He had countless makeout sessions while lounging in them.

He wastes no time spotting his friend Felipe sitting in a corner.

The Brazilian American man is wearing a navy blue three piece suit. Lucas is certain that his wife picked the clear blue shirt complementing the ensemble. She enjoys curating his analyst friend's wardrobe. Some would even say it's a true miracle that Emma Brown and her sure fashion sense fell for a man lacking one altogether.

But love is blind they say.

Lucas laughs internally at the reflection.

Back in university, he never would've thought that Felipe Soares and he could end up in the same city working for competing firms, but here they are.

His friend has an interesting future ahead of him, Lucas is sure of it.

As an Investment Banking Analyst at *Isla Miller & Co.*, Felipe has generated multiple brilliant pitch books, and provided quality market data research in the last while. If all goes well, he should now be on his way to get a promotion to Associate.

Lucas wishes he gets it soon. His analyst friend deserves it.

Felipe is also one of the few close friends Lucas has. He can count those on one hand, and he cherishes those friendships with all his heart.

Lucas greatly appreciates being able to call his college buddy at any time of day to discuss all types of matters.

From *Liberty Cove* to here, they evolved together. They've seen each other go through big wins and harsh failures.

Their bond stuck through everything.

For better or worse.

As soon as the bartender puts his drink on the counter, Lucas pays for it, grabs it and makes his way through the crowd to join Felipe.

He slides onto the seat next to his friend. "Hey, Flip."

The nickname never fails to make Lucas smile interiorly every time he uses it.

Felipe is known to become irrational in a split second. One could say that he is regularly 'flipping out' over a variety of subjects.

In this context, the occasion was too good to pass up.

Lucas felt that it was his duty to use his friend's name to make a nod to that particular personality trait of his.

Years later, it still stands.

Felipe turns to face him. "What's up, man? You were running late." He gestures at the other side of the room to point to a tall black man with a royale beard wearing a white shirt and midnight blue suit pants. The man seems to be engaged in a deep conversation with a blonde woman. "Kyan is already flirting as you can see, and Mark left with some random guy over an hour ago."

Their other friends are very vocal about loving to hook up on Thursday nights when they all go out together.

The fact that they are now both well on their way to do so doesn't come as a surprise to Lucas.

"The opposite would've been startling." He snorts. "I'm sorry I'm late. I was having dinner with a prospective new client, and it lasted longer than planned. I need to make sure I'm there for him whenever he has questions. He has a prosperous import/export company, and getting his business would be amazing for us." He brings his glass to his lips. "Or so everyone at the office keeps saying."

"Am I discerning some kind of doubt from you there?"

"You know I always trust my gut when signing new clients and deals alike." He clenches his jaw slightly. "Data is one thing, but if I have a bad vibe out of someone or a situation it's often a hard pass for me."

"But some of your clients are in another league, buddy." His friend frowns. "You're playing with fire with them sometimes."

"I know what I'm doing." The managing director takes a sip of his beer. "If I don't take risks, there's no payoff. I still need to trust the people first."

Flip locks eyes with him. "But some of the ambiguities you take advantage of are—"

Lucas cuts him off. "I don't want to talk about it. We're here to unwind and have fun."

"Fair enough." Felipe holds his hands up in fake surrender, a playful smile dancing on his lips. "I just wish it never comes back to bite you in the ass."

He stays unflinching. "I'm always careful enough for it not to."

"Bigger guys than you have been caught." His friend reaches for his martini on the table. "I'm glad you seem relaxed enough even after having dealt with this shit for some clients."

"What do you expect me to do?" Lucas shrugs, laughing lightly. "Freak out and become anxious beyond measure at the prospect the authorities could dig deeper into my transactions someday? You know me better than that. Every deal I close is legit on paper. It respects regulations that are in place. Even if some can be debatable, I always find loopholes to help my clients get what they want."

"True. And no one asked you something out of the ordinary lately? You know, those important people you work with sometimes like to..." Lucas confirms as Felipe trails off. He continues. "Good. Let's hope it stays that way."

Lucas raises his glass in a toast. "Cheers to that."

As they drink some more, songs by well-known DJs keep being played.

The managing director scans the room, nonchalantly engaging in small talk with his friend. "Em bought you this shirt, right?"

"She did." Flip exhales loudly. "She is often making allusions to how I'm lacking ambition lately. That I should be more proud of who I am to be able to get that damn promotion. Since I'm being tested on my ability to get bigger clients for the firm right now, she somehow thinks that choosing my clothes will help me look more serious to achieve it."

"You're doing great." Lucas snaps his attention back to Felipe. "Why is she—"

The analyst interjects. "I'm not as successful as others." He smiles shyly. "Like you for example." He scratches the hair at the back of his head, becoming very solemn. "You have no strings attached so you always put in the hours, and manage your career exactly like you wanted to. I've been with Em since university. I've always tried to balance my personal and professional lives." He half-smiles. "We've now been talking about starting a family, and I know she would love for me to have more free time, but also more money. Her dream has always been to be able to afford a house in the Hamptons at some point. She'd love to see the kids play in a big yard and have some actual space."

Lucas holds his glass in his lap. "Is that something you'd like, too?"

"Emma is the love of my life, and I've always wanted kids with her." Felipe breathes in. "Of course we share the same goals. I'd love to be able to offer her what she wants, you know."

"To me the Hamptons are overrated, but I understand the appeal." The managing director smiles playfully. "You guys could maybe find a cozy spot upstate or even start over somewhere else?"

"We would both like to stay in the New York vicinity if possible." His friend presses his lips into a thin line. "But I hear you. The appeal of just moving to another spot is strong sometimes. There is no shortage of investment banking jobs throughout the country, after all."

"They're just not all as glamorous as in big cities such as NYC. I get it." Lucas takes a gulp, raising an eyebrow. "Emma always dreamed of living the big life. That hasn't changed, right?"

Felipe shakes his head. "And it now feels like I can't give it to her." He inhales steadily. "I hate it."

"I wish her interior design company would've taken off sooner. She's incredibly talented." He scratches the stubble on his cheek. "I still get plenty of compliments on the decor she made for my office. Newcomers and clients absolutely love it. I'm glad the company also hired her to relook the whole floor."

Ever since Emma redid the decoration to bathe the space in a sure mid-century inspired vibe, it feels more homely.

It's still modern, but now has heart.

The place is warm and inviting while screaming of professionalism.

It helps a lot for someone like him who spends the vast majority of his time at his workplace.

Felipe smiles coyly. "That means a lot. I'll let her know." He seems to remember something. "It's been a while since we had dinner. Would you like to come over on Sunday? We could have a BBQ. I installed a new one on my balcony, and—"

Lucas interrupts him. "I'm traveling to Sabrina's and Brooke's on Sunday. It's been forever since I haven't spent time in Boston. I would be willing to go to your place any time next week though." He flashes Flip a comforting smile. "I can make room in my schedule for one of my best buds. Also, to circle back on the topic, if you ever need money you know you can ask me, right? It'll be my pleasure to help any way I can."

"I appreciate it." Felipe suddenly lightens up, downing the rest of his drink. "Enough of that depressing subject. I'm here to have some fun with you before you hit it off with a beautiful woman and end up bringing her home or going to her place."

"Who says that it's what I'll do?" Lucas teases.

"Isn't that your usual MO at every guy's night out?" The analyst snorts. "I'm living vicariously through you guys."

"You just admitted that Emma is the love of your life, bud." The managing director shakes his head vigorously. "You don't even look at anyone else, and you're perfectly happy being in a relationship." He takes another sip of his beer, smirking. "Quite like I'm enjoying not being in one."

"Touché. It's still fun to see you all go. You three are very entertaining. You all have different techniques to flirt. It's fascinating. For example, it took Mark no more than fifteen minutes to convince the man he was talking to to leave with him." He shifts his stare in the direction of where Kyan was not long ago. He realizes that their friend is nowhere to be found anymore. "And now it seems like Yanou is also gone." His friend laughs lightly. "But I'll slide into bed next to my wife later, and I won't be self-conscious about snoring or not looking my best. We know each other by heart at this point. We accept every flaw."

"How sweet. That's real life goals right there." Lucas smiles amusedly as he joins his friend in looking around the room once more. "I think the fact that Mark is a personal trainer that looks like he's been carved by Gods helps him get people's attention at first glance, and Yanou is one smooth talker. He has an effortless way to make anyone feel relaxed. No wonder women fall into his arms after three sentences."

"You're not too bad yourself, Lucas." Flip smiles knowingly, his eyes lingering on a redhead staring at the managing director. "I say you don't even have to do anything to get attention. You apparently exude enough sex appeal just by sitting."

Lucas follows Felipe's gaze.

The woman waves at him subtly while smiling brightly.

Her sequin black cocktail dress is sparkling like a million diamonds under the vibrant lighting of the dancefloor, mirroring the luminosity of her mossy green eyes to perfection.

She's certainly pretty.

She even seems to be utterly confident and lively.

All things he appreciates in a lover.

But something feels off.

Lucas smiles politely before averting his stare.

Felipe automatically gapes at him. "Really? You won't go talk to her?"

"Nope." He looks at his friend. "Don't get me wrong, she's beautiful and looks to be of wonderful company. I'm just not feeling it."

Flip searches his eyes for a beat. He ends up smiling eloquently. "Oh, I know this look on you."

Lucas furrows his eyebrows. "Which look?"

The analyst sits back comfortably. "The one you harbor every time your mind goes back to that woman you met in Greece ages ago, hoping to find her in the crowd someday. The one you still claim is the best you've ever had."

Lucas opens his mouth to retort, but no sound comes out.

He takes a sip of his beer instead, basking in the steady tempo of the music.

He could lie, say it isn't true, and dismiss the whole thing. The problem is that his friend and he both know better.

Sometimes some people leave an indelible imprint on the mind. One that can't be shaken off no matter how much time has passed.

Raven definitely succeeded in doing so to him.

Unlike any other of his lovers through the years, she lives rent free in his mind if he concentrates enough on her. This encounter dates back nearly a decade now. The fact that she's the only one who left such a mark on his psyche is bewildering.

Nevertheless, every time Lucas is feeling too tired and more vulnerable, he can't shake off the feeling of Raven's touch on his skin.

Of her lips roaming everywhere on him, and the sight of her brushing her fingers through her wavy ash brown hair as she rode him.

Of the way her body flawlessly molded into his, and of her taste on his tongue.

They spent countless hours in bed and on beaches exploring each centimeter of flesh off of each other. By the end of his vacation, her slender frame and perfect curves had no more secrets for him.

They spent days living their best lives, danced the nights away in nightclubs, and fucked each other senseless every chance they got.

He sometimes wishes he could dive back into her peaceful turquoise gaze as she comes apart.

That he could hear her moan 'Luke' laced within a curse once more as she would clench purposely around his ministrations.

No one ever called him like that before her. No one ever did since either.

He has a hunch no one else ever will. He's not even sure he'd want anyone to anyway.

Her smooth voice still resounds like the most soothing melody in his psyche.

But that's not nearly all this is.

To this day, her digits dexterously combing through his hair are unmatched. She had an effortless way of making him relax and purr as she massaged his scalp gently.

She would do it purposely during sex, idly after, intensely as they made out or peacefully whenever they were cuddling.

Every single time was pure magic.

One of the best parts of that short-lived thing between them was that when he was holding her close, it felt like she belonged in his arms and nowhere else.

For the span of one week of his life, she felt like salvation.

But it was another era.

They were both young and just out of university. She was set on becoming a big-shot lawyer and he—

Felipe's steady tone brings him back to the present. "You're thinking about her, huh?"

He decides to turn the tables a little. "What if I am?"

His friend tilts his head in questioning. "What was her name again?"

Lucas sighs. "Raven."

"Well, she clearly made quite an impression on you." The analyst puts his martini on the side table. "Why did you never try to track her down?"

"We were carefree." He can't help the melancholy from painting his features. "We both agreed it was a vacation fling. We never shared our contact information, and I never asked for her last name."

"She was from around here, no?"

"From San Diego." Lucas smiles dreamily. "She was a true California girl. Got her law degree from a world-renowned university based on the west coast: *Harriers*."

"You could look for lawyers named Raven in the area."

"And what would I tell her?" Lucas chuckles, taking his best fake business-like voice. "Hi. Remember me? We had sex during one week in Mykonos about eleven years ago. I thought I would reach out since sometimes my brain has this weird way of bringing you back into my thoughts when I'm exhausted."

Felipe bursts out laughing. "I admit you would sound like a creep. You think she's still in SoCal though?"

"I hope she is." He becomes reflective. "She loved it there from what she told me. She adores the coast, the ocean and the seaside breeze."

His friend sounds cheerful. "That's something you both had in common, then."

He hums inattentively. "A lot of people love the ocean."

Lucas can suddenly vividly recall how Raven told him all about her love of surfing in the middle of the night once.

He was gloriously naked in bed shortly after round three, the white bamboo sheets covering him from the waist down as he was laying on his stomach.

She had put on his old vintage t-shirt to go fetch some water. When she returned, she put the glass on the bedside table, climbed back onto the mattress, and stretched along his body slowly.

He was feeling delightfully wrecked. Feeling her caress him and lay soft kisses across his shoulder blades as she was drowsily telling him about her hometown made his heart swell in his chest.

It was so blissful that he had trouble formulating any coherent sentences. So he set on listening.

From her soft voice to her mouth reverently defining his muscle ridges and valleys as she talked, life couldn't get any better than that.

All his senses were focussed on her and only her.

He even remembers thinking that this was probably what Heaven feels like if such a realm exists.

Are you okay? she asked after a while.

He probably had stayed silent a little too long. He needed to rectify the situation.

Yeah. He curved a corner of his mouth upward, draping his arm around her and pulling her closer as he rolled a little more onto his side. *You feel too good for words.*

You know, you're not too bad yourself. She brushed her nose behind his ear to whisper, *I've never experienced such powerful orgasms.* She sucked on his earlobe gently before nuzzling into his neck. *Anyway, as I was saying, if you ever come to San Diego I—*

He cut her off. He couldn't stop himself from a quip while bending his right arm underneath his head resting on the pillow. *If I come to San Diego does it mean that I could come with you, too?*

Obviously. She smiled into his skin, absentmindedly tracing his tattoo on the inside of his right forearm with her fingertips. *One doesn't go without the other.*

She used to love tracing the outline of the ink every time they were close and it was visible to her. Be it at dinner tables, cuddling on the beach or in bed.

Although the one time she asked about the deep significance of it, he didn't feel like sharing it completely. He brushed off the question by telling her that it was a way for him to never lose sight of who he was, and who he was striving to be.

Truth is, it's much more than that.

To him, the intricate design of his tattoo goes from the sun to the waves, the sky to the sea, to the roots he never felt he got, and the ones he wants to remember. All of it being directed by an arrow pointing down as an eternal reminder that it stands for the path he'll make for himself.

The future he had yet to forge.

He briefly debated telling her all of it. To open his heart a little more and allow her in as he was feeling her featherlight touch painting it soothingly.

But in that moment, he chose to beam at her approval of his innuendo instead. *I'm glad to hear.*

As if I would deny myself amazing sex. She snuggled up to him. *But I was also going to offer you private surfing lessons. The ocean is one of my favorite things on Earth. I can't get enough of the duality it can offer. One second it can be completely serene, and the next it could tear you down to pieces if you're not careful.*

Mmm. I wouldn't need the lessons. He wanted to feel more of her. He grabbed her hip to pull her to him. *I know how to surf.*

Aren't you full of surprises, she murmured while flying her fingers through his hair. *How's that?*

My mother is Lebanese. He closed his eyes under her touch. *When I was young, my sister and I used to spend part of our summers visiting our mom's family.* He sneaked his hand under her t-shirt to trace her spine with his index and middle fingers leisurely. *I learned how to surf at a very young age because of it. I also adore the ocean. It brings me peace.*

From as long as he can remember, surfing has been one of his preferred ways to manage the ups and downs of life.

Standing on a surfboard is where he feels tranquil.

Where things make sense.

There's a meditative metaphor to him in riding the waves as they refract. When they change directions as they pass from deep to shallow water, unleashing their raw power that one has to tame if they want to reach the shore.

He adores how the waves are rendered silent by the coastline.

It's as if they achieve the perfect quiet convergence where they can finally be one and the same with the littoral after having been unbridled in the wild.

Lucas finds peace in such patterns while the waves find solace on the shore where they conquered chaos.

In that context, he always thought it was quite fitting that he likes becoming one with the elements.

Raven smiled brightly. *That's wonderful.* She pressed herself to his front. *You're still going to Lebanon often?*

Not so much. He opened his eyes to bore into hers. *When my dad left, things became more complicated. I haven't been to Lebanon or traveled outside of the USA in years.* He rested his palm flat on the small of her back. *This is actually the first time I've traveled in a long while.*

I'm sorry, Lucas. She involuntarily arched into him. *Is your father Lebanese, too?*

No. He clenched his jaw. *He's American.*

Assessing his expression, she seemingly picked up on the fact that it was a loaded topic.

She scratched her nails in the short hair at the nape of his neck. *You don't like talking about him, huh?* He hummed his approbation. She smiled tenderly, sliding one of her legs between his. *Let's make you forget that we ever mentioned any of it then,* she breathed out.

The moment she captured his bottom lip, he set on kissing her lazily.

A split second later as her tongue was tangling with his, she had successfully obliterated everything that wasn't *them* from his mind.

All his doubts about the possible flaws in his reasoning of becoming a better man than his father, and every uncertainty about where his future would lead him flew out the window.

She had a way to make him feel as if everything would be okay.

That he could overcome anything.

That the weight of the world wasn't—

The bright voice of Felipe cuts through his recollection. "Yeah, lots of people do love the ocean. It's just that in moments like this, it feels like you let 'the one' get away."

"I'm honestly not even sure such a person exists for me." Lucas clears his throat. "And it's totally fine, I don't need nor want to—"

He trails off, sensing his phone buzzing in his pocket. He fishes it out, frowning at the caller ID.

At this hour, something important must have happened for his—

He quickly concentrates on managing the situation. "It's my assistant." He gets up, placing his unfinished beer on a table. "I'm sorry, I really have to take this."

As his friend nods, Lucas strides toward the exit while picking up the call.

"Hey." He swiftly dodges an inebriated dancer. "What's up?"

"I didn't know what to do, boss, so I called you." The young man's voice is shaky. "I'm sorry if it's a bad time. I was panicking." He has trouble catching his breath. "It was all too much, and—"

Lucas cuts him off in an attempt to calm him. "Woah woah woah. Breathe." He inhales deeply himself as if to give an example. "One thing at a time, Paul." He reaches the door and steps outside of the club. "What is going on?"

His assistant breathes in soundly. "I came by the office to make sure everything was tidy and ready for the presentation later this morning."

"That's good." He walks down the sidewalk. "I appreciate it, thank you."

The comment seems to have relaxed Paul a little. "But then I entered your office and..." His assistant pauses briefly to gather his thoughts. "It has been ransacked."

Lucas makes a face.

His office is usually locked, and only a handful of people have the key.

He also never leaves any sensitive document in there, and makes sure to take home his laptop at the end of each day.

Even if his computer has the best firewalls and software protection he could have had installed on it, he doesn't take any chances by leaving it laying around at his workplace.

Too much confidential information is stored on the device. In the wrong hands, it could become dangerous both for him as well as his clients.

He furrows his eyebrows, stopping to lean against a wall "What do you mean? Someone went through my stuff?"

"Mhmm." His assistant swallows audibly. "The door had been broken and..." His voice starts trembling once again. "I'm really sorry, Mister Blake. I didn't know how to handle the situation and—"

Lucas decides to be firm, but reassuring as he cuts the employee off again. "Whatever it is, I'm sure we can manage. What have you done?"

"So far, I only took some photos." Paul's voice is quiet. "I'll send them to you."

"Perfect."

Lucas removes his phone from his ear to monitor incoming messages. He rapidly gets a notification, and opens the associated images.

He blinks in disbelief at the absolute mess he sees staring back at him as he scrolls through pictures.

Papers are dispersed around everywhere on the floor.

All the decorative items are either plainly broken or have been knocked over.

The frames on his walls were removed probably to check for potential hidden safes.

His desk as well as his file cabinets drawers have been forced and their whole content spread on top disorderly.

Fuck.

Someone was clearly looking for something.

Maybe whoever did this even knows about how he sometimes threads a real fine line between legal and illicit in his dealings.

As a general rule, when something is too risky, Lucas much prefers to stay legitimate and find a workaround for the sake of everyone involved whenever possible.

No one wants to get caught, after all.

But he could cross said line on a daily basis, and in a heartbeat, given the type of requests he sometimes gets from a couple of his clients.

He's certain that there's no other explanation.

One of them now clearly wants leverage to maybe force him to bend to their will.

He suddenly feels dizzy.

He put his whole soul into his job.

He can't let all his hard work crumble down.

What choice does he truly have?

And what were they looking for anyway?

Whatever it could've been, did they manage to find it?

He's careful about privacy, but maybe he—

He shakes his head.

Maybe it's a one time thing, and whoever did this won't—

He hears Paul calling out to him distantly.

He can't deal with his assistant right now. "Clean the mess as best as you can, please. I'll call you back," he murmurs into the speaker before hanging up.

He has to think of his next move.

Is he even set on taking this seriously?

If so, he definitely can't call the cops. It would be bad for business. He doesn't need any unwarranted attention at this stage.

The spotlight has to stay as far away from him as possible.

He would have to deal with this silently.

The doors from the nightclub open and close repeatedly letting the upbeat tempo of the music leak through.

He checks the time on his screen.

1AM.

He throws his head back, breathing in.

He could probably call it a night, go home alone, and let a good night's sleep take care of sorting through his thoughts.

This approach never really helped him when his psyche is reeling like it is currently doing though.

Or he could go back inside, chat with Felipe and hook up with someone.

The latter would certainly offer some semblance of normalcy that he desperately craves at the moment.

Yes.

That's exactly what he needs.

He pockets his phone, padding toward the entrance of *The Nightly Disco Room*.

As he picks up the pace, he convinces himself that this is a good plan.

He has to take his mind off of things for a minute, and partying has always been a successful coping mechanism for him in the past.

Reality will catch up with him soon enough one way or another.

He'll deal with it whenever it does.

Two

Brooklyn Antics

"**D**o you have a comb or hairbrush I could use?" The deep voice of a tall muscular man resounds in the modern monochrome bedroom as he taps the screen of his phone to press play on the music app.

"Yes," Raven's steady tone echoes from the en-suite bathroom. "Come over here, I'll give you one."

"Thanks." He fixes the golden cufflinks on his white shirt before adjusting his belt buckle in front of his black suit pants. "I'm not used to staying the night. I have no idea where anything is around here."

"That's because it's our whole arrangement, Will, remember?" She looks at her reflection in the mirror, humming in approval at her choice of clothes consisting of a scoop neck loose black t-shirt with a pair of washed indigo jeans. "No feelings. Just sex."

He walks toward her. "I quite liked waking up next to you." He stops next to her in front of the semi-recessed-sink. "I wouldn't mind doing it more often."

She half-smiles, opening a drawer to give him a wooden comb. "We'll see."

As Raven sets on applying her copper colored eyeliner, William places his brown curls into his signature side-part medium fade haircut.

"Brooklyn is an underrated neighborhood." He scratches his egg-shaped beard slightly. "I like the view you have from here."

She hums absentmindedly.

From her condominium in Brooklyn Heights, she can see the East River and both bridges leading to Manhattan Island on a clear day.

It's certainly a big selling point.

Although, what made her love this space at first glance was the open-floor plan with multiple windows letting the light from either the sun or the city in at every hour of the day or night.

One of the best parts of the overall design is the light wood flooring allowing the luminescence to travel everywhere in the space, which she greatly appreciates.

There's also definitely no denying that the brick wall with in-wall fireplace and bookcase delimiting the main living area also played a big role in her wanting to own the apartment.

She decorated her office and bedroom to take full advantage of the strengths of the architecture, blending a detached modern vibe with a more cozy and enveloping feeling.

The only minor drawback is the kitchen.

It is functional with its cream marble countertops and matching lacquered cabinets, but is a little smaller than what she would've liked.

She could've gone for something bigger.

She has the means to, after all. Her career has been on a roll these past few years.

But she always refused to buy a property that screams of opulence. She especially didn't want one anywhere in Manhattan.

She left California nearly a decade ago because of a professional opportunity that she didn't want to let pass with one of her best friends, but the noisy energy of New York City never truly felt like home.

She misses the coast, the cliffs, and the seaside breeze.

The orange and pink sunsets bathing the waves in a colorful glow, and the sky in a thousand warm hues.

On most days she'd like nothing more than to dip her toes into the sand, letting the immensity of the ocean staring back at her.

Maybe visiting her friends and family soon could—

She shakes her head to focus.

Brooklyn's creativity and diversity is the closest she can feel to home at the moment.

It's vibrant, but quiet enough to dissociate it beautifully from the island on the other side.

Plus, she would argue to anyone that the best pizza in the state can be found on Front Street just a couple of blocks away.

She smiles as she tucks away her makeup to then messily pick up her wavy ash brown hair in an ivory hair clip.

William looks at her intently, putting the finishing touches to his hairdo. "Listen, I understand that you didn't want to talk about your latest case, but if you ever change your mind, I—"

She cuts him off instantly. "It's fine. There's really nothing to say."

He creases his eyebrows. "I know we never really share personal stuff, but it's been more than a year since we're casually seeing each other, and—"

She interjects once more. "If what we have doesn't work for you anymore, you're free to go and do whatever you please. I'm not keeping you here."

"All I'm saying is that we both have demanding jobs. Being a lawyer is challenging. With the type of clients you have, it's even worse for you than for me." He puts the comb back on the counter, turning to face her. "You weren't feeling well yesterday, and you called me. Out of all the people you could've messaged, it happened to be me. Maybe we ought to try to see the sign there if there is any."

"There is none. I just wanted to empty my mind. You're good for doing that with how great you are in bed." She saunters past him to go back into her bedroom. "It was a booty call. You're on my speed dial, you know that, you do the same with me."

"I do," he confirms, frowning as he turns around to follow her movements. "But it seemed more profound this time around."

She grabs a white blazer from the top of the ottoman at the foot of her queen-sized light gray upholstered bed.

She puts it on, gazing at William. "Well, it wasn't."

An entrancing melody leaking from his phone's speakers fills her ears. The lyrics envelop her while Will seems set on waiting as long as needed for her to say something more.

She has no intention to be the one who breaks the silent staring contest. Her resolve won't falter.

He's not her boyfriend.

He's a great and kind man, but he means nothing to her besides good sex.

He clearly doesn't have to know about the dumpster fire that her life has become in the last forty-eight hours.

She breathes in, rolling the hem of the sleeves of her jacket once so the white on black polka dot inside pattern is visible.

Her work has always been punishing.

Working at a Wall Street law firm can be a dream come true given that some of the most prestigious firms in the world are based there, but it can also slowly eat at one's sanity.

It all comes down to long hours, and unforgiving clients.

To shady business practices, and loopholes to be found.

Sometimes, attorney-client privilege sucks.

She's never been blind. She knew she was slowly losing sight of the ideals she once held dear with each new trial she was pleading for in court.

When she chose to specialize in criminal law, she wasn't expecting to one day feel like she was selling her literal soul to the Devil.

Maybe she was young and naive, but she thought she could make a difference by advocating for good causes and rightful individuals.

However, the more time went on, the more she steadily noticed the flaws and corruption of the system.

Her latest case unquestionably ended up being the last straw.

She couldn't take it anymore.

She realized she couldn't keep doing that her whole life if she wanted to thrive. If she wants a chance at being what she always aspired to be when she became a lawyer.

In her practice, she's seen her fair share of scumbags, but as she was listening to witnesses' testimonies in court on Thursday afternoon, she sensed that she was close to being way past any redemption if she continued down this path.

Right before her eyes, she got compelling testimonies of whole lives being destroyed by her client.

What started out as a banking fraud trial quickly took a turn for the worse when the prosecutor decided to give a more humane dimension to the whole lawsuit.

She had her doubts about her client's scheme, but seeing it all laid out in front of her eyes showed her how much of a true monster the man she was supposed to vouch for was.

She couldn't have that.

She's not even thirty-three years old for fuck's sake. She can't waste her life defending assholes.

Her moral compass is more important than any paycheck. Or so she decided on the spur of the moment.

So she quit.

She finished her day, made sure her second counsel could handle the rest of the trial by himself, validated the move to her boss who was fuming at her departure, handed in her letter of resignation in the middle of one of the biggest trials the town has ever seen, packed her stuff, and didn't look back.

Which means that she doesn't even have a job anymore, and will probably be blacklisted from most big name firms in the country as soon as the news spreads.

She slept for the better part of yesterday, but decided to go out with her friend Jun to blow off some steam in the evening.

It was Friday, after all.

Better have some fun while her life isn't a complete nightmare yet.

In the wee hours of the morning, after hours of dancing, she decided to call it a night.

The problem that arose was that as she was walking back to her apartment, a song came out through her earphones, bringing back everything to the forefront.

She knew she needed to calm her disgust toward society, and the whirlwind in her mind.

Only one person lately has been able to offer that to her without asking for anything in return.

The same person who always makes it simple and easy because he loathes commitment.

So she called—

Will clears his throat. "If you say so. I'll respect your wishes. Just know that I'm here if you ever want to take whatever there is between us to another stage."

"You're looking for a relationship now?"

"We could be friends with benefits." He pads toward her. "You know, the type who actually discuss stuff, and open up to each other." He slides his hands around her waist. "Always with the spectacular sex though. I couldn't go without it now," he whispers, bending down to kiss her softly.

She leans back to peer into his eyes. The relaxed expression he's harboring is convincing.

She could do way worse than William if she was to ever open her heart to someone again.

Some scars run deep, but maybe she could give it a shot.

She glides her hands along his forearms. "Be careful what you wish for."

He beams. "I'm ready for whatever you throw at me, Rae."

She presses her lips into a thin line.

Rae.

It's not the first time William uses that nickname for her. There's nothing bad in how he pronounces it or anything...

It somehow still sounds wrong every time.

If she hadn't heard it first by a completely different man years ago while she was on vacation in Greece, it would maybe even sound right coming out of her current partner's mouth.

But she can't help it. It doesn't.

That handsome stranger she slept with for a week was—

She barely audibly sighs.

Lucas. That man in Mykonos was named Lucas.

And the way her name fell from his lips as he climaxed was spectacular.

The way he murmured it sultrily into her skin in the darkest of the night is eternally etched in her mind.

His laugh could illuminate the whole milky way, and his genuineness only had his tenderness as equal.

She remembers spending nights in his arms, tucked away from the whole world in a cocoon they had built for themselves out of sheer willpower.

They both wanted to treat this time as a getaway to bask into before they would catch up with the rest of their lives.

For the course of seven days, the future could wait. The only thing that mattered was *them.*

Together at every hour of every day, not getting much sleep, but compensating by the high levels of oxytocin running through their veins at any time point.

It was fucking spectacular.

She recalls how magnificent he felt pleasuring her.

How amazing his touch on her skin felt, and how skilled he was with his tongue.

How he would never let go before she was completely elated first.

To this day, she never had such an attentive lover.

Each time he made her come apart was better than the last.

Plus, she could never get enough of the sounds he was constantly making when she pleasured him, especially the ones just before he would—

She blinks in an attempt at snapping herself back to the present.

She had a couple relationships since then, but sex and pillow talk with Lucas is amongst the very best she experienced.

He had a way to—

William tilts his head in questioning. "You okay?"

"Yeah." She half-smiles. "I was just thinking."

"Well, I hope it was pleasant thoughts." He lays a quick kiss on her forehead. "I'm sorry, I have to go. I'll grab a bite on the way." He pulls away. "Do you have anything planned tonight?"

She looks at him grabbing his phone from the nightstand. "Not yet, but that might change."

"Gotcha." He pockets his device, and takes his suit jacket from the chair in the corner of the room near the wardrobe. "I'll ask you again later then."

She strides out of her bedroom. "Sure. I have a couple things I want to check today, but I'll let you know if my schedule stays clear."

He makes a beeline for the lobby. "Sounds good."

She walks through the living room to get to the kitchen. "Have a great day, Will."

He finishes putting on his loafers. "Take care, Raven."

As she saunters past her moss green vegan leather sofa, she hears the door close behind William.

She inhales deeply, swiftly taking hold of the remote on the wooden coffee table to turn on the sound system.

She then sets on having breakfast before screening for potential new job opportunities.

She does want to look into her options and next steps today.

She has to get back on the proverbial horse, so to speak. She has to figure out what she wants out of life moving forward.

If being a lawyer is truly—

She makes a face as the first notes of a too familiar tune wash over her.

Of course the amplifier connected to her phone automatically, now playing the very song that haunted her last night.

She decides to not bother skipping it.

She's less tired, and in a slightly better mindstate than yesterday.

Maybe letting it sink in will help her process some of her sentiments.

The lyrics talking about a sex worker's addiction to drugs, and struggles, still hit oddly deep as she opens her cupboard to get some ingredients.

Drug addiction can be insidious.

One can start using for a variety of reasons, and depending on events, before long it can take its toll until it's near impossible to stop.

People end up needing it as much as they need oxygen to breathe.

It's a treacherous slope.

Raven would know. Her long time friend Angie died from an overdose a few months ago.

The memory of being powerless to help her is still hurting Raven more than she cares to admit.

She carries the reminder of it everywhere she goes as a constant memento to try to do better.

If she hadn't been so busy and taken by her work, maybe she could have—-

She pinches the bridge of her nose.

There's no need to tap into those feelings right now.

At least her friend didn't slide into the abyss of forced sex work which could've fueled her addiction, like the witnesses Raven heard in court this week.

She sings gloomily, taking out a saucepan.

If she's being honest, it was very wise of her opponent to put some women on stage to talk about their awful experiences.

This line of questioning served to show a darker side of her client. It proved that he was clearly involved in human trafficking.

It was bad enough that he was using techniques to launder his money, the legitimate companies through which he was doing it were also employing and exploiting such workers who were then highly encouraged to become escorts or sex workers of all types after hours.

If she once thought it could be possible to turn a blind eye to any illicit activity their client business was managing, hearing those three women eloquently talk about their past experiences convinced her otherwise in a heartbeat.

The suffering in their voices, mixed with their fragility as they shared their truth rendered Raven angry beyond measure.

She got frustrated at the system more than she ever had since her law degree days.

Story after story, only one conclusion was echoing in her brain: no one deserves to live through that.

Especially not because of greedy individuals thirsty to get more power over others.

Raven had been unable to conduct her cross examination.

The testimonies of those brave women demanded to shine.

So she stated she had no further questions, and stayed silent.

Her client fumed by her side, insulting her under his breath.

The rest of what happened as soon as she got to her office is now history.

She opens the faucet, filling the casserole with water and clenching her jaw a little.

When someone becomes too big at the top of the societal pyramid, it's easy for them to feel invincible.

Easy for them to think they're untouchable.

It needs to stop.

Every human being deserves to be treated with nothing but respect and care throughout their lives.

Attorneys should defend the most vulnerable.

Not tear them down to pieces for the profit of a select few who use the shortcomings of a doomed system to land on top.

That's the vision she had when she started her career. The one she wanted to pursue.

As she puts the saucepan on the gas burner, she can't help but think that she obviously lost herself somewhere along the way.

Since she quit, she feels strangely more free and peaceful.

She's gradually coming to the conclusion that she doesn't want to have anything to do with corrupt leaders and their likes. Be it in Wall Street or anywhere else.

She can't—

A loud knock resounds in her ears. She perks up instantly, striding toward the entrance.

Who could be visiting her at 10AM on a Saturday?

Maybe William forgot—

She takes a peek through the peephole before opening the door.

She smiles coyly. "Hey, Ju. What's going—"

Her friend cuts her off, giving her a once over. There's a sure urgency in her tone. "Grab your boots. You're coming with me."

She frowns. "I can't—"

Jun interrupts her once more. "Don't." She holds her hand in the air between them in a stop motion. "I have my driver waiting downstairs, I know you have no job anymore thanks to your principles, and you're one of the best at what you were doing so I'd love your help on this matter."

Raven examines her briefly.

Her Japanese American friend has always carried a destabilizing assurance for people not used to her personality.

That's also why she's so successful with Hamasaki Mastermind Management—HMM for short—her Crisis Management company.

She exudes unwavering confidence and aplomb that every single one of her clients admires.

She can manage any situation with flair and by keeping collected.

There's no mountain too big to climb, nor a crisis too huge to contain quietly, she always says.

Right now, she looks to be a bit on edge, but her all-yellow suit with black shirt and matching stilettos tells Raven that Jun wants to make a good first impression wherever she's going.

Her short hairstyle with pastel peek-a-boo highlights is working wonders to complement the ensemble. It gives her friend a professional yet creative look.

If she wants to bring her somewhere at the moment, it's probably important.

But—

Raven points backward toward her kitchen. "I didn't even eat yet. Could you—"

Ju interjects yet again. "I got you some burritos. It's not your fancy oatmeal, but I figured it would do."

Raven can't stop herself from snoring as she picks up her chunky street-style Chelsea boots.

Ever since she visited Sweden and Finland, she developed a fondness for oatmeal.

So many options of toppings to put in those breakfast bowls makes them a go-to meal for Raven. It can be sweet or savory, and she can't get enough of the possibilities.

Her friend loves to make an allusion to it every chance she gets.

As Raven finishes putting on her boots, she's already regretting the sausages, beans and poached egg oatmeal she won't get to eat this morning.

It's fine. Her day was wide open anyway, and Jun needs her.

They know each other by heart at this point of their fifteen-years old friendship.

If Ju asked, there's a good reason, and she will humor her.

She makes sure she has her phone in her pocket with all her cards and essentials. "Okay, fine." She gestures at Jun to move. "Lead the way."

As her device drops the connection with the sound system while she exits her condominium, the last lines of the tune hang in the air like a shadowy prospect.

Raven locks the door to then follow a very restless Jun through the corridor leading to the elevator.

The wait for the lift as well as the descent are spent in silence.

The lawyer doesn't want to put pressure on her friend to talk.

If she knows her well enough, she won't waste any time to do so as soon as they are—

The second the door of the black Sedan parked in front of her building closes behind them, and the driver propels the car forward, Jun breathes in. "Thank you, Raven. I appreciate it."

"You're welcome." She identifies the brown bag laying on the seat between them. "Are you going to tell me what this is all about now?"

Her friend chuckles nervously. "Since you can't really abandon ship once inside the car, sure."

"Why would I—" She trails off, furrowing her eyebrows. "Does this have to do with my ancient law firm by any chance?" She scans Jun's features for any sign of confirmation. "Are you asking me for advice on how they could manage my own departure?"

"No!" Jun locks eyes with Raven. "Of course not." She shakes her head. "That would be very fucked up."

"Well, you're scaring me by not telling me what it is, but saying that I might want to run in the opposite direction when I learn about it."

"It's just that I know you quit your job because you couldn't take any more bullshit from the system." The crisis team leader inhales deeply. "But I still work within said system, and you know just how I've always wanted to collaborate with you."

"You've been nothing but subtle about it." The lawyer opens the bag to fetch a burrito inside, smiling amusedly at her friend. "For years you've been trying to hire me as a consultant."

"See?" Jun smiles knowingly. "When I got the call this morning, I figured this was my chance to work with you on this one. If you'd like to, of course."

Raven starts removing the wrapper. "If you start by explaining what it entails, I might give it some thought."

"Okay. Here goes nothing." The businesswoman never averts her stare. "A managing director of an investment bank reached out because he's been receiving threats."

Raven keeps her tone calm. "What kind of threats?"

Jun sits back in her seat, relaxing a little. "Well, his office was ransacked on Thursday night, but then last night he received blackmail."

She takes a bite. "Did he report the ransacking?"

"No."

The lawyer thinks for a beat, masticating her burrito.

When she finally talks, her voice is serious with a hint of exasperation. "He didn't want to bring attention to himself or his business because his clients wouldn't appreciate the spotlight?"

"Exactly."

Raven frowns. "So he's dealing with shady people."

Jun becomes defensive. "You know they all do to different extents in town."

"I'm still holding out hope to find someone who doesn't at some point." She looks out the window at the East River they're now crossing. "You know I hate this shit. Always have. It's just worse now."

"I know, but you were in deep." The team leader tries to sound comprehensive. "You were dealing with the same kind of financial and banking matters. Your input is invaluable to me here."

Raven doesn't say a word and stays still as they get into Manhattan.

The buildings, the skyscrapers and all the concrete look bleak to her. It's steadily making her feel like she's suffocating.

It's as if the weight of what they stand for is now closing in on her. Her body is leaving her no choice but to notice that the era when she was able to navigate the urban scenery without stopping to reflect on all the implications of a failed societal approach is long gone.

She hadn't been downtown since she left her firm two days ago. It's arguably not that long, but being back is playing tricks on her brain.

She absentmindedly takes another bite of her breakfast.

So much for wanting to stay away from power-hungry leaders.

Money runs the world. It also runs this town.

There's no escaping it.

It would be an utopian vision to think otherwise.

It's also impossible to change something without effort.

Without investing time and energy.

Chaos spreads freely. It takes effort to bring back order and peace.

Jun is a good person. She usually takes on causes she believes in. She fights for what's right more often than not.

Raven thinks she can at least see what is unfolding in this case right here.

She has to figure out what she wants to do in her future, after all. Helping a friend could be a good start to that journey.

A thought suddenly crosses her mind as she replays their previous exchange. "You said this guy received a letter?" She turns to face Jun. "Like an actual letter?"

"Yeah." The team manager hums. "He said it's made of journals and magazine cutouts."

"Doesn't that only happen in movies nowaday?" Raven squints her eyes. "I—"

Ju snorts as she interrupts her. "He said the same thing. He sounded dumbfounded, to be honest."

"As he should. That's odd." Raven reflects some more. "He kept it?"

"Obviously." Jun nods. "I asked him to have it on hand to show us when we get there." She smiles in a hopeful manner. "Does this mean that you're on board?"

"It seems like I am. It could be fun working with you." The attorney chews on her burrito before continuing. "Just for now though. I'll reassess the whole thing after we talk to this man. If I don't get a good impression, I'm out."

"Perfect." Her friend beams. "You have no idea how happy that makes me."

"Don't get used to it." She squints her eyes in fake reprobation. "I might very well leave you to deal with this alone."

"Duly noted." Jun makes a fake military salute. She turns serious once more as she observes Raven eating. "Did you tell your parents about you leaving your—"

"Not yet." The lawyer shakes her head. "I actually haven't talked to anyone back home since. I needed to process a little."

The team manager wiggles a suggestive eyebrow. "Does this mean you called Will by any chance?"

"Yeah. He left just a few minutes before you arrived earlier."

"Oooh." Jun sounds excited. "He spent the night then?"

"He did."

Her friend smiles teasingly. "You guys cuddled?"

"Not really." Raven shrugs. "Intimacy is not something I do with Will."

Ju can't help a quip. "Just doing him is enough it seems."

"Ju!" She uses a fakely offended tone, laughing lightly. "It is. He still mentioned that he noticed that I looked preoccupied. He wanted me to open up to him a bit more."

The businesswoman raises a playful eyebrow. "Open up emotionally, you mean?"

Raven half-smiles. "C'mon, Ju, you know it's solely the emotional factor that is lacking with him."

"I know you don't do feelings since Nathan, but maybe you—"

The driver's firm voice reaches their ears, making Jun trail off. "We're at our destination, ladies."

"I'll call you when we're done here, Gary," the team leader offers dryly as she gets out of the car.

After having thanked the sporty-looking blonde man in a blue suit, Raven follows her friend to stand in front of a tall Bauhaus architecture looking building covered in oversized colored windows.

She scans Jun's features as she straightens her blazer. "Are you still sleeping with Gary sometimes, or..."

Her friend strides toward the entrance. "I didn't want to bother you with the whole thing with everything happening to you, but if you must know we stopped earlier this week." They get past the revolving doors. "It has gotten complicated. He doesn't want his son to learn about us, and I'm no good at secret relationships."

"That sucks, I'm sorry." Raven quickly glances around the white marble lobby. "You'd like to be involved in his son's life?"

"Yeah. I told Gary as such, but he's self-conscious that if it ends up not working between us, his son will be caught in the middle. He's only six, and already lost his mother when she decided to leave out of the blue." Jun stops in front of the panel identifying the building occupants and their associated floor. "I understand, and I respect Gary's choice." She resumes walking toward the elevators, smiling at the security guard at the desk on her way. "For a hot minute, I thought we could truly give it a shot, you know?"

"He has his son's best interests at heart with reason, but I feel you." The lawyer catches up with her. "What you guys had was special. I've never seen you be this happy, Ju."

"Thanks." Jun presses on the button to call the lift. "I want to keep him as a driver so I'll try to get used to the fact that I have to keep it strictly professional now."

"I wish you luck with that." Raven rapidly checks her phone for any notifications out of habit. "It's always hard to do so when you can vividly remember how great it felt to have sex with someone."

Jun exhales audibly. "Please don't remind me."

"Sorry, I won't." After deciding to reply to her friend Heather later, the attorney pockets her phone, focusing all her attention on Jun. "So, where are we going?"

"Forty-second floor." The elevator's doors open in front of them. They both step inside. "We're going to meet Mister Blake."

"He's the managing director of which division?"

"Mergers and Acquisitions." The team manager selects the correct floor. "He seemed really nice on the phone." She keeps her balance as the elevator starts moving. "He had a warm and soothing voice."

Raven sounds unimpressed. "Has he been in the business for long?"

"Nearly a decade, he said." Jun states matter-of-factly. "I checked his socials. He's around our age."

"So no old man stuck in his ways to deal with?" the lawyer supplies playfully.

Her friend chuckles. "Hopefully not."

A beat passes in comfortable silence as Jun checks her emails on her phone.

Raven feels that the environment is not really welcoming.

No wonder the architect decided to put some color touches all around by using polychromatic glass. The rest of the design is chilly, and while being professional is also void of any warmth that would render it a little hospitable.

"You know, this building strikes me as being very cold." She looks around at the brushed aluminum walls of the cabin. "I'm not getting a very promising vibe out of the endeavor so far."

"I appreciate you giving this a shot." Jun hastily types on her screen keyboard. "I promise that if you're not feeling it after this initial meeting, I won't bother you further."

Raven smiles amusedly. "You sure you won't even ask me for—" She trails off intentionally.

Her friend tucks her device away as she laughs. "Okay, okay. I might still call and message you for tips once in a while." She sounds dead serious. "But I swear that I won't force you to actively participate in anything."

"Thanks. It reminds me of that case we worked on during our internship back in university when—"

The elevator comes to a halt, the doors sliding open in front of them.

Jun strides into the investment banking company floor, smiling brightly. "Let's do this."

As Raven follows suit, she is pleasantly surprised. The impersonal vibe she got from the rest of the building so far seems to fade in here.

The whole decor screams of modernity and professionalism, but is oddly cozy.

They probably hired a designer to play to the strengths of the space.

She has to admit that it succeeds in giving potential clients and newcomers a great first impression. If she was shopping around for the kind of services they offer, she would seriously consider them based on the ambience of their offices.

The business-like voice of the auburn receptionist at the front desk reaches her ears. "Yes. Mister Blake is waiting for you." The woman in a white blouse and navy blue skirt gestures at Jun and Raven to follow her. "This way"

As they navigate through a series of corridors and common rest areas, Raven continues to be impressed at the exuded atmosphere.

Maybe this won't be the nightmare she thought it could be.

To have rendered an otherwise joyless place inviting, the boss is probably not the average Wall Street guy.

When they finally reach a corner office, the secretary stops in the doorway, guiding them inside. "Here you go. If you need anything, don't hesitate. My name's Delilah."

Raven and Jun both nod as the woman leaves them alone.

The second Raven sets foot in the immense office, she can't help but notice the relaxed vibe and tidiness.

Everything seems to have its spot, and every object is blending seamlessly with its surroundings.

She's pretty sure that the few art pieces on display are real ones, and makes a mental note to ask if the pop-art painting hanging proudly behind the walnut industrial modern desk is an original.

Along with the masterpiece, two bright red file cabinets are standing on either side of the black console behind the workstation, bringing a pleasing pinch of color in the mostly monochromatic office.

Another nice splash of color catches her eye on her right where an odd surfboard is anchored to the wall.

It looks to have been used, and Raven has a thousand questions flooding her mind upon seeing it.

Finance men who love surfing are rare to come across, but one who loves it enough to put a used surfboard on display in his office might just earn her respect.

It's a secret for no one close to her that she adores the ocean and its waves. That she could surf for—

Jun clears her throat, and Raven realizes that she had started walking toward the surfboard of her own accord. She smiles shyly, correcting her course, and sauntering to go stand beside her friend in front of the desk.

She breathes in as her eyes land on their host.

In the middle of this peculiar oasis of peace, a tall man with broad shoulders in a custom tailored gray suit, black shirt and loose pink tie is standing facing away from them. He has his cellphone against his ear and a hand in his pocket.

His black locks are gelled to perfection, and Raven can see the hint of a flawlessly trimmed three-day beard defining his cheek and jawline.

She can't stop herself from thinking that he looks good, but that he would be gorgeous beyond words if he was to let his hair fall naturally without putting any products in it.

He is indeed young and—

His tone reaches her ears as he ends his call. "I'll check up with you later. I have an appointment now." He sounds cheerful. "I'll see you tomorrow anyway."

She furrows her eyebrows.

This voice.

She swears that she already—

As soon as he turns around to face them, a breath catches in her throat, and her heart skips a beat.

Time stands still.

She would recognize this soft emerald gaze and those squared facial features anywhere.

She spent too much time exploring the body currently covered by this high-end suit to forget.

She never thought she would ever see him again in a thousand years.

Just like she used to do back on those beaches in Greece, she dives into his stare effortlessly.

He seems similarly trapped.

He feels like he's staring right through her soul.

She strangely doesn't mind. He's the only one who ever had that effect on her anyway.

But people change and evolve. They're clearly in other phases of their respective lives.

She has to get it together.

When she finally opens her mouth to speak, she knows she probably sounds like she has just seen a ghost.

"Lucas?" she asks tentatively.

THREE

Creating Ripples

L ucas is not one to be easily destabilized.

Ever since his father left without ever giving sign of life again, he made an oath with himself to never let a situation throw him off balance ever again if he could prevent it.

Which means that throughout his existence thus far, he always planned ahead for all potential outcomes whenever possible. That way, he could assess, adjust, and be prepared for any eventuality.

He could be in charge.

In high school, he would complete all parts of any team projects just in case the other members of the group would end up being late turning in their work. If this were to happen, he could then swiftly include his version, and hand in a complete assignment. No grade penalty, and no useless stress about unmet deadlines.

In university, he would study with Felipe using a simulation software they coded themselves. The program would randomly generate the most challenging questions that could arise during exams for each course.

After every test, they couldn't help but notice that the endeavor had been more smooth because of this technique. The actual questions consistently ended up being simpler than the ones they trained for.

Through life in general as well as when he's surfing, keeping his balance while navigating the currents has invariably been essential to his well being.

These days, this personality trait has certainly become prominent.

He tries to nurture his more pragmatic side, especially in any professional setting, setting aside the creativity that is often screaming to be let loose.

But now life has thrown him a curveball.

A gorgeous, five foot nine with legs for days and an ocean gaze that could melt an iceberg on the spot curveball.

The last person he expected to see walking into his office to manage his blackmail crisis was her.

He breathes in deeply.

Raven.

Or should he call her Miss Collins now that he knows her last name?

As Lucas gets out of the subway at the 96 Street station in the Upper West Side, he is still trying his best to shake Raven's soft smile from his brain.

The upbeat tempo leaking through his earphones—with lyrics from the female singer describing how alluring a woman can be—is doing nothing to help him in that matter.

He inhales deeply.

Spending the evening at his friend Mark's should do him some good and clear his mind from the day he just had.

He certainly went through many emotions in the span of a few hours.

When he heard the beautiful brunette call out his name, his heart may have skipped a beat.

She was looking stunning in casual chic attire. Her vintage jeans and loose black t-shirt were flawlessly paired with a white blazer, accentuating her slender frame.

He had to smile at her boots that added the perfect edge to her ensemble.

Her ash brown hair fell messily from a bun. His eyes lingered on the industrial piercing on her left ear that he used to love so much, and he had an urge to—

He cleared his throat instead.

Raven? He peered into her eyes, his tone steady, but barely over a murmur. *What are you doing here?*

She kept her voice business-like. *I'm here with my friend Jun to consult on your crisis situation.*

She angled her head toward the Asian American woman in an all-yellow suit, black shirt and stilettos standing next to her.

He instantly recognized the team leader he had decided to contact following the reception of his threat letter.

Where are my manners? He extended a hand. *Lucas Blake. I appreciate you coming over in person on such short notice.*

Of course. Jun shook his hand before shifting her stare to her friend. *It seems like you already know Raven.* She smiled coyly. *Judging by the way she's looking at you, I'm thinking you might even be the Lucas from Mykonos?*

He laughed lightly as he walked around his desk. *I am.* He gestured at them to take a seat in front of him, staring at Raven. *I honestly never thought I would see you again.*

She sat down in the white armchair at the same time as Jun. *Me neither.*

He smiled teasingly. *But it seems like your friends know about me even a decade later.*

What can I say? She shrugged, looking sure of herself. *You left quite an impression.*

There it was. The gaze that always managed to pierce straight through his soul.

In a split second, his worries began to slowly vanish, leaving him with a pleasant warmth coursing through his veins.

He was automatically mystified.

He had no idea he had missed those eyes that much.

He had to let her know that he never forgot her either.

So did you, he whispered.

Raven opened her mouth to reply, but Jun decided to cut through the staring contest. *While it is very heartwarming to witness your reunion, we're here for work.* She crossed her legs. *Lucas, could you please walk us through what happened to you so far?*

Of course. He sat back in his seat. *On Thursday I got a call from my assistant, Paul, that my office had been ransacked.* He focused his attention on Jun. *I was out at The Nightly Disco Room with my friend Felipe when I learned about it. Paul sent me pictures, cleaned up the mess, and placed a service request to have the door replaced because it had been broken open. I have to warn you that there's no cameras in my office or on the entire floor. The company wants all employees to work in peace and not worry about being potentially watched. Although the building has its own surveillance system.*

I'll check out the building cam footage in case anything stands out. The crisis management leader hummed. *Could you send us the photos, please?*

Lucas nods, resting his hands in his lap. *Of course.*

Thank you. Jun smiled warmly, staying serious. *Did you come by the office yourself to assess the damage or check if any files were missing?*

No. He kept his tone unflinching, but still started to wring his hands. *I stayed at the club, and then went home with someone. I needed to take my mind off of things.*

Okay. Raven's friend creases her eyebrows. *Did your assistant notice anything was missing then?*

Paul didn't check for specifics. Lucas shook his head. *He only cleaned things up. I went through my files on Friday morning, and nothing seemed to be missing.* He inhaled calmly. *I don't leave sensitive information in my office to start with. Plus, I bring my laptop home with me every night.*

Gotcha. Jun put her arms on the arm rests of the chair. *So it was someone who doesn't know of your habits since they were definitely looking for something by searching your office.*

Raven perked up. *Maybe it was someone who wanted to scare him or send him a message.*

Lucas hummed in approbation. *That's also what I thought.* He pressed his lips into a thin line. *To be completely honest, I didn't think much about it at first. I do have some very high profile clients, but couldn't wrap my mind around the fact that one of them could've done this.*

Raven held his stare. *Are all your clients treading only in legality? I have to be completely truthful here?*

She squinted her eyes. *It would help.*

He raised an eyebrow. *Client-attorney privilege applies?*

Not really. She smiled playfully. *I'm a lawyer, but I'm not your personal lawyer.*

He shifted in his seat. *So I think you know the answer to that question.*

She snorted. *Spoken like a true lawyer.*

He played along. *I could've plead the fifth, too.*

Whatever you say, it proves one thing. She scanned his green eyes. *You're millions of miles away from what you said you stood for when you graduated.*

People change. He felt as if he needed to defend himself all of a sudden. *I'm sure you did, too.*

Everyone evolves. She never averted her gaze. *I would hate to have lost myself to this degree though.*

He frowned. *There's clearly a line to not cross in my line of work, and I—*

Jun interjected. *Could we get a grip? Mister Blake, I'd like to see the letter you received yesterday.*

Sure. Lucas reluctantly dropped his exchange with Raven to go open his drawer, then placed the piece of paper stored in a plastic bag flat on his desk. *Here you go. I opened the envelope, and when I realized what it was I used the ice tongs from my bar cart to put it in a bag so I wouldn't contaminate potential evidence any further.*

Clever. The team manager read the all caps message—which was made out of magazine cut-outs—out loud. *You better give in to our upcoming demands or you'll regret it. If you don't comply, we can expose you, and are powerful enough to destroy you.*

The managing director waved his finger over the piece of paper. *That's a clear threat, right?*

Jun makes a face. *It is,* she confirmed. *Do you have any idea what they could be referring to?*

He decided to stay evasive at this stage. *It could be a lot of things.* He reoriented the discussion a little. *They also haven't followed up with their demands yet.*

Contacting us was the right thing to do, the woman in the yellow suit stated. *We have a multidisciplinary team at your disposal. We'll figure this out.*

He smiled confidently. *Thank you.*

Jun took her phone out. *I'll send you the contract if you want to sign it.* She hastily scrolled through her documents. *We have the equivalent of the client-attorney privilege you alluded to before, that covers everyone working on your case.* She briefly looked up from her device at him. *Which, I'll keep to a minimum number of people. I'll personally be the team leader here.*

He flipped open his portable computer. *Is Raven officially included in the team?*

Jun sent the file through her company portal. *If she wants to.*

He received the contract in his inbox promptly, and double-clicked to open it.

Before electronically signing it, he locked eyes with Raven.

At that moment he knew that if she wasn't on board, he didn't really want to embark on this journey.

She had walked back into his life seeming a bit different than she was years ago, but still as fascinating as ever.

He felt like he needed to take a shot at uncovering all the layers of her personality this time around.

A little voice inside himself was also telling him that Raven was probably one of the best to tackle this situation.

Her friend Jun didn't ask her to consult for nothing, after all.

Jun has a reputation that preceded her. She's one of the best at what she does. Her company only has rave reviews and testimonials from past clients. That's arguably because she surrounds herself with only the finest people.

In that optic, it convinced him of the necessity to have Raven on his crisis management team even more.

He put his cards on the table. *I'm not agreeing to this contract if I can't work with you.*

She seemingly took it as a challenge. *Fine.* She reached to take one of his business cards from the card holder at the edge of his desk. *I think the first step would be to go through your client list, and I'll take care of it.* She silently motioned for a pen, which he gave to her. *I know a thing or two about shady practices, and who has the potential to be involved in them.* She scribbled something down on the card and slid it his way. *You can send it to this address.* She smiled mellowly. *Make sure it's encrypted.*

He beamed as he pocketed the card.

Soon after, both women left his office, and he attended to his business of the day before leaving.

He loosens his pink tie a little more as he takes a left turn on West 57th Street.

Even through the slight tension buzzing in the air following the exchange about the type of clients he had, Raven's presence in his office was soothing.

He didn't expect her to call him out on his practices, but reflecting on it, he had to admit that she had every right to.

It's true that he doesn't feel exactly like the person he was back when he met her in Greece.

Which is normal.

He has gone through a lot since then.

He poured his soul into his work, and his job obliterated pretty much everything else.

He climbed the steps one after the other to end up where he is now.

He built a life for himself.

He doesn't want it to crash down because of an invisible enemy threatening him.

He's exactly the man he always strived to become. That's what he'll keep telling himself.

Ideals are no good if they lead nowhere, anyway.

His life is orderly and organized. Things are good.

It has to stay this way.

Entering his friend's building, he removed his earphones, and politely saluted the doorman.

A quick check of his notifications for a potential update from Raven renders no results. She hasn't said anything back after he sent her the list she asked for before he left his office earlier.

It was only a short while ago, but he hopes she received it.

The file is protected, and he's also notified as soon as it's opened. It hasn't happened yet. Raven would've surely asked for the password by now if she had tried.

He feels like getting confirmation.

He opens his messaging app.

L: Just making sure that you got the files? Have a nice evening

He hits 'send' and wastes no time before calling the elevator and riding it up to the sixth floor, knocking on Mark's front door two minutes later.

His friend sounds joyful as he lets him inside. "Hey, man! I'm sorry we didn't get to chat on Thursday."

"It's fine." He steps inside the lobby, spontaneously removing his Magnanni formal Chelsea boots. "I heard you left with someone?"

"Yeah." The fitness aficionado closes the door. "Actually, it might also become more than a one-night thing." He grins proudly. "We're seeing each other again for dinner tomorrow."

When Lucas turns around to face the personal trainer, he can't help but fully notice the relaxed vibe he exudes.

Mark's light brown hair, usually held in a high man bun, is now completely loose and falling down to his shoulders.

He is also cleanly shaved, and wearing a plain white t-shirt with black sweatpants and neon green flip flops.

His hazelnut eyes are sparkling with anticipation at the statement he just shared.

Lucas has not seen his friend be this laid back in months.

"That's great!" He mirrors his expression. "What's his name? You know, in case it lasts I better remember it."

"Matteo." Mark starts walking through the long hallway. "He would be my first Italian boyfriend."

"That's exciting." Lucas follows suit, briefly scanning his surroundings for any new decor addition to the space. Mark loves to add some bohemian flair to his contemporary looking home. "Kyan also left with someone, but I doubt it will lead to anything in his case."

The personal trainer pads past his bedroom door on the left. "Remember when he thought the woman he hooked up with was 'the one', and it turned out she was already married with children?"

"To be honest, I think that episode still haunts him. With reason. He never would've slept with her in the first place if he had known." The managing director entered the living room with his friend. "He never wants to get attached again out of fear of getting hurt."

Mark nods, sauntering past his bar cart in front of the bay window. "We all have our coping mechanisms."

"We sure do." Lucas identifies a new Buddha statue sitting on top of the gray console under the wall-mounted TV. "At least one of us is not afraid of commitment." He removes his suit jacket, putting it on the arm of the gray couch. "Felipe is happily married and Emma is a saint for putting up with him sometimes."

"Hey!" His friend chuckles, and walks into the immaculate white kitchen. "I'm not afraid to be in a relationship either. It's just really difficult to find someone who shares the same life goals." He opens the fridge. "Speaking of Felipe, you know that he got Em a new car yesterday?"

Lucas begins rolling up the sleeves of his black shirt, sounding surprised. "A new car?"

"A luxury one at that. Em's dream car." He puts two beers on the black granite island. "I think they were taking it for a spin this weekend." He shifts his gaze to his longtime friend. "You really didn't know?"

"Not at all." He shakes his head. "Last time I checked, Felipe was talking about not being able to give Emma what she wanted, and he felt bad about it. This is a surprise."

"Not able to give her what she wants?" Mark frowns while opening the beers. "He's making good money."

"He is." Lucas sits down on the sofa as his friend walks back into the living room. "Although not the 'I can buy a house in the Hamptons' kind of money yet. Maybe he decided to tap into his savings to get a gift for Emma."

"Probably." The trainer hands Lucas a bottle. "But what's up with you, cuddy? Anything fun happened since last week?"

"Fun? Nah." He grabs the beer. "I did hook up with a voluptuous dark-haired woman named Monica on Thursday, but that's about it." He takes a sip. "The discussions I'm having with potential future clients are taking up a ton of my time. There's one in particular that I'm getting a lot of pressure to sign as quickly as possible, but I've been stalling."

"That's unlike you."

"He has a nice wallet to offer, and he's certainly influential, but he feels like a bully to me. I don't like that." He squints his eyes at his own reflection before shrugging it off. "It's a blessing that I'm not working from the office tomorrow, and that I have no meetings planned. I'll be able to go visit Sab and Brooke like I intended. It'll do me some good to take my mind off of work a little."

Mark laughs as he sits down in the velvet baby blue armchair at the end of the glass coffee table. "So work is business as usual basically?"

Lucas draped an arm on the back of the couch, placing the bottle in his lap. "Well, there's a crisis happening at the office, and I had to hire a consultant to take care of it."

No one except his assistant and crisis management team is aware of the ransacking and threat.

He hasn't even told Felipe when he went back inside the nightclub after Paul gave him the news.

He thinks that it's better this way for now.

He trusts his friends, but going into the details of the events would surely create a commotion.

Plus, the more people know, the more likely it is that it ends up getting out there one way or another, which is the very opposite of what he wants to happen.

Better keep things vague.

He would still like to be able to talk about it broadly with the ones closest to him.

Especially since Raven is part of said crisis management team.

He needs to talk about her to someone.

The trainer makes a face. "Nothing too serious I hope?"

"Not for now." The managing director stays cool. "We'll see how it evolves." He smiles coyly. "But check this out. One of the people on that crisis management team is Raven."

Mark gapes at him. "Raven as in Mykonos Raven?"

He gulps down some more of his drink. "Precisely."

"Woah, man." His friend blinks in surprise. "That's unexpected."

"You don't say." Lucas breathes in to compose himself. "She's still as gorgeous as she was, and don't get me started on her eyes..." He exhales soundly. "She emanates fierceness, Mark."

The trainer smiles knowingly. "You talk about her exactly like you did back when we met."

"I can't believe you and I have known each other for that long." Lucas reminisces about how he met Mark. "I remember I moved to New York a month after that trip to Mykonos, we met at the gym, and I couldn't shut up about Raven at every training session."

"You had no idea how to contact her, but you didn't sleep with anyone for a year." Mark laughs lightly. "I still recall that dry spell. You were sure no one would make it as good as her. You're sentimental at heart, Lucas."

"I was still right." He half-smiles. "I have never felt as good since her."

His friend raises his bottle in a toast. "Now you might have a second chance to go for it."

Lucas furrows his eyebrows. "We're both very different people now."

Mark looks puzzled. "You just said that—"

"I know what I said, but we're also clearly not in the same situation nor headspace now." The managing director takes another sip. "Our lives seem to be on very different paths."

"Maybe learn to know her for real this time?" the trainer suggests. "I mean, get to know *all* that she is."

"I have every intention to." Lucas smiles coyly. "Working with her might just be the perfect occasion to do it."

"That's the spirit, bud." It's Mark's turn to take a sip. "If you don't end up sleeping together again, maybe you guys could become good friends."

"We'll see where this goes."

"Did I just hear you say that you'll go with the flow?" His friend teases, a smile dancing at the corner of his mouth. "Who are you, and what have you done to Lucas?"

"Very funny." The managing director snorts. "Maybe I'm just keeping my mind open to possibilities. It can't hurt."

"Your sister would be proud of you for letting go a little." Mark raises a playful eyebrow. "Speaking of, have you talked to her lately?"

"No. She's still in Brazil until the end of the month for that rainforest documentary." Lucas absentmindedly plays with the rim of his bottle. "I hope to be able to go visit her and my mom when she gets back."

"Sounds great." His friend takes his phone out of his pocket. "I'm sure that film will be amazing."

"I have no doubts." He hums in approbation. "She's very passionate about biodiversity and climate change."

Mark holds his device in front of him. "Wanna order in?"

"Sure." Lucas smiles. "Whatever you want. I'm starving."

The trainer goes through his apps, beaming. "Then we'll be right on time to watch the preseason game."

He can't stop himself from cheering. "Perfect."

As his friend places the order, Lucas takes out his own phone.

Multiple work-related messages are staring back at him, but still no news from Raven.

He places the device on the sofa's armrest.

Why is he this impatient to get a sign of life from her?

It's unlike him to wait for anyone's comeback on anything.

It's debatably because Raven fascinates him, and he can't wait to talk to her more. She always had a way of captivating him with the tiniest gesture or any sentence falling from her lips.

He never had such an instant and intense connection with anyone else in his life before and since her.

He can't help it. He's drawn to who she is.

The fact that she entered his life again is sending his brain reeling in more ways than one.

He needs to keep his mind clear, and assess the situation as it comes to him.

He's not been very good at doing that in the last few years, but he feels like he still has it in him to try.

It's not like all his personality disappeared when he got his job in NYC, after all.

He reaches for the remote to open the TV.

Tonight he'll relax with his friend Mark. Tomorrow he'll deal with the rest.

After having dinner with Jun at their favorite pizzeria on Front Street, Raven walked back home and decided to take a quick shower and then change into her favorite leisurewear: her *Harriers Law* graphic sweater with charcoal leggings.

That sweater has followed her since her university days like a comfort blanket. She could never part with it. It has been washed so many times that it's fashionably comfy while showing little signs of wear after more than a decade of use.

Padding barefoot in her apartment as she sloppily puts her hair up in a bun to the beat of her playlist, she feels oddly free.

She takes a quick sip from the glass of her favorite White Zinfandel that she left on her coffee table.

This wine has the perfect blend of sweetness and tart for her taste buds. It's like lounging under the California sun.

It makes her feel at peace with the world every time she drinks it.

It's as if she's propelled back home for a hot minute.

She sighs as she puts back the glass on the surface to resume her walking.

She clearly didn't get to check for potential new job opportunities today. Her plans got derailed the second Jun knocked on her door.

But she feels good about how things went.

Seeing Lucas again was in equal measures a surprise and a delight.

When he locked eyes with hers, saying that he would not sign the contract if she wasn't on board, she took it as an invitation to kill two birds with one stone.

She could work as a consultant for Jun like her friend always wanted her to while she assesses what she wants to do moving forward, and she would get to interact more with a man that never fully left her brain in the past decade.

Bonus points for the fact that she might also uncover sketchy schemes and pursue some more assholes who think that they are all powerful in this city.

Even if Lucas doesn't feel exactly like the same man she met back in Greece, he sounded fun and confident enough for her interest to be piqued.

People do change through time. Sometimes for the best, sometimes for the worst.

She can't decide what is the case for Lucas yet.

He definitely looks like he succeeded in becoming big in the city, which is no small feat considering how competitive the financial market is in NYC. He potentially did it at the expense of leaving some of his virtuous principles to the side while dealing with big money.

She's been around long enough to be aware that this is usually how things work around Wall Street. It's difficult to make it into the highest spheres without leaving a part of your identity behind.

She considers herself lucky to have opened her eyes before it was too late for her.

Even though quitting her job has been stressful the past few days, her resentment toward the system is igniting a fire deep within her. She would very much like to channel it into trying to level the scales a little in the grand scheme of things.

To try to do better moving forward.

She takes a deep breath while making a beeline for her office to fetch her computer.

Working on Lucas' crisis management team will be a good opportunity to get to know him better.

See who he became and what drives him these days.

He was nothing but entrancing when she first met him in Mykonos.

She can confirm that he still bleeds charisma and assurance.

She's very curious to reconnect with him.

It's a professional endeavor, but she's set on seeing where this goes. She can't deny that she might very well still be drawn to him.

She can vividly recall his warm smile as he was sitting next to her at a bar counter in Mykonos. She had just shut down an obnoxious man who wanted to take her back to his hotel room.

That was quite amazing, Lucas stated while downing the rest of his cocktail.

She shrugged, tucking the front of her pink t-shirt into her denim shorts. *I can't stand toxic masculinity.*

Same. He pulled up the sleeves of his black hoodie and put his phone that was on the counter back into his bermuda shorts. *That guy deserved nothing less than what you said to him. I was about to tell him to fuck off myself if he wasn't going to get the hint.*

She smiled amusedly. *I can take care of myself.*

I'm sure you can. He peered into her eyes. *It's just that, to me, women deserve to always be treated with the utmost respect. I despise men who can't read the room and have such disgusting behaviors.*

She scanned his gaze for a few seconds, analyzing if he was full of bullshit or not. *What's your name?* she asked finally.

He curved a corner of his mouth upward. *Lucas.*

She kept eye contact. *You're here for work or pleasure?*

Definitely pleasure. He shifted on his stool to face her. *I've just graduated, and decided to travel a little on my own. My friends all decided to get drunk in Miami, but I wanted to get out of the country.*

So you're American, she affirmed more to herself than him.

He nodded. *From Chicago.*

The fact that he never pushed her to reveal anything about herself from the get-go, and let her lead the discussion, was already giving her a good reading on the type of person he was.

When he smiled genuinely at her, his emerald gaze flickering with softness, she felt like he was pulling her into his orbit.

She didn't want to resist any of it.

She left some money on the counter. *How about we get out of here?*

He agreed, and they spent the night walking in the streets, sharing their life goals and vision. Righting the wrongs of the world ten times over during that endeavor felt good.

She remembers that when he laughed bright and loud at her recollection of the first time she had watched a well-loved blockbuster movie and hated it, she couldn't resist anymore. She curled her hand into the front of his hoodie to bring him to her.

A second later, their lips were colliding and their tongues were tangling together in the most flawless kiss she had ever experienced.

As she flew her fingers through his black locks, he felt like an inferno she wanted to succumb to, and she had no intention of denying herself the opportunity.

She spent the rest of the week with him, and—

She shakes her head while entering her living room.

It's too easy to get sucked back into those souvenirs. Into his green stare she always wanted to dive into.

She has to focus on the present.

Lucas is back in her life, and she has to help him find the culprit of the blackmail he's been receiving.

Past history between them or not, she has to tackle the task at hand.

She already decided that she'd go with the flow here.

How hard can it be to follow her own decision without anticipating anything anyway?

She sits down on her couch, placing her laptop on the coffee table and then turns off the music to watch sports on the TV. A basketball preseason game is on.

There was a time where she would watch every single match with her friend Heather back home. They even managed to attend some of them when they were at *Harriers*.

With a couple other of their friends, they were—

Shit.

She forgot to reply to Heather.

She saw her friend's message before meeting with Lucas, and then forgot to follow-up on it.

While her computer boots, she checks Heather's text only to realize that it is more of a heads up than an actual message.

H: I really need to talk to you. I'll call you tomorrow.

Raven frowns. She hopes her friend is doing alright. She hasn't talked to her in the past month because of the trial she was working on.

That thing was truly taking up all of her time.

Not being part of it anymore is undoubtedly liberating.

She decides to answer affirmatively to let Heather know that she's looking forward to her call.

R: Sounds good, Haddy

As soon as her desktop lights up, she goes to open the client list Lucas sent her.

She thinks that starting her investigation while watching basketball will make for an entertaining Saturday night.

It should at least get her mind off of the uncertainty of her future past this crisis management contract.

The moment the file opens, a pop-up window appears, prompting her to enter a password.

She frowns.

Lucas took her request to secure the document seriously.

She grabs her phone to ask him for it.

R: What's the password?

As she sends the text, she notices that Lucas had already sent her another message asking if she had received the file, and to wish her a good evening after providing her the list.

The message timestamp is from an hour after she received said list.

Was he really thinking about her, and felt an urge to reach out?

She sits back on the couch, curling her legs under herself as she waits for a reply.

She's probably overthinking this. Maybe Lucas just wanted to make sure that he didn't send the file to the wrong address.

That's a legitimate concern.

She now wishes she had seen the text before so she could've answered and let him know that all was—

Her device chimes in her lap. She picks it up.

L: Remember that beer you ordered in Mykonos that one night before we ended up naked on the balcony of your room? Try that.

She doesn't have to reflect for long.

Of course she remembers how she embarrassed herself by ordering the wrong beer. Her Greek pronunciation was so bad that she couldn't make the bartender understand what she was saying.

The barmaid ended up serving her the right one after she pointed to the bottle that one of the other women at the counter was holding.

She also recalls how Lucas took all the fucking time in the world to lick his way up her legs on that balcony.

How she came apart powerfully, crashing through a wall of pure white nihility in a silent heave.

To this day, no one has ever given her better head than Lucas.

She is not ashamed to admit that his tongue is unequaled, and that she wouldn't say no to an encore.

His hair gliding through her fingers as he lapped at her and groaned into her core is still—

She pinches the bridge of her nose.

She has to focus.

Password.

She reaches to change keyboards and type hastily into the appropriate field, entering the four letters of the beer brand.

Νησί[1]

The document unlocks.

---

1. Greek. Pronunciation: ny-sy. Meaning: Island.

She smiles, grabbing her glass of wine and sitting back into the cushions once more.

R: You remember that moment?

Three blinking dots appear. She waits, taking a sip.

L: How could I forget? Best night of my life.

She pulls her bottom lip between her teeth.

R: Still to this day? I hope your girlfriend is aware of that fact.

The reply is instantaneous.

L: Yep (and I don't have a girlfriend)

He seemingly keeps typing.

L: Was it the best for you, too?

She laughs under her breath.

She always loved how bold and unabashed he is. Nothing is taboo with Lucas. He's open about his feelings, his thoughts and his beliefs.

Or at least he used to be.

It looks like he still is in regard to sex.

But it would be a lie to say that this specific night is the best she ever had in her life.

And she takes pride in the fact that she is always genuine in her personal affirmations.

R: Sorry, I can't say the same.

L: Now you got me curious. Who was the lucky gentleman?

She's not about to tell him that it was him, and that she's only thinking of another night from that week.

It could be fun to tease him a little.

R: Some witty, tall, dark, and handsome guy.

She lets her fingertips trail along the stem of her glass as he types.

L: You're still with him?

R: No.

L: He was probably not that good, then.

She laughs lightly.

This exchange feels smooth. He's effortlessly flirting with her.

Maybe Lucas didn't change a whole lot, after all.

But back in Greece there were a ton of unspoken things between them.

They never talked in depth about their families or their friends. They weren't together long enough to notice the other's quirks either.

It was fun and easy. Exactly like they had agreed on.

Now they're not on vacation. They're in each other's real lives with all it entails.

There's no more carefree sentiment of a fleeting adventure.

No matter where things lead them this time around, she knows he's Lucas Blake. One of the managing directors of a very important and well-known investment bank.

Similarly, he knows she's Raven Collins; a lawyer who clearly moved to NYC at some point and who's working on his case.

There's no hiding behind inconsequential circumstances because everything would reset the minute they would part ways at the airport.

This is tangible. It could lead them somewhere, or nowhere fast.

She breathes in, deciding to reorient the exchange.

R: What are you doing?

She takes another sip of her rosé.

L: Watching the basketball game with a friend. You?

She shifts her stare at the TV for a second to check the score.

R: Same, but alone.

She watches the game for a beat until she gets a new message.

L: Cheers

A picture of Lucas' hand raising a bottle of beer in front of a screen where the game is playing is accompanying the text.

She smiles absentmindedly.

She takes a similar picture with her glass of wine, extending her feet on the table to get them in frame before curling her legs under herself, and putting her glass back on the table.

R: Cheers I'm surprised you don't have season tickets.

L: I would be too busy to attend most days. You look very cozy. Only missing a cat in your lap.

Raven smiles sadly.

R: I had one. She passed away last year. I miss her presence in my condo everyday.

She presses 'Send' and then stares at what she just told Lucas.

She never confessed to anyone that she was still feeling the loss of Toast—her white tabby rescue cat.

It somehow felt right to share it with him just now.

L: I'm sorry, Raven. I personally always wanted a dog, but you know how it is when we work long hours...

R: I totally get it. Toast was very independent so it was easier. She definitely put life into the apartment.

L: Such a great name. Something tells me it has a fun meaning.

She feels oddly thrilled that he is interested in that particular story.

R: It did. First off because of her fur coloring, but mostly due to my annoying toaster at the time.

L: You had an infernal toaster?

R: Yeah. It kept burning toasts. No matter the setting it was on, the bread would come out of it dark as the night. I didn't take the time to go buy a new one for weeks so when I adopted Toast it was still there.

She sends the message intuitively before typing the rest, and gets an instant reply.

L: Let me guess. Your cat was a fan.

She cackles.

R: My cat was the ONLY one who absolutely loved it. She would jump on the counter and wait until it was done so she could eat it. She was a rescue who just got to the shelter the morning I adopted her. I decided to wait a bit before naming her when she got to my apartment, so it was the perfect opportunity to use one of her quirks.

L: You're amazing. I'm sure Toast lived her best life with you.

She stares at her phone for a moment.

She could honestly chat with him like this for hours.

But he's with a friend, and she considers that she took enough of his time for now.

R: I'll let you watch the game with your friend. It was fun conversing with you a little.

L: You can keep texting me. Mark is also spending a lot of time on his phone messaging his newest crush.

She smiles, but keeps her resolve.

R: Good night, Lucas

L: Good night, Raven

She puts her phone next to her, getting lost in the game for an instant.

The last thing she expected was to sense a sure serenity upon casually chatting with Lucas.

It has been a well needed breath of fresh air in her day.

If this short exchange was any indication, working with him should be enjoyable.

When a commercial break starts, her eyes flick down to her laptop.

She should probably work like she planned to.

She knows herself well enough to be aware that as soon as she starts she'll probably have a ton of questions that will appear in her brain.

She'll try to make sense of things, and will want to understand the tiniest details.

The only person able to answer all potential inquiries she might have is Lucas.

An idea crosses her mind.

She grabs her phone to send him another message.

R: Would you have some time tmrw to talk about your case?

She doesn't wait more than a few seconds to get an answer.

L: I already have something planned tmrw.

She unexpectedly feels a pang of deception.

She presses her lips into a thin line.

She shouldn't feel that way. He doesn't owe her anything, and it's the weekend, of course he has—

A new message illuminates her screen.

L: But if you're willing to come to Boston with me, I'd be happy to discuss during the drive.

She rereads it twice to make sure she got it right.

R: You're really inviting me on a road trip?

L: If you give me your address, I can pick you up in the morning. Same day round trip. We'll be back before Monday so I can start the week normally.

The suggestion is tempting.

She could spend some actual time with him to potentially quench her curiosity about who he became.

She starts typing her acceptance, but stops after two words.

She's hesitating.

A round trip to Boston is a long drive. Tons of things could go wrong. They are closer to being strangers who just met than actual friends.

Strangers who have seen each other naked plenty of times in the past though.

She snorts at her thought process, noticing a new notification banner appearing on top of her screen.

She frowns.

William is texting her.

W: Still nothing planned? Wanna meet?

Is a booty call really what she needs right now?

She inhales deeply, throws her head back, and drops her phone in her lap.

How did her uneventful and relaxing evening turn into one where she feels like she has to make important decisions?

She first decides to take a moment before replying to both men.

She has a hunch that whatever she chooses to do, it will have consequences on how her life will pan out in the near future.

She has to tread carefully.

Four

Quicksands

"You really sang *All Of Me* from Billie Holiday at your friend's wedding in front of three hundred people?" Lucas fixes the aviator sunglasses on his nose as he's driving.

"I mean... I love Billie, and it was a dare. I had no choice, right?" Raven half-smiles, pulling down the sleeves of her mint green over-sized cropped crew sweater. "It was barely on key, but Heather and her wife Zoe appreciated it. That's what counts I guess."

"For sure." He straightens the collar of his marled charcoal hoodie while briefly flicking his stare at her dark indigo ragged jeans. "I'm sure it wasn't that bad."

He remembers that when he saw her come out of her building dressed like this with her perfect subtle makeup and wearing what he's now calling her 'signature Chelsea boots' on her feet, he inhaled deeply.

He only wanted to grab her hips and pull her to him to see if her body was still feeling as flawless against his as it used to.

He wanted to bury his nose into her hair to breathe her in.

Maybe it would still smell like jasmine and lavender like it did back when he met her.

It never failed to propel him into another dimension. He could spend hours nuzzling into her neck to relax. To let the whole universe disappear around her.

In those moments she was all that mattered.

He recalls that she similarly always loved his sandalwood cologne. She kept saying that she couldn't get enough of wearing his clothes when they were alone to soak in his soothing scent.

And oh, how he loved seeing her in his garments.

The more she was approaching his black convertible, the more he wanted to give in and reach out to her.

But he didn't do any of that.

He put a hand inside his light washed jeans and opened the door to let her settle into the passenger seat of his luxury sports car as she pulled her hair up in a messy ponytail instead.

He shifts his attention back on the road.

She arguably shouldn't have left such a mark in his psyche, but he can't help it.

She did.

His whole body is undeniably drawn to her whenever she's close, and his brain is bringing back unwarranted memories every time their eyes meet.

He's interacted with thousands of people in his life so far. He got to know hundreds of them.

Raven is the only one who keeps haunting his thoughts.

Now that he has reconnected with her, he can't wait to see where it leads them.

They are potentially at very different stages of their lives, and on vastly different paths, but—

Raven's smooth tone reaches his ears as she drapes her arm on top of the door. "I guarantee you that you don't want to hear me sing."

He shrugs amusedly. "What if I'd genuinely like for my ears to bleed?"

As her laugh echoes in the habitacle of his car, Lucas flashes her a smile while changing gears.

As the sound slowly fades, a comfortable silence falls upon them.

He suddenly realizes that he happily welcomes any and all moments spent with Raven.

To him, the quietness is as relaxing as the conversations between them. Which is something rare to achieve. There's not a lot of people with whom Lucas feels content sharing quietude.

The only ones who fit that bill are his sister along with his best friend Sabrina.

The exact Sabrina he used to visit once per month by driving up to Boston alone, listening to music and getting lost in thoughts.

It always acted as a small respite to his otherwise packed schedule and lifestyle.

Nowadays, the visits are more scarce. His schedule doesn't easily allow for it most months so he hasn't done so since the spring.

A lot of things have changed in his friends' life since the last time he was in Boston, so when he realized that summer had already gone by, he decided to rectify the situation and visit.

Having Raven with him makes it even more fun.

To be completely honest, he was surprised when she accepted his invitation.

As soon as he sent it, he wondered if he was moving too fast too soon.

Texting her had been nothing but enjoyable, and he had an urge to keep the ball rolling by spending more time with her. He was reflecting on how to achieve it when she asked him if he was free to talk about his case.

He jumped on the occasion to ask her to accompany him to Beantown.

He's glad she agreed.

The whole drive has been nothing but pleasant so far, being mostly filled with smalltalk and talking about their respective professional journeys.

So you climbed the ladder pretty quick, Raven told him after he shared the story of how he made it to Managing Director three years faster than average.

I did. He maneuvered through traffic. *I was lucky they offered me a job directly when I got out of Liberty Cove.*

That's amazing! How did you end up getting this offer?

I started working with them my junior year through the work co-op program that they had. I found my niche by uncovering risks for some of our clients and that led to being asked back to work with them for my senior year, too. He tapped on the wheel to the beat of the music as he talked. *During that second time around, I did some work with the Mergers and Acquisitions team, and I absolutely loved it. I think that all the time I put in during my college co-op* and summer internships *gave me a head start. Then all the extra hours I worked since helped me fast-track to managing director quicker than the usual fourteen years it takes to get to that position.* He smiled assuredly. *Everything stemmed from the lasting impression I left on them during my internship, it seems.*

She hummed. *With your natural charm and wit it was probably not very difficult.*

Well, thank you. He couldn't help but look proud. *Coming from you, I take it as a big compliment.*

Don't tell me you don't know your own strengths. That would be bullshit. She snorted. *You wouldn't be thriving like you are if you didn't know how to sell yourself.*

I might know how to put my best side forward. He smirked knowingly. *I am aware that I can make a really nice impression if I want to.*

It's surprising that you don't have a girlfriend in that context. She made a show to look as if she was reflecting. *Maybe it's the fact that you sound so humble.*

Very very funny. He laughed a little. *I mainly don't want to get involved knowing that I can't give a relationship my full attention. I'm emotionally unavailable. It would be doomed to fail.* He furrowed his eyebrows, becoming more serious. *Also, I haven't found anyone that makes me feel like I want to settle down yet.* He took a left turn toward the highway, deciding to reorient the exchange. *What about you? No boyfriend? Also, I'm sure that you wasted no time making a name for yourself in town with your brains.*

No one in my life. It's better this way. I might be allergic to commitment at this point. I prefer to keep things casual whenever I'm with someone. She looked out the window as they merged onto I-90. *Plus, my work was my whole focus for the best part of the last seven years.*

He sounded surprised. *Was?*

Yeah. I quit last week. He saw her tense in her seat. *Working to defend assholes has run its course.*

He took his best supportive voice. *That sounds like a sensitive subject.*

She became defensive. *I don't really want to talk about it.*

He kept his tone soft. *Fair enough.*

He could feel she was closing off and wouldn't share more.

So he didn't push it. He decided to swiftly reorient the exchange to how she ended up working for Jun on his case.

Since that slight tension, they only addressed lighter topics.

Raven always struck him as being a brilliant woman with strong principles. She once told him she chose law because she would be able to bring justice to individuals who are often silenced. She wanted to make those people's voices be heard.

It was essential to her.

She clearly took it to another level, and made it into the big leagues by ending up working in NYC.

He has no idea what happened to her along the way to feel like she couldn't keep on working for whichever firm was employing her, but he's certain she had a good reason to hand in her resignation.

Maybe if she ends up trusting him enough, she'll tell him the whole story.

He'd be honored if that's the case at any point.

In the meantime, he'll continue to go with the flow like he vowed himself he would do.

He turns his head to watch her letting the wind glide through her fingers through the open window before concentrating on the road again.

He curves a corner of his mouth upward. "Speaking of weddings and music, I played guitar at Felipe's and Emma's ceremony. It was fun."

She puts her head on the headrest, angling it to look at him. "Your friend you were clubbing with on Thursday?"

"Yeah. You have a great memory. He hangs out with Mark, Kyan and I every week, but he and Em have been together since *Liberty Cove*." Lucas quickly glances in the rearview mirror as they enter Newton. "He's the only one of my friends who's married."

Raven's tone is playful. "So he basically grabs a few drinks with you guys, and goes home to his wife while you all individually hook up with different people?"

"That's pretty much it." He hums. "Thursdays are sacred for all of us."

She raises a curious eyebrow. "Only time in the week when you have sex with a stranger?"

He shakes his head. "Not always."

She snorts. "Why am I not surprised?"

He smiles coyly. "Don't tell me you don't have meaningless encounters after telling me you are allergic to commitment."

An amused smile is dancing on her lips. "Do you play guitar often?"

"My acoustic one has been sitting in my wardrobe for the past few years, and I haven't touched it." He gazes at her in soft defiance. "And don't try to evade the subject."

"That's a shame. I think having hobbies help us balance things out in our hectic lifestyles." She inhales deeply. "And I'm not dodging anything. I do have needs, and they are being taken care of appropriately, thank you."

He can feel her eyes on him as he takes an exit to avoid the toll road ahead.

It strangely doesn't bother him to be observed intently by her like this. He could get used to this dynamic. He would love to navigate this kind of banter every day.

He loves it.

Everything feels easy with Raven. That's definitely something that didn't change between them.

She still has this uncanny way to make him feel alive. To make all his nerve endings tingle in fascination.

She is truly one of a kind.

"I'm glad to hear your needs are being fulfilled." He smiles boldly. "Are they making it good for you?"

She never averts her stare. "I can't complain."

"Tsk tsk. That wasn't very convincing. You deserve mind blowing orgasms, Raven." He stops at a red light, instantly facing her with a smug smile on his lips. "Every single time."

She doesn't skip a beat answering him. "Who says that's not what's happening? William is pretty great in that department." She drops her tone to a murmur, leaning toward him as if to share highly confidential information. "If not, I have other ways to achieve it."

"William, huh?" He peers into her eyes. "Not your boyfriend but definitely more than a friend then?"

She holds his stare. "It's purely physical between us."

He scans her turquoise irises behind her sunglasses. "So do you whisper filthy things in his ear as you're lightly scratching his abs while cuddling?"

She pulls her bottom lip between her teeth. "You liked when I was doing it, yeah?"

He sighs. "Adored it."

"And do you let your mouth trace every millimeter of skin of your lovers to have them climax on your tongue alone afterward?" she breathes out, shifting her gaze to his lips.

"Sometimes." He tightens his grip on the wheel with his left hand to resist the urge to touch her. "But you know, you remain my favorite conquest."

"You're such a flirt." She smiles tenderly. "It's been a decade, Lucas. Someone surely—"

He cuts her off. "No. I'm only speaking the truth here. You've been unforgettable."

She reaches slowly to brush her fingers through the shorter hair on the side of his head. "I'm proud to learn that I hijacked your thoughts because of how good I am in bed."

"You're captivating beyond words, Raven." He leans into her touch. "Your eyes when you're falling off the—"

A car horn resonates in their ears, effectively making him trail off.

Lucas rapidly realizes that the light turned green, and focuses back on driving.

He needs to get a grip. He can't let her invade his mind seamlessly like this at every second.

He also needs to calm down, and not think of what she looks like when she throws her head back cursing his name as she—

He hears Raven clear her throat as they both straighten in their seats. "Any reason why you put so much product in your hair these days?"

He frowns, snapping back to the present. "It looks more sleek and presentable."

"I digress." She puts her hands in her lap. "Your natural locks are like velvet. Plus, having it partly untamed was giving you a perfect classy yet edgy look."

"I was looking like I was permanently on vacation." He sounds a little defensive. "That didn't make me look very serious at my job." He makes sure he's merging onto Cambridge Street. "I felt like I needed to step up my game and look like a managing director."

"I respect that. You do whatever you want." She smiles comfortingly. "You're naturally handsome, Lucas. I just personally loved your slightly disheveled look."

"Duly noted." He relaxes once more. "Circling back to speaking about having hobbies, I take a week of vacation per year specifically to go surfing."

"That's fantastic." She beams. "Do you have a favorite destination?"

"I traveled a bit all over." He continues on the River Street Bridge. "I loved Gold Coast in Australia and adored the challenge of the waves of Nazaré in Portugal."

"Agreed. Those waves are something else, right?" She sounds joyful. "I also have a special place in my heart for Jeffreys Bay in South Africa, and Aregno Beach in Corsica."

"Never went there."

"You have to," she exclaims cheerfully. "Actually, I could show you the best spots if we ever end up going there at the same time."

"That would be amazing." He looks at Charles River as they cross the bridge into Cambridge. "To this day, surfing is one of the only things able to quiet my mind. It makes me reconnect with the essential." He half-smiles. "You can't fool the waves."

"No, you can't." She grabs one of the two reusable bottles of water he placed in the cup holders for the trip. "You have to be in harmony with yourself to become one with them, and achieve the perfect balance required to feel free."

"Mhmm. It's very therapeutic."

He pauses at the same time he stops at another red light.

He usually doesn't address those topics with a lot of people.

None of his friends are as passionate as him about surfing, and the carefree sensation he has when he is riding waves is not something he talks about a whole lot.

His whole persona in town is based on being nothing but sure of himself, pragmatic and uncompromising.

He has to admit that it's the polar opposite of how he feels when he's away from the city for a prolonged period of time.

He has no idea how he ended up putting this side of himself forward for his job and—

He shakes his head to push the thought away.

He doesn't want to linger on it while he could enjoy Raven's presence by his side.

He curls his hand onto the transmission lever. "You have any preferred activities to unwind?"

"Yoga and meditation are big go-tos. Helps me to center myself amidst all the craziness of life." She smiles warmly at him. "I also read, jog, and try to travel whenever I can. At this point I've been on all continents at least once." She seemingly remembers something. "Which reminds me that Jun is constantly making fun of my love for oats for breakfast since I visited Sweden."

"Oats are incredible," Lucas states assuredly. "Most underrated meal ever."

She opens the bottle. "Right?"

"I'm personally a big fan of spicy chickpeas with soppressata and eggs for breakfast, and my mother's Shawarma's chicken with garlic cream is to this day my go-to comfort meal." He gets lost in thought. "My mom showed me how to make it before I left for *Liberty Cove*. Everytime I would feel overwhelmed, I would cook it." He smiles shyly. "It never fails to bring me to a happy place."

"That's awesome. I don't have such a wholesome story." She takes a sip. "Although I will say that I love food, I love experimenting with flavors, and so every time I'm in a kitchen I have fun."

Trafic begins moving again. Lucas presses on the accelerator, taking a right on Memorial Drive. "That's pretty wonderful. Do you think that you'll experiment since you might now have more time to—"

He stops himself short of mentioning her recent resignation.

He doesn't want to upset her or make things uncomfortable.

Going with the flow is oddly effortless with her. It comes naturally to him to just discuss anything and everything.

No holding back.

But he has to remind himself that she might not see it the same way.

He'll always respect her pace, what she's willing to share, and how she decides to orient any important discussion.

He wants her to feel it.

So he shifts gears, and lets a beat pass as he starts humming to the music playing in the car.

Raven looks around, seemingly letting his latest comment slip. "You know, I think it's very nice that you're taking the time to visit your friends like this, but you lied." He makes a face at her statement. She continues, smiling teasingly. "They're not living in Boston. According to the route we're taking, they are in Cambridge."

He snorts, shrugging. "Potato. Potato."

She laughs softly. "Cambridge sure is a beautiful spot." She starts toying with the lid of her water bottle. "You're certain that my presence won't bother them? I can totally go take a stroll downtown in the meantime. I don't want to—"

He interjects. "Stop it. As I told you the moment we left New York, I already asked them, and they're thrilled about meeting you." He hesitates for a second before deciding to carry on. "I usually never bring anyone with me."

She furrows her eyebrows. "It's not like I'm an important person in your life."

"We're now working together for a while. That makes you important." He smiles something mellow at her. "Plus, I might've mentioned you a few times because of that lasting impression you left in my psyche." He turns his attention briefly toward her. "Sab and Brooke will love you."

The lawyer suddenly becomes very serious. "Did you talk to any of your friends about the blackmail you received?"

"No, I only mentioned I had to hire a crisis management team because of a situation at work that required it." He sounds business-like. "I kept silent about all the details to everyone I told so far. I figured if I don't want it to get out there, the less people know about it, the better. Even if they're my close friends, it still feels like a hazard to tell them about it at this stage. I'll reassess depending on what happens."

"It's a good call." She takes another gulp of water. "By the way, Jun sent the letter for analysis to see if there's any potential fingerprints on it or traces of DNA."

"That's great." He changes gears. "Whoever sent it probably took all precautions to leave no evidence, but it never hurts to check."

"Our thoughts exactly." She puts the bottle back into the cup holder. "I know we were supposed to talk about your case since the beginning of the drive, and that was the whole point of being together today, but we definitely got sidetracked talking about other stuff, huh?" She smiles gently. "Do you have any idea if one of your clients or even any of your exes from your personal life could've done it?"

"I, for one, am glad that our conversations turned out the way they did. Spending time with you is not all work." He sounds serious. He wants her to know that he means it. "I don't think it ever will be." He smiles coyly. "That being said, I've never been with someone long enough to share a lot about my life with them. Even the longest relationships I've had were very casual. I doubt someone could use any of it against me." He reflects for an instant. "As for my clients, there's a few I could potentially see pull off something of this sort. Especially some who keep asking me to take more risks because they've become greedy lately. Their businesses have expanded into some more dubious territories to make fast and big money, and of course I'm the guy they'll call if they want to manage it."

Raven presses her lips into a thin line. "Do you normally give in to their demands?"

"There's a clear line I never cross." He keeps his voice steady. "Sure, I can find loopholes. As long as it stays legal. If any request involves that I have to straight out lie and make up something at any point, that's where I draw the line."

"I'm glad to hear. So I shouldn't stumble upon any smoking gun by going through your files to investigate?"

"You shouldn't," he confirms, unflinching. "You might find some things you'll find questionable, but as I said it's usually all workarounds."

"Okay." She looks to be into full work-mode now. "So, you have access to your clients financials, and assets—or at least what they authorize you to see. I have to issue a warning here. We can go check further, and also monitor their communications, but whatever we find won't be able to be used in court because we don't have the proper mandates to dig into those files at the moment."

"I know that." He nods solemnly. "I just want to know who is behind it, and deal with it silently. I want them to know I'm on to them so they can hopefully stop, and we can reach an arrangement."

She knits her eyebrows, looking at him intently. "You really think that will work?"

"Knowing my clients, it very well could." He sounds resolute. "They don't want the spotlight on them any more than I want it on myself. It's worth a shot."

"Fair enough. You're the boss here." She hums in approbation. "We'll definitely get to the bottom of this." She looks pensively out the window as they approach Harvard Bridge. "What if it's one of the bank's employees? We have no digital trace to follow so far—the letter was very old-school—but employers are in their right to check any electronic device used for work by their employees. If whoever planned this hired someone to ransack your office, there's definitely a trace of that planning somewhere."

"Ah yeah. The deceiving fine prints in contracts which allow us to legally monitor workers activities. The ones that next to no one reads." He smiles sadly. "I highly doubt it's one of the employees, though."

She tilts her head in questioning, snapping her attention back to him. "You really have that much faith in them?" She stays very serious. "I've seen people wanting to get leverage against the higher-ups more than once. Power-hungry individuals wanting to climb the ladder any way they can."

He becomes contemplative.

Raven is right, but at the same time he still has a hunch that the staff wouldn't be the type to do such a thing.

Most of them are long-time collaborators that have been around since he joined the company.

They have always been very loyal, and determined to see the business thrive.

They would know that acting in such a way with the prospect of making him commit to questionable dealings can only lead to the opposite outcome.

It's still better to entertain all possibilities, and not close off any doors.

But maybe it would be better to go one step at a time.

He decides to expose his thoughts to Raven. "Let's start by looking into my clients." He half-smiles to show her that he's on board. "If nothing stands out, we can move on to other potential suspects."

"Sounds good." She smiles back at him. "Just imagine for a minute if it's one of the employees who did it, and they weren't wise enough to not use their work equipment to plan it. Our job would be so simple."

"That would be hilarious. It would indeed be very easy to find the culprit in that case."

Quietness envelops them once more as only the music fills the space.

They're nearly at their destination, but he feels like sensing a little more of the breeze since they're not on the highway anymore.

He takes the occasion of being stopped at a pedestrian crossing spot where there's a slew of tourists to completely immobilize his car, and presses on the button to open the roof.

Raven glances at the top sliding out of view. "I like your car." She curves a corner of her mouth upward. "I have a small convertible back in San Diego that my friends are looking after, and that I use when I visit. I could never part with it."

"I love my car, too. It's great on the open road, and smooth enough to maneuver around in urban landscapes." He looks in the rearview mirror to make sure the roof is safely tucked into the trunk before starting the engine again. "I've always wanted to own a rugged truck to go offroad though."

"And bring your dog everywhere with you?" she teases.

"Yes!" He grins. "Perfect to put all the surfing equipment in it too." The last person crosses the street, and he resumes driving. "The fun part with some of the models is that you can remove the top, and even the doors when you go on sand dunes."

She makes herself even more comfortable in her seat. "The dream."

He hums in agreement.

"I miss driving along the coastline." She angles her head to feel more of the wind on her face. "I mean the Californian one. The one here on the East Coast is nice, but it's not the same."

"I've only ever spent a few days in California, but I think I get it. The vibe over there was easy-going, creative and relaxed. From what I gathered, people were mostly living life by their own rules with a beautiful open mindedness." He smiles pensively. "I felt good everywhere I went. I think it reminded me of—"

He trails off.

He realizes that it reminded him of *her*.

When he visited SoCal for a congress a couple years ago with Felipe, Lucas felt like he belonged. Exactly like he felt in Raven's arms back when they spent that week together.

Raven comes from California, and it's more than obvious to him now that they both share the same energy.

A tempestuous but peaceful aura paired with a calm, but thrilling undercurrent.

A sensation that if he was ever to abandon himself to it, he'd be in for the ride of his life, and could become whoever he aspires to be.

That it could beautifully take him to new heights.

This sentiment threatens to consume him whole if he isn't careful.

He needs to—

Raven's inquisitive intonation reaches his ears. "Reminded you of what?"

There's no need to pretend. "Of you." He flashes her a tender smile. "It reminded me of you."

"You know, when I went to Beirut with my ex-boyfriend, I understood why you were saying that in Lebanon you can ski in the morning, and go sunbathing on the beach in the afternoon." She lets her eyes travel along his jawline dreamily. "I also loved the vibe there, and I'll admit that I thought of you a lot."

He can't help but feel a gentle warmth spreading through him upon hearing her confess this. "It seems like we were both living in each other's minds rent free by moments," he whispers.

She shifts her gaze away from him, inhaling deeply. "Yeah," she murmurs back.

As some transcendent lyrics from a pop singer reach his ears, Lucas breathes in soundly.

He's never been religious nor ever placed faith in concepts that can't be explained through logic.

But maybe what he's living through right now is serendipity.

Maybe Raven's and his destinies are somehow intertwined in the grand scheme of things.

Maybe they'll always end up finding each other no matter what.

Because this powerful feeling that transcends his blood flow every time he thinks about her can't be ignored, and having her near again is playing a number on his brain.

Maybe none of it can be tamed.

Maybe he doesn't even want to control it though.

He feels more ready than ever to see exactly where this extraordinary connection will lead them.

He has a hunch that it could all end up in the most beautiful chaotic convergence he's ever known.

"Connor will be sad that you came by while he's not here," Sabrina states while serving everyone at the table some more wine.

Lucas puts his hand on top of his glass. "I have to drive so it'll be water for me for the rest of the meal." He smiles warmly. "I would've loved to spend some time with him, too. Next time I'll try my best to synchronize my visit with a week when he's with you."

As Raven is sitting next to Lucas in his friends' modern dining room, she lets her fingers trail along the stem of her glass while observing the exchange.

After the usual presentations, Raven soon learned that Sabrina recently got divorced, and that Brooke offered her to stay with her while she was waiting to move into her new house.

Now she just got made aware that Sabrina's seven year-old son Connor adores Lucas.

She can't help but smile absentmindedly while looking through the bay windows at the moon now high in the night sky.

She has to admit that she's having a really nice time.

From the minute she set foot in the luxurious Berkshire Street condo, smooth jazz was filling the air, and she felt welcomed.

The fact that Sabrina is a neurosurgeon, and Brooke an astrophysics teacher, could send off an intimidating vibe, but it was quite the contrary.

The atmosphere is nothing but homely. The Moore sisters greeted her with bright smiles, and warm hugs.

We couldn't wait to finally meet you, Raven, Sabrina told her as she flattened her A-line gray plaid dress. *There was a time when Lucas couldn't shut up about you.* She combed her digits into her long dark brown hair. *But I honestly never thought I'd ever have the chance to know you.*

It's unbelievable that he never asked for your last name or any way to contact you back in Greece, Brooke added, straightening her own flowy floral dress. *And then, he kept saying that he didn't want to try to look you up because you both agreed that whatever you had during that vacation was a fling.* She had a mischievous glint in her hazelnut eyes. *Looks like life caught up with him somehow.*

Raven smiled. She couldn't help but notice that both women have a sure resemblance.

Which makes sense since Lucas told her they are sisters earlier.

Brooke's hair is shorter than her slightly older sibling, but their similar petite frame, matching golden hearts necklaces, and comparable fashion sense are definite giveaways of their family link as well as close bond.

So you couldn't shut up about me? Raven teased Lucas as they progressed inside the house. *It's a good thing you already told me as such from the get-go. It could've been very creepy and uncomfortable if not.* She looked around at the high ceilings of the living area before her eyes landed on the fireplace. *You guys have a beautiful home.*

Thank you. The surgeon continued to walk toward the kitchen. *Although I hope to not stay here for long. Brooke has been very accommodating by allowing us to stay here until the new house I bought is available to move in.*

As Raven politely hummed her approbation, Lucas bent down to whisper in her ear, *You know just how you played a number on my mind.* He moved closer. *I could never fully erase you from my thoughts.*

She leaned back into him automatically. *Is that so?* she murmured back, deciding to play along. *I'll admit that at times I personally had trouble getting you out of my head.*

He sighed as he ghosted his hand low on her hip. *Do you think we should do something about it?*

She couldn't stop her heart from skipping a beat.

A gentle warmth was spreading along her spine.

The heat his body was irradiating was dizzying.

She wanted to feel his touch.

She was craving for him to make her melt into his embrace.

She bit into her bottom lip while reaching to trail her fingertips along his forearm. She wanted to bring their joined hands onto her abdomen to mold her back into his front as he would—

Brooke's cheerful tone reached their ears instead. *Are you all okay with Riesling?*

The moment shattered.

Raven dropped her hand to her side.

Lucas took a step back.

Both smiled and nodded at their hosts.

Now having been sitting beside him for the best part of the last few hours, she can smell Lucas' intoxicating woodsy perfume mixed with something undoubtedly *him* every time he gestures as he talks.

It's slowly driving her crazy.

She is entertaining the possibility of taking him up on his offer to '*do something about it*' as soon as they're out of here.

She has no trouble doing exactly like him, and falling into bed with someone any time she feels like it.

Sex was memorable with Lucas.

An encore would surely be amazing.

Plus, they could totally keep it casual.

She proudly admits that she's good at keeping things superficial in her personal life. That's in great part because of how she became a master at never getting attached after her previous long-lasting relationship with Nathan.

She's clearly no stranger to physically responding to attractive men, and acting on it while keeping an emotional distance.

The problem here is that she can feel not only her body responding to Lucas, but her brain sending discharges of serotonin steadily making her skeleton bask in a satisfying daze every time he looks at her.

Maybe this runs a little deeper than the usual meaningless affair.

It's dangerous.

She never felt that way in years. Actually, she's not certain she ever did at any point in her life except when she was with Lucas in Mykonos.

And she works with him, sleeping together would probably render things very—

Sabrina's sincere voice cuts through Raven's thought process.

The neurosurgeon seemingly finally decided to reply. "Our respective schedules were hard to coincide as it was." She smiles joylessly. "I now worry that with the divorce Connor won't get to see his uncle Lucas as often as he used to. You're a good influence on him. You push him to become better, and pursue what is dear to his heart."

The managing director flashes her a soft smile. "So far that mostly involves playing football, and building alien spaceships."

Brooke chuckles, placing her fork in her plate signifying that she's done with her meal. "No matter if he becomes an astronaut or a professional football player, his future looks bright."

"Very true." Lucas sits back into his seat, putting his hand on his knee under the table. "It could all change in the blink of an eye though. Look at me. I used to play music, draw a ton, and reinvent the world with you both back in college." He grabs his glass of wine. "Today, I'm nothing but rational and efficient."

"As long as you're happy, it's the only thing that counts." Sabrina raises her glass in a toast. "I personally couldn't imagine my existence without operating patients. Knowing that I help them get a better quality of life, or even save them from impending death is very satisfactory."

"You're making a huge difference in people's lives, Sab." Lucas meets her toast with his glass. "I arguably don't, but I love my life." He takes a gulp. "Who wouldn't like to have all the money they can to achieve whatever they set their mind to?"

Raven can't stop herself from frowning. "Although money isn't everything." She turns to look at him. "Being successful comes with a price. There's a cost to reaching the highest spheres of the societal pyramid. One you have to be ready to pay."

"I agree." Lucas locks eyes with her. "Once you succeed though, you don't really want to go back, right?"

Raven scans his emerald gaze. "Well, it depends."

He furrows his eyebrows. "On what?"

She doesn't flinch. "On if you're still able to look at yourself in the mirror at the end of each day, and recognize the person you once aspired to be."

He turns silent for a beat, never averting his stare.

He's looking at her with the mellowest expression she has ever seen, but he indubitably stands for everything she wants to distance herself from.

Her recent soul-searching rendered her more intransigeant toward the quirks of the system.

She doesn't want to go back to entertaining every demand from an elite who abuses their power more often than not.

Lucas might very well embody the most blatant example of those failed societal structures.

Her mind is actively battling between the definite blissful pull Lucas excerpts on her, and her logical notion that he—

Brooke's sudden inquiry snaps her back to the present. "You're a lawyer, right?"

She shifts her attention to the teacher, straightening in her seat. "Yeah." She half-smiles. "I've been defending questionable individuals for far too long. I'm trying to reorient my practice now."

"That's great." The younger sister offers her a coy smile. "Any idea in which sector you're going to—"

Lucas cuts her off. "This was delicious, by the way, Brooke. I think it's one of the best recipes you have ever made."

The teacher beams contentedly. "Thank you."

As the astrophysicist goes on to tell Lucas about her cooking experience, Raven breathes in.

She's glad Lucas interjected.

She certainly doesn't want to get into the specifics of why and how she resigned and what the future might hold.

She is still trying to get her footing, and she's certain that talking about any of it in casual conversation won't do much good.

She didn't even tell Lucas back in his car when they stumbled upon the subject. She definitely isn't about to openly share her resentment toward her old job at that dinner table.

Plus, Lucas himself seems set in his ways of loving the lifestyle his work is giving him. He might say that he doesn't tread in illegality, he still pursues the perks that come with the glamor.

For her part, she knows she's way past that now.

The minute she made her decision to quit, there was no holding back on her principles.

If one thing is made clearer by the second ever since, it's that she doesn't want to go back to how things were when she was working for her old firm.

She brings her wine glass to her lips, observing the moonlight reflecting on the quartz countertops of the kitchen.

It was very considerate of Lucas to have picked up on her unease earlier, and swiftly reorient the discussion another way.

They might not stand for the same things, but he's still observant.

Quite like he always did in the past, he seems set on respecting whichever pace she wants to go for.

She can't stop the smile forming at the corner of her mouth as she puts the glass back on the table.

No matter how people might evolve, maybe some things never change, after all.

Lucas is certainly one of the most thoughtful people she has ever known.

He has a remarkable way to be nothing but attentive and kind.

He's always been in phase with his emotions.

It's one of the things that drew her to him in the first place.

His bewitching assurance pairs flawlessly with his tenderness in a captivating whirlwind she could abandon herself to a thousand times over.

She has to keep reminding herself that she needs to tread carefully here. Things could get complicated fast if she's not.

She idly glances at him from the corner of her eye only to notice that everyone is now quiet.

She looks around, seeing Brooke staring at her sister. "That song still gets to you, huh?" The teacher pulls back her chair to get up. "I'm sorry, I can change it, it's—"

"It's fine." Sabrina curls her hand around her sister's forearm to stop her. "It'll just take some time getting used to what my life has become, but it's strangely cathartic listening to this music now."

Raven focuses on the powerful lyrics about heartache, and learning to accept who one is really past their romantic relationships, washing over them.

Lucas smiles comfortingly at his best friend. "I'm really sorry, Sab. I know you insist that there's nothing I can do to help, but I'm here if you need me. Please never hesitate."

"I appreciate it, but you barely have time for yourself." The neurosurgeon breathes in soundly. "Just the fact that you pick up my calls when I need to vent or chat is a lot." She half-smiles. "I can manage with the rest."

The managing director grabs her hand on top of the table. "It's always an honor when you reach out to me. I wish there was something more I could do."

"It's fine. Honestly, it's going to be better this way. We couldn't keep lying to ourselves." Sabrina squeezes Lucas' hand. "It's just that breakups are never easy. Especially after so much time spent with that person, and even more so when you have children together. The worst is when Connor misses him. He ended up being a lousy husband, but he's a great father to our son."

Lucas frowns. "He was a fucking idiot for cheating on you."

"You know what?" The doctor laughs heartlessly. "I should've doubted him sooner." She lets go of Lucas' hand, sitting back in her chair. "He was getting lazy in bed since he had started seeing that other woman."

"You can't blame yourself for that." The investment banker shakes his head. "You loved him. You trusted him. You're not the one who decided to not address the issues you were having as a couple heads on, and went on to sleep with other people instead."

"Reflecting back on it, I can see clear as day that I've been way too busy with work to make him feel like I was invested in our family." Sabrina takes hold of her glass of wine. "I know that it's too late now, but I'll try to get a better balance. If only for Connor and myself. I owe it to both of us to try to do better."

"Your ex should've still talked to you about it." Lucas peers into his friends' eyes. "Communication is everything. Especially when two people love each other."

"Maybe he had fallen out of love without me noticing it?" The surgeon shrugs dismissively before smiling shyly at Raven. "Look at us with that depressing subject in front of our guest."

"I really don't mind," Raven answers honestly. "If you can't talk about that sort of stuff with your friends, then what's the point?" She curves her lips into a comforting smile. "I've had similar discussions more than once with my own friends after breakups or when just musing about relationships in general." She briefly looks at the man next to her. "I also agree with Lucas. Communication is everything."

She hears Brooke hum. "Are you with someone at the moment, Raven?"

"No." Raven shifts back in her seat to face the two sisters. She hesitates for a split second before deciding to share some part of her personal life. This conversation hits close to home. "But what's funny is that Cambridge feels familiar to me for a variety of reasons. One of them being that I spent time here with my ex Nathan. His family is from around here."

Sabrina makes a face. "Hope you're not getting too many weird vibes from being in town."

"It's okay." Raven's smile morphs into something nostalgic. "We're better apart. None of us was willing to make any compromises so it was doomed to fail one way or another."

"You've always been headstrong." Lucas angles toward her, smiling softly. "It's one of the greatest things about you. He was a fool for not embracing that side of you."

"Says one of the most stubborn guys I've had the pleasure to meet," Raven retorts playfully, boring into his eyes. "I honestly thought I could build a future with Nathan. I was prepared to meet him halfway, but he made his choice. We parted ways."

She knows she's being cryptic. She's doing it on purpose.

She's not ready to share the whole debacle of her failed relationship with Nathan yet.

Those scars still run deep somehow.

At their cores, Nathan and her were all about their work.

She remembers that he was ready to leave everything behind for the sake of his impending promotion as if it was yesterday.

He was wholly ready to move abroad for a few years while she didn't want to embark on a long distance relationship. She also had no intention to quit her job, and abandon everything she had worked so hard to build.

Back in those days, she was still thinking that she could make a difference by working within the system.

All in all, it led to long sleepless nights and excruciating arguments.

To endless fighting and self-questioning.

And if all of that wasn't difficult enough in itself, she can also recall the subsequent pregnancy scare clear as day.

She inhales deeply at the souvenir.

Even if it turned out to be a false alarm, it forced Nathan and herself to not only butt heads about their professional goals, but also confront their broader visions of the future.

Which turned out to be vastly incompatible.

She didn't necessarily think that having a child at that exact moment was the best outcome, but having to deal with the idea of the possibility made her question herself.

She loved Nathan. She realized that, for once in her life, she was ready to attempt to invest herself in something with someone for another purpose than work.

But that was the whole problem.

He wasn't.

While she finally concluded that she could maybe spend some time in Europe with him, and use the occasion to make a name for herself there, Nathan made it plain clear that even years down the line, his job would always be the most essential part of his life.

That he would never be willing to compromise anything to achieve any kind of balance. Work was and would always be his whole life.

Not her.

Not any potential kids.

Not anything else.

She decided to call it quits, and vowed to never let herself feel something akin to love ever again.

At the end of the day, feelings are not worth it.

She was exactly like Nathan before all the soul searching this whole situation brought upon her. She could go back to it in a heartbeat and live a very happy life.

That's exactly what she has been doing ever since.

Now Lucas is searching her gaze for any kind of explanation, and the mellowness in his eyes is nearly making it impossible to not give in.

She opens her mouth to hopefully swiftly reorient the discussion, but has no time to before Lucas retorts.

"He was still a fool for letting you go," he breathes out.

Here it is again, the sparkling stare that contains all the softness in the world. The one she could never fully resist.

He's so close.

She could reach out, and comb her fingers through his hair once more. Scoot closer, and skim her nose along his.

She could curl her hand around his thigh, and gently slide it up. Toy with the hem of his hoodie, and sneak her fingers underneath to define his abs.

How she would love to feel him react under her touch.

Heat is pooling low in her belly at the mere thought of him cradling her head, kissing her senseless, and pressing himself against her.

She would moan against his tongue, and—

Sabrina laughs echoes in her ears. "I keep telling you to stop using so much gel, Lucas. You're gorgeous without, and this proves that it clearly doesn't always fulfill its purpose."

Raven instinctively leans back as she registers that Lucas is replacing a strand of hair that is falling on his forehead.

He snorts. "See?" There's a mischievous glint in his eyes. "You might've found an ally here, Raven."

She smiles shyly.

How many times will they have to be interrupted by outside events before she has enough?

It's a slippery slope to keep being close to him like this.

She's not entirely sure she trusts herself to be able to have any kind of self-control for very long if they continue on this path.

She has to become better at reminding herself that they both stand for different things.

He loves his life. She fled her similar one.

But if they were to only sporadically hook-up like she contemplated earlier, maybe it could be doable.

The neurosurgeon gets up. "I see you have great taste, too, then." She flashes Raven a knowing smile, striding toward the kitchen. "Time for dessert now."

Lucas flips his phone that is laying face down on the table to quickly check the time. "And then we really have to go if we want to be back in New York in time to start the week."

"It's a shame." Brooke picks up the empty plates. "You could've slept here. I have a great guest bedroom."

"You know how Lucas dedicates himself to his work," Sabrina shouts from near the fridge.

The teacher looks at him in fake reprimand. "Very true."

Raven gestures at the items on the table. "Do you need any help with that?"

"Nah. It's all good. You're our guest. Your only task is to relax." Brooke grins. "Dessert coming up!"

"She really means it." Lucas scrolls through his messages. "They both never let me lend a hand, but I sometimes find a way. Judging by their attitude today, I would say now is not the moment to try though. They are very enthusiastic that you're with us."

As Raven laughs lightly, she slumps a little in her seat.

She can feel the tiredness catching up with her. She hasn't slept a whole lot in the last few days.

Between the stress and angriness of her resignation, the sex marathon she lived through with Will on Friday, and her brain keeping her alert at all hours of the day, her body is now steadily showing her that she needs rest.

She wasn't in the mood to see Will last night when he messaged her, but she was kept awake by a thousand thoughts colliding in her psyche until dawn was breaking through her windows.

Tonight, she has a hunch that for the first time since Thursday, she'll fall into bed to sleep soundly as soon as she gets home later.

It will be a blessing.

It might even help her reset her mind of the ghost of Lucas' entrancing presence.

As she looks at him typing hastily on his screen keyboard, she breathes in.

Who is she kidding?

Even if she's exhausted, she'd love to fall into bed with him.

In the past few hours, he managed to make her feel a little bit more peaceful.

She'd love for this sensation to last longer.

Plus, she knows how it feels to spend hours in his arms alternating between sex and slumber.

She's convinced that it's probably another thing that didn't change.

He would make her feel tremendously good.

She shakes her head.

It's the fatigue talking, and positively bypassing her rationale.

She needs to focus on something else.

So she grabs her own phone to check her notifications.

That will maybe prevent her from climbing him like a tree while his friends are preparing the next course.

But the second he puts his device back on the surface to look at her keenly, she's not too sure about anything anymore.

FIVE

Life Is a Highway

Nighttime driving has always been something Lucas loves to do.

He can crank up the music, let it wash over him as the scenery passes him by, and bask in the calmness of the nearly empty roads.

He could drive on open roads, highways or along any coastline as the stars shine bright in the sky forever. He adores the contentment it brings him.

Although at the moment, he loves it for a completely different reason.

Raven is sleeping peacefully next to him, and every time his eyes fleetingly land on her facing him in her slightly reclined seat, he can't help but smile.

She's totally unguarded, she trusted him enough to doze off, and she's strikingly gorgeous.

It's an honor that she allowed herself to relax enough to take a nap in his car.

He's now keeping the volume of the sound system low, maneuvering his car as smoothly as he can to not wake her up.

He wants her to get some rest.

He recalls that she mentioned she was tired while they were alone at the dinner table.

Did you receive any important messages? he asked when she picked up her phone.

No. She inhaled deeply. *Since I resigned I have a ton of emails and texts I don't even feel like looking at.* She sounded preoccupied. *I'm just texting a friend I was supposed to talk to today, but didn't. I hope she's doing okay.*

I hope so, too. He offered her his best comforting smile. *Was something happening with her?*

I don't know. She frowned, sending the message. *And I might be getting worried, but it's possibly only the exhaustion talking. I have barely slept since Thursday.*

If you want we can leave now, and be in New York before 2AM. He looked at her with some concern. *It's not optimal, but it's arguably better than arriving during the dead of night? I'm sorry I assumed staying was alright for you. I should've—*

She cut him off. *It's all good. Believe me, if I had a problem with the schedule I would've said something.* She smiled coyly. *I'm having a good time. I'll rest when I get home.*

He scanned her eyes. *You sure?*

She hummed. *Positive.*

He let her deal with her other notifications as his own phone lit up again on the table.

He had replied to Felipe a minute or so before. His long-time friend was asking him about this crisis situation he has to deal with.

That's another sure sign that news travels fast.

Mark already told Felipe the small piece of information Lucas divulged to him last night which means that soon Emma will know as well as all her book club.

Mark will potentially also tell Kyan when he'll see the analyst at the gym tomorrow.

In no time the fact that something is going on at Lucas' office will have made the rounds.

He made the right call not wanting to overshare anything with his friends for now. This is already getting out of hand.

Lucas messaged Felipe that everything was taken care of. He expected the analyst to let it drop, but his latest text was showing that he sounded alarmed instead.

F: Are you sure you're going to be fine? Who did you hire? I hope it's nothing too serious. Man, you don't need that in the middle of signing up with new clients...

Lucas frowned and ignored it.

Every time something important occurs, Felipe gets apprehensive.

Lucas was not in the mood to entertain his friend's concerns. He decided to just give him some time to let it sink in and calm down.

The whole interaction still managed to piss him off a little.

He's always careful to respect what others are willing to share or not in general. He expects the same treatment from his closest friends.

They should trust him to do what's right for himself, and understand that he'll talk to them about what he wants—nothing more.

By doing the complete opposite, Flip has a way to get under his skin in the worst ways sometimes.

Unlike Raven who effortlessly gets under his skin for entirely different reasons.

He snorts quietly.

His mind easily circled back to her of its own accord.

He won't complain.

He quite likes it when she creeps into his thoughts. It brings him a peace he wasn't even aware he was missing.

She even seemed to get along nicely with Sab and Brooke, and he's sure that if Raven had met Connor she would've liked him, too.

He's happy about that fact. Sab is definitely an important person in his life. Moreover, she is a good judge of character.

More than once during university she had a bad feeling about someone that turned out to confirm itself later on.

Plus, they always had each other's backs.

He looked out after her following a plagiarism incident she was wrongfully accused of. He found out who did it by conducting his own investigation and hacking into the correspondences of Sabrina's classmates. He then made sure the culprit was exposed publicly along with the proof.

Similarly, Sabrina was the one who went to spend time by his mom's side when she had to go through a minor surgery. He couldn't because of his internship, he was getting worried, and Sab offered to accompany his mother through the procedure. She gave him regular updates, and when he could finally join them in Chicago, his mom was ecstatic at having had someone take such good care of her.

Sabrina and he lived through a lot together.

It also means that he is aware that it doesn't happen often that his friend genuinely likes someone.

Especially after only one meeting.

It's heartwarming to know she had that feeling about Raven.

She's a good one, Lucas, Sabrina whispered into his ear while hugging him goodbye. *If I was in your shoes, I wouldn't let her go.* She pulled away, smiling knowingly at him. *But I'm not the boss of you.*

He smiles absentmindedly at the souvenir old of only a couple hours.

As the lyrics of a dark and sultry alt-pop song wash over him, he internally agrees with his friend.

Raven is unique.

During one week from what feels like ages ago now, she creeped into his brain to leave her mark, and now she could very well be able to carve a place into his whole life.

He hears Raven hums inattentively beside him on the tempo.

He half-smiles.

Maybe she knows this song.

She is potentially slowly getting into the REM phase of her sleep or through hypnopompia. She's getting more aware of her surroundings so she—

He shakes his head to focus.

Reminding himself of the whole explanation Sabrina once gave him about sleep phases is useless at the moment.

He stomps a little bit more on the accelerator, crooning under his breath, and letting each line resonate.

Raven is definitely the most stunning woman he ever met.

There's just something about her facial features with her hooded eyes, delicate nose slope and square jaw that makes him go mad.

He wants to take it all in every time he stares at her.

He wants to register every single detail as if he'll never have the chance to look at her again.

He breathes in as his brain summons a mental map of her body.

Every one of her curves is engraved in his mind.

He knows he could spend eternity defining the slopes of her perfectly rounded breasts over and over.

He yearns to travel down her toned abdomen and slender hips to bury his head between her thighs once more.

He sighs.

But this attraction is way more than just physical.

Her wit is unmatched, and her spirit indomitable. He adores how she challenges him when they're word sparring.

He loves her repartee, and her authenticity.

From what he gathered, she has the biggest heart. Her core personality doesn't look like it changed as the years went by.

She still radiates the perfect blend of intensity and kindness.

Plus, each of her gazes is able to make him weak in the knees because it feels like she peers right into his soul.

He furrows his eyebrows.

Was he starting to fall in love with Raven back in Mykonos?

It only lasted a week. Surely it hadn't been long enough to—-

No.

He wasn't.

When he was in his twenties he entertained relationships with women he liked, but he debatably wasn't in love with any of them even after months of being together.

No chance in hell he was falling in love in such a short span of time.

Although he can't deny that he was feeling *something* for Raven.

And whatever those sentiments he ended up having toward her were, they were strong.

He recalls that parting ways with her at the airport was more difficult than he would care to admit.

That last embrace they shared felt like a curse after having been granted a once-in-a-lifetime opportunity.

He didn't want to leave her.

He nearly asked for her phone number, but decided against it. They wanted something uncomplicated with no-strings attached. He didn't want to break that promise.

They had their lives in front of them anyway. They could both find someone and build something truly serious in the future with someone else.

He clearly didn't, but she got into a serious relationship.

With a certain Nathan.

He has no idea what happened exactly with her ex, but it sounds bad enough to justify not wanting to get into anything serious moving forward.

He understands a little better now why she says she might be allergic to commitment.

But there's now William in her life who is apparently good in bed. Even if she says there's nothing between them at the moment, maybe she could develop a fondness for that man.

Actually, for how long has she been sleeping with him?

It might be new and—

Approaching New Haven, he checks the fuel gauge. He curses under his breath. He should've made sure it was full before exiting Cambridge. That was a stupid oversight.

He'll have to stop to fill the tank or they won't make it to New York City.

A rapid look at the GPS on his dashboard makes him identify the nearest gas station at the next exit.

The deceleration as he navigates through a turn looks to be enough of a change to pull Raven out of her slumber.

He sees her stretch out of the corner of his eye.

"Hey υπναρού[1]," he whispers as to not rush her awakening.

She snorts softly. "You still remember how to call me a sleepyhead?"

He takes a right turn at the intersection. "I do recall how you used to be able to be a late sleeper in another life, and how I enjoyed teasing you with it." He makes sure he's following the right direction by reading the sign. "I thought it would be a fun way to greet you back into the land of the living."

"You enjoyed staying in bed late just as much as me, mister." She stays in the same position laying on her side, looking at him drowsily. "And it's not as if I was very far away in dreamland," she teases.

"You tell me." A playful smile is dancing on his lips. "Were your dreams any fun?"

She yawns. "If I had any, I don't remember."

"It's a shame." He glances at her briefly. "I wish you'd dream of me."

She breathes out a laugh. "You're so full of yourself."

He changes gears, smirking. "You used to love it."

She hums. "Who says I don't right now?"

He grips the wheel a little tighter. "Don't say that."

She tilts her head slightly. "Why?"

Later he may blame it on his own tiredness, but at the moment he chooses to share an undeniable truth. "You're always beautiful, but when you allow me to be the guardian of your sleep, I just want to feel you against me."

"Oh, really?"

"Mhmm. I want to mold my body to yours." He inhales deeply at the image his brain summoned of how perfect she feels in his arms. "I want to slowly undo your ponytail to brush my fingers through your hair." He gets lost in thought, deciding to be nothing but honest. "I want to let my thumb trace your jaw, and see if your lips are as soft as I remember. I want to feel the warmth of your tongue as you wake up. I'd kiss you for hours on end, Raven." He shifts a little in his seat. His jeans might be becoming a little more uncomfortable as his imagination runs wild. "I would let my mouth explore every inch of you lazily." He sighs. "I want

---

1. Greek. Pronunciation: ipnarou. Meaning: sleepyhead.

to feel you scrape your nails into my scalp as I pleasure you. I want to see you climax again." He barely audibly groans under his breath. "I want to hear you moan my name, and feel you coat my taste buds."

He swears he sees her press her legs together a little more as she bites into her bottom lip. "What if I want that, too?"

He keeps his voice steady. "Then I would do it all night."

She reaches to trail her fingertips along his bare forearm. "So what are you waiting for?" She curls her hand on top of his on the gear shift. "There's probably a ton of hotel rooms in the—" She trails off when he takes a turn into the gas station parking lot. She furrows her eyebrows as she suddenly realizes they were going somewhere. "What are we doing?"

He stops in front of a pump. "I need to fill the tank." He turns off the engine, and unclips his seat belt. "It's nearly empty."

It feels like another moment just shattered.

She drops her hand, and straightens in her seat. "Yeah, that's a great idea."

He watches her rub her forehead. "I was also thinking of getting coffee while I'm here." He scans her features. "It's not very good quality versus real coffee shops, but it'll help carry me through the end of that drive. Do you want anything?"

She smiles shyly at him. "Surprise me?"

He flashes her a soft smile. "Sure thing."

He exits the car, and while he walks around it, he takes a deep breath.

Raven straight out told him that she wanted him just like he wants her.

He remembers her boldness, but he wasn't expecting that.

He has to calm down.

They're both exhausted.

The moment they end up having sex again—if it ever occurs—he doesn't want her to regret it.

Which would potentially be the case right now.

As he completes his payment and sets on filling the tank, he looks at Raven navigating through her phone in the car.

He lets his eyes travel to her hand curled at the back of her neck. She's stretching and applying pressure points on her vertebrae there.

He'd like to be the one massaging her sore muscles. He would make sure to rub in a circular motion just like she used to love, and wouldn't stop until the knots dissolve completely.

Sensing her relax under his touch is special to him. He cherishes every time he had that effect on her.

How come are you so skilled? she once asked him while he was massaging the small of her back as she was laying on her stomach in bed.

She had mentioned a slight pain in that region after dodging a jellyfish on the beach during their morning run.

It probed her to do a false-movement that caused a twist in her back.

As soon as they got back to the room, and after their shower, he had offered to try to help make her feel better.

Having her half-naked under him as he was straddling her in only his boxer briefs was making it difficult to not turn that massage into caresses.

I took some classes. They were offering them as an extracurricular activity during my second year. He dipped his thumbs slightly under her black polka dot shorties. *I thought it might come in handy.*

Well, I'm certainly glad you did. She bent into an arc at the motion. *Your hands are like magic.*

He smiled warmly as he bent down to murmur into her ear, *Feels good?*

Feels amazing. She sighed. *I don't feel pain anymore.*

I'm glad. He laid soft kisses up her jugular as he continued massaging her hip bones. *I also felt you seek me just now.* He skimmed his nose behind her ear. *Was that on purpose?*

I said your hands are like magic. She angled her head to give him more access. *I meant it not only to soothe the pain. I have little control over how my body responds to you sometimes.*

He slowly defined her cartilage with his tongue to end up gently sucking at one side of her industrial piercing. *My body has a mind of its own when it involves you.*

She whimpered as she leaned into his not so subtle arousal against the small of her back. *I can feel that.*

I'm sorry. I'll try to—

She cut him off. *Don't.* She reached for his hand lingering at the hem of her panties. *I want you inside me, Luke.* She helped him slide them down her legs. *I think there's one or two condoms left in the box.*

He captured her bottom lip to kiss her lazily as he daintily traced her core. *We'll go buy some more later?*

She moaned as she grinded into his palm while kissing him. *Mhmm.*

She was on the pill, but preferred to always use condoms.

He still recalls how sexy she looked when she was the one rolling them onto him as she bored into his eyes.

Never has someone treated his cock with such care and—

He hears the valve shut off signifying that the fuel tank is now full.

He wastes no time removing the nozzle. He wraps up the transaction by asking for the receipt, and strides toward the building.

Once inside, he goes to stand in front of the self-served coffee selection, where he grabs two cardboard cups with matching tops.

He's glad that this station has some choice past the usual Arabica blend. He chooses the darkest roast available to fill the tumblers, placing them both in a tray once he's done.

On his way to the counter, he takes stock of the available selection of food in the aisle.

He grabs a bag of roasted almonds for himself along with a pack of two wrapped cinnamon buns.

Picking up some more snacks—a bag of salt and vinegar chips as well as sour worm gummies—for Raven, he curves a corner of his mouth upward.

It only took her waltzing back into his life for him to long for her to an insane degree.

Having sex with her is a phenomenal experience.

He has no doubt she would once again feel spectacular arching underneath him as he would undulate his pelvis slowly just like she loves.

He would do anything to feel her make a mess out of his hair while she moans deep into his mouth as they make out.

He forces himself to stay in the present by looking at the cash register while the clerk scans the articles.

He and Raven work together at the moment.

Sleeping together could complicate things. Maybe it's even a deal breaker for her.

But she seemed very willing to fall into bed with him tonight.

The cashier asks him for the total amount of the transaction that he quickly pays before making a beeline back to the car.

No matter what happens during the rest of the drive, he has to remind himself that he vowed he would go with the flow, and not overthink things.

Which is exactly what he decides to do when he plops down into the driver seat.

He still double-takes when he notices that Raven removed her hairband, letting her wavy hair flip mostly on one side, making it cascade down her shoulders exquisitely.

The second she sees him, she drops her phone in her lap and smiles coyly at him.

He inhales steadily.

He has to get a grip.

He places the snacks on the middle console. "Here you go." He hands her the tray with the cups. "I hope you still like your coffee black?"

She takes one from it. "Yes, thank you."

"You're most welcome." He takes his, puts it in the cupholder and discards the tray on the side of his seat. "I hope it'll be drinkable." He puts on his seatbelt to then start the engine. "I took the dark roast."

She holds the cup with both her hands to bring it to her nose. "Just the comforting heat and smell will do wonders in themselves."

He exits the gas station lot. "I saw you stretch your neck muscles." He changes gears. "Is your back okay? You can turn on the heated seat if you have any discomfort or muscle soreness from having slept in the car."

"I'm fine, Lucas. Really." She combs her fingers through her hair. "I appreciate the concern, but I'm good." She raises a playful eyebrow. "And wow for stalking my every movement."

"I'm not stalking you." He sounds dismissive. "You're in the car, and I happened to be outside of it with nothing to do so I glanced inside."

"I hope the view was worth it," she teases.

He smiles tenderly. "That view will always be worth everything."

She snorts. "You're one smooth talker." She takes a sip. "Does this kind of line truly work?"

"I never use lines. I hate them." He frowns. "I always try my best to be nothing but honest."

"It doesn't surprise me." She grabs the bag of chips. "You probably don't even need anything of the sort for women to fall into your arms to start with."

He becomes pensive. "I don't recall exactly what I did for you to want to—"

She cuts him off. "Just being you was enough." She goes through the rest of the snacks. "There's just something about you that connects with me."

He smiles absentmindedly. "Connects? Present tense?" He sees her check the snacks. "I apologize, there was no hummus to go with whichever crackers I could have chosen." He blindly reaches for the pastry bag. "I also thought you'd like to have the choice to have a bun with your coffee instead of the chips or gummies, but I wanted you to have the liberty to pick whichever you'd prefer."

She smiles coyly. "Yes. Present tense. I can't deny that things feel easy with you whether it's years ago or now." She takes the cinnamon buns, dropping the roasted almonds in her lap. "And you obviously took the almonds for you. I might steal some." She unwraps the pastry. "I'm amazed you remembered about the hummus as well as salt and vinegar being my favorite chip flavor."

"You can take the whole almond bag if you want." He smirks. "Don't forget the sour gummies. I know you like your snacks to have a kick."

"Obviously." She takes a bite, humming appreciatively. "That is surprisingly good for a commercial cinnamon bun."

"Really?" He sounds surprised, once again shifting gears. "Would you mind giving me the other one?"

"We can share this one, I'm not that hungry." She takes a piece from her cinnamon roll and holds it in front of him so he can eat. "I merely wanted to taste it."

He doesn't hesitate to angle his head to take it into his mouth. He's aware that his lips might linger a little bit too long on her fingertips before he leans back.

He doesn't mind.

He might be hallucinating but it feels like she also didn't want to remove her fingers. She lightly traced part of his bottom lip before retracting her hand.

He gets lost in thought as he masticates.

He would've loved to gently suck on her thumb to swirl his tongue around it and clean it from the glaze.

But from the corner of his eye he can see her do it herself.

He curses internally.

He has no idea how she can render this simple gesture so sensual. Maybe it's because he knows how magnificent her mouth feels.

How she can flick her tongue over—

He can't concentrate on that. He needs to drive.

He summons all his strength to focus. "You're right. It's pretty good."

She smiles something mellow at him. "I remember how we both tremendously enjoyed the food in Greece, but kept saying that the one thing we missed was cinnamon rolls."

"Yeah." He merges back onto the highway. "I even said that if we were to find some in the region we were in, I would eat it off of you."

She takes another piece to bring it to her mouth. "Coming from someone who inclines toward savory dishes versus anything too sugary, I took it as a big compliment."

"It was." He changes the satellite radio channel. "You're probably the only person who could make me eat pure sugar."

She sounds surprised. "You're serious?"

"Mhmm." He grips the gear shift a little tighter as he changes speeds to stay composed at the naked image of her that his brain unwarrantedly brought him. "You'd just have to sprinkle it all over you."

She makes a face. "It would get sticky."

"I would make sure every millimeter of skin has been taken care of appropriately to not leave you with that gluey feeling."

"Mmm. That's a happy prospect." She finishes eating the bun. "I would still need to take a shower afterwards."

The more she goes on, the more he's having trouble staying collected. His mind is living through a fantasy he doesn't want to snap out of. "Then I could help wash you to make sure the sugar is properly dissolved."

"I wouldn't dare take a shower without you." She pulls her bottom lip between her teeth, putting her head on the headrest to look at him. "Especially since we both know how it usually goes. You end up kneeling before me."

For a minute he wonders why it's so easy to have this kind of exchange with her.

He concludes that he doesn't want to question it.

They always had this way of interacting. He clearly doesn't do as such with anyone else.

It's yet another thing that makes Raven unique.

He can be himself, lower his walls a little, and just navigate each interaction as they come.

"Making you come apart feels even more exceptional under a water stream." He shifts in his seat a little. "And I recall you also trailed down my body quite a few times."

"What can I say?" She reaches to comb her fingers through the hair at the back of his head. "You always felt amazing, Lucas." She scratches her nails smoothly on his skull. "I enjoyed every time, and each second of it. By the way, I would also eat anything off of you. Something tells me that any food would just be more delicious when licked from your abs or—" She trails off herself, inhaling deeply and dropping her hand. "I'm sorry. I'm exhausted, and flirting with you is too easy. You make everything feel natural."

He instantly misses her touch, but wants to reassure her as rapidly as possible that this was all fair play for him. "Don't be sorry. I'm also gladly contributing to the exchange." He smiles warmly. "The fact that I'm tired makes the images just more vivid in my head."

"You think it doesn't do the same for me?" She exhales soundly. "I'm also being nothing but honest at every comment." She picks up her phone and unlocks it. "It's crazy that our paths crossed all those years later, and that it still feels like yesterday I was wrapped up in your arms watching the waves crash on the shore in Mykonos." She navigates through her notifications. "We both lived through so much since then, and—" She frowns. "Fuck," she breathes out.

It's his turn to frown. "Are you okay?" He quickly glances at her. "I don't want to push, but I'm here if there's anything—"

She interjects. "You remember that friend I was texting earlier because we didn't get to chat today like we were supposed to?" He nods. She carries on. "It's Heather. I was getting worried at the time because she was the one who told me she would call. She apparently wanted to discuss, but didn't say what." She looks out the window. "She just replied."

He definitely doesn't want to rush her into talking about anything.

So he stays silent, and waits.

As the last piano note fills the space, Raven's voice is unsteady. "Her wife Zoe is in the hospital." She closes her eyes. "They've been running a series of tests. They think it might be cancer."

"I'm so sorry, Raven." His tone is soft. "If you want to call her and have some privacy I can take the next exit to stop somewhere, and—"

She interrupts him. "It's fine." She snaps her eyes back open. "It's three hours less for them on the West Coast, but she said she was heading to bed to be rested to accompany Zoe for the remainder of the scans tomorrow." She picks up her cup of coffee. "I told her to keep me posted." She seems to become reflective. "She must be devastated."

"Obviously." He wants to sound as comforting as possible. This is harsh news to get. "I can only imagine how difficult this must be to navigate."

"They've been together for nine years." Raven smiles absorbedly. "Married for five. They're the most beautiful supportingly couple I know." She takes a sip of her beverage. "Zoe was there during all of Heather's struggles when she founded her law firm. Without her, Haddy wouldn't have been able to make it."

"You studied with Heather?"

"Yeah. *Harriers* is where we met. We went through a lot together. Quite like you and Sabrina, I guess." She analyzes his features before continuing. "We were a small group of four inseparable friends. Heather, Angela, James and me."

He is curious. "Jun was not studying with you?"

"I met Ju during my last year of high school. She studied programming at another college. Although, she became fast friends with that group when they all met."

"That's awesome. You still all talk to each other?"

"Not really." She exhales while shifting a little on her seat. "A year after we graduated, I left California for New York because I thought I could make more of a difference if I was to join the big leagues here." She brushes her fingers through her hair, sounding a little jaded. "James let me know about an opportunity that was opening up at the firm he worked at, and I jumped on the occasion. Looking back on it maybe I should've hesitated a bit more, but it is what it is." She laughs heartlessly. "For her part, Heather worked a few years before deciding to found her own firm specializing in civil rights law. She is the Davis in 'Davis, Specter and Garcia.'"

"That's truly amazing. Does she like it?"

"Yeah. A lot. She focuses on matters such as housing discrimination, individual liberties and rights, and all kinds of equality concerns. She even added an Environmental and Natural Resources branch to her practice last year with her new name partner." Her expression morphs into a contented one. "She's doing such important work. I'm very proud of her."

"As everyone should. It's an essential part of society. She's fighting the good fight." Lucas smiles brightly. "So you were working with James until last week?"

"No." She shakes her head. "James left about three years ago to go practice in Europe with his wife. We rarely hear from him these days. He's more the 'send a virtual card at Christmas and a message on birthdays' type of guy."

"Gotcha. We all have those types of friends who tend to disappear through time." He half-smiles. "Our paths separate to never cross again, but the memories live on."

She hums. "It would've been the case for you and I if we hadn't fortuitously met again."

"I don't believe in destiny and all that crap." He gazes at her as if to share a secret, murmuring, "But please don't tell my mom."

"Your secret's safe with me."

He directs his attention back to driving. "I'm still thankful for whatever it was that made our roads collide once more." He chooses to tell her a bit about his own journey. "The only friend I kept from university except for Sab is Felipe, and that has come with a lot of hurdles." He puts his index finger in the air as if wanting to stop her from saying something before he has finished his point. "Don't get me wrong, I love the man. He's like a brother to me, but he can be intense in the worst ways sometimes."

"Oh, no worries, I get it." She takes another sip of her coffee. "Is Emma able to bring out the best part of him?"

"Mostly, yes." He grabs his cup from the cupholder. "Lately it's been a little more difficult because they want to start a family." He drinks some. "The problem is that he says that Em wants a house in the Hamptons, and I personally know that Flip always wanted to make a name for himself. Now he can't afford the house, and his career is going great, but not to the extent he wishes it would."

"What does Emma do for a living?"

"She's an interior designer." He puts the tumbler on his thigh. "She's the one I hired to do the decoration of my office, and the company hired her to also do it for our whole floor."

"She's clearly very talented." Raven toys with the lid of her cup. "Your floor is the only one in the whole building where I felt welcomed. It feels cozy."

"Maybe it's because of my presence." He smirks. "Your body could sense that I was near."

"Always so humble." She snorts. "Really, I love your office decor."

"Thank you." Lucas turns on the cruise control. "So yeah, Flip is making good money, but not the kind that can afford any big bold buy yet."

"As long as they're happy with what they're doing, that's the most important thing." She becomes slightly more serious. "Money is essential, but it's also not all there is as I previously stated."

"For sure." He furrows his eyebrows. "It helps though. Mark, Kyan and I keep telling Flip that he could move out of the city and thrive, but he doesn't want to."

"So Mark and Kyan are also working in finance?"

"Kyan is an Investment Banking Associate who works for the same firm as Felipe." He sits back a little in his seat. "Mark is a personal trainer and gym instructor."

"Met him while working out?"

He laughs lightly. "You know I love my workouts."

"You sure do." She smiles amusedly. "I can see at a glance that you're keeping fit."

He automatically shakes off the vision of Raven outlining the ridges and valleys of each of his muscles with her fingertips or her tongue.

"I'm trying my best." He mirrors her expression. "Mark is a great guy. I hope it works out for him with Matteo. He deserves a win in the personal department. He's been very unlucky these last few years."

She raises her cup in a fake toast. "I also wish it turns out for the best for him."

As they both drink, Lucas can't help but recognize once again that it's effortless talking to Raven about anything.

Such straightforwardness is not something simple to come across. It doesn't happen with just anyone.

He can truly navigate anything and everything with her.

It's intoxicating.

She opened up about her own friends, a little bit of her past, and—

He suddenly remembers something. "What about Angela? Did you and Heather keep in touch with her?"

Raven tenses.

He frowns.

She stays quiet.

He regrets his question. It clearly upsets her. He shouldn't have asked.

He sees her fidgeting on her cup as she breathes in.

He was caught up in the discussion. He thought it was a good follow-up subject.

She now looks uncomfortable.

He can't have that.

He has to rectify this.

"I didn't want to overstep." He smiles hearteningly. "I legitimately thought that—"

Raven's voice is barely over a whisper when she cuts him off. "Angie died." She swallows. "Of an overdose. Seven months ago."

He feels like the air has been sucked out of his lungs upon hearing her confession.

That's certainly a demanding event she lived through.

Judging by her reaction, it's still difficult for her to talk about it.

He's honored that she felt comfortable enough to tell him.

He'd like nothing more than to reach out to her. He wants to press her close to him so she could feel the sincerity he has of wanting to share her sorrow.

However, he doesn't know if she would welcome his touch.

So he takes his most tender voice instead. "Again, I'm so sorry, Raven."

"She had been struggling with addiction for years." She keeps her eyes on her coffee as if it's the only thing keeping her from breaking down. "Her drug consumption had been a constant roller coaster throughout her life. She was clean for five years, but then had a really bad relapse." She knits her eyebrows to keep her composure. "She lost her job. Isolated herself. She got some bad stuff on the street that was cut with some illicit fentanyl, and—" She breathes in. "She didn't make it. I wish I hadn't been consumed by my work to be there for her. Maybe she wouldn't have—"

He cuts her short. He can't let her blame herself. It will slowly eat at her if it isn't already. He can't have that. "I'm certain you did everything you could."

"I tried, but I feel like it wasn't enough." She smiles sadly. "Even if she shut me off, and wouldn't reply to my messages or calls, I could've visited more often." She clenches her jaw slightly. "I could've forced her back into rehab." She sounds annoyed at herself. "I could've done a million things differently."

He decides on a new approach. "Do you think it usually works when people are obligated to do something?"

She is taken aback a little, but answers without any hesitation. "No."

"You can lead a horse to water but you can't make it drink as the saying goes." He flicks his stare at her for a second. "Sometimes we feel powerless and it's the worst feeling ever. I might sound harsh, but you can't help someone who doesn't want to be helped." He grips his cup on his upper leg a little more to resist the urge to slide his hand on the side of her face. "Someone who is not ready and emotionally available to accept help."

"You're right." She presses her lips into a thin line. "I know you're right." She takes a sip of coffee. "But it still hurts, you know?" She smiles sadly. "Now with what I learned about Zoe, it brings back my whole 'I have to do more' feeling."

"I get it." He concentrates on a shadow on the road a few dozen feet ahead. "The fact that you're still close with Heather and Zoe versus what it was with Angela should make it a little better, no?"

She hums distantly. "It will certainly help to be kept in the loop."

"Exactly. You'll be able to know what's happening, assess what you can and want to do for—" He trails off. "Shit."

In a split second, he instinctively puts both hands on the wheel, pressing on the brakes swiftly to cancel the cruise control, and quickly analyzes the surroundings for any other vehicles.

Once he confirms the space is clear, he sharply changes lanes.

The car vacillates briefly but stays gripped to the asphalt as Lucas deftly maneuvers it around the obstacle.

Once he stabilizes the speed and gets back into the right lane, Raven looks behind them through her window. "Was that a raccoon?"

"I think so." He frowns, confused at the dampness he feels in his lower body. "I'm glad I was able to dodge it."

She sits back straight in her seat. "He or she seemed to have been startled and was fleeing the road."

"Let's hope the raccoon stays safe, and goes back into nature." He looks down to see that his coffee spilled everywhere on his lap. "Could you please give me some tissues?" He points in front of Raven. "There are some in the glove compartment."

She follows his stare. "That made quite a mess. At least it's not sticky since you also take your coffee with nothing in it." She reaches to grab the Kleenexes. "Unlike if it had been me covered in sugar like you fantasized about once upon a time."

"You should become a comedian." He holds out his hand. "Once upon a time? Who says I'm not still daydreaming about it?"

"Concentrate on driving." She ignores his gesture to go absorb some of the spill on his thigh with the tissues. "I'll take care of it."

As she does so, Lucas tries his best to not get distracted by her delicate motions that steadily move dangerously closer to his crotch.

He inhales deeply to keep his composure.

He should be better than this at not invoking images of Raven in bed with him.

Who is he kidding?

She's too staggering in the throes of passion for him to ever forget about it and not want to repeat the experience every chance he gets.

He already made peace with the fact that he probably won't ever be able to not want to spend hours tangled with her.

He contracts his quads in an effort to not rock into her.

How they were able to navigate through this crescendo of talking about serious topics to him having trouble keeping any control is mind-boggling.

He breathes in. "It's a bit hard for me to focus on the road at the moment."

"Hard you say?" She retracts her hand to take some more tissues. "I'm legitimately sorry." She cleans up the liquid from the side of his seat as well as the middle console. "I honestly didn't want to tease you or anything. I didn't think it would elicit any kind of reaction from you."

"It's okay." He half-smiles. "It's not your fault that I'm apparently fifteen years old when it comes to you."

She snorts. "I'm sure it would've been great knowing you at fifteen."

Hearing her laugh after the heavy discussion they had feels incredible, but he can't fully enjoy it.

"I beg to disagree." He frowns. "At that age I was still struggling from my dad leaving us."

"I'm sorry." She discards the tissues in the map pocket of the door. "I didn't know. I—"

He interjects. "It's fine. No need to talk about it at 4AM."

"As you wish." She tilts her head, a mellowly amused smile dancing on her lips. "You prefer that we go back to discuss our other past depressing subjects?"

It's his turn to snort.

Just like that, Raven once again managed to bring him back to a more serene place.

By respecting the boundaries he set.

By smoothly reorienting, but still acknowledging what happened.

She is utterly one of a kind.

For the remainder of this drive, he will concentrate on her.

Just like all those years ago, she should be all that matters every time he's with her anyway.

While Raven looks out of her kitchen window at the city lights starting to illuminate the skyline, she stretches.

As her loose hair sways with every step she takes, she pads toward the oven in only an oversized long sleeves black graphic t-shirt and fuschia shorties.

She feels rejuvenated.

She woke up not long ago after the most restful sleep she had in months.

She's aware that she has Lucas to thank for it. And it's not resulting from the fact that they got physically intimate again. It's because he succeeded in making her feel relaxed enough for her mind to quiet down just enough to get some actual rest.

Even during the drive home when they had more difficult conversations, he navigated those with respect, comprehension, and tuned into every emotion with her.

She's certain that if she had given him more information, he would've been even more comforting and understanding.

He always had this peculiar way of matching her energy, and balancing her feelings.

It's dizzying to experience it again.

No one since him had that effect. It feels like he could take back his rightful place in her life.

She shakes her head.

There's no rightful place for Lucas in her life. They only just reconnected. They have a hundred things to address and take care of. She can't entertain the fleeting possibility of keeping him around.

The truth is that they both have no idea what the future holds.

She hums idly to the music she put on, grabbing oven mitts to take out the Mac & Cheese she cooked from the oven where she put it for the parmesan to broil on top.

She places it on a cork trivet, removes the mitts and breathes in.

Plus, Lucas' life seems to be set in New York, while she is thinking more and more about leaving the Big Apple once his case is done.

Learning about Zoe sent her mind into a tailspin.

It brought back a slew of memories along with a series of conflicting sentiments. She realized that she misses home. Badly.

And home to her is in California.

She might've tried and succeeded in making Brooklyn her home for nearly a decade, but San Diego won't leave her alone. It's present in every part of who she is. In every node of her body and each thought process.

She should visit soon.

She owes it to herself as well as to her family and friends.

Nothing is keeping her in New York City now. Once it was her job acting as an anchor. Nowadays she's free as a bird to do what she wants moving forward.

Jun is her only close friend in the area, and Raven knows that Ju would understand if she decided to go for a change of scenery.

She grabs a bowl from the cabinet behind her along with a large serving spoon. Facing the island once more, she portions some pasta into her plate.

Sure, with Lucas they could have fun and sleep casually together in the meantime.

But whatever is rushing through her veins at only a gaze from him makes that potential endeavor risky. She has a bad feeling that she could get attached.

She doesn't want that.

Especially not with him. He's addicting, but he's engaged on a different path than hers.

She picks up her meal along with the glass of wine she poured herself earlier to go sit in front of the TV.

Walking inside her living room, the song keeps resonating within her psyche, bringing her back into Lucas' car.

She remembers how she couldn't stop herself from kissing him on the cheek before exiting his car.

The way he closed his eyes as he sighed in response made her want to curl her hand around his throat and kiss him for all she is worth on the spot.

The ghost of the roughness of his scruff is still lingering on her lips if she concentrates enough.

She has to admit that she adores it.

William also has facial hair, but it somehow doesn't feel the same.

Lucas' beard is a special kind of deliciously numbing on her nerve endings.

She could never get enough of the softness of his mouth paired with the coarseness of his stubble anywhere on her.

Apparently that's yet another thing that didn't change.

She exchanges her glass of wine for the remote, turning on the TV.

The TV automatically lands on a docu-series about patients going through a variety of health issues.

She rapidly changes the channel.

She doesn't want to spiral into dark thoughts thinking about Zoe and her condition.

Heather still hasn't given her any news. Raven told herself she would wait until tomorrow to ask for an update.

Heather clearly has a lot to deal with at the moment. Her friend will contact her when she can.

Raven sits back into the cushion, making herself comfortable.

She settles on watching the news in case she missed anything in the past few days. She used to listen to everything that was happening in town at any given moment to make sure she was on top of everything.

Especially when she was in the middle of a trial.

She always wanted to be certain that no harmful information that could be related directly or remotely to any of clients was circulating. She needed to be able to contain potential crises faster and be quick to react.

As she sees the wife of her last client smile widely at a journalist on screen, Raven clenches her jaw.

The tall Italian brunette is giving an interview about her latest donation to a children's hospital on the red carpet of the event. Raven can feel her blood boil slightly upon seeing her chocolate irises sparkle with joy as the interviewer compliments her golden cocktail dress and signature rings on her right hand.

How can someone burst out laughing when their husband is tried for money laundering? When they know all too well about the human trafficking part of the business, and participate actively in it?

Raven knows. Her client told her he and his wife were a team. Even if it was vague, it was all she needed to know.

She can't stand the audacity of that woman.

She rapidly changes the channel once more.

Since Thursday, she hadn't checked news outlets a whole lot.

Reflecting on it she has to admit that it felt liberating.

The constant stress was slowly getting grueling to manage.

She puts the remote back on the coffee table next to her laptop and her phone.

She takes a bite of her meal.

It didn't take long for her brain to oscillate between her uncertain future, Zoe's health, her past job, and an attractive, tall, dark and handsome man that seems to occupy every corner of her mind.

She wants to empty her head of that whirlwind.

Working a little might help in that regard.

On a whim, she decides to look through Lucas' client list.

That should keep her focused on something productive.

She opens her computer, instinctively picking up her phone to text the managing director as her laptop boots.

R: I'm about to check your client list for real this time lol.

In the meantime, she checks her other notifications, opening her conversation with Jun which has two new messages.

J: I interviewed Paul. Everything Lucas said checks out. The man still looked a little on edge with the whole thing. Talked to other employees. They all had confirmed alibis for that night. Waiting on potential DNA and fingerprints results. Can't wait to see if anyone stands out to you from looking at the client list.

J: Also... Gary wants to talk. He invited me to dinner on Sunday. Should I be worried?

Raven smiles idly, typing her answer.

R: Going through the list as we speak. Will keep you posted. RE: Gary; I'm sure he only wants to talk about you two in a positive way. My guess is that he must miss you like you miss him. Just be honest, and tell him how you feel at each step.

The second she sends the text, she lets out a breath.

She knows that it's easier said than done in most cases. While she's being honest herself in all her interactions, situations and relationships are never single-layered. There's a beautiful complexity to them.

Which also means that to stay genuine one has to remain true to themselves, and also take all those factors into account.

It's an intricate puzzle to piece together.

A banner flashes on top of her screen notifying her of a reply from Lucas. She instantly clicks on it.

L: Sounds good How are you doing?

The corner of her mouth curves upward of its own accord imagining his soft voice asking her this.

R: I slept for twelve hours straight. Needed it. I was exhausted.

L: I wish it would've been bc you were exhausted from our nighttime activities...

She pulls her bottom lip between her teeth as her fingers travel across the keyboard.

R: It was totally bc of that.

L: You very well know I'm not referring to *those kinds* of activities...

She can vividly imagine him smirking while saying it.

She smiles.

R: I still think it was very pleasant.

L: Ditto.

She extends her hand to take hold of her glass of wine.

R: What are you doing right now?

L: I'm still at the office. Since I took off yesterday to go to Boston, work has piled up on my desk (figuratively bc it's all digital as you know)

She takes a sip, looking at the time in the corner of her screen. 8PM. She frowns.

R: I'm sorry you have to work late.

L: It's fine. It's not that late.

She receives the message, but three little dots keep blinking in the window.

L: The same probably happened to you all the time, no?

She can easily recall having worked until past midnight on occasions. Definitely not optimal, but essential sometimes.

R: Yep. Don't miss it yet.

L: I bet.

She lets her phone drop on the cushion beside her to go take a bite of her mac and cheese.

His office is potentially empty except for him still working.

She pictures him sitting at his desk, probably wearing a tailored suit with the jacket resting on the back of his chair, and sporadically looking out at the skyline while messaging her.

She's certain that he's strikingly gorgeous.

She'd like to be there with him to go sit in his lap, flying her fingers into his hair to feel the strands glide through her digits as she would kiss him lazily.

She would make sure to scratch her nails exactly like he loves as she would grind gently into him to elicit the most beautiful groan from him against her tongue.

Feeling him respond to her is one of the best sensations she ever experienced.

She can't deny that she loved pleasuring him. She was proud to see him splinter under her care. He was a sight to behold every time he did.

She pinches the bridge of her nose to shake the thought off.

She surely doesn't need to summon any fantasy of having sex with him in his office. But it would be so easy to do so since she knows exactly what the decor looks like, and—

She unexpectedly remembers something. She grabs her phone.

R: I've been meaning to ask if the pop art painting on your wall is the real deal?

She doesn't wait very long to get an answer.

L: It is. I love how pop art shook conventions, and made art more accessible to appreciate. I saw that one at an auction a couple years ago, and I had to have it.

R: That's amazing. My dad used to be inspired by pop art a lot. He was mostly painting for fun in his spare time.

L: Was?

She hesitates for a beat. This is yet another deeply personal topic.

She decides to let Lucas know.

He's heard a lot from her past in the last day or so, after all. It feels oddly good sharing some parts of her life with him.

He welcomes them without any judgment or snarky remarks.

R: It was his escape from the world. Sadly he stopped doing it when my mother got sick.

L: I'm sorry (and I'm saying this way too often lately). Is your mother better now?

R: Yes. She recovered well after they removed her tumor. She also went through some chemotherapy, and has officially been in remission for four years now.

L: I'm glad to hear.

She keeps typing.

R: But my father never painted again. I think it reminds him of when he was doing it and wasn't there a lot for my mom. I always tell him that it's unrelated, but you know how the brain works...

L: Yeah. In mysterious ways.

She moves to sit on the edge of the couch. Her family is not an easy topic to discuss for multiple reasons. Her parents have always been really great at not communicating, and—

She shakes her head.

She has to focus, and not let other loaded conversations sneak up on her.

R: Exactly. I'll let you work, and dig into your client list

The next message appears instantly.

L: Speaking of my clients, I had an idea.

She raises an inquisitive eyebrow while typing.

R: Do tell.

L: There's a fundraiser tomorrow night. You could accompany me and meet directly with a bunch of said clients in a very neutral setting.

She stares at the blinking dots in slight shock.

L: I know it's short notice, but I'd love for you to be there

She can't help herself.

R: Did you just 'puppy dog eyed' me?

L: I did. You would make everything more fun. I usually go alone.

She thinks for a moment.

It's a great idea. She could get a vibe to put with the names, mixing business with pleasure.

Because a night out with Lucas is sure to be enjoyable.

Plus, her schedule is wide open.

R: I'd love to. Any dress code? Is it like a fashion runway level dress up or more like a little black dress event?

L: Somewhere between the two?

She laughs lightly.

R: Perfect.

L: You have no idea how happy that made me. I'll send you the details. I can pick you up around 6PM?

R: Sounds good. Ttyl

L: Take care, Raven. Just send me a message if you have any questions.

As she puts her device next to her laptop, she notices that she is smiling wide.

She won't question it.

Lucas makes her feel good.

She'll enjoy it for as long as it lasts.

SIX

Evanescent Eclipse

"**Y**ou must be kidding me saying that this man is trustworthy," Raven snaps as she looks at a blonde middle aged man with an aquiline nose, stern features, and wearing a powdered blue suit walking away from them.

"He brings great business opportunities." Lucas stays unflinching. "We're very happy he chose our bank to deal with his finances."

Standing in her sage green long flowy dress in front of the managing director at a cocktail table, her blood is boiling.

The chilly night time breeze on the north terrasse is definitely not even able to calm down her frustration.

She takes a sip of her champagne while distantly listening to the Disc Jockey starting his live set.

The five thousand square feet venue is chic and modern at once being divided in four terrasse levels; each having their own purpose for the fundraiser they're attending.

While the North and East Terrasse are full of bar height tables, outdoor sofas, string lights hanging from the roof to the edge of the balconies, and music entertainment to provide a fun place for people to chat and party, the Main Room is where the more serious dealings take place.

It's inside the building with its modular sofas, low coffee tables and dual bar counters that the bidding is taking place for the silent auction to amass funds for research and local non-profits.

Finally, the small Reception Room—adjacent to the Main one—acts as a boudoir where people mostly sit down to enjoy the evening in a slightly more quiet setting.

Raven loved the vibe of the place as soon as she set foot in it.

Now, the view of the Manhattan skyline might be breathtaking from where they stand, it does nothing to alleviate her annoyance.

Lucas might look irresistible dressed in all black with a maroon tie—and with way less gel than usual in his black locks—it currently can't tone down her irritation.

They clearly are on different life paths.

It's not as if she hadn't predicted it.

It shouldn't come as a surprise to her.

Somehow getting confirmation pisses her off way more than it has any right to.

She inhales deeply.

She has to stay composed.

The overall mood of this evening just shifted in the blink of an eye.

When she woke up this morning, she was excited for this fundraiser.

She had spent a few hours going through Lucas' client list last night while eating.

Since Jun is taking care of running detailed background checks and going through the building camera footage, it leaves Raven with the opportunity to see if she is familiar with any of the names.

She's been dealing with a lot of powerful individuals in her career, after all, and a lot of businesses are interconnected.

She has to admit that Lucas' clients spawn a wide range of both local and international moguls.

No wonder Lucas is financially thriving and has no trouble getting by in life.

With those kinds of connections, pretty much all doors can easily open up to him. It's no surprise that he likes what this existence brings him. People would go to great lengths to even just flirt within those higher spheres of society.

As expected, some stood out to her from past cases she had worked on as well as from general media coverage.

But all in all, from memory, the vast majority of the names she recognised were not the grade A assholes type.

Prone to questionable behaviors? Sure.

Being able to entertain shady financial relationships? Certainly.

Wanting to coerce someone to do something for them? Not their type.

Maybe Jun will find something more on her side of the investigation.

Still, the mention of two people directly made Raven frown.

Thomas Keller who she managed to exonerate from insider trading claims, and Dick Adams for whom she did the same from mortgage fraud.

Both CEOs are willing to go to great lengths to convince anyone of the importance of their visions. She once was front row to notice exactly how they can become borderline violent when formulating demands.

Dick slammed his fist on the table more than once during their exchanges, while Thomas was all about snarky remarks and passive aggressive comments.

They were both very direct in their approach.

Which also made her think that acting in the shadows by sending threats would maybe not be their *modus operandi* to get what they want.

They both always were very vocal about their demands. Never shying away from looking her straight in the eyes, and try to instigate fear.

She then made a mental note to ask Lucas about their interactions with him later, and called it a night.

Flipping close her laptop and leaving her phone on the table, she watched some episodes of a TV show she likes from a streaming platform before finally going to bed.

In the morning, she called Jun to ask if she could borrow the exact dress she's currently wearing.

She knew her wardrobe was full of appropriate gowns of all types for every occasion, but she wanted more.

Deep down she had a hunch that 'somewhere between fashion runway aesthetics and little black dress' was potentially requesting more than her usual go-tos.

Wearing the same size as her best friend also comes in handy in times like these. More than once through the years they borrowed each other's clothes for events around town.

This particular garment was bought jointly by Jun and herself during fashion week two years ago.

They couldn't get the design out of their heads.

Since Jun knew the designer because she had helped her brother get out of a rough patch with his communication firm, they were able to negotiate a price.

So far, the sleeveless dress with a thigh-high slit and floating cleavage has only made her appearance once when Raven wore it to the opera.

Her firm was a big donor, and they gave away tickets. Jun couldn't accompany her so she went alone, and called dibs on the dress.

She knew that the gown would make her blend in at that high profile venue.

She was right.

All evening, the dress became a topic of interest and wonder.

Reflecting on it, one of the best selling points about it to her are the hidden pockets inside the silk of the skirt. No need to carry a matching handbag to accentuate the look. Phone and essential personal belongings can be kept handily close at all times.

That was truly a flash of genius from the female fashion designer right there.

Raven can clearly recall the conversation she had with Jun earlier about it.

I never had a chance to wear it yet, her friend stated teasingly while giving her the dress.

The crisis manager was just back from the gym, wearing her most comfortable purple tracksuit. It was a great match to Raven's black leggings and pink knitted sweater that she had put on top of her sports bra.

The lawyer had just finished her own training routine, and was en route to have her nails done when Jun had called to answer her inquiry about the night gown. Ju only had one hour free in her schedule when Raven could go pick it up before her work day became too crazy.

She jumped on the occasion before stopping for her french manicure.

I honestly thought you'd have an opportunity before me. She grabbed the dress. *That's why it's currently in your wardrobe and not mine.*

But that's not how life works, is it? Her friend supplied playfully. *Of course it has to be you who has been invited by a handsome man to a jetset event.*

I'm going for business purposes. She held Jun's stare. *I'll be able to meet a bunch of Lucas' clients*

Mhmm. It's definitely all there is. The manager raised a knowing eyebrow. *I can call any of your bluffs, Raven.* She crossed her arms over her chest. *And you know it.*

Her friend knows her too well. Along with Heather, Jun is like a sister to Raven. They've been through thick and thin together. Obviously she's able to tell when she's not telling her the whole story.

There's no need to be cryptic about what she's thinking about Lucas anyway.

Things are usually better off being in the open. Especially between friends.

Honestly Ju, having him around again is playing a number on my brain. She smiled coyly. *But I also do think this gala is a perfect opportunity to dig further into this case. I already spotted two names who could potentially—*

Jun interjected. *Only your brain?*

She snorted at her friend's not-so-subtle allusion. *My brain kinda controls all the rest, right?* She bit into her bottom lip. *Yeah, that's about it.* She became slightly reflective. *Lucas and I might be on very different paths, but I can't deny that I'm still as attracted to him as I was a decade ago. Which is insane. I've never felt such a magnetic pull toward someone.*

It's impossible to control what the heart wants, huh? Her friend relaxed and started walking out of her walk-in. *There was clearly something special to him back then, and it hasn't faded because he's still the same man. But as I said, we probably are incompatible in so many—*

Jun tsk-ed her while cutting her off once again. *No. Don't serve me that bullshit before you truly get to know who he became.* Once in the doorway, she turned to face her again. She scanned Raven's eyes, a smile forming on her lips. *I'm sure you even already got a glimpse, and you liked what you saw so far.* She wiggled her index finger from head to toes at the lawyer. *You wouldn't be standing in front of me right now asking for that killer dress if not.*

Fair enough. I might've had trouble keeping my hands to myself lately in his presence. I keep thinking that, in the worst case scenario, we could just hook up casually.

That's the spirit. Jun hummed. *From what I remember from your recollection, he was wickedly good in bed, and also a true delight to have pillow talk with.*

Yeah. She shrugged. *We'll see where all of this leads us, I guess.*

I say there's only one logical outcome if it continues on this trend. The crisis manager tilted her head in questioning. *But what about William?*

I've never been serious with Will to begin with. It's not like I'd be cheating on him. It's our arrangement. Raven was serious. The thought had made some rounds in her head in the past few days, and she came to that exact conclusion. *I'm sure he slept with other people in the past year, too. Plus, Lucas already knows about his existence.*

Her friend sounded genuinely curious. *What did Lucas say?*

Nothing, Raven stated dismissively. *He acknowledged it, and we sort of moved on from it.*

Sort of moved on? Jun repeats, putting the emphasis on 'sort of'.

There was once more no use trying to deflect or ignore the subject.

She could recall that discussion clear as day in her head. How Lucas casually told her about things she was doing when they were sleeping together that drove him mad, and how she reciprocated.

They built the whole exchange like an exquisite crescendo that only had one possible outcome: that the tension simmering into the air between them beautifully snapped.

Alas, they were stopped by—

She decided to answer Jun truthfully. *We might've had some kind of moment when we were going to Boston where I totally would've kissed him if a car hadn't honked at us.*

Wow. Her friend smiled something warm at her. *You really have it bad.*

You have no idea how I just effortlessly melt into his gaze when he looks at me with all the softness in the world. I wanted him so badly in that moment.

Only then?

He unabashedly flirts with me just like I do with him. It's so natural between us that it sends my mind spinning. Raven pinched the bridge of her nose. *Can I plead the fifth to all your questions?*

Jun snorted. *Okay, I'll let you get away with it this time.*

Her tone was nothing but amused. *How generous of you.*

You know me. Her friend made a show to flip her ponytail on one side as if she was starring in a shampoo commercial. *The epitome of benevolence.* She chuckled lightly at her own joke before looking at Raven intently, pointing at the bag draped on her lower arm. *So, what will you wear in addition to this gorgeous piece of clothing?*

Raven took no more than a split second to reply. *I will obviously put on my pair of gray and purple stilettos.*

Her friend nodded her approbation, dropping her voice to a whisper. *He'll go insane.*

We'll see about that. She smiled shyly. *No matter what, I still have to be attentive to my surroundings during the evening. I have some work to do.*

Sure. Jun half-smiled at her. *But you may very well end up sprawled out in his bed, and not get much sleep. Don't tell me you haven't thought about it.*

The fundraiser is actually closer to my apartment than his. Raven looked around the wardrobe. *It's in Williamsburg.*

Her friend stayed solemn. *Then you'll end up tangled with him in your own bed.*

Who says I'll be able to make it to the bedroom before climbing him like a tree? She shifted her stare back to Jun. *My sofa is also very comfortable, and I could be at a perfect angle to kneel before him and—*

Raven! Jun exclaimed in fake surprise, interrupting her. *You really weren't kidding when you said you loved going down on him, yeah?*

I would never joke about something like that. She remained serious. *To this day, Lucas has been unmatched for giving me head, but he also feels beyond amazing swelling in my mouth.* She pulled a corner of her mouth upward. *Or gloriously stretching me.*

That's not something we're able to say about just anyone. Her friend leaned against the doorframe, squinting her eyes at her. *You think he'd still feel the same?*

I do think it's one of the numerous things that hasn't changed through time. She half-smiled timidly. *If he's still able to make me warm all over by bantering with me, I'm certain we could have mind-blowing sex.* She let her thoughts roam free, speaking them out loud. *I also always felt like we had more than just this physical craving for each other. Everything feels natural with him.* She inhaled deeply. *But I somehow still let him go back then.*

Jun flashed her an understanding smile. *Maybe now is your chance to see if he could really be the whole package.*

Raven hummed non-committedly as she walked by her friend.

They spent the rest of their short instant together to discuss Jun's upcoming 'date' with Gary.

The crisis manager is still unsure about calling it as such, but Raven keeps insisting it is.

She's convinced that the driver wouldn't have asked to talk to her friend for anything less. Those two are way too infatuated with each other to not decide to give that relationship a chance.

At least that's what the lawyer thinks.

She also has to admit that it felt good to talk about her conflicting feelings toward Lucas out loud to someone.

Especially a close friend like Jun.

Later in the day, when Raven was getting ready for the fundraiser, she put on the exact heels she said she would.

She also took her time in front of the mirror to render perfect smokey eyes, and glossy lips.

She is a firm believer that less is more when it comes to makeup. Keeping it subtle with a few accents is her preferred way to go.

The beat of her favorite singer's first studio album was resounding in her ears like a perfect mantra.

It made the whole moment peaceful.

Raven loves mezzo soprano voices. She has a clear preference for this type of vocals.

Female singer-songwriters with this range of tonality paired with any tempos have a way to connect with every fiber of her being. Listening to that music always brings her to a place where she feels like she's on top of the world.

Her mind went to her conversation with Jun as she analyzed her options of what to do with her hair.

Raven was not kidding when she expressed her concerns about her and Lucas being on different life journeys to her friend.

The thoughts have been making rounds in her head to a point where she second guesses what her next moves should be.

Under any other circumstances, she knows she would've already slept with him.

This constant doubt about the fact that she could potentially get attached as well as realize that their aspirations are incompatible is constantly prompting her to take one step forward and two steps back.

It sometimes feels like the Sword of Damocles is hanging over her head, ready to drop at the first wrong decision.

Truth is, choosing between her principles and this powerfully deep attraction that binds her to Lucas is a zero-sum game.

Things were so much easier back in Greece.

Maybe she should've listened to her instincts, and asked for his number back at the airport. She clearly didn't want to kiss him goodbye for good that day.

If they would have evolved together, perhaps things would have turned out differently.

But it's too late for that now.

She just has to deal with the fact that he haunts her thoughts for better or worse.

She pushed all the reflections away as she pulled up her hair into a messy low bun.

The finishing touch was to put on her golden bar earring. This particular one makes a nice change from her usual silvery one. It's also amongst her favorites with its pearls in the middle as well as elegant chains and a half moon pendant dangling from it.

She only had time to put on her dress before Lucas texted her saying he was waiting in front of her building.

Now a few hours later, she can still recall that the cool autumn night did nothing to calm the rush of warmth that coursed through her veins upon seeing him.

She's seen him twice in suits so far.

She has to admit that this one is her favorite to date. There's just something about him dressed in all black that does things to her.

The way he always leaves the first button of his shirt unfastened to let his tie slightly loose is a small detail she picked up on.

She absolutely loves it.

It shows off his more laid back and relaxed side. She knows all about those layers of his personality, but he doesn't seem to want to let it out to the world.

This tiny particularity in his way to dress acts as a subtle tell-tale sign that this part of him still exists somewhere underneath all the professional armor he built throughout the years.

She had to gather all her strength to not reach out to him when she approached the car.

She only wanted to sneak her arms under his suit jacket to pull herself flush to him.

He was looking a little awe-strucked as she walked before him while he was holding the passenger door open.

He's the one who bent down to murmur into her ear, *You're gorgeous, Raven.* He breathed in. *But again, you would be stunning wearing anything.*

She saw him curl his free hand by his side.

He was probably also trying his best to not touch her in case she didn't welcome it.

She slid her fingers on top of his fist softly. *So I could've put on a paper bag, and it would've been acceptable?* she teased.

He sighed into her hair as he became less rigid. *Totally.*

She deftly intertwined their fingers. *A bag is also easier to remove I guess?*

He hummed. *That, too.*

She placed his palm low on her hip. *I swear to you that this dress just falls on the floor by itself once unzipped,* she whispered back into his neck.

She heard him barely audibly groan.

She pulled her bottom lip between her teeth, trying to contain the heat that automatically started pooling low in her belly at the sound.

It was astounding that they only just reunited after a day, and they were undeniably drawn to each other in ways she can't even begin to describe.

Having him near unwaveringly means she wants him as close as possible.

She couldn't help it. She curled her fingers into the lapels of his tailored coat. *You also look handsome as hell, Lucas.*

He let go of the door to slide his other hand around her waist. *Hearing you say that is like music to my ears.*

She leaned back to lock eyes with him. The heat of his body irradiating through her was making her dizzy.

She had to focus.

She smiled coyly, patting his chest. *I think we better get going if we want to make it on time.*

Getting through the evening was top priority, after all.

They had clients to meet, and business to attend to.

Dragging him up to her condo right on the spot to fuck his brains out would've defeated the whole purpose.

He laid a kiss on her forehead before gesturing toward the inside of the car. *As you wish.*

As soon as she walked past him, she felt his fingertips trace the first few letters of the tattoo on her back softly. *You have a tattoo on your spine?*

She turned her head to see him stare at the ink. *Yeah. All along it.*

His eyes followed the trail of his touch down her vertebrae until it reached the hem of her dress under which the rest is hidden. *What does it say?* he murmured, flicking his gaze back to her turquoise pools.

She wanted to tell him all about why she has a sentence tattooed in latin script down her spine, but felt like it wasn't the right time to address the subject.

She chose the next best option.

Maybe someday you'll see all of it. She pulled her bottom lip between her teeth. *I'll tell you then. Deal?*

He glided his hand up, smiling coyly. *Deal.*

The gesture was so delicate that she can still feel the—

She shakes her head one more time, taking another sip of her drink.

She's aware she's been silent a beat too long as she was reminiscing about everything that happened today when she sees Lucas furrowing his eyebrow.

"You okay? You look mad. Talk to me, Raven. What do you want me to do?" He gestures in the air between them. "Not sign up with him based on an assumption?" It's his turn to shake his head. "I'm warning you right now that it's not gonna happen."

She has to get a grip.

Right now, all her reflections and doubts about Lucas being on a path of his own are making a violent comeback.

Getting introduced to Gabriel Smith as the managing director's newest most influential client has sent her mind into a tailspin.

The import/export magnate is certainly not someone she would qualify as a good guy.

The minute she saw Mister Smith shake Lucas' hand, she had to swallow around a lump in her throat.

The last time she saw Gabriel, he was in deep conversation with one of her clients. The exact one who made her quit her job last week because his dealings were too reprehensible for her to ever want to defend them.

Exploiting people, and dealing in human trafficking is a hard pass under any circumstances.

It disgusts her to the highest degree that such people can roam free and thrive by building empires by cashing in on the hardships of others.

Every time her brain brings back snippets of that case, it makes her sick.

The sensation never receded to date. She doesn't think it ever will.

What is even worse at the moment is the fact that Gabriel Smith is in business with that scumbag of a human being, and now she just learned that Lucas will soon be in charge of Mister Smith's finances.

How can she have made such a blatant oversight?

No. It wasn't a misstep.

She never saw Gabriel Smith appear on any of Lucas' firm documentation she analyzed. She would've identified Smith's name if she had come across it prior to—

She frowns. "You know he's doing debatable shit and you hide him by not putting his name on your client list? Is that what it is?"

Lucas stays determined. "The only reason why he's not on it is because we haven't fully finalized all the paperwork yet. I've been somewhat delaying signing it since I met him. I'll admit that he seems to like to intimidate to get his way, and I'm not the biggest fan, but my bank really wants us to close that deal. He's a powerful CEO with lots of assets. It's good for us." He straightens his jacket's sleeves. "I received the partial draft that will lock him in as a client last night, and forwarded it to him. He said he wants everything to be concluded asap, but he also wants his lawyer to add clauses to it. I'll have our own legal team—and you if you're up for it—look that one over before closing the deal."

"But as soon as you sign this, you two are bound together anyway, right?"

He confirms. "Yeah."

She lets out an annoyed snort. "You didn't think that letting me know that such a big name was going to imminently become one of your clients was important?"

"Honestly, no. As I said, he isn't a client yet." He scans her eyes. "But he came highly recommended just as we also got recommended to him by some of his business contacts. As long as it brings good business, I don't know why I should—"

She cuts him off. "From whom do all those recommendations come from?"

"Smith confessed to me that a very influential woman told him he should bring his business to us. He said she's named Roni, and I didn't ask for more details. He also wants to transfer some assets pretty urgently it seems." He shrugs. "As for who vouched for him on our side, it's some of the biggest wallets in our portfolios. Those guys have been with us for years." He sounds as resolute as ever. "They always trusted me, and treated me with respect. We developed a great partnership based on mutual understanding."

She knits her eyebrow, wanting to make him realize that those people might be clients, maybe they're still not above all suspicions. "You're not friends with any of them."

"Not close friends, no." He picks up his own glass of champagne from the table. "They're my top clients though." He raises it in a toast to her. "You'll have to deal with the fact that I trust them just like they trust me."

There's not a hint of hesitation in her reply. "Well maybe you shouldn't."

He puts the champagne down after having taken a sip, looking puzzled. "Why's that?"

Lucas looks sincere in his desire to grasp what she's thinking.

But she doesn't want to tell him about Gabriel being in business with her prior client. It would open a can of worms.

She's not ready to address that subject yet.

Plus, it would give Lucas the opportunity to turn the tables on her right now, and this discussion needs to be about him.

It's kind of like questioning witnesses.

When doing so, she never opens up fully to be able to steer the topic in the direction she wants it to go. Through tightly negotiated questions and answers, her goal is to bring the witness to have no choice but to follow along her reasoning.

Hopefully, this usually all ends up in her getting some important information from them.

Here, things are slightly different.

She wants to make Lucas reflect on potential outcomes.

She'll thread carefully to direct the exchange while using her interrogation techniques.

She keeps her resolve. "Well, if—"

Lucas suddenly extends a hand in her direction. "Care to dance?" She looks confused. He tilts his head toward a small man with salt and pepper hair walking toward them. "This is one of my clients. He'll want to talk, but I want to see this conversation with you through." He softens his features. "No one will bother us on the dance floor."

She can't argue with that logic.

Actually, is it more about being able to or *wanting* to?

No matter what, she has no intention to let any more of Lucas' clients divert them from having this talk right now.

She takes hold of his hand, circling the table to join him on his side. "Let's go."

As they stride in direction of the made up dance floor, she notices that the house DJ started remixing lascivious tempos.

The moment Lucas stops and faces her, she instinctively wraps her arms around his neck.

He grabs her hips. "Is this okay?"

"Yeah." She nods. "You can touch me, Lucas." She half-smiles. "I'll always welcome your touch."

He smirks. "Always?"

"Mhmm." She starts swaying slowly. "Unless I snap your hand away."

She bores into his eyes only to fight the urge to drown into his soft and deep gaze.

"Duly noted." He follows her lead. "So, would you mind telling me what it is about Gabriel Smith that gets you all riled up?"

He's holding her with a flawless blend of tenderness and intensity.

Her body only wants to arch into him at each undulation of his hips.

She wants to kiss off the playful smile dancing on his lips.

She wants to brush her fingers through his black locks to make a mess out of it.

She wants to loosen his tie to—

She closes her eyes briefly.

A minute ago she was outraged beyond measure at the situation. Now she's battling with herself to not throw everything out the window, and just grind to the beat with Lucas.

Let everything else disappear.

He makes it too easy for her to want to give in.

She has to stay determined, and carry through the discussion at hand.

It is essential that she sees this through.

She snaps her eyes back open. "You ever thought that Mr. Smith's 'clauses' he wants to add to your contract, and his eagerness at wanting this done with soon might be tied to that threat letter and the ransacking of your office?"

Lucas frowns. "You really think he'd think he can get leverage that way?"

"Maybe." She absentmindedly scrapes her nails into the short hair at the nape of his neck. "He would at least know more about you by doing it." She can't stop herself from brushing her nose along his. "This type of guy is not one to suddenly get into business with just anyone. He probably ran a background check on you."

The managing director puts one of his palm flat on her lower back, purring under her ministrations. "I have nothing to hide." He sighs as she grinds gently into him to the tempo. "Although, if Gabriel did run that background check, why would he send threats and try to go through my stuff?"

She thinks for a beat. "He might've wanted to push the concept further, and see how you react in the face of adversity or under pressure."

He sounds amused. "You think I passed the test?"

"It's not funny." She furrows her eyebrows. "Hypothetically, if Gabriel is willing to go to those lengths, he might very well be willing to go further, too." She leans back to peer into Lucas' eyes. "He must know you usually find loopholes when needed, but he might require more than that. The fact that he wants to move fast is also a red flag to me. With someone as powerful as him, things can get dangerous for you."

"I never told anyone about the threats, and our company has an impeccable reputation." The managing director idly traces up her spine with his index and middle fingers. "No matter if Gabriel did something to me—whether it was a simple background check or more—I can't do anything about it. He probably saw that I conduct business steadily, and am not easily troubled. I'm getting a lot of pressure to reach an agreement with him. I worked hard to get where I am. I don't want it to vanish because I didn't respect instructions."

The lyrics wash over her at the same time Lucas smoothly starts playing with a loose strand of hair that fell from her updo.

She's annoyed once again, but his proximity makes it difficult to keep her mind clear. "You really still want to get in business with that guy?" She quickly assesses his expression. "Even if everything we just theorized about is true?" She slides her cheek along his stubble to stop herself from getting lost into his gaze some more. "Even if you feel like he acts like an intimidator?"

"It's more complex than meets the eye." She feels him shrugs while he turns his head to speak directly into her ear. "No one is truly void of any flaws. As long as he pays, and my employer is happy, I see no harm."

She inhales slowly. "Wow."

He stiffens a little. "What?"

She swallows down her irritation.

Getting closer to Lucas by nearly burying her nose into his curls was arguably not the greatest decision.

Her body molding perfectly into his is bringing back a thousand souvenirs.

It's as if every single one of her skin cells remembers what he feels like when he abandons himself to her. She wants to experience that feeling again.

She wants *him*.

Badly at that.

She swiftly turns into his embrace in another attempt at getting her head back in the game.

Lucas basically admitted that he's all about money.

She picked up on each time he alluded to it before throughout various conversations, but this is the most direct he's ever been.

She has to call him out on it. "I thought your standards were higher than this." He follows her movements to position his hands low on her hips. She intuitively places hers on top. "The man I met back in Mykonos had higher ones at least."

She can vividly remember that he once confessed to her over dinner, *Money can corrupt the soul. I want to make enough of it to go by and live a good life, but I won't make a deal with the Devil to make it happen.* He took a bite of his Moussaka. *I would rather work for a smaller investment bank, and be able to look at myself in the mirror than reaching the highest spheres and helping corrupt people.*

How could he have forg—

He drops his voice to a whisper, oscillating his pelvis to the rhythm. "Sorry to disappoint."

She inattentively trails her fingers along his forearm. "Do you think that everyone who's here tonight is doing it for the most righteous reasons?"

"Of course not."

"I don't think so either." She leans more into his front. "You and I both know that a bunch of them are only here to show that they want to help people, but in their daily lives they only care about profit and themselves. They're inherently egoistical" She toys with his matte black skull shaped cufflinks "They're here because they can deduct it from their taxes. All this hypocrisy is making me cringe."

He bends down to brush his scruff below her ear. "People do whatever makes sense to them."

She breathes in to stay composed, deciding to throw him back his own words from years ago. "As long as they can look at themselves in the mirror, right?"

If he picks up on the reminder, he doesn't let it show. "Something like that. It's how people roll." He curls his fingers around her hip bone to bring her flush to him. "Some are still well intentioned."

She hums.

He's steadily driving her out of her mind.

Only him could make her feel like dancing that ardently while talking about compelling topics is natural.

She can feel him respond to her as she sways into him in sync with the thumping bass.

Her entire skeleton is screaming at her to do something to release the tension coiling in her belly.

Her mind is shouting that it's a way too dangerous thought to entertain if she wants to keep her sanity in the long run.

If they continue this, she has no idea which part of her will take over.

She tries to keep her increasingly ragged breathing under control. "The line between having good intentions and genuinely not giving a shit about others is getting blurrier by the second for a slew of people." She has an urge to feel him caress her bare flesh. She glides his hand down her thigh. "I just couldn't act that way anymore. Been there, done that, and saw it all before my eyes. I'm never going back." She sighs as he tentatively sneaks his fingertips under the slit of her dress. "Which also prompts me to suggest that if I were you, I would run my own background check on Gabriel Smith. He's not clean."

"You're so fucking headstrong." Lucas nuzzles into her neck. "I love it."

She can't stop herself from reaching behind her to comb her fingers through his hair. "You like a challenge, you mean?"

"There's a ton I don't know about you yet. I want to understand everything you are, Raven." He smiles into her skin. "You're the most beautiful puzzle I'd like to solve."

She can sense that she's slowly losing any rational thoughts she has left.

She lets her head drop slightly onto his shoulder as the last notes of the song wash over her.

She softly massages the back of his head. "Maybe you would regret uncovering the layers," she murmurs.

"I highly doubt that." He traces her quad with his thumb gently. "You know, when I first came here, I didn't want to let the city swallow me whole." He skims his nose along her jugular. "You made me remember that pledge just now," he whispers.

Her mind is spinning.

She knows that the connection they have feels special. It's all consuming. It feels like it's greater than the both of them.

Surely Lucas must sense it, too.

But there's no way he can—

She leans back a little. "What are we doing, Lucas?"

He mimics her action, locking eyes with her. "I think we're grinding on the dance floor." He brushes the pad of his fingers up her thigh some more. "And pretty incredibly well if I might say so myself."

She slows down her movements. "You know very well what I mean."

He looks serious as hell. "What do you want, Rae?"

Hearing him call her 'Rae' makes her sigh.

He used to do it in intimate settings, and it never failed to make her heart flutters of its own accord.

She had the reflection a couple days ago. It sounds wrong when anyone other than Lucas uses that nickname.

There's a reverence to his tone when he pronounces it that resonates with every fiber of her being.

She can't get enough of the lustfulness that blends with the intrinsic softness of his voice which appears when he talks to her and her only. It transcends her blood flow.

Now he said it like he wants to spend all night worshiping her.

Fuck she would let him.

But what does *she* truly want?

She'd love to get reacquainted with his body for hours.

She'd love to admire him as he falls off the edge because of her.

She'd like to render his mind completely blank, and join him in oblivion too many times to count.

But the truth is that it's much more complicated than just admitting that *he* is all that she wants at the moment.

They're nearly standing still at the edge of the dance floor now. She feels him slide his hand on the side of her face.

She holds his stare, feeling his thumb beginning to trace her jawline. She leans into his touch instinctively as she inhales deeply.

She has to make him understand just how complex her thoughts are before this gets out of hand.

Her voice is barely over a murmur as she reaches to curl her hand around his throat. "You feel phenomenal, Lucas." She can't help to flick her stare down to his lips. "But you also chose to—"

A bright male voice resounds in the space, effectively making her trail off. "Lucas, my man! I was looking for you."

Lucas and she both straighten while shifting their attention toward the Latin man in a navy blue suit, white shirt and assorted tie striding in their direction.

Her heart is beating like a bass drum.

Each of her nerve endings is tingling as if electricity is trailing along them like through a livewire.

Her whole body is alight and aching for Lucas.

She somehow has to stay collected. They are still in public, and this man clearly wants to talk to the man who's making it damn near impossible for her to keep her desires in check.

She quickly examines the newcomer's frenzied demeanor. He seems to be highly energetic, and the way he beams at Lucas tells her that both men are probably close.

"Felipe!" There's a pang of annoyance in Lucas' tone. "I didn't see you around when we got here. I thought you decided not to attend at the last minute."

"We finally made it. I nearly had to give my tickets to Kyan because Emma and I got into a stupid fight, but it seems like we haven't missed out on all the fun." Felipe looks at Raven as he stops in front of them. "Who is this beautiful lady you were dancing with?"

The managing director keeps is composure as he buttons his suit jacket. "Felipe, meet Raven." He turns to face Raven, angling his head toward his friend. "Raven, this is Felipe. My long-time friend."

She extends a hand to greet Lucas' college buddy. "It's a pleasure to meet you, Felipe."

Lucas' friend takes her invitation. "Likewise." He briefly shakes hands with her. "You mean Raven as in Raven from Mykonos?"

She half-smiles. "That would be me."

"Woah. It's an honor." Felipe grins, putting his hands in his pockets. "You have no idea how much of an impression you left on my boy here."

She acts innocent, smiling at Lucas playfully. "Really?"

"Oh, yeah. He couldn't shut up about you for weeks afterwards." The analyst trails off, chuckling. "What am I even saying? For months!" He flashes Lucas a knowing smile. "He had it bad. I think Mark and Kyan could corroborate that he didn't go out with anyone for a whole year or something."

As they start walking to vacate the dance floor area, Raven feels the ghost of Lucas' hands on her hip bones.

She smiles coyly. "I have to admit that Lucas was pretty memorable himself."

"Well, I'm glad you ran into each other." Flip furrows his eyebrows, seemingly having an enlightenment. "Actually, how did you two re-connect? You've been keeping that from me, buddy!"

Lucas jumps on the occasion to answer. "Raven is part of a team I hired to address the issue I've been dealing with lately." He grabs two champagne flutes from a tray a server is carrying around. "I had no idea she would be part of it, but it's funny how things work out sometimes."

Raven takes the champagne Lucas holds in front of her. "It's been quite the surprise."

"I bet." Felipe stops to look at them behind him in alternance. "Would you guys mind if we go join my wife Emma? I left her with one of my colleagues to go fetch some drinks."

"Sure.'" Lucas gestures in front of him. "Lead the way."

As they resume walking to follow Felipe, Lucas bends down to whisper into Raven's ear, "You and I will have to finish that conversation."

She's instantly propelled back onto the dance floor, getting inexorably pulled into Lucas' orbit.

Of course he won't let that one slip. They will definitely need to address the subject at some point.

They can't continue to flirt inconsequentially forever.

She still feels like making sure they are on the same page about what needs to be discussed.

She slows down to get to his level. "The one about Gabriel Smith or the one about us?"

He sounds sure of himself. "Both."

At least he's not only willing to hear about her personal feelings, but also about her concerns toward the import/export businessman.

It's oddly heartwarming.

She opens her mouth to agree, but gets interrupted by Felipe who suddenly turns around to flash Lucas a concerned look. "You're still dealing with this crisis thing, man?"

The managing director stays composed. "Yeah, but I'm thinking more and more that it was potentially only an isolated incident."

Raven is slightly taken aback. "For real?"

"Well, nothing new has occurred since." Lucas shrugs. "It would still be nice to understand what happened, and track down what could have caused the events." He smiles warmly at Raven. "You know, so it doesn't reproduce itself."

She hums. "Obviously."

Felipe is confused. "So cryptic. Still don't want to share what it's all about, Lucas? Maybe I could help."

"No. I'm good. It's nothing. Plus, with Raven on the team it can only go uphill from here." Lucas seemingly decides to reorient the conversation. "What about you? You wanted to grab some drinks, you said?" He looks at his friend tauntingly. "You'll really go back to Em empty handed?"

"Shit." Felipe looks around frantically. "You're right, I—"

"Here. Calm down, Flip." Lucas hands him his champagne flute. "That way you'll have one for your wife."

"Thanks." His friend takes it. "I don't know what I would do without you, bud."

"We both know that you'd have lost your mind by now," Lucas teases.

As she lets out a polite laugh, Raven looks at Felipe. "Your firm also had tickets to this fundraiser?"

"Yeah." He nods. "Mine is smaller than Lucas', and has way less high profile wallets to manage, but this is for a great cause. Which means that my boss thought it would be a good idea to mingle with the 'creme de la creme' of the banking world for the span of an evening, and also give money for research about orphan diseases."

Lucas slides his hands into his pockets. "It would be great if you could make a good impression on some people to get new business." He gazes at Raven beside him. "Felipe is a great investment banker. He was at the top of each class."

She feels playful. "Oh, it wasn't you?"

"I wasn't far behind." The managing director leans toward her as if he's about to share confidential information. "I wouldn't dream of letting anyone outcompete me that easily."

"There you are." It's her turn to snort. "I was wondering when you would finally admit about your competitive side."

He puffs his chest a little, an amused smile dancing on his lips. "I totally own it."

She mirrors his expression. "Glad to hear."

Raven knows that Lucas is fundamentally driven when something is dear to him. He wants to be prepared for all eventualities, and smoke any competition he might have along the way.

He once told her about a surfing trip to Oahu with some friends. Trying to ride Pipelines was unforgiving. They don't say that those waves are the absolute best to prove one's abilities for nothing. Everyone would end up engulfed by the sea without fail. Some even injured themselves.

Lucas was as obstinate as to do it again and again until he was the only one ending up tube riding inside the giant.

The only one who succeeded in *becoming one with the ocean*, he said.

Nowadays he was even able to ride the ones from Nazare. He told her as such. He probably did the same with multiple other scary but surfable waves through the years.

She smiles absentmindedly. She'd love to hit the Mavericks of Half Moon Bay with him someday.

She teased him about it a few minutes ago because it's true: Lucas Blake loves a challenge. He will always do everything in his power to come out of it victorious.

She always connected with that drive he has. It's highly sexy and attractive when it balances out the other layers that make him who he is.

Thinking about it now, she appreciates that it also serves as a great metaphor to his own life journey as a whole.

He's working in a very competitive field. He still managed to climb to the very top of the pyramid in record time.

He blends into this world to perfection. He clearly chose to put those specific facets of his personality forward to become the best.

That's a deliberate choice he made, and it might mean that the other parts of—

Lucas' cheerful voice pulls her out of her musings as they reach the East Terrasse. "Emma!" He opens up his arms in invitation. "Good to see you. It's been a while"

The average height ginger haired woman in an A-line rusty brown dress hugs the managing director. "I'm happy to see you, too." She looks to his left as she pulls away. "I didn't know you had a plus one, Lucas."

Her husband replies before Lucas has any chance to. "It's Raven, Em. You know, *the* Raven..."

Realization slowly paints the interior designer features. "Oh." She looks genuinely shocked and thrilled at once. "I wasn't expecting to ever get introduced to you, Raven." She smiles brightly, getting closer. "I'm very happily surprised."

The second the lawyer accepts the welcoming embrace, she can feel that Emma seems to be a very warm and calm person.

She looks to be complementing her husband's more buoyant energy impeccably. It's probably no wonder that those two have been together for years.

Raven smiles as Emma pulls away, and puts her glass on the bar table to her right. "Lucas and I will be working together for a while." She keeps her fingers on the foot of her flute. "It's also a pleasure to meet you, Emma."

Emma stares directly at Lucas. "So you invited her here only for professional reasons?"

The managing director hums in agreement, staying vague. "Mainly."

Felipe glances at his friend, too. "Have you seen yourself dance just now?" He gives his wife the champagne. "You should've been there, honey. It was electric." He alternates pointing his index finger between Lucas and Raven standing in front of them. "I have no idea how they are able to platonically stand next to each other after what I saw."

Lucas acts fakely offended. "And you dared interrupt us?"

"In my defense, I only noticed that your dancing session was heated once I had called out to you." The analyst puts his hands up in surrender, smiling teasingly. "I'm sorry, it's—"

Raven cuts him off, laughing lightly. "It's fine. Nothing was going on."

"If you say so." Felipe raises a mischievous eyebrow. "I'm still unconvinced, but I'll let you get away with it this time."

Raven fleetingly focuses on the music booming in the distance.

Saying that nothing was going on on that dance floor is not a lie, but she knows that it is also a cop out.

She doesn't want to entertain the meddling of his friends. When she puts her cards on the table, it will be with Lucas and Lucas alone.

Things might be incertain and more complicated than she'd like in her brain, but she owes him that much.

It's unlike her to hesitate and second guess.

But can she really take the risk to get attached to Lucas? Is she even *willing* to?

It hurt a whole lot with Nathan. She has no desire to reproduce the pattern.

Meaningless sex, sure. Feelings? Certainly not.

She sips on her champagne. Her mind is a mess. She won't be the one to pick that conversation back up.

After a beat of silence, Emma reorients the exchange. "So did you guys bid on anything at the silent auction yet?"

Raven and Lucas both shake their heads, but the managing director decides to entertain the small talk. "Not yet. I was eyeing the one week stay in Switzerland."

Raven turns toward him, trailing her fingers along the stem of her glass. "Is it because of the celebrity chef cooking every meal or because of the two included in-house massages per day?"

"I don't know." Lucas bends down, a sure spark in his eyes. "Would you like to accompany me?" He slides his hand to rest on the small of her back, dropping his tone so only Raven can hear him. "Because in that case I would much rather prefer to be the one performing those massages." He brushes his nose into her hair. "On you," he breathes out.

"That's very tempting."

He groans. "You'd really want me to—"

Felipe's laugh echoes in her ears. "See? I swear those two are not to be left alone."

The analyst's wife chuckles. "Or maybe that's exactly what they'd like."

"True." Lucas' friend nods. "We can totally—"

It's Raven's turn to interjects. "No. It's okay." She flashes them a warm smile while Lucas and her both readjust their postures to keep a respectable distance between them. "It's just this thing we have to always tease and flirt with each other. As soon as we reconnected it all came back naturally."

Emma grins. "That's actually amazing."

Raven hums absentmindedly, returning the initial question back to the interior designer. "So have you bid on anything?"

"I looked quickly, and maybe will place a bid on the trip to Fiji and stay at a villa." Emma brings her glass to her lips. "It requires the permission of the island owner to go there so the fact that they got it to put this package at auction makes it special." She scoots closer to her husband. "I also eyed the fully restored Special Edition vintage car, but we wouldn't be able to afford it. It will probably go for a price near seven digits." She slides her arm around Felipe's waist. "Plus, Felipe bought the newest model from that brand last week anyway."

"Mark told me about it." Lucas bows his head in acknowledgment. "Congrats, buddy."

"I got a bonus at work so it was a no-brainer." Felipe smiles shyly. "Emma always wanted that car."

Raven suddenly feels like asking. "You guys never thought about working together?" She stares at the two men in alternance.

"We nearly did." They both answer in unison. Lucas continues the explanation. "When I became Managing Director, some other positions opened up. I told Felipe, but he decided not to apply." He glances at his friend. "It was for the best, I think. We have way too different energies for it to go smoothly. Plus, his investment bank is my most direct competition. A couple of my clients hesitated between his and my firm, but I managed to convince them to sign with me. It would be dull without him around." He smiles smugly. "Less challenge, and all that"

The lawyer snorts. "Fair enough. At least you're lucid." She takes a sip of her drink, deciding to circle back to the previous point. "Speaking of the auction, I personally also looked at the restored coupe, but would have no use for it in the city. Plus, I love the convertible that I have back home."

Felipe drapes an arm around Emma's shoulders. "You're from the West Coast, Raven, right?"

"Yeah. San Diego." The lawyer smiles politely. "I have a house there along with my car. One of my best friends is looking after both, and I do my best to visit as often as I can."

"That sounds fantastic." The analyst grins. "Most of my extended family is still in Brazil. My parents, brothers, and grandparents live upstate, and I'm lucky that all my closest friends are also here."

"Do you go to visit them often?" Raven sees Filipe's inquiring look. She adds some precision. "In Brazil, I mean."

"Once every two years or so?" He shrugs. "I'm not really close with any of my aunts, uncles and cousins." He stares at his wife. "But Emma loves my hometown as well as the subtropical climate so we go whenever we have a chance."

The lawyer looks at Felipe's wife. "And where are you from, Emma?"

"Vermont." Emma smiles cheerfully. "My parents still live there while my brother now lives in Germany, and my sister in Tennessee. I will go visit her at the end of next week. She and I are pretty close."

Felipe doesn't miss a beat. "Speaking of sisters, how is yours doing with her filming, Lucas?

"I haven't gotten news in a few days, but last time she reached out she was doing great, thank you," Lucas responds proudly.

Raven turns toward him. Seeing the pride in his eyes, she's genuinely curious when she asks, "What is your sister filming?"

"A documentary about rainforest and its changing biodiversity and impact on climate change." Lucas smiles heartily. "She studied cinematography in the hopes of being able to do something like this someday."

She smiles back at him. "That's amazing."

He takes it as an invitation to explain further. "She created a few documentaries through the years, and worked on smaller projects, but her and her husband finally got the funding for this big one." Delight is painting his features. "I'm proud of her. She wants to bring more awareness about underlying issues about what human actions provoke."

"We can never have too much of those," Raven agrees. "She's doing important work. People need to be aware of what our choices and politics entails concretely. We only got one planet. Better live in harmony with it."

The managing director locks eyes with her. "You'd get along well with Lena."

She can't stop the words before they fall from her lips. "I'd love to meet her."

Lucas beams. "She's in Brazil until the end of the month, but I was thinking of visiting her and my mom in Chicago when she's back. Maybe we could—"

Felipe's voice resounds in their ears once more. "Woah, would you look at that. I think Lucas here never brought anyone home in ages." He looks at his friend in fake reprobation. "And you tell me this thing is strictly professional, man?" He tsk-ed. "Do I look dumb to you?"

Lucas' tone is nothing but serious as he faces Flip. "I said inviting Raven to this fundraiser tonight had professional motives." He shrugs dismissively. "I didn't say anything past that statement."

His friend laughs. "You're sly."

He sounds amused. "I'm trying my best."

Emma continues to look at Raven. "Do you have any siblings, Raven?"

"No. I'm an only child."

The designer scans Raven's features. "Ever found it difficult?"

"To be completely honest, not really." She tilts her head in reflection. "I had amazing friends and this found family I built through the years. I can't complain."

The interior designer seems to think of something. "I didn't ask, sweetie, but would you like to come visit my sister with me?" She rubs her husband's back. "It's been a while since you saw them. My mom is also in town for the grand opening of my sister's bakery, and—"

Felipe stiffens. "I can't."

Emma frowns. "It's during the weekend, you surely can take a few days off."

The analyst's tone is dripping with exasperation. "I need to double down on the extra hours if I want my Christmas bonus at the end of the year. Plus, I need to sign some fresh blood if I want that promotion."

His wife makes a face. "C'mon, you're one of their best employees, you'll get it even if you don't burn yourself down. I'd really love you there with me"

"You'd also love a new house, and we want kids and it all costs tons of money, and both our salaries might not be enough to get what we want," Felipe snaps.

Raven takes a sip of her champagne, wishing she could subtly flee the private conversation.

She met Sabrina and Brooke not long ago, and felt like she was strangely fitting in that part of Lucas' life. Now interacting with Felipe and Emma, she also felt like things were going well until this awkward moment.

The couple either feels very at ease in her presence to start bickering unashamedly like that, or it's their overall attitude to just do it whenever it happens no matter the circumstances.

Felipe did say that they were late because of a fight. Tension was probably already flying high. It only took a tiny spark to reignite the whole thing.

How could she graciously—

While his friends argue about money, work schedules, and their future, Lucas shifts his stare to Gabriel Smith who's waving goodbye at him as he strides toward the exit. "Please excuse me for a moment, I have to go chat with someone."

Before Lucas starts going after Smith, Raven looks at him with a puzzled expression. "What are you—"

He interrupts her, angling his head so as to be shielded from Felipe and Emma's potential prying eyes as they stop quarreling to look at them. "I have to let him know that I won't sign the paperwork before I make some more verifications myself," he murmurs.

She blinks in confusion. "You're going to run that background check?"

He smirks softly. "It can't hurt, right?"

As he walks away, Raven can't stop the smile forming on her lips.

Did she really get through to him?

He definitely listened to her advice, at least.

Maybe all is not lost.

Maybe the Lucas she knew with all his beautiful complexity and strong ideals is not that far away, after all.

SEVEN

Lust for Refraction

"**Y**ou really think that Thomas Keller or Dick Adams could be good candidates for having sent that threat letter?" Lucas shifts gears as he takes a left turn while exiting the underground parking garage.

Raven analyzes his features as he drives. "As I said, they're usually pretty direct in their approach, but they're also very impulsive and have a tendency to become borderline hostile"

He frowns. "Sounds like you personally dealt with some unpleasant things with them."

She inhales deeply. "I did."

He stays silent. He's dying to know how she knows them, and what they put her through.

As always, he won't push.

If she wants to share, she'll do it on her own terms. He feels way too content at the moment to risk ruining it by potentially overstepping.

The second she walked out of her building earlier when he arrived to pick her up, he knew he would only want one thing throughout the night: to have her as close to him as possible.

He's happy that it seemed utterly reciprocal.

He noticed how she seeked him herself. How she leaned into his touch every time without fail.

They spent an incredible evening chatting, drinking, meeting with some of his friends and clients alike as well as dancing.

Dancing.

The mere reminder of how Raven felt pressed against him is sending his mind into a daze.

He would give anything to be back on that dance floor right about now.

She was matching the rhythm and the movement of his hips to perfection as she grinded into him.

They were having a very important discussion, but her way to flawlessly blend with his energy was steadily overriding his thought process.

Only Raven is able to make such an essential conversation feel natural while swaying sensually on a dancefloor.

They were word sparring, clashing ideas, and acting like they wanted to tear each other's clothes off all at once.

He loved it.

The minute she turned in his arms, there was no use trying to calm down his arousal.

The way Raven directed his hand on her thigh and welcomed his touch when he slipped it underneath her dress is making rounds in his head.

Her fingers were expertly combing through his hair. She was caressing his scalp in this unique way she has that makes him purr.

He wanted her to do it all night.

He was craving to kiss her for all he's worth right there in the middle of that endless sea of undulating bodies around them.

He was yearning to feel more of her. To sense just how she was responding to him.

He wanted to take all of the time in the world to pleasure her like she deserves. To show her that he longs to dedicate himself to her and her only. To make her come apart until dawn breaks.

Judging by the way she told him that he felt phenomenal, he is pretty sure they desired the same thing.

But she also started expressing a concern just as Felipe interrupted them.

They both agreed to address the subject again in due time, but had no chance to do so so far.

As soon as they entered his car, he removed his suit jacket and told Raven that Gabriel Smith looked pissed off when he told him about wanting to take more time before signing the documents.

Plus, the import/export CEO of Products Daring Adventure—PDA for short—Cargo warned Lucas that he was going away on a business trip for a few days, but hoped that he would've received a contract to review from Lucas in a timely manner. Smith even added that he wouldn't entertain the possibility of meeting with Lucas again unless the managing director signed the documents, and he officially became a client.

It made Raven reflect.

As he took off his cufflinks and rolled up his sleeves, she started to tell him about other names that stood out to her from when she went through his list the night prior.

Lucas is certain that Raven's opinion of Mr Smith is based on more than just a bad vibe and general public information.

Just like the rest, she'll probably share it if or when she feels like it is important to.

For now, he got the prevailing message. That's all that matters.

He trusts Raven's readings of situations and her instincts.

He personally wants to thrive and make good money. He worked hard for that to happen.

Raven seems to have a more careful outlook on things, but it's enriching to exchange with her.

They might not always see eye to eye when business practices are the topic of interest, but he respects and welcomes her views. She is able to make him examine the facts differently. He greatly appreciates that fresh dynamic.

With the way they're interacting, he's sure that—

Raven clears her throat as she glances outside through the window. "I had to defend Keller from insider trading, and Adams from mortgage fraud. They've both been very aggressive when I had to talk to them." She half-smiles. "I noticed that they're amongst your newest clients so you might've not noticed."

"I'm sorry they acted like assholes with you." He clenches his jaw. He's not liking that those men treated Raven that way. "They were indeed brought to the company by some other employees in my division." He quickly checks in the rearview mirror. "I haven't looked at their files in detail yet." He furrows his eyebrows. "Maybe I should."

"Maybe." Raven hums. "You don't have to approve of every new client?"

"I do." He nods. "But some of the managing directors, associates, and analysts, I trust nearly blindly at this point. Through the years they proved to me that they deserved it."

She turns her attention toward him, smiling amusedly. "So no need to prepare for all possible outcomes, and double check everything in those cases?"

"I did learn to delegate a little through time." He laughs lightly. "I still quickly go through every file personally. I sign off on documents to authorize the business afterwards." He thinks for a beat. "What happened with Keller and Adams? In regards to their trials, I mean."

She clenches her jaw slightly. "They were both exonerated."

"Obviously." He snorts as if he just asked a useless question. "You're good at your job. No surprise there"

She becomes even more serious. "*Was* good."

"You're still a lawyer." He frowns, sounding determined. "Your skills didn't vanish overnight. Any firm would be lucky to have you."

"Thanks for your unwavering faith in me, but you weren't around the past few years." She tenses a little. "You didn't get to see just how many scumbags I defended. How trying to be the best at it was slowly eating at my sanity."

He decides to ask tentatively. "That's what made you hand in your resignation?"

She hums in approbation. "I couldn't continue working to defend that kind of people."

He remembers she mentioned it vaguely before, but things are suddenly making more sense all of a sudden.

Her constant need to want to do better.

Her apprehension about potentially working with questionable individuals.

Her apparent quest to dissociate herself from her past.

He keeps his voice mellow. "Hence why you keep saying that principles are important."

There's melancholia dripping from her tone. "I felt like I had lost myself."

He flashes her a comforting smile. "I'm sure you'll find yourself again, and get a job that aligns with your aspirations."

"Maybe I'll also end up blacklisted from most firms with what I did." She breathes in. "I resigned in the middle of a big trial."

He takes a left on Wythe Avenue. "Knowing you, something tells me that you still made sure the client was well represented, and that things were in order before doing so."

"I did. I left my colleague Sara to take care of his defense. She was already the second chair anyway." She curves a corner of her mouth upward. "Not that I didn't think about just leaving him in the mud."

"You weren't very fond of that client it seems."

"That's an understatement." She exhales loudly, knitting her eyebrows. "Were you serious when you told Felipe that you think the threat you received might've been a one time thing?"

He flicks his stare at her briefly. "Yeah, but no matter what, I want to see it through."

She examines him for a moment before replying. "Still be careful. You never know what can happen once the hornet's nest is shaken."

"I'm well aware that I can get new blackmail anytime." He stops at a red light, turning to smile coyly at her. "I also know I have the best team to deal with it."

"We'll certainly do our best." She looks at the screen of the head unit as the song shifts. "Speaking of, do you want to ask Jun about checking

Gabriel Smith's background? I think she's the best one to reach out to for it. She'll keep it private and all."

"Sure. I'll contact her tomorrow to ask." He looks at the time on the dashboard. "I mean, later today."

She gets lost in thought, humming to the music leaking through the sound system. "Thank you."

He tilts his head in questioning. "For what?"

"The invitation." She smiles tenderly. "I'm beyond tired, and might have drank a glass too much of champagne, but it was fun spending the evening with you."

His eyes bore into hers as he stretches his arms a little to release some tension. "We could do it more often in less official settings if you want."

He sees her briefly shift her stare to his tattoo before averting it to look straight ahead.

He suddenly remembers that he never told her the true meaning of each component forming the design of the ink on his skin.

Maybe he could try to share some—

He hears her start singing under her breath at the same time he revs up the engine as the light turns green.

He smiles absentmindedly.

He could get used to listening to Raven humming to songs like that. It's wonderfully soothing.

Especially paired with that singer's deep haunting sultry voice and enthralling harmonies.

Which reminds him that—

"Do you like that singer?" He is genuinely curious. "You seemed to react to another tune by her that was playing when we came back from Boston. You were asleep, but when the song came on, you—"

She interjects "Yeah. I absolutely love her." She smiles shyly. "Her vocals, her beats, her whole artistic approach. It just connects with me." She lets her head drop on the headrest. "I have all of her albums on vinyl. I can't explain it, but listening to them always brings me to a peaceful place."

"That's amazing. I have to admit that I also like her." He turns the volume up a few notches by pressing the appropriate button on the wheel. "I used to have that feeling you described when playing old school jazz or blues on my guitar."

"The one that's been sitting in your closet for years?" she teases.

He snorts. "Yeah, that exact one."

She stares at his hand on the gear shift inattentively. "What have you been listening to lately?"

"I'm really into 60s inspired jazz song structure these days." He looks at the Brooklyn bridge to their right. "Gotta love a good blues riff, too."

"I also greatly enjoy that." She gazes at him intently. "You can feel classic rock, and some R&B in some musicians' works. I love to hear those associations. It makes for a lovely listening experience."

He beams. "It's like we were made to get along, you and I."

"It certainly feels like it." She gets lost in the tiny specks of white in his scruff. "Do you think you're ever going to dust off that guitar?"

"Probably." He reflects for a second. "I think about it sometimes, but then I run out of time in a day."

"I get it." She lets her eyes travel along his jawline. "You have to make room for it. I had to do the same for reading, yoga and workouts." She yawns lightly. "I try to do all physical exercises first thing in the morning, and good books are for when I go to bed."

He can't help himself. "So you still like morning sex as much as you used to."

The lyrics wash over them as she breathes out a chuckle. "You know very well what I was referring to with 'physical exercises', but if you must know..." She drops her tone to a murmur, leaning forward. "Yeah. I still love morning sex."

"The very best way to wake up, yeah?"

"Can't think of a better feeling." She takes a short pause as if she's hesitating to finish her thought. "When done right," she finally whispers.

He frowns. "You had bad experiences?"

She shrugs. "Don't we all?"

"Fair enough." He maneuvers to get onto her street. "I hope I wasn't part of those."

"You very well know you weren't." He can feel her gazing earnestly at him. "Was I?"

His answer is instantaneous. "I told you multiple times I couldn't get you out of my head."

He grips the wheel tighter.

An unwarranted image of Raven kissing him lazily in bed first thing in the morning is flooding his mind.

Sensing her body heat was blissful.

Feeling her touch on his bare skin was heavenly.

His arousals were anything but subtle when he was waking up next to her. He couldn't help it. His whole skeleton was alight as soon as he was feeling her close.

He can clearly recall that she would curl her hand around his cock to deftly pump him as they made out.

When she would move south to leave open mouthed kisses across his pecs, down to his navel to finally lick her way back, it was driving him mad.

She usually ended by teasing his nipples in the most erotic fashion, rubbing and gently sucking on them before blowing lightly.

He inhales deeply, shifting into his seat.

From all the lovers he had, Raven is the only one that has ever been able to enhance his sensitivity in riveting ways.

Every time they were having sex, she would bring him right on the edge of ecstasy to a point where he had no choice but to splinter powerfully.

He shakes his head. He has to focus. "My friends even vouched for it. I think it's safe to say that you've been nothing short of memorable."

"So were you." Her voice is laced with softness. "Do you know what I particularly loved?"

"Do tell."

"You had a way to delicately let your hands caress me..." She trails off purposely. "And then your tongue..." She bites into her bottom lip.

He breathes in to stay composed.

She doesn't need to say more. He knows exactly what she's referring to.

To this day, there hasn't been a better sensation to him than to feel Raven coming apart on his tongue no matter the hour of day.

But the way she was cursing his name with her sleepy tone when she climaxed at sunrise is forever ingrained in his brain.

The little moan she would always emit when he was kissing her afterward is still one of the most beautiful sounds that ever graced his ears.

So he decides to share an undeniable truth. "I loved every second of it."

"Lots of men don't enjoy giving head."

"That's because they're fools." He feels very serene having this discussion with Raven. Just like the rest, it's natural to speak his mind with her. "They should make sure to know how to pleasure their partners. There's few more satisfying sensations in life than to achieve that."

She hums, smiling brightly. "I couldn't agree more."

"Sadly, some are just too eager to get to their own orgasm when it's truly all about mutual pleasure." He decides to test her reaction. "And you, Raven, are in a class of your own when it comes to it. I wasn't kidding when I said that I loved every second of it. Making you shatter is spectacular."

She's unflinching. "A lot can have changed in a decade."

He stays unyielding. "I have a hunch that this is not one of them." He pulls up in front of her building. "We're here." He stops the engine, seeing Raven unbuckling her belt and reaching for her door handle. "Please let me get that."

He rapidly exits the car, circling around it to get on her side where she is already standing on the sidewalk.

He smiles amusedly. "I told you I'd open it."

"I'm not a damsel in distress, Lucas." She mirrors his expression. "I can take care of myself."

He half-smiles. "I only wanted to be a true gentleman."

"You always are." She gets closer to him. "Thank you again for tonight."

He locks eyes with her. "Thanks to you for agreeing to come."

The moment the last word gets spoken, he can't stop himself from snorting.

She picks up on the double-entendre, smiling playfully. "I've always been happy to come with you, Lucas."

"I'm glad to hear." He scans her gaze, getting inexorably pulled into the icy fire of her turquoise pools. He drops his tone to a murmur. "Same for me."

She matches his intonation, boring into his stare as she becomes serious. "'Night."

Her speech tells him that she is saying goodbye, but her body language is telling a different story.

She's not moving. She even lets her digits trail down the silk of his tie until they reach his belt buckle.

Her ocean blue irises are slowly disappearing in profit to her dilated pupils.

He takes a step forward, reaching to slide his hand softly onto the side of her face. "Good night, Rae."

She leans into his touch nearly imperceptibly. "Please don't," she whispers.

He furrows his eyebrows, letting his index trace the helix of her ear between the tips of her industrial piercing. "What?"

She places her palm flat on his pec. "Call me Rae."

He presses their foreheads together. "Why?"

She glides her hand around his neck to go bury her digits into the black locks at the back of his head. "Because I like it, and that's dangerous."

"Dangerous?" He smiles shyly. "It can't be more dangerous than me nearly coming apart untouched at the ghost of your voice calling me 'Luke'."

Her tone is tender as she traces the beard along his mandible. "Really?"

He grabs her hip with his other hand to pull her flush to him. "Mhmm."

The instant she curls her hand around his throat and captures his bottom lip, he sighs.

She quickly asks him for an access that he fervently grants her. The second their tongues begin battling for dominance, it's even better than he remembered.

He never thought he'd have the chance to kiss Raven ever again in this lifetime.

She feels like salvation all over again.

It's like he's finally breathing after years of being on artificial oxygen. He's steadily melting into her, and he wouldn't want it any other way.

He's glad that he decided to put less product in his hair today. He can feel the strands glide through her fingers smoothly, and he's seeking more of it.

Her tongue is warm and insistent.

Her nose is skimming along his.

One of her hands is trailing down his chest, curling around his tie knot to loosen it some more gently.

Her touch is soft and assured at once.

Her kiss is sensual and lascivious.

He fucking can't get enough of her.

She's superseding all of his senses.

As he caresses her jaw, he marvels at feeling every one of her muscles exquisitely move under his thumb.

The second he brushes the pad of his fingertips down the vertebrae of her neck leisurely while kissing her back, she moans deep into his mouth.

He involuntarily grinds into her.

Damn.

That sound.

He wants to hear it a thousand times over.

He wants to make it fall from her lips repeatedly.

He wants it laced with his name as she chases her pleasure and then falls apart.

The moment he feels her untuck his shirt while scraping her nails in the short hair at the nape of his neck, he can't help but groan.

She leans back, pulling her bottom lip between her teeth. "Wanna come upstairs?" she whispers in the infinitesimal space between them.

"I'd love to."

She sneaks underneath his shirt to trace his abs with her fingertips. "Why are you hesitating, Lucas?"

"You expressed some concerns before that we still haven't addressed together." He can't help his muscles twitching under her attention. He breathes in to stay composed. "We're both beyond tired, and—"

She cuts him off, laying a soft kiss on the underside of his jaw. "I'm sure I would sleep incredibly well in your arms after having fucked you."

He closes his eyes, gliding his hands down to her ass. "Don't make this harder than it already is, please."

"I can sense *exactly* how hard it is for you right now." She rocks into him lightly. "Let me help you with that."

He lets out a small grunt. "I don't want you to regret anything."

She defines his cupid's bow with the pad of her index finger. "How could I—"

It's his turn to interject. He snaps his eyes back open. "Is there even the tiniest possibility that you might regret this?"

He can feel the ghost of her lips on his as she stays silent.

He knows she wouldn't lie. Her silence is the only confirmation he needs.

Whatever is going through her head he wants to learn about, and then he hopes to be able to fall into bed with her.

But not right now.

Not at 3AM when they're both exhausted, and she arguably had one drink too many as she freely admitted.

If he has sex with Raven this time, he knows it has the potential to become more than just a fling.

His mind is yelling at him that she's different from everyone else. She could carve her place in his life.

Fuck. She already feels like everything he needs after only that one kiss.

He only hopes that she won't take it as a—

She exhales. "You're right." She pulls away. "My mind is a mess."

He kisses the pad of her finger. "And you hijacked mine."

She kisses him tenderly once more. "I'm sorry?"

"Don't be." He chases her lips. "I quite like having you live there. It makes life more enjoyable."

She inhales deeply while disentangling herself from his embrace. "Good night for real, Lucas."

As he watches her walk away, he puts his hands in his pockets.

He already misses her body warmth and her touch.

He would've loved to keep her molded into him all night. He's certain that, just like she said herself, he would've slept incredibly well after they'd have fucked each other senseless.

He wonders why he insisted on being the sensible one right now.

When she disappears inside her building, he strides toward the other side of the sports car.

He knows why he acted that way: it felt like the right thing to do. Especially after she admitted that her brain was a mess.

He doesn't want to ruin whatever this has the potential to be between them.

Seating into the driver seat, he shifts uncomfortably. He'll definitely have to take care of his arousal when he gets home.

There's no way it's going away with the thousand images of Raven that are submerging his psyche, and with how he can still sense her tongue in his mouth.

The minute he presses on the keyless push-button start, he's met by the last notes of the song.

He starts driving with the phantom of Raven's voice singing beside him, and her caresses lingering over his flesh.

He breathes in.

He can feel that this night's sleep is going to be a short one.

As Raven plops down on her sofa in a pair of tie dye leggings and a long-sleeved black shirt, she hums to the melodies of music from her favorite playlist.

She had an urge to listen to familiar tunes today to keep her mind in a relatively calm state.

She puts her bowl down on the coffee table, and combs her fingers through her loose hair.

Quickly taking stock of her surroundings, she puts her phone on the arm rest of the couch. She has her glass of wine next to her couscous salad, a book she has yet to finish reading, the universal remote and her laptop in case she feels like working.

This should be a relaxing evening at home exactly like she intended.

She switches the stereo for the TV, grabs her meal, and starts eating while watching the latest movie release from the first streaming service she comes across.

Her mind takes no more than a few minutes to wander back to what she did today.

She has to admit that it was nice despite her thoughts circling back to a certain managing director more often than not.

As soon as she got home in the middle of the night, she took a quick shower before climbing into bed, but her brain couldn't shut up about Lucas.

Plus, the ache between her legs never subsided.

She knows herself well enough to be aware that it wouldn't have gone away unless she released the tension herself.

She briefly hesitated in reaching into her bedside table drawer to grab one of her toys, but decided against it.

She wanted to feel the exact effect he had on her. So as she caressed down her abdomen leisurely, she reminded herself of how she liquefied as soon as their lips collided earlier.

How his hands were reverent as they roamed over her body and into her hair.

How he kissed her like his life depended on it, being just the right kind of passionate and tender.

It was everything she didn't know she needed.

No.

It was better than that.

It ignited an inferno she had no idea could still exist deep within herself.

With one make out session, she got reminded of how exceptional he feels.

She hungered to undress him slowly. To kneel before him to sense him swell magnificently on her tongue, and then ride him into oblivion.

She needed to feel more of him.

She wanted *all* of him.

Every doubt that had been making rounds in her head for days flew out the window at the split second his groan reverberated through her bones.

She whimpered as she dipped her hand under her shorts to trace her core, imagining Lucas' fingers doing it.

She recalled how he would let his middle and ring fingers part her folds finely to then slide and curve them expertly.

How it was even better when it was his mouth pleasuring her.

He was never trying to restrict her movements, but was welcoming each undulation of her hips with renewed ardor. The way he would purr into her as she combed her fingers into his hair never failed to drive her crazy.

He could lap at her unrelentingly as his nose would brush her clit with each swipe, bringing her closer and closer to climax.

When she started rubbing tight circles on her bundle of nerves, summoning a souvenir of him sucking on it lightly, she got propelled into ecstasy.

She remembers she took a hot minute to come back down from it.

She can't even begin to imagine what it would've been like if Lucas had literally been in bed with her.

Just fantasizing about him gave her a sensation of pure bliss she hadn't felt in ages.

If he had been physically there, she would've surely ended up delightfully wrecked.

Instead, the residual oxytocin running through her veins made her get a few good hours of sleep.

She won't complain that twice in the span of a few days Lucas managed to have a positive impact on her slumber. The first time was for vastly different reasons than now, but still.

No matter what their interactions look like, he undeniably has a soothing effect on her.

Upon waking up around lunch time, she checked her messages only to see that she received a bunch of them, including one from him. She automatically opened it.

L: Morning, υπναρού. I hope you had a good night. I had an early meeting so I barely slept. Wishing you a good one. Ttyl.

She smiled softly.

She can sense that calling her υπναρού will become his thing. She doesn't mind. She has to admit that she likes that it's something referring to their history, and to stolen moments spent together.

The fact that he sent her a good morning text is also heartening.

She checks the timestamp of the message before replying.

5:50AM. He indeed didn't get a lot of sleep. That is if he got any at all by the time he got to his apartment.

R: Just woke up so you can judge by yourself. I'm sorry you probably don't feel rested. Hope your day goes by quickly. Call me when you're done?

She hesitated putting emojis or some kind of fun salutation, but he kept his tone mostly business-like in his message so she did, too.

Since she sent it, she hasn't heard back from him. Even if he's normally very responsive when they communicate, they don't owe each other anything.

She highly doubts that she scared him off by asking if he'd like to chat at the end of the day.

The way he's been acting with her bleeds of nothing other than understanding and interest. They both agreed they need to talk, and she's convinced that they will.

He's probably been ultra busy, and had no time to reply.

She just hopes he's doing okay.

She also had a slew of other notifications from Jun telling her about Lucas' request to look into Gabriel Smith more closely. Her friend signified that she would like for Raven to call her at the end of the day once she'd have a moment.

She quickly told the crisis manager that she would do so.

All in all, it means that she spent the rest of her day running errands, and called Jun back on her way home.

So you're saying that you're the one who gave Lucas the idea of running a detailed background check on Gabriel Smith? her friend asked as she was removing her makeup in front of her bathroom mirror.

From the angle at which Jun had put her phone on the counter, Raven was seeing the beautiful marbled white tiles of the crisis manager's shower wall as well as the purple shirt her friend was wearing.

Raven was trying her best to keep her phone in hand during the video call. It was not an easy task to achieve while juggling with bags draped on her shoulder on top of her plaid pink blazer she had put on top of a black scoop neck t-shirt. *Yeah.* She looked down at her boot-covered feet while climbing the stairs to exit the subway station. *And I didn't tell Lucas, but it's because I once saw Gabriel Smith deep in conversation with my last client: Cameron Wallace.*

Jun frowned. *The one who was into human trafficking?*

Mhmm. Raven removed an earphone to tuck it into her jeans pocket. She likes to be able to hear what's going on around her as she walks on sidewalks. One AirPod would do. *I didn't want to get into the details of everything that made me quit my job, and my whole thought process in the middle of this formal event.*

I get it. Her friend looked back at the screen. *But know that Mr Blake can't shut up about how he loves interacting with you.*

Does he now?

You should've heard him when I asked if he liked how we handled things so far. Jun smirked. *He said he was loving how you were challenging him. To which I replied that I wasn't surprised. You're the fiercest woman I know.*

Raven smiled warmly at her friend. *You're not too bad yourself, Ju.*

I try. She laughed, going back to removing her eyeliner. *Speaking of Lucas' case, there was nothing that stood out from all the cam footage I looked at. The only person who entered the building who might've ransacked his office was a tall man dressed in all black with his hood on. From more than ten cameras, there's not a single good angle that I can use to identify him.*

Mm. The lawyer reflected for a beat. *He either knew where the cameras were, or he was lucky. Was he wearing any face covering?*

I have no idea. Jun shrugged. *None of the footage is showing even a part of his face. He mostly kept his head down.* She shifts eyes with her green cloth, seemingly remembering something at the same time. *And, he was wearing gloves.*

If we needed more proof that this was carefully planned, we have it. Raven frowned. *It would be surprising that he just decided to go search Lucas' office on a whim.*

I agree. Her friend concentrates on wiping off her eye liner. *I also forgot to tell you that the envelope of the threat letter can't give us any more clues. The stamp only says that it was mailed two days before Lucas received it.*

And whoever posted it probably dropped it into a mailbox anyway. She pressed her lips into a thin line. *We won't watch every single one of them to potentially get—*

Jun cut her off. *It would take lots of time, but we actually could.* She dropped the cloth to focus on Raven. *I could ask someone from my team to check and cross reference the surveillance images from the city with the envelope we have. If the definition is good enough—*

It was Raven's turn to interject. *You think it could be?*

It's worth a try?

If that person was as careful mailing it than they were when going into Lucas' firm, I think we won't see much, but as you said it might be worth it. She stopped at a street corner. *Maybe whoever did it was hired by someone, too.*

True. Jun nodded. *We'll only be sure of that once we find out who did it though.*

Raven looked around her only to see two teenagers deep in discussion. She still dropped her voice a few octaves. *Could you also keep an eye out for Dick Adams and Thomas Keller?*

Sure. So far, nothing stood out a lot from the background checks I ran, and all the employees had good alibis. Her friend stared at her. *Any specific reason why those two?*

Let's say I dealt with both, and they employ a variety of techniques to get their points across. She breathed in. *From all the clients I had to defend, those two stood out because they were very aggressive.*

Gotcha.

Lucas said they were brought in by some other employees lately. Raven saw the pedestrian crossing signal turn green. *He hasn't interacted with them so far, but every new client knows that he needs to approve and verify every transaction.* She started striding across the street. *It would make sense that they'd want to make it clear that they want their business to be run a certain way.*

I agree. I'll take a look. Thanks for the tip, Raven. Jun raised a curious eyebrow. *So how was the fundraiser?*

She assessed her friend's expression. *Lucas didn't kiss and tell?*

We barely know each other, of course he didn't... The manager trailed off, gasping. *Wait.* She beamed. *Did you—*

Raven interrupted her. There was no use letting her finish that sentence. *Yeah.* She smiled at Jun's enthusiasm. *Yeah, I kissed him.*

You only kissed him? Jun gives her her best fake reprobative look. *Girl...*

I know. I feel like a teenager right now.

Her friend turned very serious. *Why didn't you have sex with him?*

I had started telling him during the evening that I'm drawn to him, but that he's also on a very different journey than me. Hence me not necessarily wanting to entertain thoughts about us going down that path again. Raven got lost in thought at her recollection of events nearly bumping into an incoming walker. She stopped near the entrance of a store to finish her story. *Although I never had time to explain it all before one of his friends interrupted us while we were grinding on the dance floor. One thing led to another, we were standing in front of my condo both tired as hell and making out.* He acted all considerate, and comprehensive, saying that he wanted to hear what I had to say before going any further because he didn't want me to regret anything.

Fair enough, I guess. Jun scanned her eyes. *It must've been hard to stop, no?*

Mhmm. Raven can't stop herself from a quip. *You have no idea how hard he was.*

Her friend snorted. *And he wasn't the only one who was aroused, yeah?*

Obviously not. She inhaled deeply, remembering her early morning activities. *I took care of it by myself.*

Oh, you didn't call Will? Jun teased.

Very funny, Ju. She let out a small laugh. *Very funny.*

I wish Lucas wouldn't have been such a gentleman. Jun smiled wilfully. *I know you crave him.*

To be completely honest, I briefly internally cursed at him, but it's truly better that way. Raven sounded at peace with the whole situation. *As I admitted to him, my mind is a mess right now.*

The crisis manager sounded impressed. *Life goals: meet someone who accepts every quirk, and embrace each unease with you as a united front.*

Yeah. She hummed inattentively. *I guess he feels a little like that.*

Jun took her phone in hand. *I hope you two get to talk it out sooner rather than later.*

I hope so, too. Raven began walking again. *Listen, I'm just a block away from home, but if I want to stay focussed on my route I'll have to let you go.*

No worries. We'll talk again soon. Her friend's tone switched to being very solemn. *Before you hang up, just be warned that I've been thinking about making you an official job offer.* She grinned. *I'd love to have you be part of my team, Raven.*

She half-smiled. *We'll discuss it later, okay?*

For sure. Just know that my offer is on the table. Ju smiled brightly. *Take all the time you need. I think we're not close to wrapping up Lucas' case anyway. We still have time in front of us.*

They both said goodbye, and Raven pocketed her device.

As she now takes a bite of her couscous, she realizes that she has a lot to ponder about.

If she hadn't formulated any kind of "but you also chose to…" that she had to leave in suspension because of Felipe during the gala, she would have woken up next to Lucas this morning.

Truth is, Jun is totally right. She craves for Lucas with every fiber of her being.

She was completely ready to just give in to her desires. See where it would lead her, and how they would handle it all.

She could still just fuck him, take him out of her system, and hopefully move on, but she is clearly aware that whenever Lucas Blake is concerned, things are not as easy as that in her mind.

She definitely has to talk to Lucas. *Really* talk to him.

He deserves that she shares her apprehensions with him.

She exchanges her bowl for her glass of Riesling to take a sip.

Then there's Jun.

Working with her wouldn't be the craziest thing in the world. She always refused to consult for her friend's company before, but thinking about it there are way worse possibilities.

Jun lives by her ideals, and only takes on cases she believes in.

The crisis manager would've never accepted to help the kind of people Raven's old firm used to get as clients. Which is a definite advantage.

But Jun is also in the big leagues, dealing with lots of influence and money. Raven has to admit that she doesn't know if she has it in her to continue within those circles.

Since she resigned, she's been analyzing her options and there's a sure appeal in making a more drastic change to her professional ventures.

One where she would be farther away from greedy individuals, and power games.

One where—

Her phone chimes beside her. She picks up the device, instantly validating the caller ID and accepting the video call.

The second she sees the familiar features of her Australian-American friend appearing on screen, she smiles comfortingly. "Haddy, I'm glad you called. How are you guys?"

She knows it's nearly a rhetorical question. Heather and Zoe are going through tough times at the moment.

If the circles and puffiness of Haddy's almond shaped hazel eyes are any indication, the fellow lawyer has spent significant time crying, and not a lot sleeping.

She replaces a strand of her sandy-brown hair which had fallen from her ponytail. "Raven, it's good to hear your voice."

"It's good to see you." She gazes at the gray concrete building with a glass entrance behind Heather. "Are you at the hospital?"

"Yeah." She fixes the collar of her blue floral blouse. "Zoe is going through some extra scans, and I couldn't stay inside anymore. I went out to get some air, and thought I'd call you." She smiles warmly. "Things have been a whirlwind the last few days. I wanted to talk to you before, but I didn't find the—"

Raven cuts her off. "Stop that. It's okay. Don't worry." She offers her friend a comforting smile. "I totally get how consuming those situations are." She sits back into the cushions. "Remember how it was with my mom? Until we knew she had gotten a diagnosis it was hell, and then it became another kind of hell to see her go through treatments and all."

Her friend smiles back at her. "And she did it. She beat cancer."

"She did. She's still more fragile now than she was before, and it's threatening to come back at any time—fuck cancer for never fully going away—but at least she's in remission." Raven takes a sip of her wine. "And you were there for me every step of the way." She raises her glass in a toast to her friend. "I still can't thank you enough."

"It was only natural." Heather reaches the corner of the building. "We're besties, remember? Even if you're on the other side of the country, that never changed."

"It will never change." Raven lifts a corner of her mouth upward. "I wish I could be closer to help."

"So far there's not a lot you could've done even if you were in San Diego." Her friend sits down on a bench. "We should get an official diagnosis by next week. Her doctors want to send some of her results to other oncologists and neuropathologists to confirm their suspicions."

"Did they share any of those hypotheses with you?"

"They pronounced some long-ass words that my own brain hasn't fully integrated yet. Gimme a sec." Haddy takes out a bright pink Post-It from her jeans pocket, flattens it and starts reading. "Oligodendroglioma, meningiomas and schwannomas." She shifts her attention back to Raven. "At this stage, they basically have to assess which type it is and assign the grade to know what our treatment options are."

"I'm hoping it's a tumor that can easily be removed."

"I hope so, too." Heather throws her head back, letting out a breath she looks to have no idea she was holding. "You know, what hurts the most?" She goes back to stare at Raven. "It's how Zoe closed herself off since she learned about the tumor." She knits her eyebrows. "She barely talks to me or anyone. She acts like she's on autopilot, and no matter what I do I can't get to her like I usually do."

"Remember my mom's reaction when she got the diagnosis? She had no idea how to treat the subject. That kind of news is a lot to process, I'm sure it's stressful for Zoe." Raven keeps her voice encouraging. "I'm beyond certain that she'll come to you when she feels ready. You two are unbreakable."

"I hope so. It's really hard having to deal with all the uncertainty nearly by myself, but I have to be strong for her." Heather breathes in as if to compose herself. "She is the one going through it. She deserves that I be patient, and go at her own pace."

"You're also going through it, Haddy. Albeit differently, but it's still emotionally difficult. Both your feelings are valid here." She gazes intently at her friend. "The best you can do at the moment is to show her that you're there by her side, ready to tackle whatever life throws at you. You two have always built on each other's strengths. It's beautiful to see."

"Thank you for saying that, Raven."

She never averts her stare. "You know I mean it."

"That's the best part." Heather smiles coyly. "What about you? What has been going on?" She slumps a little in her seat. "Tell me everything, it will help divert me from all the anxiety I'm going through for a minute."

Raven doesn't feel like potentially burdening her friend with everything that happened in her life lately. "Oh, not much."

"Raven, c'mon." Heather pouts. "I really need to hear all of it. How's work?"

"If you insist." She decides to humor her. "I resigned last week."

"Wow." Her friend gapes at her. "What happened?"

Raven presses her lips into a thin line. "Let's just say that I couldn't keep defending the type of clients I was working for."

"You've finally had enough after years of doing it?"

"It did take me a while, but I came back to my senses I guess." She smiles shyly. "You remember how I used to question certain things, but always ended up sweeping it under the rug because I somehow had to keep on moving forward?" Haddy hums. She continues. "Well, there's no more rug and no more sweeping now."

Her friend seems to analyze her facial features. "Clean slate."

"Nearly." Raven takes another sip. "I'm in the process of assessing what I want to do next."

"All doors will open up to you, Raven." Heather grins, "You're brilliant."

"Thanks." She puts her glass of wine down on the table. "In the meantime I'm consulting on Jun's latest case."

"How fun!"

"Yeah." Raven hesitates for a second before choosing to tell her friend about Lucas. "You'll love that part: the client is Lucas. As in the Lucas I met in Greece a decade ago."

"No way!" The manager beams at her. "How is he? Did he age well?"

"He's not a bottle of wine, and he's no older than me." She bites into her bottom lip. "But yeah, he aged really well."

"That's insane." Haddy shakes her head in disbelief. "What are the chances?"

"I know." Raven hums. "And the most amazing thing is that he feels even better than he did back in Mykonos." She smiles dreamily. "Everything flows naturally with him. It's like we parted ways yesterday."

Heather raises a questioning eyebrow. "When you say that he feels even better, does it mean that you—"

She cuts her off. "We didn't hook up." She pulls her bottom lip between her teeth once again before adding, "Yet." She exhales soundly. "It's complicated." She brushes her fingers through her hair. "We only made out."

"That's still something." Her friend is now wiggling her eyebrow suggestively. "I recall you said he was amongst the best kissers ever." She gets closer to the screen as if she's about to share a secret. "Does he still live up to the hype?"

"Totally." Raven nods. "I would venture to give him the very top spot."

"Raven!" Heather gasps." Get him into bed asap!"

"I really want to, but as I said it's a tad—"

It's her friend's turn to interject to finish that sentence. "Complicated." She laughs lightly. "Yeah, I heard." She stares at Raven seriously. "You do you, but if this guy feels as amazing as you say, and he wants you as much as you want him, don't deny yourself that." She smiles wistfully. "Life is short. Look at my wife and I. We—" She trails off, checking the time on top of her screen. "Actually, I should probably go check on Zoe. She should be done by now."

"Take good care, Haddy." Raven smiles reassuringly at her. "We'll talk again soon, yeah?"

"Sure thing. Bye, Raven."

As they both hang up, Raven slumps into her sofa a little more.

She really wishes she could be there for her friends. They are going through a real rough patch, and she's multiple thousands of miles away. A little voice in her head is telling her that her rightful place is in San Diego with them.

Plus, she misses California.

She longs for walks on the beach and surfing sessions. Emptying her mind while defying the waves.

Bathing in the California sun and driving along the coast.

She feels like this zen setting could do wonders for her current introspection. She could become one with her surroundings, let the chill atmosphere and peaceful setting help clear her thought process.

She grabs her Riesling from the table. Going to San Diego could—

Her phone rings beside her from where she dropped it. She smiles absentmindedly at the caller ID.

Lucas.

She drapes an arm on the back of the sofa to angle the device in front of her as she presses on the green button. "Hey, you." She smiles something soft at him. "Had a long day?"

Her screen instantly fills up with the image of a very tired looking Lucas wearing a gray shirt with a loose blue tie that accentuates the specks of yellow in his green irises to perfection.

Oh, how she would love to remove that tie and unbutton that shirt right about now. To let her fingertips trail down his bare chest while kissing him.

She breathes in. She has to get a grip.

He seems to be alone in an elevator she doesn't recognize. Maybe he's going to see someone, or—

He combs his fingers into his hair. "It's been *a* day. I'm glad it's over." He suddenly focuses solely on her, smiling warmly. "You're a sight for sore eyes, Raven."

She wishes it was her that was combing through his black locks. She would make sure he can feel the tension from his day recede under her touch.

She drinks some more wine. "Thank you. You look exhausted, but always irresistible."

"I'm glad to see you relaxing." He points his index finger at the screen. "Please keep some for me?"

She follows his gesture approximately to end up swirling the alcohol in her glass in front of the camera. "You want wine?" He confirms before she carries on. "Does that mean you'd like to come over?" She locks eyes with him. "I'd love for you to join me."

He steps out of the lift. "I'm nearly home, but if you give me an hour I can hop in the shower and then drive to your place."

"Why wait a whole hour?" She smirks. "You can take a shower here."

He barely audibly groans. "Don't tempt me."

She shrugs. "It's not tempting if I intend to follow through on it."

He stops in front of a door, never averting his stare. "So this offer includes you with me in said shower?"

She rests her head on the arm holding her phone. "It might."

He opens the door and stands in the doorway just looking at her for a moment. "You have no fucking idea how much I—" He trails off, abruptly shifting his attention to the floor. He bends down to pick up something. "Fuck."

She frowns, sounding concerned. "What is it, Lucas?"

He holds an envelope in front of the camera. "Looks familiar?" She focuses on the paper to identify many resemblances with another letter she saw not long ago. She nods as he continues talking. "Seems like that asshole knows where I live." He clenches his jaw as he deftly rip it open, peeking inside. "This is clearly another threat."

EIGHT

None Of It Matters, but It Does

I t's crazy just how many things can happen in twenty-four hours.

At least that's what Raven tells herself as she soaks in her bubble bath.

Under the dim lighting of her modern slate blue and white bathroom, she made herself a cozy setup. She poured herself a glass of Zinfandel that she put on the bamboo bathtub caddy tray along with a book, reading glasses, and her phone.

As the soothing fragrance of lavender and mint fills the room, and the entrancing music tempos she chose to listen to resound in her ears, she reaches out for her glass of wine to take a sip.

She usually opens one bottle of wine per week and indulges in finishing it in the course of those seven days. It's definitely her preferred way to unwind at the end of a long work day.

Even if out of a job for now, she has every intention to keep that tradition alive.

Sitting back in the clawfoot bath, she drapes her arm along the lip of it, and softly leans her head against the rim behind her.

She inhales deeply, closing her eyes.

The lyrics of the latest tune about how people change or not hit oddly close to home at the moment.

This whole setting is because she wanted to relax, but if she has to be completely honest, she is also a little pissed at the whole situation unraveling under her eyes.

Although there's not much she can do about any of it now.

When she answered Lucas' video call yesterday, she thought her evening would turn out to be filled with fun conversations, maybe some more serious ones, and she was determined to fall into bed with him.

She had made peace with the fact that she only wanted one thing: him.

No matter her concerns, and probable complications this would lead to, she couldn't take it anymore.

Screw the consequences, and all it would entail. She would deal with it as it would've unfolded.

She would not back down this time.

Or so she thought.

She was looking forward to having him join her at her apartment. She was fully ready to undress him slowly between kisses before stepping into the roman cubicle of her shower with him.

She could already picture her hands painting every inch of his body under the water stream, and his mouth everywhere on her.

She wanted to make him feel good just like she's certain he would've accomplished for her, too.

The night was promising.

However, the instant Lucas picked up the threat letter that had made it under his door, that whole plan flew out the window.

That's also when things started taking a turn for the worse.

She frowns at the reminder while the song continues to echo in the space.

Lucas gave her his address, she called Jun, and they both joined him in his penthouse to discuss the next steps.

Raven didn't bother changing. She just tied her hair up in a messy ponytail, and made quick touch ups to her makeup before putting on her boots. She then grabbed her phone, wallet and keys, and left her apartment.

Upon setting foot in Lucas' home in Chelsea, she couldn't help but take in the grandness of the space.

The open-floor plan was inviting the outdoors in similarly than her San Diego house does.

Except that this is NYC.

Which means that the outdoors are not palm trees, sandy beaches, and cliffs emphasized by the coastal breeze. It's neighboring buildings, concrete, and the Hudson river that stretches at the end of his balcony spanning the whole back of the apartment.

She thought it was still stunning.

His penthouse gives a sensation of freedom in the heart of the busy city. She could easily see why Lucas bought the property.

The neutral tones of the walls and furniture were accentuated by well chosen accessories.

From where she stood in the lobby, the chocolate brown ottoman delimiting the side of the living room, matching leather couch and wood coffee table in front of the in-wall fireplace created an inviting area.

Jun was already there, wearing her royal blue suit with a white blouse and sitting in one of the two Barcelona chairs placed in front of the oversized windows. She looked deep in thought, staring at a paper in a plastic bag on the side table.

To Raven's right, the kitchen with its gray quartz island and counters pairing matching open shelves holding his plates, glasses and spices was also offering a welcoming vibe to just enter it and start cooking.

The modern white bar stools—that she owns in charcoal coloring at her home on the West Coast—at the end of the island acted as a wonderful transition into the adjoining dining room where the modern trend continued.

The round nordic-style dining table with mid-century inspired chairs probably saw its fair share of enjoyable dinners between friends, family or date nights.

Although Lucas admitted to entertaining fleeting relationships more often than stable ones. In that context, maybe his penthouse has not seen a lot of gentle intimacy and sweet moments.

Her eyes kept wandering around while she removed her boots to leave them under the black console next to a pair of ankle boots and some designer sneakers.

Two doors on either side of the fireplace and wall-mounted TV were giving peeks into Lucas' bedroom on the left and office on the right. From where she stood, the dimensions suggested that the bathroom is probably an en-suite.

All in all, she felt as if she could've been the one living in this penthouse.

It was a flawless blend of her California digs and her Brooklyn condo, with touches that made it uniquely Lucas' here and there.

The few frames on the walls that she identified as being from other pop art legends—probably originals based on their previous exchange about the piece in his office—were certainly great examples of it.

She briefly hesitated hugging Lucas as he closed the door to go stand in front of her with the sleeves of his gray shirt rolled up, his loose blue tie and his slightly untamed hair, but he put his hands in his black suit pants pockets.

He looked fragile and mighty all at the same time, but his posture was not inviting any physical contact so she refrained from it.

Plus, Jun was waiting for them a few dozen feet away.

When he smiled at her, it was laced with preoccupation. *Welcome to my humble abode.*

She raised an eyebrow. *You call that humble?*

He half-smiled playfully, starting to walk toward the living room. *It's a figure of speech, but you gotta admit that there's way more luxurious penthouses in Manhattan.*

Agreed. She slowly padded inside, following him. *It's still very sumptuous. I like what you've done with the place.*

It feels like home to me after being here for eight years. He gestured at her to take a seat. *Please make yourself comfortable.*

That's great. I'm glad it does that for you. She sat down beside Jun on the other Barcelona chair. *I love my place in Brooklyn, but I adore my house in La Jolla. I bought it during my fourth year working for my old firm. I wanted a place where I would feel good when I went back to San Diego, and not rely on always staying with friends, you know?*

I totally get it. He strided into the kitchen. *I acquired this one when I signed my hundredth client. I felt like things were going great at work by then, and I always wanted a fine piece of real estate in the heart of Chelsea, so here I am.* He opened the fridge. *I'm sure your property in California is amazing.* He turned around briefly. *Would you both like something? I know I could use a drink right about now.*

Jun answered idly as she typed on her phone. *I'll be fine, thanks.*

I'm also okay, thank you. Raven watched Lucas grab a beer before closing the refrigerator. *I love my house on the West Coast. It's not outrageously big or anything, but there's a rooftop pool, a cozy balcony, and it's basically situated directly on the beach. I get a direct view of the Pacific through the oversized windows that form the majority of the back wall. Waking up with the ocean breeze sneaking in is the best feeling in the world.*

Lucas smiled warmly at her. *Sounds like an absolute dream.*

She's also lying. The crisis manager put down her phone to join the conversation. *I'll agree that her house is not outrageously huge, but it's nothing short of spectacular. The whole place just has this chill vibe that fits her so well when she's over there.* She looks at Raven, curving a corner of her mouth upward. *I swear, she's a different person when in California.*

I beg to disagree. The lawyer frowned. *I'm the same person. Other sides of me just come forward more easily when I'm on the West Coast.*

I know, I was teasing you. Jun offered her a comforting smile. *It's just always fun to see you be more carefree, Raven, and it turns out that it tends to happen a lot on the other side of the country.*

What can I say? Raven shrugged. *My brain dissociated my professional life from the rest for a long time. New York is for business.*

Lucas took place at the end of the couch closest to them, beer in hand. He seemingly decided to let himself known by staring at Raven. *You could mix business and pleasure here, too.*

Oh, I've done that plenty. She remained unflinching. *You know exactly what I mean. Brooklyn just feels less like my true home than San Diego.*

I get it. He placed the bottle on his knee. *I made NYC my home, but that's because I wasn't feeling like I fully belonged anywhere else. Looks like I found the whole package in Manhattan.*

There was a pang of deception in Raven's tone. That's yet another thing that separates her from Lucas. *That's great for you.* She sat back in her seat, breathing in. *That you found everything you were looking for here.*

He hummed absentmindedly as he brought the beer to his lips.

Jun reoriented the conversation. *Not to crash the soul digging party, but we're all here for a specific reason, yeah?*

Right. Raven directed her full attention toward her friend. *You're right. So what does this letter say this time?*

Her friend gestured at the item laying between them on the table. *You can take a look.*

Before Raven eyes, a letter in all points similar to the first one was laying on the surface.

Her eyes traveled on the magazine cutouts forming a grim message.

Finding loopholes. Closing risky deals. Protecting clients' weirdest assets. Giving in to some over-the-top demands. Making insane profits.

Surely you can facilitate things for us, Blake?

Remember: the higher you climb, the harder you can fall. If you don't give in to our demands, we will make sure that the ones closest to you suffer & we will bring the spotlight on you.

Instructions will soon follow. We look forward to our collaboration.

She blinked repeatedly. This was bad.

She shifted her stare to Lucas who was now sitting with his elbows resting on his knees, his hands intertwined in front of him.

He looked pensive and irritated. She could understand why. There was a ton of important information in that letter, but the worst part was—

She kept her voice soft when she chose to speak the undeniable truth aloud. *They definitely know where you live so they're surely aware of who you're closest to.*

That's the thing that frustrates me the most. The managing director clenched his jaw. *I don't want any harm to come to my friends and family because of the career I chose. They don't deserve to be dragged into whatever sick game those people are playing.*

Raven searched his eyes. *My take is that they want to destabilize you hoping you'll make a mistake.* Lucas lifted his head a little more to hold her gaze. She continued. She wanted to lay it all out on the table. *I think they want you to give in to their demands, but we don't even know what those are. They could potentially be something illegal, and if you commit to it they'll have more leverage against you afterward.* She scanned his expression. He was closely listening to every word she was saying. It spurred her on. *Plus, if your clients learn about that scheme, they might embark on this journey too, and ask more out of you than what you already give them. Then it would be a never ending game of perpetrating more felonies waiting for you.* She pointed at the letter beside her, sounding solemn. *Those people know it. We have to stop them.*

I agree. There was a tick in his jaw. *But I also don't want to alert authorities or make this public.* His tone was annoyed and angered. Unpleasant even. *My reasoning hasn't changed since the beginning. I need this to be dealt with quietly. I want to keep thriving.* He was speaking through gritted teeth at that point. *I don't want to lose everything I worked so hard to build.*

Raven decided to go down the rabbit hole with him. *So your reasoning is that if you go public, show that something is bothering you right now and that you are taking care of it, a bunch of clients won't like that? Your employer won't like it either?* Lucas hummed, his eyes boring into hers. She carried on. *And that is because it will put the spotlight on you and your bank and so also on them?* He hummed again. She crossed her legs as she nodded in approbation. *Following this trend, in this scenario, your debatable, but not illegal, practices would be questioned and the media would dig into your bank's activities.* She kept her tone as calm and casual as possible. *That's definitely something big names and powerful clients don't like. You do risk losing their business.*

Exactly. That was a great rundown. The managing director sat back on the cushions. *And I don't want any of that to happen.* His tone was nothing but determined. *I think I can keep my affairs prosperous, my loved ones safe, and find the culprit of those threats before anything comes crashing down.*

Fair enough. Raven crossed her arms over her chest. *But what if you're not able to achieve all of that? Sometimes life doesn't go the way we want it to. Sometimes sacrifices have to be made.*

They entered a short-lived staring contest where Lucas seemed to be searching for some kind of profound answer to her inquiry.

She was set on waiting for as long as it would take for him to speak his mind.

She wanted to get to the bottom of his thought process.

But Jun cut through the silence before a single word was able to leave his mouth. *Wow.* She smiled coyly. *If it's how you two are in sync and challenge each other all at once, it's electrifying to see.*

The comment snapped both Lucas and Raven out of their daze.

The managing director cleared his throat, focusing on the crisis manager and redirecting the exchange. *You think whoever is sending those threats will follow through on them?*

We'll assume that they are prepared to. Jun tapped rhythmically on her cellphone case. *There's certainly been an escalation between the two letters. We can't take any of it lightly.*

Tomorrow, it's going to be a week since my office was ransacked. Lucas took hold of his beer again. *Do you think they're on some kind of schedule?*

The crisis manager furrowed her eyebrows reflectively, grabbing her phone. *Maybe.*

Raven suddenly had an enlightenment. *Urgency.* She alternated looking at Jun and Lucas. *They acted with a sense of urgency to come deliver this straight to your door. It makes a statement.* She directed all her attention to Lucas. *Which brings me to the fact that Gabriel Smith was pissed yesterday when you told him you wouldn't sign his documents directly. Maybe it could be his twisted way to pressurize you?*

But if it is him, he's not part of my roster yet. Lucas frowned. *I could just as easily not sign with him, and kiss goodbye to the whole problem.*

He knows how you deal with stuff for your other clients. He made that plain clear. Raven felt like her brain was working in overdrive trying to piece together everything. *He doesn't have as big of a leverage as he would if he was already your client, but the whole 'going public' and drawing attention could still happen one way or another if he is behind all this blackmail and decides to expose you. Banks don't like that kind of attention on them, you said it yourself. The mere mention of looking into one of their Managing Directors would be enough to want to dissociate themselves from you to keep their head high.*

You're right. He took another sip. *This is so fucked up.*

Jun picked up the subject. *I still haven't looked into Mr. Smith's business because you only asked me about it today so it's fairly new, but I'll do that asap. The letter clearly wasn't there when you left this morning, so we'll also check the cam footage from your building for today.* She hastily typed on her device. *There's some, right?*

Only at the entrance downstairs. My elevator is private as is the hallway leading to my door and small storage room. I like that there's this space and that the lift doesn't arrive directly in the middle of my living room even if all this side of the floor is mine. Lucas started toying with the rim of his bottle. *I assume you're hacking into those so I won't ask any more questions on it. They also said that they want me to hide something for them. That could help you?*

Yes. It's a good clue that we'll thread with the rest. Jun continued to compose her email while talking. *There was no trace of DNA on the other letter, but we'll also check this one.* She looked over her screen for a quick moment. *Thanks once again for having extracted the letter with some clips to not tempter with any potential evidence, Lucas.*

No problem. It was a no-brainer. Through his visible rumination, he still kept his speech joyous. *You really have a multidisciplinary team, I'm impressed.*

The crisis manager beamed. *Let's say I have plenty of contacts, and working quietly without raising suspicions is our specialty.*

Lucas smiled knowingly. *The CIA should be afraid of you guys.*

Jun raised a playful eyebrow. *Who says I don't have an in with them already?*

He acted fakely surprised. *You're not messing around.*

Jun is never messing around. Raven nodded, turning toward her friend. *Maybe check for cat or dog hairs on that paper, Ju? It gets everywhere, and would at least tell us if the person writing those has a pet and if so even the breed. You could then check if any of our suspects are matches. I think it's worth a shot.* She had another idea she wanted to get out there. *Also identifying from which publications those cutouts come from could give us a slight hint.*

Brilliant. The manager glanced at Raven with pride. *That's precisely why I want you to be a permanent member of my team, girl. You have this outside the box thinking I love so much.*

Lucas didn't hesitate one second to add, *Raven would be an amazing addition to anyone's team.*

Thank you both for the vote of confidence. The lawyer half-smiled. *In this specific case, I just got reminded that one of our clients once got caught because of cat hair DNA on the crime scene.*

Her friend snorted lightly. *That's hilarious and sad at the same time. She was totally guilty so honestly, I'm glad she got caught.* Raven uncrossed her arms to place her hands in her lap. *But going back to the situation at hand here, I think we have our work cut out for us once again.*

Yes. Jun stared intently at the managing director. *Lucas, you should go to work tomorrow like you usually do so as to not raise any suspicions. Also it will help appearances just in case someone from your office is keeping score.* She sounded resolute. *You want to keep your job, continue thriving and keep your clients so I think this is the right course of action. We'll single out the individual who's sending you those threats.*

That's the plan. The managing director's nostrils flared in slight annoyance. *I can't imagine having everything I worked so hard to build being demolished because of that.*

Jun offered him her best supportive smile. *We'll make sure that doesn't happen.* She got one of her custom devices out from her purse. *Also, please give me your SIM card.*

Lucas complied. *What are you doing?*

She slid the card into the portable hard drive-looking apparatus. *I'm cloning it onto this blank one so it's impossible for people to tap your phone or track you. Just in case.*

Clever. He hummed. *Your team came up with this?*

She looked proud. *Yeah.* She gave him the new SIM, letting the gadget destroy the old one. *I have some great engineers working at my company.*

Lucas put the card into his phone, and Jun and her left not long after, leaving him alone with his thoughts.

As Raven swirls the alcohol in her glass while trying to relax, she recalls how Lucas seemed devastated during that whole discussion.

He was feeling distant and clearly disconnected from any emotional connection. There was no getting through to him, which is why she kept the exchange mostly factual.

For the first time since he walked back into her life, she hated this sensation of helplessness toward him.

It was as if he had built giant walls around himself that no one would be able to knock down.

Following the tumultuous evening, she hadn't heard back from him all day today. No even a text message.

When she decided to send him one to ask if he'd like to grab a bite after work—thinking it might've helped him cope with some of his feelings—he didn't reply until twenty minutes ago.

If she's being honest, reading that message is probably what prompted her to take a bubble bath.

It stung so bad that she memorized every word.

L: I'm going out with Mark and Kyan. Thursdays are sacred, you remember? I need it right now. Hope you have a good night.

She knows perfectly well what Thursdays entails. He'll drink, chat with his buddies, and end up hooking up with someone to forget his troubles and have a good time.

They say that in the face of adversity it's possible to see what people are truly made of.

Apparently Lucas made his choice.

The fact that she feels annoyed right now is arguably unjustified. She keeps repeating to herself that there's nothing going on between Lucas and herself.

They only kissed for fuck's sake.

He can fuck anyone he wants. She doesn't mind. It was only one moment they shared, and it clearly didn't mean anything.

He's not her lover. Even less so her boyfriend.

She shakes her head. How did her mind go there?

It's not like she is falling for Lucas Blake.

No. She never falls.

Even before Nathan, back in Mykonos, the strange feeling that was starting to take hold toward Lucas in her psyche wasn't that. She's certain of it.

She can keep a cool head.

She's known plenty of people in her life. Each one had his own way to deal with stressful situations.

The worst coping mechanism to her is when they decide to act as if nothing is wrong, and don't communicate.

She dealt with that bullshit all her life. Her own parents are masters at it.

Too many people she met didn't care about discussing problems so everyone could move forward. They highly prefer to stifle all feelings.

Her first boyfriend in high school had a knack for doing that. He ended up spiraling so bad that he broke up with her without any explanation. She learned months later that it was because he had caught his dad cheating, and didn't know how to deal with the information. It led him to internalize all his emotions, not open up to anyone, and endlessly reminisce about the events.

By the time he had been able to speak about it, he had pushed away more than half of his closest friends who had tried to help him.

She takes a sip of her rosé.

What Lucas is doing right now is vastly different. He is not cutting ties with anyone. Not yet anyway. He's simply using a well proved coping mechanism he feels good with.

He even admitted doing the same thing after his office was searched last week. He ended up having sex with someone he met at the club because he needed to 'get his mind off of things', he said.

Objectively, she shouldn't feel that strongly about that kind of decision from him.

She still can't stop herself from wishing she would be the one he would've come to to deal with this newest threat as well as all the feelings it brought to the surface.

She wrongly thought there was something forming between them. Be it a strong friendship or more.

She lets out a breath, putting her glass back on the tray.

Who is she kidding? It's impossible to sexually crave someone that much and call them a friend. Inconceivable to get off while fantasizing about what said 'friend' would do.

No matter what, a part of her definitely wished he would have reached out to her.

Now she can't get the images of him and some unidentified woman having sex out of her head.

She inhales deeply, sinking into the water a little more.

She knows exactly how his hands feel when they glide on bare flesh, and how he paints and caresses every curve with devotion and wonder.

She knows just how spectacular his tongue feels when kissing, and how his mouth is pure witchcraft between her thighs.

She knows perfectly well how his cock hits at just the right spot with each thrust.

He always holds off on his own release until his partner climaxes. At least that's what he was doing with her. Every single time.

He was fucking phenomenal.

And when he would finally let go, the way he spasmed inside her as he was groaning was—

She closes her eyes.

There's no use lingering on any of it. He'll do it all tonight with a stranger.

No matter how many times they flirted lately or how often he told her that she was unparalleled in bed, he'll still end up fucking someone else.

No matter if he admitted having trouble getting her out of his damn head or how he described what he'd want to do to her, he'll do it all to his latest one-night conquest.

She snaps her eyes back open.

She needs her own distraction, and she has a very precise idea on what it will be.

Two can play that game.

She props herself up, and grabs her phone to text Will.

As Felipe puts his phone back in his black suit pants pockets while turning on East 94th Street, he loosens his navy blue tie and unbuttons the first two buttons of his white shirt.

He had an excruciating day, and he clearly needed some fresh air. The stress of his work as well as the money he knows he isn't making is stressing him out to the highest degree.

The latest fight he had with his wife is also clearly not helping.

He hastily canceled his plans with his friends as soon as Emma went into their bedroom to get some peace and quiet. He thought that he was better off trying to show her that he wanted to try to make things work out for the best between them by staying in her vicinity instead of going out with his buddies.

While she was recentering herself by spending some time alone, he watched at least three episodes of his latest TV addiction before his mind grew restless. Their whole heated conversation was making rounds in his head.

He needed to do something.

Anything.

He had to find a partial solution to their problems.

So he went out for a walk to call his bookie Charles.

He inhales deeply.

Lately with Em they've been bickering about a bunch of different things, ranging from the best moment to try and have kids all the way to the time he apparently won't take to raise them.

Emma is pissed that he doesn't want to go with her to visit her family this weekend. She keeps saying that it just shows that he's not dedicated to them, and that he is turning into his father.

His father who basically spent his entire married life working eighteen hours per day, and valuing money more than his family.

Felipe knows he's been progressively more distant on multiple accounts, but he is not his dad. It's preposterous of Emma to make that comparison.

He would truly love nothing more than to have the life he dreams of and give his wife everything she wishes for in the process. They've been together for so long at this point that he can't imagine his life without her in it. He can't even remember a time when she wasn't an integral part of his every day routine.

He wants to prosper while making her happy. That's always been his ultimate goal.

Getting her one of her dream cars was certainly a start, but he is determined to not stop there.

If the call he just placed to Charles pans out, he should be able to bring her on nice vacations anywhere she wants to for at least a month. That should make her happy. Showing her that he can pair being physically there for her, and getting them the life they've been pursuing.

That is if he's able to take that much time off of work.

He frowns as he lets the lyrics wash over him.

He's definitely not in the same leagues as his friend Lucas. The clients Felipe deals with are rich, but not as rich as the ones his friend signs on a monthly basis. He has to work his ass off for what the vast majority of people would consider a very nice salary, but it's nothing that can compare to what Lucas earns.

He's not complaining.

Not really.

He loves his job. It's the societal pressure, and his internal struggle to not be enough, that is slowly eating at him. He's always been competitive, but through the last few years his desire to fight tooth and nail to try to make it into the highest spheres of his field has eroded.

The problem is that his ambitions did not.

He hates this toned down version of himself he became. Seemingly resigned to not pursue his ultimate goals.

So he finds himself at a crossroads between settling for a comfortable life, and finding a way to quench his thirst to get all that he ever wanted with Emma since they met.

He always desired to make a name for himself, and his wife always craved living the big life. The two are pairing very well together in themselves. The only problem is that none of them panned out so far.

Old ideals and dreams are sometimes made to be rethink, he muses as he breathes in the chilly evening air.

But he has no desire to put all his aspirations on the backburner just yet.

Back in college, he had his whole future ahead of him. Between pulling all-nighters to study or write assignments, the weekly poker games, and spending time with his friends, he legitimately thought he was going to reach the highest spheres of finance. That his name would mean something. That it would be talked about with respect and admiration.

He was going to be a *Liberty Cove Business School* Alumni, after all.

His dad being a successful hedge fund manager who always valued hard work meant that he was overjoyed his son was graduating from the prestigious university. The look of esteem his father harbored when he showed up at the ceremony is still ingrained in Felipe's brain to this day.

And maybe it's because of the absence of his father at every important event in his life growing up, but from this moment on the analyst vowed to himself to become someone his dad would be honored to call his son.

Thinking about it, he was in constant search of his dad's attention when he was younger, but the old man never gave him any. It then reached a point where Felipe just abandoned any hope of it ever happening.

Having his father sit in the audience beside his mom that day changed everything. It was as if the little boy who was driving his bike around the driveway late at night to show his father his perfect scorecard from school to make a statement of his existence was finally being seen.

It made him feel like, for once, he was on the right path.

By the time his last year rolled around, he even had a job lined up at one of the biggest investment banks in NYC.

It was a point of pride for him.

His journey ahead in the world was promising.

The future looked bright.

After some time working for that bank, he climbed the ladder, and gained the respect of his bosses.

Before long Lucas got promoted to Managing Director of Mergers and Acquisitions, and told Felipe that new opportunities were opening up at his company. The analyst toyed with the idea of throwing his hat into the ring, but he legitimately thought he was in a good position to achieve his planned objectives with his current job so decided against it.

Plus, at the time Emma was being burned out from working in the fashion industry, and decided to pursue her dreams of founding her own interior design company.

Pursuing a higher position at another investment bank back then was not the best call. Success was not absolutely guaranteed for Lucas either. Being managing director comes with bigger stakes, and higher risks. That was making Felipe feel better about his decision.

Although the moment Lucas started getting all the biggest clients because of his natural charm and wit, Felipe recalls having slightly regretted his choice.

However, he reminded himself of an undying truth. Lucas and himself are both very different individuals with strong personalities. It was working well during university to study, but professionally working together would've been a nightmare. They would've argued more often than not about their different approaches. They were being very honest when they told Raven as such at the fundraiser.

It still means that the years passed by, and while Lucas became more and more prosperous, Felipe stayed stuck in the same position he was.

He is still happy for his friend. Things are not atrocious for him and Emma by any means.

Lucas is right, Emma *is* insanely talented. Felipe would've loved for her endeavors to be fruitful earlier, but she's slowly doing better and better. He's immensely proud of her.

But he is convinced that getting more money in general would solve most of their problems.

He is certain that if he manages to get Emma the life she dreams of, he'll then be able to be less occupied, and show her that he can be the whole package: a wealthy as well as present husband and father.

The way to get there just requires a little more sacrifice at the moment while he tries to consolidate his day job—which asks more and more out of him with his boss constantly wanting them to recruit more powerful clients—and his gambling hobby.

Although he thinks that the whole new plan he came up with to attain his goals is working pretty well so far.

It might encompass multiple layers—and be very risky on several accounts—he feels good about his chances to come out of it in a better financial position than he was when he started.

It would be a lie to say that said plan doesn't make him anxious, but the pay off is potentially going to be legendary.

Gambling-wise, he already won big. He feels like he's playing into his strengths by betting on specific events. He knows his way around sports teams. Using that knowledge to continue to quickly make his money fructify to great extents was a no-brainer for him.

He wants to see more of that look of pure joy on Emma's face. The one she got when she realized that he had bought her the car she had been dreaming of. Between her increasingly more frequent silences, and their unavoidable arguments, he hasn't seen her be a whole lot carefree. The fleeting moment where she was when she took possession of the car was blissful.

He wants more of that.

He'd also love to witness the look of pride on his father's features a little more often. Saying that their relationship went through a rollercoaster in the last decade would be an understatement. Felipe remembers how good he felt when his dad was calling him every week, and discussing as if he was his equal. He misses it.

He wants more of that, too.

The unexpected, but very welcome win from his bets last week, allowed him to give Emma some small respite from the whirlwind they've been going through. He wishes to do it again soon with this trip.

Then there's the whole other part of his strategy where he has to kick it up a few notches for it to—

The lines of the last verse of the song echo in his brain like an ironic callout.

He shakes his head.

In the spirit of wanting to get more money even faster right now he could probably up the stakes a little to make things more interesting.

He fishes his phone out to message Charles without delay.

As Lucas is walking toward *The Amber Remedy* on West 28th Street, he keeps his hands in his pockets.

He wonders why he agreed to go out with Kyan and Mark tonight.

Yes, Thursdays are sacred. But now it feels strange to think that he'll be expected to drink, have fun and hook up with someone like he usually does under such circumstances.

For a split second when he agreed to the outing as he was tucking his black shirt into his light indigo jeans, he thought that it would do him some good to bury his troubles partying. It has been his go-to coping mechanism for years at this point, after all.

He's not too sure about it anymore.

One thing is for sure: past the blackmail he's receiving lately, he loves the direction his life took the last few years. He comes from a very humble not even middle-class family where everything was tightly budgeted, and any extra money was very scarce. Having enough of it to now be part of the wealthiest people in the country is a definite sign of triumph.

He frowns as he crosses 8th Avenue.

Actually, is it really?

If he focuses enough, he can vaguely recall a time when he was questioning himself constantly. He was auto challenging himself to try to stay on a path that he would be comfortable with.

Making good money, but never losing sight of the big picture and of his values.

Maybe he ended up on the path he's currently on because at some point he turned a blind eye to some signs along the way? He wonders. This life he willingly chose is uncompromising, and it doesn't always feel completely right.

Maybe he found the biggest loophole of them all for himself by convincing his mind that dealing with rich clients in ambiguous ways was acceptable.

It seems to catch up with him right now.

Those conclusions are probably why he usually keeps those drawers closed shut in his brain. There's too much at stake. He's too engaged on the journey he chose to stop now and examine it in detail.

He has to put the lid back on this Pandora box, and keep it tightly sealed.

He breathes in.

He can't deny that there's a whirlwind in his gray matter.

He doesn't want his whole existence to come crashing down in front of his eyes. The threats he's receiving are resonating deeper than he cares to admit aloud.

Plus, the prospect of having his work destroyed, his loved ones hurt, and a psycho set to wreak havoc on the loose is unappealing.

He has no other choice than to trust that he'll be able to save it all. If not, what would be left for him anyway? He has to force himself to hope that everything will be okay. That he'll succeed in his attempt at protecting both his professional and personal lives.

But past the fear and rage at the whole situation, he can't shake off Raven's question from his mind.

What if you're not able to achieve all of that? Sometimes life doesn't go the way we want it to. Sometimes sacrifices have to be made, she said.

What would he truly be willing to sacrifice?

She definitely asks him the hard questions he doesn't dare ask himself lately.

He was very close to telling her that he would never forfeit anything one way or another, but then he hesitated as he got lost in her eyes.

He smiles inattentively as a bridge of the song resounds in his ears.

Ever since Raven waltzed back into his life, he's been submerged by a feeling of wholesomeness he hasn't experienced in years.

When he told her she was a puzzle he wants to solve, he wasn't kidding. He adores how they challenge and match each other at once at every step.

She constantly shows him that she supports him, but also wants him to live up to his own ideals.

Raven feels like she believes in his capacity to stand up taller than the rest.

Every relationship he entertained in the course of his life so far has been void of such ease and care. Maybe the fact that the longest one he entertained since his mid-twenties lasted no more than six months has something to do with it.

Each liaison was void of any true emotional involvement.

Looking back on it, it also felt very empty.

Sure, before all those flings there has been his girlfriend Stephanie back at Liberty Cove who was different, but they parted ways of a common accord and—

He clenches his jaw.

No need to resuscitate the past right now, especially when Stephanie is totally inconsequential as soon as he remembers Raven.

After college, when he met Raven, she reconnected him with the world in a phase where uncertainty was roaming free through his veins. Nowadays, it feels as if she is now slowly reconnecting him with a part of himself he had forgotten about.

It's scary and thrilling at once.

Maybe he should've agreed to go have dinner with her. Chatting could've been a good escape from his thoughts. She surely would've been able to calm him a little.

However, he made a decision a couple hours ago and he's going to stick to it. His friends are expecting him to join them so he will.

Having just passed 7th Street, he pockets his earphones as he approaches the club.

He can certainly have an enjoyable night and forget about his problems in a trial and tested way. There's no need for more soul searching. This is about fun.

So he strides toward the building to navigate his way up to the 35th floor.

The second he steps inside the rooftop venue, the warm decor filled with floral and leather couches, wooden tables and encircled by window walls envelops him of a welcoming sensation.

The place is packed, people are colliding around the copper-clad bar counter, under the vintage disco ball or crystal chandelier. He makes a beeline for the bar to order a scotch.

As he waits for his drink, a quick look around has him identify Kyan dressed in a hunter green silk suit with white shirt who is seated in one of the leather wraparound sofas near a window.

When the bartender puts his drink in front of him, he pays for it and automatically strides toward his analyst friend, smiling brightly as he sits next to him. "Hey, Yanou. Glad to see you. It's been a while."

Kyan beams at him. "Lucas! I'm sorry we didn't get to chat last week."

"No worries." He smiles knowingly, remembering how he saw his friend flirting animatedly before leaving the nightclub. "You looked busy."

The analyst laughs lightly. "One could say that I was." He looks in the distance dreamily. "It was a memorable night. She called one of her friends to join us and I think I lived up to expectations because she asked me if I was free this upcoming weekend."

Lucas takes a sip. He's no stranger to threesomes, but he only agreed to one a handful of times.

Now thinking about it, his mind automatically circles back to Raven. It never crossed his mind to want to invite someone else in bed with them. It was a short-lived thing they had, but it still absolutely hadn't presented itself as an option in his brain.

Even right now, as he's remembering how she felt kissing him in the dead of night in front of her apartment, he has to be truthful and confess that he would hate for anyone else to see her come apart while he's in the room. Unless she would be the one asking him to indulge in such an activity. Then he knows himself well enough to be aware that he would agree because above all he wants for her desires to be fulfilled.

He frowns slightly. This strange thought about wanting to potentially have a committed exclusive relationship is something he hasn't felt in a very long while.

It's perplexing.

It's as if—

Kyan's voice reaches his ears once again, bringing him back to the present. "So you can imagine I didn't get much sleep that night. Completely worth it." He gulps down some of his Old Fashioned. "What about you? Felipe told me about this situation you have to manage at your firm. I hope it's nothing too serious."

Lucas snorts. "Of course he told you."

"He shouldn't have?" His friend furrows his eyebrows. "You know him..."

"And you know I love Flip, but he's a bit much sometimes." The managing director swirls the amber liquid in his glass as he takes a look around. "He reacts so instantly to everything. He keeps trying to push to help me with this thing when I clearly told him that it was being taken care of."

Kyan raises an inquiring eyebrow. "I might've also learned that a certain 'Raven' was part of the team managing the situation?"

"It's true."

His friend smiles joyously at him. "Now, I wasn't around when you were apparently not able to shut up about her after you went to Greece, and I hope you've been able to spend some time together and catch up."

A dozen recent souvenirs flood Lucas' mind. He's transported back in his car going to Boston, and driving back from it with her sleeping form next to him in the passenger seat.

He can easily feel the ghost of her touch in his hair, and of her voice as she sings softly.

He can't get enough of her sweet laugh. Of how perfectly she word spar while conversing with him.

He also knows that he probably looks dumb when he smiles automatically every time he sees that she messaged him. He loves their text exchanges. It's a breath of fresh air in his otherwise very serious days.

How can he begin to explain that he feels a little more alive since she walked back into his life?

He chooses to go for a general truth, bringing the glass to his lips once more. He doesn't feel like sharing much tonight. He's oddly protective of whatever is going on between Raven and him. "It's been nothing short of amazing so far."

Yanou half-smiles. "You look under the spell already, Lucas."

"It's that visible?" His friend nods as he continues. "It's complicated. Let's just say that I'll see where it brings us."

"Well, I hope that whatever this situation is, it resolves itself quickly." Kyan hums comprehensively, taking the cue to move on from the topic. "I don't know if you've heard the latest insane rumors? Important assets that once belonged to a real estate magnate should apparently change hands soon. Huge transaction. The kind that can make or break a career spending on if you manage to close the deal successfully or not."

He suddenly remembers the latest threat letter. "Any idea what it involves exactly?"

"There's only fragmented information across the city on the matter." Yanou shrugs. "The assets are managed by a woman at present, and she has to move quickly to transfer them from what I've heard. No idea why she's in a hurry, but everyone is wondering if they'll be the ones to be lucky enough to close that deal."

Lucas hums absentmindedly. Could this be what the person behind the blackmail refers to?

Usually when word gets out like this about affairs, it's tangible intel that can be taken seriously. It occurred multiple times before, and Lucas was often a prime witness of the veracity of those rumors.

There's a clear sense of urgency in that endeavor Kyan mentioned. The stakes are undoubtedly high.

It would tie in nicely with the messages he's receiving through those letters. Maybe he is the 'chosen one' to carry on that gigantic transaction which he still hasn't heard of in any details.

If it is really Gabriel Smith perpetrating those menaces, what is he waiting for to come forward, and tell him exactly what he wants?

Smith can't keep looming in the shadows forever, and—

Lucas forces himself to concentrate on the ambient music for a beat. He has to get into a peaceful mindset. This busy club might not have been the best choice, after all.

A relaxing meal with Raven could've—

He breathes in to keep his composure. "I hope someone skilled enough is able to profit from that business if it really happens." He has to calm down. He decides to reorient the conversation. "Speaking of Felipe, he will hate that he missed out tonight. He loves this place."

"He's in the dog house, man." Kyan shakes his head. "Marriage is no joke."

Lucas can't stop the words before they fall out from his mouth. "I guess if you can find someone who matches you and navigates every hardship like a crescendo it could be worth it."

His friend stares at him with a playful expression. "When have you become so soft, cuddy?"

"I was just thinking out loud." The managing director dodges the question. He's not about to admit that his mind constantly brings Raven and all she elicits in him back to the forefront. "I know Flip and Emma are strong. They will overcome what they're going through at the moment."

"I hope so. They've been together for so long and went through so much already at this point, it would be a shame to see them not work it out." Kyan starts looking around. "But we're here for fun and drinks, so let's leave Flip alone. Those two ladies seem very interested in getting to know us better."

As his friend beams at two blonde women in red and black cocktail dresses and stilettos waving at them while standing at the bar, he feels like asking. "Mark is supposed to join us, no?"

"He said he would be delayed because he was having an impromptu dinner with Matteo. Maybe he'll even bring him along, who knows?" Kyan gestures at the two women to come sit with them. "I say we can start the festivities ourselves."

Lucas makes a face. "You don't feel weird thinking about potentially flirting and sleeping with one of those women when you'll also go see your last conquest this weekend?"

"Life is short, man." His friend scoots over to leave some more space between them. "It's made for having fun. It's nothing serious between me and any of those women anyway."

"I still tend to only sleep with one at a time." He rests his glass on his thigh. " If I know that I'll see her again, it wouldn't feel right to me to go and have sex with another unless we both agreed that we were done or okay with an open relationship."

"That's very considerate of you. I also try to make things clear from the start." Kyan grins as the blonde bombshells stand in front of them. "Hello, ladies." He tilts his head toward the managing director. "This is my friend Lucas, and I'm Kyan."

The woman in the red sparkling dress looks at Lucas while presenting herself. "I'm Megan." She extends her hand holding a martini toward the woman next to her. "And this is my friend Claire." She points at the empty cushion beside him. "Mind if we join you?"

Kyan jumps on the occasion. "Of course not."

As Megan sits between the two men and Claire beside Kyan, Lucas rests his hands in his lap.

He inattentively hears his friend start flirting unabashedly with the women in the black cocktail dress as some club music leaks through the sound system.

Megan bores her green eyes into his. "So what are you doing for a living, Lucas?"

He forces himself to smile. "I'm a Managing Director at 'B.A. New Empire Group'."

She perks up. "So you're working for one of those big investment banks downtown. I'm impressed."

"It's not always as glamorous as they put it out to be. I often have to work more than a hundred hours per week, and I'm always on call." He keeps his tone gentle and interested. "You?"

"I'm a chef." She looks proud. "I wish to open my own restaurant soon, but so far I've been working at FireCoals Grilling House."

"The fusion cuisine restaurant that got a special mention from multiple renowned cooking magazines?"

She hums. "That's the one."

"I like that place a lot." He flashes her a coy smile. "They totally deserve all the praise, it's fabulous."

"I agree." She suggestively flips her hair on one side. "I moved here from Tennessee not long ago, and I was thrilled to be hired."

"I bet you were." He takes a quick sip of his scotch. "Are you enjoying New York so far?"

"I am." She rests her elbow on the back of the couch, leaning her head into her hand. "I also love the nightlife. It's so fun and animated."

"There's certainly a lot of great nightclubs around Manhattan." He studies her features as he's talking. "This one is honestly one of my favorites."

She acts very interested. "You're a regular?"

"I wouldn't say I am." He half-smiles. "Some of my friends and I usually go out every Thursday, and we pick a different venue every time to mix it up a little."

"That sounds like a nice idea." She extends her arm along the cushions, her fingers grazing the nape of Lucas' neck. "My friend and I have a similar tradition, but we mix up the day of the week instead of the spot. Last week we were here on Tuesday."

"There's plenty of nice bars around where you and Claire could go to." Lucas angles his head slightly away from her hand. "You really never go anywhere else other than here?"

While Megan retracts her fingers to make them trace patterns on the leather instead, she goes on to tell him all about her experiences in the city during the last few months.

Lucas keeps gazing at her, but steadily disconnects from the conversation.

She sounds compelling, and she is indubitably pretty.

But her green eyes are not the tempestuous and calming ocean ones of Raven's.

Her lips are not as voluptuous and inviting.

Her idle touch was doing nothing to kindle a flame deep within himself either.

The thought suddenly hits him like a freight train: he'd love to be here with Raven right now. There's no use trying to contest it anymore.

He hums distractedly at Megan who said something about swimming at a rooftop pool with her ex as the music envelops him a little more.

He's certain that Raven would enjoy the botanical decor and chill vibe pairing with the perfect cityscape everywhere around.

He would drape his arm over the back of the seat and brush through her hair to gently massage her scalp if she'd let him.

He'd whisper naughty things into her ear just to see her reply witty remarks while biting into her bottom lip. The way her lip slowly gets pulled between her teeth drives him mad. His brain nearly short circuits at the sight every time.

He always has to summon inhuman strength to not kiss her senseless on the spot every time she does it.

He inhales deeply.

He wonders what she's doing right now.

He used to have fun being Kyan's or Mark's wingman. To flirt with willing individuals, and end the night in bed with them.

Now he doesn't care about any of it.

He has no intention to bring anyone back home or go to their places. He doesn't want to have sex with just any woman.

He wants Raven. No one else.

For the past two days he's been wanking himself blind at night thinking about how he wants to pleasure her, and how amazing she feels when she falls off the edge.

How could he have been foolish enough to entertain the possibility of hooking up with someone else by going out tonight?

No matter what is going on in his life, it's ridiculous to believe that he could've suddenly erased Raven from his mind. He's been splendidly lying to himself for the past few hours thinking he could disregard his thought process when it comes to her.

It apparently took him having a discussion with an attractive woman to convince him of the futility of the whole exercise at play here.

The tune leaking through the speakers is also currently doing nothing to quiet his senses.

He lowers his eyebrows.

He must not forget that Raven has concerns they haven't addressed yet. That's another layer of complexity in the great scheme of things.

She made it plain clear that she wants him, but said that her mind is a mess.

Worst case scenario, they could be friends that casually sleep together once in a while, right?

But who is he kidding? Once in a while won't do. He yearns for Raven every time they're together. That lust won't easily go away.

If he doesn't talk to her about any of it, he'll never know.

Maybe he should—

Megan's voice resounds in his ears. "Are you okay, Lucas? You seem distracted." She chuckles lightly. "If I'm boring, you can tell me. I won't take it badly or anything."

"No. You're not boring." He smiles shyly. "It's not you, it's me."

"Wow." She curves a corner of her mouth upward. "That has to be the record for the shortest time in which a man used that excuse on me." She looks at him teasingly. "Don't you think it's a bit early in our relationship to use it? We only met a few minutes ago."

"You're funny. I like that." He downs the rest of his drink. "But you see, my mind is full of someone else, and I shouldn't be here right now. I should be with her."

"What are you waiting for then?" She gestures in the air between them. "Go."

He sees her smile at him as he puts his glass on the table. "Megan, you're a wonderful person, and I hope you'll find someone equally great tonight."

"If you ever come by FireCoals Grilling House, ask for me." She drops her hand in her lap. "If I'm there, I'll have something fun delivered to your table."

He gets up. "Will do."

She winks, bringing her martini to her lips. "Now go get her."

He quickly excuses himself to Kyan and Claire before striding toward the exit.

He has no idea how Raven is going to react upon seeing him randomly appear at her door, but he has to be true to himself.

He has to feel her presence next to him. Her soft touch brings him a serenity he longs for.

Even just talking to her while sitting on her sofa will be better than the agony of going out without her at the moment.

He presses on the button to call the elevator, waiting no more than a few seconds for it to open in front of him.

The beat fades through the space as the doors of the lift slide close in front of him.

He breathes in deeply.

Going directly to the subway is his best bet to get to Brooklyn as fast as possible.

He's hopefully going to be able to hold Raven close and not let her go all through the night.

His whole being needs it.

NINE

Step Into the Unknown

As Raven walks to the other side of her kitchen, she gazes through the window at Manhattan while fishing her phone out of her coal camo leggings.

She puts the device flat on the counter, acknowledging no new notifications.

The lines of the song currently playing resonate deep in her psyche as she sets on finishing to prepare her grilled tomatoes, goat cheese and thyme sandwich.

Humming to the verses loaded with existential questioning, she inattentively slides the sleeves of her pink knitted sweater up her arms before grabbing the bread knife to slice the baguette.

Shifting her stare at the cutting board in front of her, she tries her best to focus on the task at hand. Her mind has been distracted for hours by now, and she's mostly functioning on autopilot at this point.

She wonders what Lucas is doing.

He hasn't answered any of her messages all day. Even the ones she sent late last night went unacknowledged.

She inhales deeply.

She can't really blame him. He knocked at her door at a very unfortunate moment.

I'll grab some wine, William called out to her.

She was sitting on her sofa, pressing pause on their movie. *Okay, but we need to talk.*

She wasn't really looking forward to him being back from the kitchen. The whole evening felt weird.

As soon as Will arrived dressed in a tailored black suit and white shirt, he was very ready to get down to business. He bent down to kiss her the second the door closed behind him, sliding his hands on her shorts-cladded hips only to not waste any time sneaking them up and underneath her t-shirt.

Usually they would have removed their clothes in a hurry, and stumble onto the nearest surface in a fist of passion.

William is a good kisser. He's also great in bed.

He's always been able to make her forget about anything else than chasing her pleasure for the short span of when they're together. That is why he's a great lover.

Somehow, the very instant his tongue traced the seam of her lips, she felt that something was different.

Her body was not reacting to him in any way.

She wondered why biology was failing her, but instantly dismissed from her brain the obvious answer to that question. Instead, she forced herself to act as she normally would by sliding his suit jacket off from his shoulders to then unbutton his shirt.

When her fingertips trailed down his chest, he growled into her mouth, which still didn't elicit any response from her.

She frowned slightly into the kiss.

Her mind was clearly not having it, and maybe she would be better off—

The minute he grabbed her hips more forcefully, bringing her flush to him and his arousal, she pulled away.

She remembers how he looked dumbfounded, but when she explained that she thought that maybe taking it slower for the night would be a good idea, he agreed.

He didn't bother buttoning his shirt up again, they settled down in the living room, and picked a movie to watch.

They chatted about their days and very general topics all throughout. He said he was happy that she looked to be open to the possibility of sharing more of her life with him by spending a casual night in.

Truth is, she was wondering why she invited him over at every minute that went by.

His company was not awful nor annoying.

She definitely wasn't dying of boredom or anything.

It was more as if she had a colleague over for drinks and they happened to want to watch something together. Purely platonic would have been the best way to describe it.

When Will draped his arm behind her to tentatively caress the nape of her neck, she just couldn't keep lying to herself.

He wasn't Lucas.

That's why everything felt off. Why her body and her mind weren't complying. She wasn't craving William either physically or emotionally.

She shifted in her seat, flashing him a small smile. *Will, I think that—*

He cut her off while removing his hand, excused himself, and blurted out something about her not being used to intimacy so it would probably take time.

He got up, saying that he was ready to wait.

She saw him ruffle up his hair nervously as he was padding toward the kitchen before announcing that he would be back with drinks.

Sitting there alone, she automatically thought that she needed to tell Will that she didn't want to continue seeing him, and that tonight was a bad idea. Their arrangement was bound to end one way or another at some point anyway. It wasn't anything serious to begin with. She clearly didn't want for it to become something more.

That was the exact moment Lucas knocked at her door.

She automatically went to answer.

Not looking into the peephole because she was too caught up in how to break the news to William was her first mistake.

The bright smile that Lucas was sporting when she opened the door could've illuminated the milky way. *Raven. Listen, I was at The Amber Remedy, and I couldn't—*

He trailed off, creasing his eyebrows as he tilted his head to shift his stare behind her.

She mirrored his expression, spinning around to follow his gaze only to internally curse at herself.

As if she had been staring in a bad romcom, William was standing in the middle of the hallway with two glasses in hand, his shirt hanging open, and with his hair peeking at odd angles just as if—

The fellow lawyer grinned. *I didn't know you were expecting more guests, Rae.*

She cringed at the nickname coming out of Will's mouth. *I wasn't.* She turned her attention back to the managing director. *William, this is Lucas, and he came by for—*

He interjected. *For nothing.* He stepped back, gesturing at William in the distance. *I'll let you two do whatever you were doing.*

It took a split second for her to regain her senses. *Wait, we can—*

She stopped herself short from finishing that sentence. Watching him turn on his heels to rapidly disappear in the elevator with his hand raised in a stop motion directed at her was a little surreal.

Will popped up beside her. *Is Lucas okay?*

She secured the latch on the door. *Probably.* She walked back inside. *But you and I really have to discuss.*

He strides after her. *You don't really want to try to build intimacy with me, do you?*

I don't think intimacy should be built to begin with. She stopped in front of her living room coffee table. *It should come naturally, and it's definitely not the case between us, is it?*

I respect your feelings. He put the glasses down on the surface. *To me, I could've easily seen myself with you for the long run.* He smiled warmly at her. *You're smart, fierce, witty, and incredibly beautiful. Sometimes it's just not meant to be.*

She smiled sadly. *We both knew it was destined to end at some point.*

There was indeed a high possibility of at least one of us never wanting more. He started buttoning up his shirt, peering into her eyes. *I still have to ask: when you messaged me earlier, did you really want me?*

She breathed in. *I think I wanted to want you, but I can't dictate to my body who to crave.* She frowned, feeling the whole burden of her bad decision weighting on her. *I'm sorry, Will. I shouldn't have texted you. You deserve better.*

You're sure it's only your body? A playful smile was dancing on his lips. *Don't live in denial, Raven. Your brain is in charge. If I'm not able to make you feel good anymore, I'm sure it's because someone else already crawled into your head.* He raised a curious eyebrow. *Maybe it even has to do with Lucas who just left?*

She thought there was no use trying to deny it. *I just connect with him.* She exhaled soundly. *I can't explain it.*

The best things in life often can't be explained. He tucked his shirt back into his pants, turning very serious. *I know you don't do feelings. We never talked in depth about why that is, because it wasn't our type of relationship, but maybe you had bad experiences before.* He straightened. *You could say it's none of my business, and you'd be right.* He snorted lightly. *But the sparks in your eyes when you saw that man don't lie. You never had them with me, and something tells me it was the same with all your lovers.*

She smiled shyly. *You're observant.*

You might not want to get attached, Raven, but it might be too late. He stretched. *No matter what is going on between you two, you clearly care about him a great deal.*

I met him years ago. She sat back down on the sofa. *I honestly didn't think I would ever see him again.*

William put his hands in his pockets. *You're happy your paths crossed once more?*

There wasn't a hint of hesitation in her tone. *Yeah.* She combed her fingers through her hair. *But I don't know where it will lead us, and I don't feel like talking about it right now.*

Fair enough. Now do you mind if I stay to finish the movie? He smiled softly at her. *I'd love to see the end.*

She agreed, and they spent the next two hours having a good time laughing and chatting.

Without the added pressure of expectations between them, spending time with Will was very satisfying.

Although, the first thing she did upon sitting back on the sofa was to reach out to Lucas. She kept looking at her phone every couple of minutes for a reply that never came.

She takes out the cheese from the fridge.

The take away now is that it's over for good with Will, and that Lucas was supposed to go out with his friends, but somehow ended up at her door late at night.

He wanted to see her, and he stumbled upon her half-naked ex-lover in her apartment in the process.

If for a fleeting moment she thought that Lucas wouldn't care about her inviting her fuck buddy over, she was obviously mistaken. The look of equal parts disbelief, irritation, and hurt on his face is haunting her.

Lucas knows about William.

He knows she's been having casual sex with Will. He probably assumed that she invited the lawyer over for that very purpose. Which was the initial plan. It just turned out very differently.

She would've liked to be able to at least explain herself to him.

She tried calling and texting thinking that going to his penthouse was arguably not the best decision if he seems set on not talking to her.

She's been dumb to act impulsively. It was a bad call to not double check with him what he really wanted to do instead of assuming he would hook up with the first willing individual to fall into his arms the night prior.

But that's maybe exactly what he ended up doing anyway once he left her place.

She knows that Lucas has a ton going on through his mind. He's dealing with some harsh shit lately. He possibly came by to chat with her about all of it, and she deceived him by not being available.

Maybe he found what he was looking for in the arms of someone else.

She pinches the bridge of her nose.

She brushes the cut bread with olive oil, shaking her head.

She's making up hypotheses, and assuming things. She has to stop doing that. She has no idea what happened to Lucas since last night.

This could be simply fixed if he would dare give a damn sign of life.

She grabs her phone out of habit, leaning against the counter.

Still no notifications from Lucas.

She hasn't sent more than four messages to him so as to not overplay it. She's still dying to know what has been going on in his head.

Opening the conversation, she rereads them to make sure she didn't sound too insistent to make him feel any kind of pressure.

R: Is everything okay?

00:11AM

R: If you ever feel like talking, I'm here for you.

00:37AM

R: I know it will sound very cliché, but what you saw last night is probably not exactly what you think. Whatever that might've been. Please call me when you have a minute?

7:46AM

R: I hope you're having a good day. I have to be honest and say that as your friend I'm getting a little worried now. Wishing all is well. Take care, Luke.

12:27PM

Looking at those, she feels as if the evolution of her whole thought process is pretty clear.

At first, she was tired and unwilling to address exactly what he might've thought upon seeing William at her place. So she left her formulations mostly open ended.

Lucas had decided to visit her for a reason, but she had no idea what it was exactly. She didn't want to presume.

Then, she thought that he could've needed some kind of embryonic explanation on her part before feeling comfortable enough to open up himself.

Finally, there was no point in beating around the bush anymore so she told him directly her state of mind.

She even called him 'Luke' in hopes that he would maybe react favorably to the nickname. He admitted loving when she was using it in Mykonos, after all.

She can also very clearly recall how it used to fall from her lips in ecstasy or during gentle intimate moments.

Using it always sounded natural to her. From the very first time he made her climax to the last embrace they shared.

To her he was 'Luke'.

A part of herself thinks he might very well still be.

Raven puts the device down on the island as the captivating tempo of a song by her favorite singer.

She finishes putting the cherry tomatoes, olives, thyme, garlic, pepper and pecorino on top of the sliced goat cheese on one side of the baguette before putting it in a tray.

She slides it into the oven, idly checking the time to start a twenty minute countdown.

It's in moments like this where she feels like she needs a break. She has to find herself very far from NYC for a while, and attempt to reconnect with all that she is.

Chill out.

Get a new perspective on things.

Her life has been nothing but a maelstrom for a long time. It's only gotten worse in the last week.

She knows precisely where she wants to go and what she needs to do to regain some sort of normality and peacefulness.

She opens the refrigerator to take out a bottle of sparkling water. She'll check for flights to San Diego while eating.

Jun will understand she needs a week away from the craziness. Plus, her friend has a ton to do concerning Lucas' case, and Raven can't be of much assistance in person at this stage.

Heather will be surprised to see her, but hopefully pleased. It will also allow Raven to be there for her and Zoe for a little while like she was thinking about doing.

As she stares at her sandwich grilling, she is utterly convinced of her decision.

Taking a week of vacation in California seems like the right thing to do.

Sitting on his couch in a pair of gray sweatpants, wearing his favorite charcoal baseball cap, and his bordeaux *Liberty Cove Business School* hoodie, Lucas is playing guitar.

He finally took it out of the closet, tuned it, and idly started strumming.

Following the day he had, he felt like trying something new to unwind. He still doesn't want to go out any more than he was feeling it yesterday, nor did he feel the need to see anyone.

Truth be told, he hasn't looked at his phone for nearly a whole day now.

He completely disconnected from everything the instant he left Raven's apartment.

Of all the things he thought might happen by paying her a visit, coming face to face with William was not even on the list. It completely blindsided him.

He briefly contemplated staying, confronting her about the situation, and taking it as a challenge to have her choose him instead of her usual lover, but he decided against it. His goal was not to make her feel bad or potentially complicate things so he chose to leave.

She had wanted William in her bed, so that's what she would get.

Even if it hurts a whole lot to think about it.

His concerns about where his life is headed, and the implication of the threats he's been receiving on his future also flew out the window at the same time.

Since he didn't really know how to deal with all his conflicting emotions, he focussed on the blues rhythms resonating in his ears.

When he got home, he put his phone on his bedside table to never be looked at again.

When he left for work this morning, he didn't even pick it up.

He felt numb.

Too many thoughts were still colliding in his brain. He had to force himself to get his head back in the game.

He went to his scheduled meetings, and accompanied Mark to a late lunch.

His friend had called his office directly after getting no response to his texts, insisting that they go grab a bite.

I can't believe you forgot your phone at home, the gym instructor stated while waiting in line at the food truck. *Who even does that nowadays?*

Mark was done with his clients for the day, but didn't change from his cobalt blue track suit to meet with Lucas.

It was a great contrast to the managing director who was in an arguably unexciting gray three piece suit with black shirt and assorted tie.

Me, apparently. Lucas' voice sounded flat. *I've been having a lot on my mind lately.*

Does it have anything to do with the reason why you didn't stay at the club last night? Mark scanned his eyes. *When I arrived with Matteo, Kyan told me you had left a half-hour prior.*

He decided to be straightforward. This was one of his closest friends. Mark would understand. *It isn't the only thing in my head right now, but yeah, it's part of it.* They walked forward as a customer got his order and padded away. *Last night I left because I wanted to see Raven.*

Were you able to?

I saw her alright. He furrowed his eyebrows. *She answered me when I got to her place.*

That's awesome! His friend's gaze was joyous. *Did you two end up—*

Lucas cut him off before he could get too enthusiastic. *She wasn't alone.*

Comprehension suddenly painted Mark's features. *Oh.*

So I left. He half-smiled. *I went directly home.*

I'm sorry, buddy. His friend patted on his shoulder reassuringly. *Have you talked to her since? Maybe it wasn't what you were thinking.*

The man was half-naked with bed hair fetching wine. Lucas chuckled heartlessly. *I know appearances can be deceiving, but that was pretty clear. I haven't talked to her because I don't have my fucking phone with me, and I feel kinda good about it. We owe nothing to each other anyway. We're not going out or anything.*

Mark frowned. *You say that but your eyes are telling a different story, man.*

Betrayed by my own eyes. How lame. Lucas tried his best to be sarcastic. *No matter what, I probably shouldn't feel irritated, there's really nothing between us. She's free to have sex with anyone she wants. Just like me.*

She is. And yeah, so are you even if you clearly didn't want anyone other than her yesterday—and I think it's been like that since she walked back into your life, huh? Mark searched Lucas' eyes for some kind of answer. *It's legitimate that it renders you jealous seeing her with someone else.* He squeezed his distracted friends' triceps before dropping his hand. *You care about her, buddy. You like her a lot. It's normal that it hurts.*

Thanks, Mark.

Talk to her, man. His friend stayed very solemn. *She'll tell you exactly what was going on, and you'll know.*

I didn't have the intention to never talk to her about it. Lucas breathed in deeply. *You know I always say that communication is everything. I wanted to give her time with that man before doing so, and then I just forgot my phone and was in meetings all morning. I'll call her later.*

The trainer beamed. *That's my boy.*

Lucas changed the subject, they shared an enjoyable meal, and both went their separate ways.

While it is true that Lucas thinks communication is key in any relationship, the problem was that he got caught up in work for a few more hours digging into Thomas Keller's and Dick Adam's files to conclude that nothing out of the ordinary was standing out.

When he finally exited his office, it was late. He grabbed some takeout on his way home, and when he finally got to his penthouse he ate in front of the TV, trying to not imagine Raven's exquisite body caressed by another man.

William is clearly attractive. He can see why Raven likes him. She even alluded to the fact that he's good in bed. That's a definitive plus in anyone's book.

Lucas needed to calm down before being able to chat with her. If not, he would probably sound like a fucking unhinged lunatic.

The feelings Raven elicits in him are strong and vehement.

She makes it easy to forget that they separately both built lives for themselves in the past ten years. He feels like a freer, better version of himself when he's with her.

It doesn't matter if they are in New York City and not Mykonos nowadays, the feeling is still present every time he dives into her eyes.

He has no idea what to do with the overwhelming sentiment.

All he knows is that he has to tone down his resentment toward the whole situation a little before picking up his phone to message her.

In that context, music intuitively seemed like a good place to start to ease the annoyance he was feeling.

The instant he picked up his guitar, he automatically got reminded of how liberating it feels to him to play.

He didn't bother using a pick. He wanted to feel the warm sound of playing with his thumb, and the fun of mixing up the downstrokes and upstrokes with a fingers and nails approach.

His fingertips are gliding and pinching the strings with practiced ease as soft jazz fills the air.

Playing old classics from memory is doing wonders to steadily calm him. He should be able to text Raven soon to—

He frowns as he misses a chord.

He stops for a brief moment to replace the old baseball cap on his head, smiling absentmindedly at the texture.

The fabric is worn in a similar fashion than his favorite hoodie is. Both items have become his favorite leisurewear through the years.

He can vividly recall how his sister gave him this hat when she accompanied him on vacation in Australia. The exact travel during which she met her now husband, and where Lucas spent most of his days surfing and playing volleyball on the beach.

The logo on the front of the cap is also special to him.

It represents abstract waves laced with an open and fluid infinity symbol. Lena told him that it reminded her of him as soon as she saw it. Of how he makes one with the power of the elements when he surfs. Of how he constantly challenges himself in an endless cycle of finding balance.

She told him that the symbol being open was because to her he was still trying to find the perfect equilibrium for his inner self.

She kept insisting that even if he tends to think that his life is orderly, it's actually closer to tumult than he might be aware of.

That constantly running around making a name for himself, pursuing recognition and leaving a part of him behind doing it was not the way to go.

That when chaos reigns free, peace cannot be achieved.

He inattentively starts improvising chords on some blues classics.

Lena might've been up to something all those years. Ever since those threats started appearing, and Raven walked into his office, he is forced to connect with layers of his personality he thought he had forgotten about.

And just like that, his mind spontaneously brought Raven to the forefront of his thoughts again.

As he starts humming to the beat he's strumming, he curves a corner of his mouth upward.

Raven told him she sang a song from a jazz legend at her friend's wedding. He would've loved to be there to hear it.

Picturing her on a stage late at night smoothly crooning to a small crowd in a festive mindset brings him joy. Knowing that she enjoyed herself, and was probably smiling with that tender smile of hers he adores during the whole performance, makes a pleasant tingling travel along his spine.

There's no denying that she is alluring beyond words, and that her wit only has her kindness as an equal.

If she was on the sofa with him right now he wishes that she would join him in singing. That she would playfully try to put her feet in his lap to distract him.

He knows he would definitely put his guitar to the side to lean over and kiss her leisurely, stretching on top of her to envelop her slender frame with his bigger one.

He loves how she used to trail her foot along the back of his leg while they made out in such a position. How her fingers constantly brushed through his hair making him groan deep into her mouth.

Now that she's back in his life, he can fully appreciate that there's no denying that once his body knew Raven's, there hasn't been any more comparisons possible.

As he pronounces the last word of the chorus, he thinks that maybe he could send her a message. He does feel more relaxed than he was before.

He also hopes she's doing well. He missed interacting with her today.

He realizes that she might just bring him that slight balance he desperately lacks most days. He should've gotten over himself faster and reached out to her.

No matter what happened last night, he can't imagine moving forward without her in his daily life. Chatting with her would've been a great thing to do from the get-go.

He sets out to remedy that.

He puts his guitar on the cushions beside him before getting up to stride inside his bedroom.

Once he has his phone in hand, he ignores the multiple messages from his assistant as well as from all of his friends to solely concentrate on the ones from Raven.

Assessing the time stamps, he acknowledges that she did text him not long after he left her apartment. She possibly wasn't as caught up in William as he originally thought.

She also seemingly messaged him when she got up, asking him to call her.

R: I know it will sound very cliché, but what you saw last night is probably not exactly what you think. Whatever that might've been. Please call me when you have a minute?

7:46AM

He frowns as his eyes read over the 'exactly' precision of the first sentence. To him, the situation is either black or white here. No shades of gray possible. She either slept with William, or she didn't.

Either way, it shouldn't matter because—

His gaze stays stuck on the last message.

R: I hope you're having a good day. I have to be honest and say that as your friend I'm getting a little worried now. Wishing all is well. Take care, Luke.

12:27PM

Luke.

Did she do it on purpose? He did tell her it was driving him crazy when she called him that.

Similarly, he remembers that she told him that she loves when he calls her 'Rae'.

But William used the nickname last night. Lucas recalls cringing internally upon hearing it. Does Raven just love the moniker, or does she specifically appreciate when *he* says it?

He inhales slowly. He certainly won't stop using it no matter what.

As his thumb selects the field to start typing, his stare lingers on the 'as your friend'. He shakes his head. He has to make an abstraction of it, and just chat with her. There's no other way to get to the bottom of this.

L: Sorry for the delayed reply, I had a long day and had forgotten my phone at home.

He puts his device on the arm rest to grab the container with some leftover Chow Mein Fun from the coffee table.

A chime resonates while he takes a bite. He looks at his screen.

R: Who forgets their phones these days? Are you sure you're okay?

He chuckles, taking hold of his phone and not losing a second to answer.

L: Mark told me the same thing. I just had a ton going on in my mind. I am good, thanks. You?

The answer is nearly instant.

R: I'm also good, and I'm sorry to hear your brain is overwhelmed. You do have a lot going on.

He half-smiles. If he knows her at all, she is taking it slow to let him share whatever he wants, when he wants to. He did show up at her door for a reason that he never got to explain, and then didn't give a sign of life all day, after all.

She might feel as if she has to tread carefully. He still thinks that addressing all of it in person would be best.

He decides to leave it very general for now.

L: I do. I wanted to talk to you last night, but you were otherwise occupied so it's no big deal.

R: It IS a big deal. I want to be there for you when you need me. You could've stayed, William was about to leave anyway.

He hesitates on how to navigate this new information.

Did Raven already have sex with William when he got there? Did he end up leaving as she's implying?

Lucas has a thousand questions that he's unsure he wants the answers to.

He plays it unemotionally.

L: It's all good.

Three little blinking dots appear in no time on his screen.

R: So you saw Mark today?

Reading this next message convinces him that she picked up on the cue that he doesn't want to talk about William at the moment.

He smiles softly.

L: Yeah. We had lunch together. We grabbed something from *Skewers Wagon* near my office.

R: Love that food truck!

He grins.

L: Same! The souvlaki platter is delish.

R: Don't forget their burgers.

L: Basically their whole menu is amazing.

R: It is . Me and Jun often go there when we're in the area.

His thumbs hover on the virtual keyboard. He has an urge to see her. He hastily types before he can convince himself otherwise.

L: Want to go grab a bite somewhere tomorrow night?

R: I can't

He makes a face, but sees that she's still typing so he waits.

R: I'll be in California by then. Just booked tickets for a week in San Diego today.

He doesn't know exactly why he doesn't stop his fingers, but he couldn't care less.

If this day showed him one thing, it's that he wants to be with her as much as possible. How they spend their days is of little importance as long as he's close to her.

Plus, he could use some time to breathe.

For once, he'll follow what his heart is dictating him to do.

He presses send as soon as the last punctuation symbol appears.

L: Mind if I tag along?

TEN

Dare to Dive

O nce in a while in life, one has no idea why they agreed to something, but they did because it felt right.

That's exactly what is happening to Raven at the moment as she's sitting in the back of a taxi in San Diego next to Lucas.

The late afternoon sun is bathing the sky in stunning orange hues reflecting through the window of the car onto her mid indigo ragged jeans and white loose scoop neck t-shirt to create a warm atmosphere.

She removed her off-white cardigan with caramel, brown and bisque stripes that is now resting in her lap as soon as they stepped outside of the airport terminal. The breeze being warmer than in New York at this time of year made her instantly happy. She felt as if she could finally breathe.

She knew that being back in California would work wonders to bring her to a more peaceful state of mind.

Although having Lucas with her is making the whole experience feel surreal.

She lets her eyes travel from his black training hoodie, geometric patterned gray cargo shorts down to his high top sneakers as if she wants to take it all in. To make sure she is not hallucinating.

A quick glance to her left confirms it: she isn't. Lucas Blake is truly currently on the West Coast, in her hometown, with her.

They landed no more than an hour ago at San Diego International Airport, and they are now on their way to a liquor store before going to join Heather and Zoe for dinner.

They both agreed to not arrive at her friends empty handed. Getting a couple of good wine bottles seemed like a good idea.

Heather had been thrilled to hear that Raven was coming to visit, and even more so when she learned about Lucas tagging along.

Raven has to admit that the reason why she agreed to Lucas' spontaneous suggestion to join her on her trip is still a mystery to her. The only thing she knows is that it's been lovely to travel with him so far.

She hopes it continues.

Jun has also been very supportive of their plans. While at first she thought that it would be better for Lucas to continue working as if nothing was going on, she revised her position the minute he told her that he needed to clear his mind.

They were all on the same call earlier today to warn the crisis manager of where they were going.

I do agree that it'll do you both some good to be away from the craziness for a while, Jun stated when they broke the news. *What will you tell at work, Lucas?*

That I'm going away for personal matters. I'm always on call anyway, and they all know how to reach me if need be. I don't have any important business to attend to in the next few days. Lucas' annoyed breathing was less than subtle. *I couldn't care less what they'll think of the whole situation, I feel like I need a break.*

Understandable. Ju hummed loudly. *I'm glad that you're taking some time for yourself.*

His tone was unexpressive. *I arguably should've done it sooner. It's pretty rare that I take vacations.*

Raven couldn't help herself as she was finishing putting her makeup in her toiletries bag. *I feel you. Getting time off was a constant struggle for me before.*

Mmm. He redirected the exchange. *Jun, I looked into Keller's and Adam's files. Nothing stood out. Maybe there's more that I didn't have access to, but it really seems like both of them are actually cleaner than a lot of my clients.* He took a small pause before adding, *I have no doubts they are assholes for dealing with people if you say so, Raven, but from a business standpoint they don't look to be good candidates for threats. Maybe they calmed down after their trials?*

It would be plausible. The lawyer exhaled soundly. *Doesn't want the spotlight back on them just yet.*

Her friend jumped on the occasion to follow-up on the information. *I'll still take a closer look. Better be safe than sorry.* Her voice was concerned, but steady. *Thank you for the heads up. I'll keep both of you guys posted on everything I find that's of interest, and we'll monitor your mailboxes, Lucas. In case any more letters arrive while you're not there. Thank you for trusting me with it.*

Lucas didn't miss a beat. *Raven blindly trusts you, and you've proven to be very professional so it was a no-brainer. I'll drop you the keys before going to the airport, Jun.*

Sounds great. Jun's tone shifted to being joyous. *Now, you two be careful out there.*

It's not like we are at risk of much. Raven chuckled. *It's San Diego, not a war zone or the shark capital of the country. We shouldn't get eaten while surfing.*

Such a nice sense of humor you have, Raven. Her friend snorted. *Take time to relax, but not too much. Don't let California spoil you to the point where I'll never see you again.*

I'll be back. I promise. She looked at herself in the mirror, confirming that she really needed that vacation. *I just need to reset my mind.*

Now being en route to have a nice dinner, and hopefully good times with some of her best friends, Raven feels as if she made the right decision.

She is more relaxed than she's been in ages.

Letting her eyes define Lucas' jawline as it ever so slightly tenses while he removes his sunglasses, folding them into his collar, makes her sigh.

The last time she spent some time alone with Lucas, she trailed her fingertips along the scruff there as his tongue was battling hers for dominance.

The nerve endings of her hands can still recall strands of his hair gliding through her fingers like silk while he was softly sucking on her bottom lip.

So many things have happened since, but she'd be lying if she was to affirm that the ghost of his lips are not still lingering on hers.

That she hasn't been craving an encore.

He must've sensed her gaze on him. He turns his attention to her, smiling coyly. "I wish you'd have had a better seat neighbor aboard the plane. I am sorry you got uncomfortable."

Raven had just told their driver about her discomfort during the trip before the muscular man had to answer a call in his earpiece.

Since Lucas booked his tickets after Raven, they spent the whole flight separated and not interacting.

Which also means that the woman sitting next to her was not as considerate as Lucas would've been.

She mirrors his smile, adding some playfulness to her expression. "At this point I'm nearly used to people removing their shoes as soon as we take off to put their feet up, then having one too many drinks, and finally falling asleep on my shoulder during flights."

"It's a trifecta of bad behavior no one should ever be submitted to while traveling." He smirked. "Although it's a true shame that it wasn't me sleeping on your shoulder."

She ignores his comment. "The best part was when she woke up, read the page I was on, and spoiled the ending for me."

"Rude." He frowns. "I guess you don't have to read the whole book now. Knowing how it ends and all."

"I'll still read it. The appeal is in the journey. The ending is only part of it. Seeing how everything unfolds is where the real fun is." She lifts a corner of her mouth upward. "Kinda like when having sex." She leans forward, dropping her tone a few octaves. "Do you only care about the orgasm?" She smiles teasingly. "Do you not give a damn about everything that happens before?"

"There's indeed beauty in the journey, they say." A knowing smile is dancing on his lips. "You know I adore foreplay. With you, I could've spent all night just letting my hands define your curves and caress every inch of your skin." He meets her halfway on the seat, locking eyes with her. "Could kiss you for hours on end," he whispers in the small space between them. "And let my mouth pleasure you without ever seeking release myself. Because your own cry of ecstasy is the sole discharge of serotonin I need."

She scans his eyes only to see the emerald pools slowly disappearing as his pupils steadily dilate with each word he speaks.

She also noticed that the fundraiser started a trend of him putting progressively less gel in his hair. She wonders if he'll end up putting none someday.

She'd certainly love to feel his product-free locks slide through her fingers as his head is buried between her thighs.

Massage his scalp and nudge him back up to her because she'd want to—

"If I remember correctly, giving me head had a way to build you up." She bites into her bottom lip. "You'd be uncomfortable after a while."

"I wouldn't mind." He shrugs, sounding dead serious. "You're all that matters."

She tilts her head onto the headrest. "But I would love to kneel before you to help you with it. I'd prefer you climax than me."

He groans.

He's so close. She would love to curl her hand around his throat and close the gap between them right now.

Forget that they are in someone else's car, straddle him, and just make out like horny teenagers.

This flirting is so natural between them that it supersedes every other thought.

But he might say all of that, they both have no idea what happened to the other on Thursday night. Maybe he hooked up with someone else because there's nothing going on between them anyway.

It would be totally legitimate, and shouldn't bother her.

Plus, he's clearly still the same Lucas who values his clients and lifestyle even if it involves some questionable activities.

That didn't change. If she thinks too much about it, her concerns are as present as ever.

But they somehow hopped on a plane together to spend a week away from the Big Apple.

Thinking about it, it possibly could lead to—

He seems to sense her inner battle. "We're both truly selfless, aren't we?" He smiles shyly, clearing his throat, and reorienting the conversation. "Circling back to books; I have this thing that I'm unable to not finish a book even if I find it not that good." He sits back in his seat. "It's as if I have to see if it gets better as it goes along, you know?"

"Mhmm." She quickly follows his lead. "Heather has to read the very last page before going back and reading the whole story." She straightens. "She says that this way she knows the final destination so she can be at peace as she reads through the events."

"That only works in the case of happy endings though." He furrows his eyebrows. "If the ending sucks, would you really want to go through the whole journey?"

The occasion is too good to pass up. She smiles at him amusedly. "Well, you for one would still read since you can't put down any book even if you think it's unsatisfying."

He laughs brightly. "Touché."

She can't stop herself from snorting. "So, what did you do during the flight?"

"See, I had this gorgeous woman sitting next to me and we really connected." He makes a show to tell it with the most engaged intonation. "We joined the mile high club together. It was incredible." He sighs fakely as if he's now daydreaming. "She apparently also lives in La Jolla. I might give her a call when we are at our destination."

"Show off." Raven can see through his made-up story, but wants to play along. "Mile high club is overrated in my opinion. The thrill of being thousands of feet into the air in a super small enclosed space doesn't do it for me."

He raises a curious eyebrow. "You need room to fully enjoy it?"

"Not really." She sounds dismissive. "I can do it in a confined area, but the one time I tried it the experience was underwhelming."

"It only means you had the wrong partner." He fetches his phone. "I'm sure I could fix that and make it memorable for you."

"Oh, but you already did it with that amazing woman." She acts innocent. "I wouldn't want to get in the middle of a beautiful blossoming love story." She pretends to be deep in reflection. "What's her name again?"

He instantly dismisses the notification, placing his device back in his short's pocket. "Kimberley."

"Mmm." She knits her eyebrows. "Kimberley wouldn't appreciate you having sex with me when you had an incredible experience with her."

He peers into her eyes. "Why's that?"

"Because you wouldn't be able to get me out of your head afterwards." She pulls her bottom lip between her teeth on purpose this time. "That's how good I would make it for you."

The way he instantly looks at her with untamed lust and genuine hunger makes her nearly regret having pushed the exchange that far.

They are in public. They can't—

His tone is warm and sultry. "I'm already unable to get you out of my head, Raven, and we haven't had sex in more than ten years." He sighs for real now. "There's no way my mind will let me fuck somebody else."

Raven analyzes his gaze. He looks as genuine as can be. He's unwavering.

Does this mean that he didn't hook up with anyone on—

Their shaved head driver makes himself known. "Are you two married?" He laughs brightly. "Ten years is a long time."

Lucas and Raven both burst out laughing. The sudden unexpected inquiry pulls them back to the present.

Lucas is the quickest to respond. "No. We were together years ago, and we just happened to reconnect lately."

"Gotcha." The driver's brown eyes look at them through the rearview mirror. "I couldn't spend more than a few days without having sex with my husband. It's been six years, and I'm still as heads over heels for him as I was at the beginning."

Raven smiles gently at the man. "That's wonderful."

"That's what true love is, I guess." He keeps driving, his grin visible through the mirror. "Getting through the hardships with the desire to have no one else by your side for all of it. Good or bad. Still craving the same person even decades after having first slept with them. Wanting to share all that you are, and all of what your life is made of with them." He lets out a breath, laughing nervously. "Sorry, I got carried on."

"No worries." Lucas smiles genuinely. "I agree with everything you said. It's beautiful to see you be this passionate about your relationship."

"Thanks, man." The driver takes a left turn. "Please carry on. I want to know what happened with Kimberley."

"She has three kids and a very loving husband at home waiting for her. We had a lovely conversation when I gave her some investing tips." The driver laughs as his phone chimes. The minute the man picks up the call, Lucas turns toward Raven, boring his eyes into hers once again. "I would never dare have sex with anyone else when my head is full of only you, Rae."

She stretches her neck to keep her composure at hearing him call her 'Rae'. She has to keep the ball rolling, and not get into dangerous territory. "So what did you do during the six hour flight?"

"I did chat with Kimberley, then I watched a movie, listened to music and tried to come up with interesting chord arrangements to create a nice melody." He taps rhythmically on his thigh. "I will need to try them next time I have access to a guitar."

She is surprised. "You're playing guitar again?"

"I might be." He looks a little timid. "I picked it up yesterday, and played. It was very fun. I had forgotten how liberating it feels. I promised myself I would do it more often from now on."

She beams. "What did you end up playing?"

"Some classic jazz." He's clearly joyful of her enthusiasm. "Some Billie Holiday."

"We could make a duo at the next wedding either of us is invited to."

He smiles something soft at her. "It would be my honor."

She scans his gaze. "So your head is full of only me, huh?"

He's unflinching. "It is."

This is the moment to address whatever happened on Thursday night.

She feels that he seems relaxed enough to be willing to indulge her questions. Better put all cards on the table.

She half-smiles. "Then how come you—"

The car comes to a halt. "Here you are lady and gent." The driver's voice resounds in their ears. "At your destination. *The Marvelous Liquor Room.*"

Raven automatically diverts her attention away from Lucas to un-buckle her belt intuitively, thanking the driver.

As Lucas also extends his gratitude, and proceeds to the payment on his phone, Raven drapes her cardigan over her shoulders before exiting the electric vehicle to grab their respective carry-on luggages from the trunk.

A split second later, Lucas appears next to her. "Let me get that." He picks up his slate gray and electric blue duffle bag. "I know you can take care of it, but please let me help for once." He gestures at her own waxed canvas khaki weekender. "It'll make me feel better."

"If you insist." She closes the door. "I'll certainly let you carry your bag, but not mine."

He places his hand over his heart in fake hurt. "Chivalry is truly dead."

She snorts. "Stop that. It's also way more practical that way." She wiggles her fingers in the air between them. "We both have at least one free hand to grab wine bottles."

"True." He starts walking toward the brick and glass façade with wooden pillars. "How many should we get?"

"I was thinking at least two?" She follows suit. "I know they have their own stash, but I want to bring them something nice." He opens the door for her. She steps inside. "You know, when Heather and I were in our last two years at *Harriers*—so we were of legal drinking age—every time we would come back to visit, we would come here and buy their best bottle of margarita to go drink it with Jun on the beach."

The beat of the latest song collaboration from one of her pop idols reaches her ears as she gets farther into the store, making her smile.

She can't stop herself from humming to the tempo.

He catches up with her, smiling mellowly. "Would've loved to be there."

She glances at him beside her. "You and I did it a couple of times in Mykonos."

"But this whole town here is special to you. It's where you have your roots." He looks around at the aisles with wooden shelves stretching to the back of the store where the refrigerators are. "I never really had any roots myself, but I know how important it is."

He alluded to it before when talking about his penthouse. She didn't inquire more at the time. It wasn't the focus of that discussion—he had just received another threat letter. Now it is different.

She wants to know all those parts of him. "You really never felt like you belonged somewhere?"

"No. Even if I spent most of my childhood and teenage years in Chicago, the moment my dad left it just felt weird to me. From that day on, I tried my best to be there for my mother and sister, not knowing where I was fitting in the world exactly. That was before New York." He breathes in, his expression morphing into something more cheerful. "I'm honored that you'd let me join you for this week. Thank you."

He also mentioned his father back when they were in Greece, and it sounded like a loaded subject. She recalls him being very glad when she had decided to brush it off in profit to go for another round in bed.

She's dying to know what's the story there, but the fact that he just casually said that might be enough for now. Talking about it under the neon lights of a liquor store doesn't look like the best course of action.

Instead, she chooses to share a truth with him in return. "I smiled when I saw your message. I feel good at every moment we spend to-gether." She navigates toward the wooden cabinets lining the exterior walls. "So instinctively I knew I wanted you to come with me."

He bends down to murmur in her ear, "I'll definitely make sure you come multiple times."

She scans his eyes, and can't repress the pleasant warmth spreading through her skeleton at the words.

Of course he went for an innuendo.

Two can play that game.

She smiles warmly. "So confident. What if you don't succeed?"

He smirks. "I will."

She shrugs, staring at the wine selection in front of her. "I have to admit that I never faked it with you."

He sounds curious. "Which implies you did with others?"

"Faking it to play to their ego?" She shakes her head. "Nah. If I don't climax I just don't call back."

He frowns. "I'm sorry you had to have those experiences."

"It's easier for you men, right? Rarely happens." She curves a corner of her mouth upward amusedly. "It's fine, it's part of life. It lets us choose the right partner, I guess."

"Foolproof way to do so for sure." He laughs timidly. "I'm very proud to—"

A clerk calls out to them. "Need any help guys?"

Lucas reformulates his sentence to reply to the young man standing at the end of the aisle. "No, we're good." He gazes at Raven. "Are we going for a bottle of your favorite margarita, some rum, and a fancy wine?"

"Thinking of mojitos with the rum?" He nods. She smiles brightly. "Sounds perfect."

"Want us to bring some dessert, too?" He reaches to grab a bottle from the shelf. "I think it would be great."

She hums. "You like cheesecake?"

"Love it." He holds a bottle of Cuban rum in front of Raven who gives her approbation at his choice. "Also love tiramisu."

"Same." She takes stock of her margarita options. "There's an amazing bakery on Union Street that makes the best cheesecakes. We can also buy a tiramisu because Zoe adores those."

"Getting both sounds like the best plan." He lets out a snort. "We should've told our driver to wait."

"We'll just ask for another, it's no big deal." She picks up some margarita. "That shop is close enough to Heather and Zoe's home that we'll ask the driver to wait when we get there." She swings her duffle on her shoulder to fish out her phone from her jeans pocket. "I can't wait to get my car back."

He strides in the direction of the wine selection. "It's at Heather and Zoe's?"

"Yeah." She pads after him. "They look after it, and in return they can also use it." She quickly asks for a lift in her app. "It's a deal we came up with when I bought it because we all love driving."

"It's great." He grins. "I can't wait to meet your friends."

She stops next to him. "Trust me, they can't wait to meet you, too."

As she looks at Lucas examining the wines, she smiles inattentively.

He's handsome as hell, and is irradiating a wellbeing she hasn't felt from him yet.

It's fabulous to witness.

Being in San Diego with Lucas might bring a slew of unexpectedness, but she feels that she's ready to just go with the flow.

See where it leads her.

The whole point of this vacation was to leave the craziness behind.

When he turns to face her with his signature charming smile, that's exactly what she vows herself to do.

ELEVEN

Serene Stillness

Being on the second floor wooden terrace of Heather and Zoe's house in Point Loma after a nice dinner is precisely what Lucas would call a perfect evening.

The stars are high up in the sky, Raven is laughing beside him at an anecdote Heather just told her while she puts her cardigan back on, the waves of the Pacific are crashing on the shore in the distance in a beautiful symphony, and he feels completely peaceful.

A distant captivating melody reaches his ears. He recalls how the two women currently sitting in front of Raven and him said that they put on a special playlist just for their friend. To welcome her home.

Which means that since the beginning of the evening, he's been basking in jazz, alternative, recent as well as old school pop, and obviously a ton of Raven's favorite singers.

He has to admit that he loves it. He even finds himself humming at most of the songs.

As the lyrics about generational differences resonate, he briefly wonders if he feels old enough to consider himself to be part of the past.

He's in his early thirties. His twenties have certainly been fun, and occupied building a name for himself, but he still got the future ahead of him.

He only hopes to be able to make the most out of it.

It's funny how being in such a relaxed setting makes him reflective, but never apprehensive. He had a couple of those thoughts throughout the night, but unlike when he's in Manhattan, it's as if he's in harmony with every single one.

Progressively, from the flight to the liquor store and bakery visit up to when Raven and him pulled up in her friend's driveway, Lucas has steadily forgotten all about New York and the threats plaguing his life recently.

Having Raven near him is doing wonders to make everything else around vanish. It seems like the sensation is amplified from being in California.

Jun was right. Raven is more carefree.

She's at ease with everything around her in a way where nothing is susceptible to bother her anymore.

It's enthralling to see, and might very well bleed into his own state of mind.

He'd very much like for this contentment to persist.

The instant he entered the Craftsman-style house of Raven's friends, he was seduced by the high coffered ceilings, light oak flooring, and modern touches throughout.

The open oversized designer living room giving into the dining room and dual island kitchen was inviting with their neutral tones and stylish furniture.

The white marble counters and islands are paired wonderfully with the same color wood lacquered cabinets, also making the cobalt blue stools, long chestnut dining table and green Walton chairs with metal frame stand out.

The fireplace and TV in front of the modern European sectional gray sofa, two off-white lounge chairs, persian rug and the rond veneer and metal coffee table is making the living area nothing but cozy.

The big windows on every wall finishes to create a warm atmosphere everywhere on the first floor.

Once up the L-shaped staircase, a modern bathroom, two individual bedrooms and an office are making up the second floor.

Two sliding doors then lead to the very balcony they are seated on right now.

The landscaping downstairs is pristine with a small garden, outdoor kitchen, and a pool, but the upstairs terrasse is where the custom BBQ is so that's where their hosts decided to have dinner.

Lucas can't complain.

The Bay view is magnificent from up here, the solar torches flicker with fake LEDs flames ever so often, the teak furniture is comfortable, and the company is delightful.

Life can't get better than this.

Heather and Zoe welcomed him as if he was part of their close circle of friends. As soon as they saw him, the two women hugged him one after the other.

The hazel eyes of Heather lighted up as she tucked the front of her copper t-shirt in her skinny jeans before doing so. *Lucas. Glad to finally meet you. An encounter a decade in the making.*

He smiled, and Zoe brushed her fingers into her short brown curls with blonde highlights beside them. *We were starting to think you were an urban legend.* She fixed the collar of her purple v-neck shirt, her heterochromia eyes sparking playfully. *From what Raven told us you were one of a kind.* Heather released Lucas, prompting Zoe to open her arms in an invitation. *It sounded too good to be true.*

He bent down to hug her. *The honor is all mine.*

She pulled back, fetching her ringing phone from the back pocket of her black floral shorts. *Well, I'm happy to see you're very real.* She checked the screen. *Excuse me, I have to take this.*

She went to answer the call while Heather showed Lucas and Raven around to finally put him to contribute at the grill while everyone prepared dinner as a team.

A few hours later now, he can affirm that the food was delicious, and that the bottle of Italian red wine he chose back at the liquor store was a perfect pairing for the meal. Everyone praised the selection, except Zoe who chose to only drink water in preparation for the small chirurgical procedure she undergoes tomorrow.

In that context, he's glad that they decided to bring some dessert for her to enjoy since she didn't taste the alcohol.

After he introduced Raven to his own closest friends, sitting with some of hers feels amazing.

He lets his eyes travel to Raven's fingers who are idly trailing along the stem of her glass as she listens to Heather tell her all about her latest outing where someone stopped at her level at a street corner, and invited her to dinner.

"So you can see that it's all your car's fault." Raven's fellow lawyer friend sits back in her chair, laughing. "I get flirted with for no reason when I drive it."

Earlier, when they walked past Raven's black compact convertible with all black interiors parked in front of her friend's contemporary garage, he could vividly picture Raven driving it.

The slight red accents at the mirrors, brakes, and front bumper grid confirmed that the car has the same elegance and edge as its owner.

He's certain that she also gets plenty of attention when she drives it.

He is eager to see what her house in La Jolla looks like.

Something tells him that it is equally refined and vitalizing.

He feels as if she's allowing him to slowly step into every part of her life, and he couldn't be happier.

Raven joins her friend in laughing. "And it doesn't happen at all with your own car?"

Heather shakes her head. "Never."

"To be honest, I blame the fact that her own car has tinted windows and a regular solid roof." Zoe shrugs teasingly. "No one sees her in it. If they would, she would get asked out constantly." She looks at her wife. "She's gorgeous."

"Thanks, baby." Heather turns to face her partner. "I think that's pushing it, but I'll take the compliment."

"You're too humble." Zoe stares at Lucas. "When I met her, she was the only person in that bookstore who existed for me. She was radiating so much power and beauty, I just couldn't not be drawn to her."

"You met at a bookstore?" Lucas takes a sip of his wine. "That's nice."

"Yeah. I was there for the launch of a book series my friend had hired me to do the covers for, and Haddy was shopping around." Zoe smiles dreamily. "Never thought that being a freelance graphic designer would lead to such a wonderful encounter. I usually work mostly from home, and am not the outgoing type much."

"Love will always find a way, I say." Haddy curls her hand around her wife's thigh under the table, adding teasingly, "Plus, I can recall that there was someone else hitting on you at that event. I had competition."

The graphic designer rolls her eyes. "That was nothing. I might be bisexual, I wasn't attracted to that man to start with."

"The poor guy had no chance from the get-go." Heather chuckles soundly, removing her hand from her partner's upper leg to wave it at Raven's. "It reminds me of that time when a handsome guy made advances to Raven out of nowhere."

"That was slightly different." Zoe half-smiles. "Unlike us who had just met, Raven was already in a relationship, and her boyfriend was only a few feet away."

Lucas is curious. "What happened?"

"We were on the beach one night at one of Jun's famous parties." Haddy locks eyes with Raven. "This man who hadn't been invited came by and started flirting with Raven..."

Raven picks up the tale to continue telling it. "Long story short, I was slightly drunk and flirted back with him for a while before refusing to go back to his place."

Heather toys with the foot of her glass, smiling fondly at her. "I can remember Nathan laughing at your awkward drunken flirtiness."

Raven snorts, taking a gulp of her drink. "As if Nathan wasn't getting all flirty himself when he had too much to drink."

Haddy looks at her knowingly. "He was lucky you aren't the ultra possessive type."

Raven hums absentmindedly. "It was another era. We were young and insouciant. That all changed fast enough."

Lucas is reminded that she only talked about her ex once in his presence so far, and she was very cryptic when she did.

Maybe he could get to the bottom of it. Get some answers as to the reason they called it quits.

He wants to know her. *Everything* about her that he missed in the past decade as well as each event that defined her life even before that is of interest to him.

"Is that why you two broke up?" He treads carefully, scanning her features. "Did he—"

She instantly cuts him off. "No. He didn't cheat on me." She breathes in deeply. "It was something else entirely that made us part ways."

"Okay." He senses the uncomfort in Raven's tone. He decides to not push it. He at least managed to eliminate the cheating hypothesis from the table. He chooses to redirect the discussion, smiling comprehensively at her. "I had no idea Jun had a reputation for throwing memorable parties."

She seems to relax instantly. "I tell you, you haven't lived if you haven't attended one of her beach gatherings."

He beams. "I'd love to see it."

"Maybe someday you will." Raven angles more toward him on her chair. "We'd have to invite Ju over with us."

Zoe's fruity voice fills the space. "She wasn't available this week?"

"No, she's working on Lucas' case." Raven snaps her attention back to her friends. "And I think she's supervising another crisis management for a video content creator who got hacked."

During the car ride to Heather and Zoe's place, Raven and Lucas concluded that it would be a good thing to let her friends know about his situation.

They would spend the majority of the week together, might get important updates from Jun throughout, thus affecting their mindsets, and Raven vouched for both women's trustworthiness.

Lucas is oddly glad to have the information out there for them to share and discuss if need be.

"We'll have to invite her at another time, then." Haddy grabs the sparkling water bottle. "Is she still seeing Gary?"

"Yes." Raven nods. "Although Gary called it quits not long ago because he didn't want to present her to his son. He's worried that he'll get attached, and that it will awaken difficult emotions about his biological mother. He did ask Jun out, and they are having dinner together soon to hopefully discuss everything. I say it's a date, but Jun's been reluctant to call it as such."

Lucas frowns. "Gary's wife left them?"

"Yeah." Raven's tone is mellow. "I can't blame Gary. It must be very challenging to deal with that kind of trauma for both him and his son."

"Especially when it happens out of nowhere." The managing director clenches his jaw. "The feeling of powerlessness is the worst to deal with."

Raven gazes intently at him, and Lucas has no idea why he blurted that out.

It's definitely something he feels deep within his soul, but he never shares it aloud.

He's very private about anything that has to do with his own father, and that part of his life.

No need to reopen old wounds.

Even if they honestly never truly healed, he doesn't see the point in digging deeper.

But he knows he feels good at this table. Everyone is enveloping him with the sensation that he belongs. Maybe it's not that far-fetched to think that he suddenly thought opening up might be a good idea.

He still tenses slightly out of habit.

Heather stares at him, having picked up on his unease. "I really hope those threats stop coming in, Lucas, and that Jun is able to discover who is sending them."

"Thanks." He inhales steadily, trying his best to not let the whole situation come back to haunt him right now on top of being reminded about his father. "I hope so, too."

"But we said we were here to have a good time, so let's not talk about it." Haddy gestures in front of her as if to dismiss the subject. "What prompted this whole conversation we just had was that I drove your car today, Raven, and I wanted to say that its fuel tank is now full." She raises her glass in a toast. "I also took care of putting some essentials in your fridge, but you might want to go run some errands yourself." She raises a knowing eyebrow. "And last but not least: your surfboard is in the garage. I even waxed it. It's ready to be used."

Raven meets her toast, smiling brightly. "You're the friggin' best, Haddy."

"Anything for you, sister." Heather takes a sip before glancing at Zoe. "It also helped both of us get our minds off of things for a little while there."

Raven frowns, putting her glass back on the surface. "I can only imagine how hard it must be for you to navigate all the uncertainty."

"We should be fixed about what type and grade of tumor it is this week. It's a blessing that you'll be around with us. I actually feel happier since you're here, Raven. I missed you." Zoe smiles shyly. "They said that after the biopsy tomorrow, the results shouldn't take more than two or three days to be confirmed." She makes a face, looking as if she remembered something. "Oh shit."

Raven and Heather inquire in unison. "What is it?"

The graphic designer presses her lips in a thin line. "I just remembered that we're supposed to babysit our neighbor's eight year-old daughter Sandy tomorrow morning."

"Damn." Haddy throws her head back. "I totally forgot about that."

"I'd like for you to accompany me, baby." Zoe suddenly sounds determined. "Maybe if we tell Brenda and Darek right now they could find someone to—"

Lucas cuts her off. "We can do it. We can take care of an eight year-old for a few hours." He gazes at the lawyer to his left. "Right, Raven?"

"Sure." She smiles coyly. "No problem."

"That's very generous of you." The graphic designer grins genuinely. "You know Brenda, Raven. She'll be glad to know that you're visiting."

She wiggles her index finger between Lucas and Raven. "You two could sleep here tonight to not have to come back super early."

Lucas stares at Raven. He's set on letting her take that decision. She briefly glances at him before replying to Zoe. "Sounds great."

Heather looks a little concerned. "We have only one guest room, but—"

Lucas interjects. "I can sleep on the couch."

Haddy's voice resounds in his ears. "Awesome." She is joyous. "You'll see, Sandy is a joy to be around. Amongst her favorite things to do, she loves video and board games, playing house, baking cookies, and going to the zoo."

Lucas automatically perks up. "We could take her."

"We could." Raven half-smiles, looking reflective. "My mom used to bring me to the zoo every month. I have very fond memories of it."

Zoe furrows her eyebrows. "Have you told your parents you were in San Diego?"

"No." Raven inhales steadily. "I was debating going to see them or not. Worst case scenario it'll be a surprise if I do."

"They'd love to see you, I'm sure." Heather tries her best buoyant tone. "I saw your dad at the mall the other day. I didn't say anything about your resignation, but he asked me if I had heard from you. I told him that you were very busy. Which is technically not a lie. You always are. Even when unemployed."

Lucas feels like asking. "You don't always go see them when you're around?"

She shakes her head at him, hesitating before talking. "It's complicated. I love them, but ever since my mom's been sick, my father is not the same and I feel like they're the only people who are fake with me when I visit." She fidgets on the foot of her glass while locking eyes with him. He keeps his expression soft to show her that he's ready to support everything she is willing to share. After a minute, she carries on. "They try to put on a front when they clearly shouldn't. I'd appreciate it if they could talk freely, and not pretend like everything's okay, you know? Even if I confront them, they won't budge. It gets tiring."

"You mentioned that your father blames himself for not having been there enough for your mother." Lucas harbors his best heartening look. "He even gave up painting altogether because of it?"

Raven blinks in surprise. "You remember?"

"I remember every single thing you told me." He hums. "I pay attention when you talk, Raven."

"I had no doubts, but I only mentioned it super quick during a text exchange, and—" She shakes her head to compose herself. "Anyway. Yeah, that's part of it. He closed himself off, and while he's there for my mom, he also suffers from not having any hobbies anymore. Plus, I'm sure my mom is suffering from him being overprotective of her. It's not as if she has always been the easiest to deal with when she was sick knowing what she—" She trails off seemingly on purpose.

Lucas knits an eyebrow, wondering what was the end of that sentence, but has no time to linger on any of it.

Heather quickly makes herself known. "He certainly went from a balanced approach to an extreme where he wants to be there for everything in case something happens to her." She becomes very serious. "I recall when he didn't want her to use a hammer to install a frame because he thought it could potentially be dangerous."

Raven exhales soundly. "I just wish he would process his feelings better. I can see that it's hurting my mom." She pinches the bridge of her nose to keep calm. "I wonder if someday I will just learn that they separated because she couldn't take it anymore. She went through all of her cancer treatments probably not imagining this would be the aftermath."

"People all deal with sickness differently." Lucas pulls up the sleeves of his hoodie. "Your father was probably very afraid of losing your mother, and now that he has become aware that it was a real possibility—and also a finality because let's face it we'll all die someday—he overreacts in the worst ways to compensate."

"I agree. It's unhealthy at this point, but they both won't hear it." Raven smiles sadly. "They never want to talk about any of it, so I've been keeping my interactions to a minimum. I often try to call home during my dad's work shifts to chat with my mom alone."

Lucas feels privileged that she is candidly discussing her family issues with him. He intuitively extends his arm to drape it on the back of her chair. "What does your mother do for a living?"

"She's a music teacher." Raven smiles warmly at him. "She gives private piano lessons. She has about thirty students at the moment."

"That's amazing."

"It is." She reaches to grab her wine. "I always loved listening to my mom play in the evenings when I was young, it was the best way to fall asleep."

He watches her take a sip, never averting his gaze. "I bet it was."

"You know, once in a while she used to make her own versions of Billie Holiday songs." Raven angles toward him, and puts the glass in her lap. "When she was doing so, it was an instant favorite for me."

He half-smiles. "Now I understand your fondness for Billie."

She hums amusedly. "There are other very talented Billies."

"True." He scans her ocean pools intensely. "You never learned to play piano?"

"No." She trails her fingertips around the rim of her glass. "I never had any desire to, and my mom never forced me. Which I'm grateful for. I was mostly spending my days at the beach surfing."

"I can understand." Lucas drops his tone to a whisper of his own accord. "Nothing tops the feeling of riding waves, right?"

"Well..." She bites into her bottom lip. "I can think of something—or rather someone—else I rode that—"

Zoe clears her throat to catch their attention. "This is all very sweet, guys, but this biopsy also means that I can't eat anything past midnight so I'd very much like to eat that tiramisu you brought now."

Lucas and Raven both straighten automatically in their seats.

He clearly got carried away. It's becoming way too easy to do so around her.

"I'll go help you." Heather gets up. "It'll also give these two a moment alone."

The graphic designer strides inside. "Are you afraid that it might be dangerous to climb down the stairs?"

"Very funny." Heather catches up to her. "I swear to you that I'll never become like that."

Zoe stops, turns around and kisses her softly. "You better not," she murmurs against Heather's lips.

As they disappear to go fetch the dessert, Lucas' phone chimes in his pocket. He fetches it, looks at the caller ID, and puts it face down on the table without answering.

There's no way he's talking with Felipe at the moment, no more than when the analyst tried calling earlier when Lucas was in the first Uber with Raven.

Whatever his friend wants to discuss he can send a text, and Lucas will reply later.

When he has actual time.

Right now he only wants to enjoy this moment with—

Looking to his left, he sees that Raven got up, and is now standing at the end of the balcony near the railing. She looks deep in thought as she watches the ocean on the horizon.

He is dying to know what is going on in her head at the moment. He smoothly pads in her direction, stopping to stand just behind her. "Are you okay?"

"Yeah." She combs her fingers through her hair. "I'm glad to be here with you."

The softness in her tone only makes him want to hold her close.

He tentatively slides an arm in front of her to wrap it around her shoulders. She instantly leans back into him, curling her hand around his forearm, and letting her thumb gently caress his extensor muscle.

The fact that she welcomes his touch means more to him than she could possibly imagine.

He smiles while pressing his nose into her hair. "Me too," he whispers before laying a kiss on her temple.

He hears her sigh, staying silent.

He knows there's probably a thousand things running through her head. She probably won't tell him about any of them right now.

He doesn't mind.

He could spend all night enjoying the quiet with Raven like this. This sentiment of plenitude is nearly unknown to him.

That's what tells him she's unique.

Any potential other lover in her life, or plausible complications they might run through in the foreseeable future are inconsequential.

He has no idea what the week ahead will bring, but he has every intention to follow it wherever it leads.

Because the only certitude he holds is that it will begin and end with Raven.

And she is all that matters to him in this reality.

TWELVE

Reposeful Casualness

"You really think you have a chance at winning against me?" The eight year-old girl wearing a yellow graphic t-shirt, and turquoise floral sweatpants challenges Lucas from her spot on the sofa.

"I do." The managing director who is sitting on the floor with his back against the couch turns to look at her. "You've only beaten Raven out of pure luck." He fixes the charcoal cap on his head. "I'm an even more difficult adversary."

"When we visit some of my dad's family in Jamaica or my mom's in Memphis, I always win every racing tournament against my cousins." Sandy starts toying with the bantu knots on her head. "And I'm so good, I beat my friends here, too."

Lucas takes his phone out of his gray denim bermudas to put it on the coffee table. "Let's see if the trends continue then."

"I feel like I'd have to wish you good luck, but I'm not sure it would be enough," Raven calls out from the kitchen. "Sandy is good at this game, Lucas." She looks at him straightening his white shirt as he grabs a controller. "Don't underestimate her."

As soon as Lucas and herself asked the girl what she wanted to do this morning, her enthusiastic answer of gaming on Heather and Zoe's console couldn't be refused.

Raven understood soon enough that Sandy was a fierce opponent. It was probably no coincidence that she had expressed her desire to partake in that particular activity.

Now Lucas will go head to head against the young girl, and be able to see for himself.

It should be highly entertaining.

He flashes her a soft smile. "I won't."

Raven mirrors his expression as she rolls up the sleeve of her cardigan, and makes sure her black tank top is well tucked into her boyfriend cut jeans.

It's wonderful to see Lucas casually playing and interacting with Sandy. His friend Sabrina did mention that her son Connor loved him a lot when they visited her in Boston last week, but actually witnessing how good he is with children is heartwarming.

It's also not something someone would expect if they met him in New York. He has this way to put his serious and business-like side forward for the world to see back in Manhattan. This playful, relaxed, and more serene side of him he leaves tucked away.

He does let it out when alone with her—she's seen it plenty of time lately—but she's infinitely glad to see it shine more and more since yesterday with no barrier holding him back to let all his personality layers converge.

This is the Lucas she met in Mykonos. Just a few years older.

As she gathers all the ingredients to put together a quick mezze plate for a snack, she smiles inattentively.

She recalls how unguarded and handsome Lucas was when she climbed down the stairs earlier while he was still sleeping on the sofa.

A bright thistle colored throw was covering him except for his bare feet who were peeking out of the cover because of his height. His head was resting on the pillow Zoe had brought him before they all went to bed; his hair peeking out at odd angles from having finished drying while he was asleep.

She resisted the urge to crouch next to him, run her fingers through his black locks, and wake him up slowly.

Heather joined her in front of the fridge, finishing to put the back of her Jersey shirt into her high waisted light jeans. *He's wonderful to be around, and he is gorgeous,* she whispered as she stared at Lucas. *I can see why you were attracted to him.*

Raven didn't think much before answering. *I still am.*

The way he looks at you tells me it is very much reciprocal, my friend. Haddy kept her voice low. *I told you before, but I'll say it again: life is short. If you both crave each other that much, enjoy it while it can last.*

He's phenomenal, but he's also on a very different path than me. She shifted her gaze from Lucas' sleeping form to her friend. *I left my job because I couldn't deal with shady practices and power games anymore. On the contrary, he is in the middle of all of that, and he doesn't seem to want to back off.*

So what? Heather shrugged, opening a cupboard to get some plates. *Having incompatible life goals was never a deal breaker for you before. You can still have fun, and—*

Raven cut her off. *That's the whole problem. He feels too good.* She inhaled deeply, leaning against the counter. *I feel differently when I'm with him. I'm scared that if I have sex with him repeatedly I'll want more than what he's willing to give.* She furrowed her eyebrows. *Or that we'll end up tearing each other apart because we want very different things out of life.*

Haddy smiled teasingly. *Then just have sex once?*

Are you insane? She chuckled quietly, looking at her friend in fake horror. *You truly think I'd be able to sleep with him just once?*

Just trying to help here. Heather snorted. *If you want my honest opinion, don't let irrational fears stop you from pursuing what you want.* She stood in front of Raven. *Truth is, you have no idea what could happen. None of us can.* She locked eyes with her. *Sure you can end up feeling more than what you were ready to allow yourself to, but maybe it's worth it?* She sounded very solemn and supportive at once. *Don't let Nathan define your life forever.*

Raven hummed absentmindedly. *I was thinking of going surfing later. I missed Black's Beach a whole lot.*

Her friend curved a playful corner of her mouth upward. *The waves or the nudists there? I recall a man who was set on showing us that his dick was way longer than average. You seemed unimpressed.*

Very funny. As if you were awestruck at all either. She laughed lightly. *Apart from that isolated incident, I always thought it was a fun mix to have surfers and nudists alike on that semi recluse beach.*

Heather grabbed a bag of coffee beans. *You're going to bring Lucas with you?*

I'm certainly going to ask him if he wants to. Raven smiled shyly. *I'd love to surf with him.*

He can borrow one of my boards in the garage if he wants to. Haddy fetched some cups from a shelf. *If he doesn't like them, he can ask our neighbors. Danek has multiple boards, too, so I'm sure he wouldn't mind. Especially since I remember you telling me that Lucas was an experienced surfer. Probably won't damage a board.*

Thank you. I'll let him know. Raven analyzed her friend's demeanor as she walked around the kitchen. *How are you this morning?* She opened the pantry. *With Zoe's biopsy coming up and all.*

I'm trying to stay hopeful. Until we have more news there's no need to anticipate, right? With Zoe, we agreed to take one step at a time. Heather stopped, putting her palms flat on the kitchen island. *Having you around is great. Zoe talked to me a little last night before going to sleep. She hadn't done that in a week.* She smiled gently at Raven. *When she said that she was happy that you are here, she wasn't kidding. I think we all missed you more than we realized. You bring a sense of normalcy with you that we desperately needed.*

I'm also very happy to be here. She faced Heather. *Even more so that I'll be around when you get updates this week. I was feeling very disconnected being in New York while you guys are going through all of that. I had to do something about it.*

Her friend spontaneously hugged her. *I love you so much, Raven.* She squeezed her a bit tighter. *Thank you for flying here.*

I love you, too, Haddy. Raven held her close. *You guys will get through this, you'll see.*

As she now puts a skillet on the gas stove to preheat it, Raven hopes that everything is going well for her friends at the medical center.

They haven't talked about it, but she knows that Zoe despises hospitals.

The graphic designer lost both of her parents at a very young age following a car accident. Every time she talks about it, the trauma of having waited for hours in the aseptic waiting room only to be told that there was nothing doctors could do to save them is palpable. Moreover, since her parents had no will at the time of their death, Zoe ended up in limbo until the court decided who was best suited to become her legal guardian. The absence of living grandparents made matters worse, as well as all her aunts and uncles on both sides not wanting to get custody. Some close friends of her parents were finally officially allowed to welcome her into their family after years of drama and legal battles.

To Zoe, all of this started because of what happened in that hospital waiting room, and so for years, she had panic attacks upon setting foot into any medical building. Therapy helped a lot on that front, but things are still challenging.

Raven thinks that it must be slight torture for Zoe to have to go through all those scans and procedures. Heather's wife is very courageous to overcome her distress to get a diagnosis and then be treated appropriately.

The racing game's bright and jovial sound effects reach Raven's ears as she brushes both sides of some pitas with her freshly made mix of olive oil and za'atar.

Sandy's joyful voice soon fills the space. "You really thought that taking Duchess Sunflowers would be a good choice to win?"

"Yes." Lucas is focussed on the screen as he maneuvers his motorcycle. "I love that her special abilities in this game are based on flowery spells. Plus, she was one of the most difficult characters to unlock in the previous console version of this."

"A past console?" The girl makes a disgusted face. "You're old."

"Excuse me?" He acts fakely hurt at her comment. "Old? I'm certain your parents have gamed on those earlier consoles, too."

"It doesn't count." Sandy shrugs nonchalantly. "My parents are old, too."

Lucas chuckles, deciding to push it further. "So when do people start to be old?"

"I don't know." The little girl frowns, pressing on a button to propel a coconut at a vehicle in the game. "High school."

Lucas smiles amusedly, making his character accelerate. "So people in college are like elders?"

Sandy giggles. "You're funny."

"Just trying to make sense of your reasoning." Lucas moves the joystick of his controller to make a sharp turn. "I might finish this race in front of you, little driving wizard."

"There's still one lap left." The girl leans toward the screen more, letting her competitive side show. "Would you accept a bet?"

"What are you thinking?"

"If I win, you accept one dare from me."

"Sounds legit." He concentrates on dodging a mud puddle. "What if I win?"

Sandy remains serious. "I will play the next tournament with Duchess Sunflowers even if I find her dull."

"Deal." Lucas puffs his chest a little. "Prepare to be amazed by the power of flowers."

Raven chuckles as she toasts the pitas in the pan. "Don't take your victory for granted, Lucas."

He shushes her teasingly. "I'm focussing here." He half-smiles. "Sandy is going to love driving with the Duchess."

"I prefer my character." The girl stays unflinching. "He looks like Peter Pan. I love Peter Pan."

"Because he wants to stay young?" Lucas drives through a tunnel. "Since you seem to have something against old people." Sandy laughs brightly. Lucas beams. "You know, when I was young, I would read bedtime stories to my sister. One of her favorites was the old Peter Pan books. I would never read her the ending because the original tale is pretty dark, but she loved the imagery."

"You have a sister?"

"Yep. Her name's Lena." He cashes in on a powerup he collected. "She's six years younger than me, and she's currently filming a documentary in Brazil."

"That's so cool."

"I think so, too. I'm very proud of her." He inclines his head up in Sandy's direction. "She's also the one who gave me this hat."

Raven feels like commenting "It suits you well. You had it for a while, right?" She seasons the Greek yogurt. "I'm basing my observation on the worn out fabric."

She has to admit that seeing him in casual attire, and looking as peaceful, is making him even more attractive to her.

At every moment, he's a perfect blend of kind, tender, strong-willed, funny, and smart. Every fiber of her being is drawn to him.

Heather is right. Life is short. She can't repress the—

Lucas' reply instantly brings her back to the present. "Lena gave it to me when we went to Australia together." He smiles coyly. "As you probably noticed, it's been my favorite cap to wear ever since."

Sandy looks pleased with herself as she gets a boost herself by executing a risky maneuver. "Do you have any brothers or sisters, Raven?"

"No." She takes out the hummus. "I'm an only child."

The young girl grins. "Like me!"

"Yes." Raven puts roasted red peppers, tomatoes, and olives on the serving board. "Like you."

Lucas takes the last turn before the finish line. "I know you briefly mentioned it before, but you truly never wished you had someone in your corner growing up?"

"I had friends for that my whole life." Raven cuts and divides the toasted pitas. "Some siblings don't go together well either. I never had the chance to know if I would've had a nice relationship with any potential brothers or sisters, but I'm very at peace with having navigated life with my found family."

"That's nice. When my dad left, I felt even more responsible for my sister, and so I—" He trails off as his character gets overtaken by Sandy's, who activated her special power. "Hey! That's unfair," he shouts at the screen in incredulity while she finishes first.

The girl beams beside him, jumping off the couch, and walking to her backpack resting on the console in the entrance. "I won!"

"The algorithm helped you win." He frowns, speaking loudly so Sandy can hear him. "It wasn't a clean win."

Raven snorts. "As if this racing game's wins are not always hard-fought to begin with." She pushes the plates on the side of the island with the stools. "The snack is ready by the way."

"True. This game is evil." Lucas gets up, striding toward the kitchen. "I love it, but it has a way to get under my skin."

Raven tilts her head in questioning. "Do you own any gaming consoles?"

"I had one, but I was barely using it so I gave it to Kyan." He takes a seat in front of her. "Sometimes I'd like to play more. Time is what is lacking in my life."

"You can always make time, no?" She scans his features. "It's like guitar. You played again, and it felt good. Gaming could be the same."

"I will definitely always try to make time for the important things in life." He locks eyes with her. "And I can think of a few that would be more vital than gaming."

"Oh, yeah?" She pulls her bottom lip between her teeth, leaning forward, and putting her elbows on the counter. "Like what?"

He smiles tenderly. "Well, if we were together, I would certainly—" He trails off as he shifts his stare to Sandy who is climbing on a stool, a unicorn manicure set resting in her lap. "You're going to paint your nails?"

"No." The girl shakes her head. "I'm going to paint yours."

He chuckles lightly. "Oh, really?"

"Yes." Sandy nods vigorously. "I won so you owe me a dare. I want to paint your nails."

He hums. "Fair enough."

The girl gets some bottles out of her kit, placing them on the island. "Which color do you want?"

He swiftly examines them before turning to Raven, raising an inquiring brow. "Which one do you think would suit me best?"

She makes a show to reflect really hard while assessing the choices in front of her. "Sparkly pink?"

"Extra sparkly!" Sandy squeals.

Lucas smiles at her excitement. "You ladies think I can pull off extra sparkly nail polish?"

"Mhmm." Raven dives into his emerald gaze. "You can pull off anything. You're always sexy."

As Lucas sighs, Sandy alternates her stare between him and Raven. "Are you two together?"

"No." Raven shakes her head, half-smiling. "We aren't."

Lucas doesn't avert his eyes from Raven. "Not yet."

"Not *yet*?" Raven frowns confusedly. "What are you—"

The young girl takes Lucas' hand to put it flat on the island next to the polish. "You would be cute together."

"Did you hear that, Raven?" He acts proud. "We would be *cute*."

Raven points at his nails being painted. "Cute and glittery."

He wiggles his eyebrows at the same time he taps his fingers on the surface. "I'd definitely be ready to dazzle you."

Sandy puts her hand flat on top of his, exhaling loudly. "Stay still."

"Yes ma'am." He clears his throat to sound serious. "Sorry. I'm being undisciplined."

Raven hums comprehensively, dipping a slice of pita in the hummus. "It's probably because you're old."

"Yes." The young girl giggles. "That's exactly why."

Lucas falsely gasps. "Are you two teaming up against me?"

Raven takes a bite, an amused spark illuminating her eye. "I would never dare."

As Lucas smiles softly at her, she feels a smooth warmth spread along her spine, and lets the faint music leaking through the small radio in the corner near the sink wash over her.

Every moment with Lucas feels natural. There's no denying it. She's been constantly reminded of it every time they find themselves together.

She recalls how amazing it felt last night when he spontaneously slid his arm around her to press himself into her back. Her body instinctively followed the lead of her mind to melt in his embrace.

Even if she was reflecting on a thousand things at once in that instant—wondering if her dad would ever evolve past his trauma, if Heather and Zoe would get on the other side of this ordeal they are living through stronger or weaker than before, if she herself would find any rhyme or reason to her life moving forward—Lucas managed to soothe her by holding her close.

Truth is, she always got by really well on her own, and never needed anyone to smoothen any hurdles or questionings she might've had through life so far.

But she was glad that Lucas silently agreed to share the quiet with her until her friends came back with the tiramisu. She recalls having wanted to stay in his arms for hours.

When he pulled away, she instantly missed his body heat along her back, and his steady breathing into her hair.

Which is unlike her.

Each moment with him reconnects her with a bliss she thought had vanished from her existence a long time ago.

But this right here is a surprise.

She didn't expect to take care of a child with him anytime soon, and for the endeavor to feel so normal.

She lifts a corner of her mouth upward seeing him marvel at the nails of his right hand that Sandy just finished painting.

Maybe Lucas is showing her one event at a time that they could overcome everything life can throw at them.

If it was anyone else other than him, she would've already given in to temptation.

She would've jumped head first.

She wouldn't even have looked back once.

Maybe it's time she fully accepts that part of herself that yearns for Lucas, and sees where it leads. She vowed to herself no later than yesterday to go with the flow, after all.

This is the biggest leap of faith she could take to live by her oath.

Past her concerns, she ought to be true to herself.

As Lucas puts a cherry tomato in his mouth with his free hand, looking directly at her while making slightly muted filthy sounds, something tells her that he would probably be more than willing to take that leap with her.

And a part of her is dying to know where they would end up.

When Jun steps out of the private elevator in her Manhattan offices to the thumping beat playing in her headphones, she straightens the jacket of her bright green suit, and smiles warmly.

She always liked to wear solid colored suits. It quickly became her signature around the city. People know at a glance who she is just by her clothing.

She loves it.

As her black stilettos echo against the concrete flooring, she takes a look around to notice that mostly everyone left a few hours ago already, or just didn't come in. It's Sunday, after all. Only she, and a few others, are zealously dedicated to their work to the point of working on weekends.

She knows that, for one, her employees with families won't ever be around on those days, and it's perfect. She wants all of them to have a great work/life balance. Which is also why she instigated the policy where everyone is free to make their own schedule.

As long as their work is done, she's not one to complain. The whole arrangement works wonderfully well, and people are grateful for the leeway they get from it.

She thinks that she could also benefit from it if she truly wanted to.

At first she was working long hours to build her company, and make herself known. Then it became a habit to bring some work home.

Her ex-boyfriend would despise it.

She recalls that after a few arguments she saw the validity of his points, and ended up taking some days off here and there.

But old habits die hard. She got back into her pattern soon enough, which led to complications in her relationship, and a break-up.

Maybe it was insecurity making her always throw herself into her work. She wanted her business to thrive and grow so much that she had forgotten about living for herself.

With Gary she thought that maybe she would have a new chance at it, but the moment it threatened to become too serious, he backed off.

Although, they're going out to dinner tonight. Raven is potentially right. Maybe it *is* a date.

Even if she keeps insisting that it's *not* a date to Raven, Jun honestly can't think of another reason why the driver would've invited her. She doesn't want to get her hopes up, but logic points to it probably being one. He sounded solemn when he asked, which tells her that he wants to discuss something important. But he could easily hand in his resignation in person at her office. He could address anything while driving her. He obviously wanted a more personal setting.

This must surely mean that—

She breathes in.

She has to focus.

She starts absentmindedly humming to the music.

Crooning under her breath, she pushes her existential questioning away as she navigates toward her office situated on the far south corner of the building.

Years later, she still loves what she made out of the space. It's modern without being too cold. She thinks it's welcoming, and full of spirit thanks to the multiple programmers working by writing on the whiteboards walls every time they have an idea to share. The small research and analysis laboratory at the end of the hallway is her pride. The forensic scientists she recruited to work there are amongst the best at what they do, and they bring a new dimension to every case her team works on.

This whole community vibe of brainstorming, and building on each other's works is precious to her.

When she founded her company, she wanted to try to make a difference for people who were going through a crisis situation, but didn't have a lot of options offered to them. Society can be harsh, and she's been striving to bring a little hope to people facing the kind of hardships which can unequivocally destroy their lives or careers—or both—unwarrantedly.

Her programming background comes in handy more often than not, but she would be nothing without her multidisciplinary team. Through the years, she also made contacts with outside companies and agencies, and she's proud to be a household name in her niche field because of the hard work everyone has put on for every case.

If most of her clients are from the entertainment industry dealing with looming image crises or social media menaces carried on by obsessed fans, she occasionally has to deal with businessmen and women as well as politicians for the same kind of issues.

Investigating, interrogating, digging deeper into each piece of evidence they receive, and putting the pieces of the puzzle together to help their clients brings her a sure satisfaction. Creating software, and troubleshooting code when she was solely a programmer never had that effect.

She receives dozens of requests per week, but single-handedly picks only the ones she believes in. She doesn't want to get involved in debatable endeavors.

When Lucas contacted her, she saw the opportunity for her company to continue to expand its horizons. He works in finances, and didn't seem ready to cross the red line to please one of his clients. He sounded exactly like the type of individual she wants to help on a daily basis.

She never thought his case would become that intricate.

As the last of the lyrics echo in her ear, she reaches the door to her office. She positions her eye for the retina scanner next to the frame.

It's another thing she takes pride in: the high-tech custom security they got installed for their whole floor.

Their workplace is located in an industrial building which is owned by one of Jun's friends who runs a non-profit organization. They use the place mostly as a warehouse for shipments, and some scattered offices. Most of the floors are unoccupied by the organization except for the ground and the second one.

Jun signed a lease for the top two floors as soon as she needed an address for her activities.

Hamasaki Mastermind Management's floor is only accessible through a private lift dubbed of a fingerprint scanner, and a six-digit numerical code that changes each week. She didn't want to take the chance that any information they stumbled upon while working on cases would be made public or could be leaked. Their clients hire them because they value their privacy, and want to deal quietly with their troubles, after all. Having an easily accessible office would kill the purpose of caring about the private intel they gather.

Every employee has a thorough background check run on them from the get-go, and Jun vowed to herself that she would keep her roster small. No more than twelve individuals at a time. Whatever they can't achieve on their own they can ask their outside contacts for.

The beauty of collaboration.

As soon as the door slides open, she steps inside her minimalistic decorated office, smiling at the mid afternoon sun peeking through the oversized mirrored windows.

She loves that the exterior of those panels are reflecting for anyone looking from the outside. No one can see inside while she can observe her surroundings at any time of the day.

Upon striding forward, she notices a bright yellow flash staring back at her in her parallel vision. A quick assessment of her surroundings makes her see a note beside her feet.

She squints her eyes.

It's from one of the best hackers on her team. She picks it up from the ground as she walks toward her oak and black modular desk.

Go check the new folder I shared with you. I think you need to hear all of it. It might be a game changer. Pw: Tin042Foil*

PS. Make sure you're securely logged in.

Cheers,

Gam

She snorts.

Graham is a huge sci-fi fan. He always makes fun of movies where the protagonists fabric hats to block foreign electric fields from reading their minds. In that context, the password he created makes total sense.

She automatically boots her computer while taking a seat in her custom designed ergonomic desk chair. She spins around to quickly assess that her birch side console, industrial bar cart, metal file cabinets, and the landscape pictures on her walls are all exactly where they should be.

She's not going to lie to herself by thinking that since she heard about Lucas' office having been searched thoroughly—and the following threats that ensued—it hasn't changed her level of awareness. Even with top-of-the-line security protocols, she feels as if it could still happen to her at any moment.

Better be vigilant.

She faces her computer again. Another rapid retina scan later, she's connected to her internal server, and identifies the folder Graham told her about.

She opens it without delay.

A bunch of audio files are classified by date in it, all labeled as being from Gabriel Smith official personal devices. She mentioned to the hacker that Smith could have other less easily traceable ones, but having access to those is a great start.

She switches the connection of her earphones from her phone to her computer, and presses 'Play' on the first recording.

The people talking are using clever metaphors, but Jun knows her way enough around those to know that in reality they're discussing trafficking, and—

As soon as she hears his interlocutor mention a specific name, she curses. She can't believe that this theory is confirming itself.

She has to tell Lucas. Raven won't be pleased.

She inhales deeply.

She'll take her time to listen to all of the files, go to her dinner, and then decide on the best way to break the news.

No matter what is in the other recordings, she wants to gather as much information as possible before acting on it.

It's not as if they need to act in a hurry. The wheels are already in motion one way or another.

They have to be rational.

She's certain that they can outsmart their opponents.

THIRTEEN

The Harmony of Surrender

As Lucas surfs the perfect barrels of Black's Beach at sunset in his black long-sleeved wetsuit, he feels free. Getting barreled over and over for the last hour or so has been highly liberating.

The waves keep coming, and he doesn't stop committing to ride them.

While he maneuvers the white shortboard with a painted octopus on it he borrowed from Heather through a smaller than usual tube, he sets on keeping his shoulders square and open toward the exit as he bends his knees a little more.

He loves it.

Those are easily amongst the best waves he's ever surfed in his life. They are beautifully challenging, and definitely not for beginners. Even with his extensive experience, he got wiped two times so far mainly because he pushed himself a little too much. He became bold after a while. The ocean reminded him that he needed to tread within his own limits.

No matter how skilled he might be, he's not invincible.

This is one of the multiple reasons why he adores surfing. It has a way to bring him back to channel what's essential to keep thriving.

He's glad that he packed his attire to be ready to comply with any surfing request. The waters of SoCal are certainly chilly enough year round to justify wearing a wetsuit.

Most of all, he's beyond happy that Raven dared ask him to accompany her.

Once he's out of the tunnel, a quick look around makes him identify her nearby in her gray, black and pink wetsuit. The broad smile she harbors as she also surfs the barrels is a good indication that she is enjoying herself.

Lucas' beams to himself in return.

He adores seeing her like this.

From the very moment he woke up this morning until now, his day has been nothing but marvelous. It's in great parts because of Raven. She made babysitting Sandy super fun, getting ready for surfing wonderful, and driving to the beach was a pure delight.

Although Heather and Zoe told them they could stay for the evening, they decided to give the couple some time alone, and let Zoe rest. The graphic designer looked positively exhausted from her one-day procedure.

Plus, Raven wanted to go surfing in addition to going to her house after. She said that she missed her own bed.

Lucas can recall that feeling the coastal breeze on his face when they drove into La Jolla listening to upbeat music in Raven's car put him in the best mood.

Such a nice California vibe to this song, he stated, letting the wind glide through his digits that he was holding out of the open window.

The band is from Los Angeles, so it makes sense. She grinned at him. *I love their sound on some of their tunes. Especially when I'm back home like this.*

He looked up at the sky, enjoying the sun on his skin. *I can see why.*

They were on an episode of this show where celebrities spontaneously talk and sing as they navigate the city a while back. She shifted gears. *It was a very fun one.*

He redirected his attention to Raven. *Love that show.*

Right? Raven looked cheerful. *Every time I get the chance, I watch it live.* She half-smiled, reflecting. *When I was working, I would spend most of my weekends digging into files, and preparing for trials. It was a breath of fresh air to put it in the background for those nights.*

He hummed comprehensively. *The job has a way to occupy every single ounce of free time we might have, right?*

She merged onto North Torrey Pine Road. *It's like we were saying this morning: you have to make time for what you want.*

He felt like asking. *Would you say that after one week after your resignation you feel better about where your life is headed?*

Well, I'm definitely not as busy as before, which should give me some time to think things through, but I barely did that yet. I still have no idea what I want to do moving forward. My only certitude is that I don't want to go back to the same system I left.

You think it's possible to fully escape it?

I do. She inhaled deeply. *There's options out there, and if someone puts their minds to it, I feel like it's all very attainable. I gotta stay hopeful.*

Here's somewhere your stubbornness might come in handy. He sounded encouraging. *You still have time to find something that you like.*

Yeah. She took a quick look in the rearview mirror. *Jun offered me a position at her company. I'm thinking about it.*

That would be great, no? He smiled warmly. *You two seem to be working really well together.*

We are. She became very solemn. *But if I'm being honest, a big part of me also doesn't know if I want to stay in New York at all. Except for Jun, there's nothing really keeping me there.*

Against his better judgment, he couldn't stop the words from getting out. *There's also me. I'd hate for you to go.*

She smiled shyly, and stayed silent.

He instantly regretted having said that on a whim. It's nothing but the truth, but if she's feeling like New York doesn't feel like home anymore, it's certainly not him that will be able to convince her otherwise.

Which is totally normal. She should do whatever feels good to her. That's the most important thing. He'll be happy if she is.

Plus, they are not together. They only made-out once since they got into each other's lives again.

Even if everything feels natural with her, those small moments can't be enough for her to consider him to be part of the equation of her future.

He listened to the music some more before deciding to change the topic in an attempt at clearing out the awkwardness. *I feel like I'm twenty years-old again right now.*

It seemed to work. She chuckled. *How were you when you were twenty?*

A little more carefree, and a whole lot more fun. He ran his fingers through his hair. *At least that's what my sister always says. You met me in my early twenties. Maybe you can tell me how I was.*

You were indeed very relaxed. Raven bit into her bottom lip. *You've always had this laid-back energy that paired well with your determination and drive. It made you instantly irresistible.*

He smirked. *Irresistible, huh?*

Mhmm. She quickly glanced at him. *There's a reason why I never managed to get you out of my head, Lucas. Multiple reasons actually.*

After the slight unease he had created, he chose to stir the conversation into another direction instead of flirting back like he would've usually done. *Oh, and I had a steady girlfriend when I was twenty. But we parted ways to pursue internships, and the distance didn't help us.*

What happened?

I guess we realized that what we had wasn't really solid to begin with. He shrugged. *We were having fun, but that was about it. She slept with someone else during that summer, and we decided to split.*

I'm so sorry.

It's fine. We don't talk a whole lot these days, but we broke up on good terms. It just wasn't meant to be, honestly.

Raven frowned. *I'm still kinda wondering how she could—*

He couldn't help himself from cutting her off. *You're saying that you don't understand how she could've wanted someone else than me?*

It sounds awfully humble of you to think that, but yes, that's what I was going to say. She nodded. *For having been with you a little, and knowing you, I would've never done that. I feel like it would've been dumb to just throw all of this out the window if we had been seriously dating at the time. You were crazy good in bed, amazing to discuss with, you made me laugh as well as felt supportive like no other.*

His heart skipped a beat at the way she casually admitted all of that. He was surprisingly left speechless.

Word sparing he can do.

Flirt with innuendos and vivid images of what he'd like to do with her is second nature to him.

Genuine deep confessions always hit differently.

Thank you, he whispered back for lack of a better and more meaningful answer coming to his mind.

Plus, I don't really get the whole cheating thing in general. She furrowed her eyebrows, shrugging. *If you're craving someone else, be honest and tell your partner about it. Don't lie to their face while you're fucking another. If so, just make it clear that you're not into a serious relationship or want a polyamorous one from the start so everyone knows where to stand.*

Agreed.

The song soon shifted to one of the hits from last summer about breakups and female empowerment, and Raven sighed heavily. It prompted him to listen closely to the lyrics.

He analyzed her expression before daring to ask her about the flash of despondence and the clear resolve painting her features. *This resonates with you?*

It does. She smiled pensively. *I feel every line deep within my soul. You get burned badly enough one time, and you realize that you don't only not want to go through that anymore, but it's also not worth it to. You can get by by yourself perfectly well.*

He curved a corner of his mouth upward. *You've always been strongly independent anyway, no?*

Yeah. She looked deep in thought. *But at some point I was ready to go all in with a relationship to see what the fuss of being stronger together is all about, you know? I thought I loved him enough to do that. To go the distance, and not just put myself and my work first because we would've been a team.*

Nathan? he asked tentatively.

Mhmm, she confirmed dismissively. *As I said, been there, done that. Going through such bullshit is not worth it to me anymore.* Her expression tensed. *Unless you're with someone who makes the balance between blissful happiness and potential pain worth it. Then I guess committing could work.*

He stared at her. *You ever felt that?*

No. She sounded unconvinced. She rapidly added, *Maybe? I don't know. I've been pretty good at not feeling anything the past few years.*

Maybe somebody will sweep you off your feet someday. He refrained from saying that he wished it was him. That he would like to have a shot at being that person she'll abandon herself to again and again. *Then, you'll feel that maybe the plausible hurt you might encounter because of letting yourself feel something is indeed worth it. That life is a balance, and one feeling can't exist without its counterpart.*

Says the guy who's never getting attached himself.

Oh, but I would be willing to do it for the right person, I'm sure. His voice was determined as he kept thinking out loud. *When the thought of not having a particular someone in your life becomes unbearable, you know you have to do something about it. So you commit, and accept that you are better together than apart. At least that's what I think happens in such circumstances.*

A teasing smile was dancing on her lips. *So you never felt that way either?*

No. He found himself funny to also throw her own words back at her. *Maybe?*

You're hilarious using my own answer against me. She chuckled once more. *Well played.*

He grinned. *I try my best.*

Well, keep some mental energy for surfing. She smiled amusedly. *What you're going to encounter at Black's Beach is nearly unique.*

Not long after they reached the South Beach Lot of the Torrey Pines State Natural Reserve Parking, changed into their wetsuits, grabbed the portable shower along with their boards, and started walking toward the beach.

Even if it's a nearly three mile walk to get to the water, he can now affirm without a doubt that the experience is worth everything.

Raven was right. Those waves are something else.

Having replayed parts of their car discussion in his head through the last double-ups, he can wholly appreciate how Raven opened up to him a bit more.

He still has no idea exactly what happened to her, but Nathan clearly hurt her badly when she seemingly had given him a part of her heart. Lucas can't blame her for having put up walls around herself.

She's also right: she is the type to be able to get by just fine on her own. Just like him.

But he knows deep within himself that what Raven and him share could—

He furrows a brow as he sees her get back on the shore in the distance. He automatically sets out to join her.

There's no use staying in the ocean if Raven has decided to take a break or go home altogether. Maybe she's also starting to be hungry. They haven't eaten since lunchtime, after all.

When he steps onto the sand, he looks around only to realize that there's a few surfers still in the water, and no more than a dozen people on the beach.

The sun is dawning on the horizon, its pinkish shades bathing the whole sky into a fiery lavish blaze.

Raven is standing beside their portable shower, letting her damp hair loose from her ponytail, and looking gorgeous beyond words as it cascades down her shoulders.

This right here feels as close to perfection as he ever dared dream living through. Nothing could bother the serenity running through his veins at the moment.

Raven smiles brightly at him as he approaches. "Hey, you. You liked the waves?"

"They were incredible. I could've kept surfing them for hours." He instantly beams at her. "I also saw you attack some of those barrels. You're captivating."

She brushes off the compliment. "Want to rinse the sea water off before we go back to the car, and go grab a bite?"

He stops a few feet in front of her. "With pleasure."

She swiftly uses the hose on herself before giving it to him so he can do the same.

While he does so, she unzips the top of her wetsuit to let it dangle at her waist.

His grip tightens on the nuzzle before he stills completely.

He sighs involuntarily.

He is utterly enthralled at the sight in front of him.

He tried his best to not peek too much at her in her black bikini with multicolored tropical flowers as she was putting on her wetsuit on top of it by the car earlier, but now it's completely impossible not to.

Her flawless curves are on full display, and there's a mermaid tattoo peeking out tantalizingly from under the top of her swimsuit and around her rib cage.

The hues from the vanishing sun rays are reflecting on her bare skin like shimmering diamonds.

Her perfectly rounded breasts are following the heaving of her chest as she tries to regularize her breathing.

Her lips are slightly parted, glistening in the late afternoon light, and inviting him to just kiss her as if his life is depending on it.

A single water droplet is sliding down her throat to disappear in her cleavage, and he wishes it was his mouth mapping that trail instead.

Judging by Raven's expression as she reaches to take back the hose, he's probably not doing a very good job at hiding his interest.

She chuckles softly. "Want some help?"

She doesn't let him answer before she starts pouring warm fresh water on him from head to toe. Once she's done it once, he does the same as her, and removes the top of his wetsuit, only keeping the bottom part on.

She continues rinsing him gently. She seems set on taking all her time to do so. Her eyes are painting his torso, and he can feel himself slowly losing control.

He curls his hands by his sides to refrain from reaching out to her.

She smiles shyly at him. "I used to come here every few days when I was living in San Diego." She starts defining his chest idly with her fingertips as the water ripples down its ridges and valleys. "I miss it greatly. And I'm sure you can now understand why." She shifts the spray to his hair for a second, scratching his abs lightly. "You know, this beach has seen some intense action from me through the years."

He can't stop his muscles from twitching under her touch. "All kinds of action?" He peers into her eyes, smiling tenderly. "Not only surfing?"

"Mostly surfing and sunbathing." She pulls her bottom lip between her teeth, combing her fingers through his black locks to rinse them well. "The rest is illegal, Lucas. Who do you think I am?"

He purrs. "Raven Collins." He grabs her hips. "The woman who lives rent free in my mind at every hour of every day."

She drops the hose, curling her hand into the waistband of his swimsuit, pulling him to her. "Really?" she breathes out.

"Mhmm."

She skims her nose along his, rolling her lip between her teeth. "And what do you want to do about it?"

He groans. "I want to fuck your brains out."

She captures his bottom lip, whispering, "What are you waiting for, then?"

As she kisses him leisurely with her nails scratching the short hair at the nape of his neck, and her body slowly molding into his, he cradles her head to feel her even closer.

It's astounding how every time their lips collide, she's the perfect blend of intensity and softness.

How she effortlessly rules over his whole body.

Her hand gliding down dangerously close to his ass is making him growl against her tongue.

Her delicate moan in response makes him automatically grind into her, and her delicious whimper deep into his mouth at his movement prompts him to kiss her even more passionately.

He could make out with her forever.

She's fucking unmatched.

The second he circles her rib cage, she arches into him, seeking friction. It transcends his blood flow to send his mind spinning.

She's truly making him feel like he's the only one able to have that effect on her.

The only one she moans like that with.

That no one else will ever—

He leans back, slightly out of breath. "Were you responding to William like this?"

"William?" She blinks in surprise. "What are you—"

He curls his hand around her throat, letting his thumb define her jawline. "You slept with William that night when I got to your apartment."

She shakes her head steadily. "I didn't."

He raises a brow in incredulity. "You didn't?"

"No." She kisses the underside of his mandible, grazing the pads of her fingers up along his spine. "I did call him because I had the intention to." She sighs against his scruff. "I thought you were going to hook up with a random stranger."

He smoothly rakes his fingers through her damp ash brown locks. "So picturing me pleasuring someone else made you lose it?"

"Mhmm." She lays open-mouthed kisses up his jugular. "And apparently imagining William's hands caressing me made you go mad?"

He exhales soundly as his only answer.

She brushes her nose below his ear. "I just couldn't have sex with him," she murmurs.

He puts his palm flat on the small of her back. "What stopped you?"

She lightly sucks on his earlobe. "He wasn't *you*."

He groans as he caresses her scalp finely. "He wasn't—"

She interjects briskly. "I wanted *your* hands on my body." She runs her digits through the longer strands at the back of his head. "*Your* tongue in my mouth." She leans back to lock eyes with him. "Feeling *your* cock as you—" She effectively trails off as she purposely rocks into him lasciviously. "I wanted *you*, Lucas." She ghosts her lips over his. "I still do." He feels her barely audibly moan in the infinitesimal space between them. "I want you so bad," she whispers.

His brain is fuzzy, but he remembers her past concerns that they never addressed. He traces her clavicle with his index and middle fingers. "You're sure?" The way she hums as she kisses him sensually tells him all he needs to know. He groans once more, letting his hands slip under her wetsuit and onto her ass. He has to make her understand one thing. "I want to take my time with you, Raven."

She presses herself flush to him, smiling. "Wanna go to my place?" Her tone is sultry as she traces his bottom lip with her thumb. "You think you can make me scream in ecstasy all night?"

As he kisses the pad of her finger, he can feel himself responding to her in strides.

Having her in his arms right now is already playing a number on his psyche. He can't begin to imagine how elated he will be to explore every inch of her body lazily on each surface of her house she'll allow him to.

He undeniably wants to take hours to make it good for her.

He wants for her to end up fabulously spent beside him as the dawn breaks through the windows.

There's nothing in this world he wants more than to hear Raven come apart repeatedly under his ministrations.

As he's the one crashing his mouth to hers to make his intentions clear, he can feel that the peak of darkness is going to be nothing short of sublime tonight.

Sleep is overrated. They can make better use of the night.

Fourteen

Drunk On Bliss

As Raven reaches the front door of her home in Neptune Place in La Jolla, she feels Lucas press himself into her back as he buries his nose into her hair.

She sighs.

She is aware that his hands are otherwise occupied. He graciously volunteered to carry up both their luggages to her house from the parking garage. She still can't wait to feel his touch on her as soon as they step inside.

She wants to melt into him.

She wants to do it soon.

It's all because of the little irresistible things he does since they left the beach.

It's how he gently slid his hand into hers as they were walking back to her car earlier.

How he kissed her tenderly when she had finished buttoning her shorts, and was putting on her cardigan directly on top of her bikini by the car.

How he only kept his swimsuit on, and didn't bother fastening up his white shirt completely, displaying his chiseled chest flawlessly.

How he stole touches all through the drive, toying with loose strands of her damp hair that was drying off in the wind.

The delicateness and consideration in every one of his movements made her briefly contemplate just stopping on the side of the road so he could make her arch underneath him on the hood of her car.

She decided against it, but every time he would smile softly her resolve was faltering a little bit more.

It was about time they reached her house.

"So the property is a co-ownership?" he breathes out next to her ear.

"Mhmm." She unlocks the door. "It's so close to the ocean that I couldn't care less about the fact that there's four units here, and that I don't have my own big backyard." She smiles coyly. "I'm sure you'll enjoy the private balcony with a Pacific view as if you were sitting directly on Windansea beach."

It's his turn to sigh. "If it involves you snuggling up with me on it, I already know that I'll adore it."

She hums as she walks past the threshold to then flip two switches on to bathe the whole first floor in a warm glow as she removes her shoes.

A quick look around makes her feel instantly peaceful.

She missed the vanishing windows walls that transform indoor spaces into open-air living. The outdoors invites itself in everywhere inside her home.

It's one of the main features that made her buy it in the first place.

She lets her fingers fidget on the cream marble top of the kitchen's curved island while she pads around to fill herself with a sense of inhabiting the space. She's eager to use her kitchen again with its dual sinks, as well as white lacquered and mahogany cabinets and Thermador appliances. Maybe even invite Heather and Zoe over for a meal in her formal modern dining room.

She's excited about sitting on her oversized ivory-white vegan leather couch in the living room in front of the Bubinga wood wall panels making the recessed fireplace and wall-mounted TV blend seamlessly within it.

She loves relaxing and watching movies while basking in the white noise of the ocean, and the enveloping natural sky luminescence.

Although her very favorite part is the second floor.

Accessible through the floating staircase beside the corridor that leads to a Brazilian granite steam room as well as a small gym, it leads to her master bedroom, a guest one, and an office.

Every room is accentuated by exotic materials, and has been professionally decorated.

Her bedroom is where there's her private balcony. The one that she mentioned to Lucas a few minutes ago. The ocean view is stunning from it, and she is excited to soak in its calmness for the week.

She is equally enthusiastic to spend time in her all-slate ensuite bathroom with white double vessel sinks. She likes to leisurely read in her soaking tub, or enjoy the quiet under the stream of her walk-in roman shower.

Having Lucas with her will only make things even more perfect.

It will also potentially lead to her showers being less quiet than usual, and her baths involve less reading.

No matter what, she's totally ready to indulge in every single moment she spends with him for the foreseeable future.

Looking behind her the minute she gets to the other end of the living room, she notices that he dropped the bags next to the door that he also closed. His slides are now resting beside her own sandals under the console of the entrance.

As he walks barefoot toward her, she sees him glance around. "Jun was right. The whole space screams of you." He seems to be taking it all in. "I love it."

"You haven't seen the second floor yet." She smiles mellowly. "Nor the infinity pool on the roof or the spa and wet bar."

He smirks as he stands before her. "Nor your bedroom."

"I'm sure you'll appreciate my California King Berlin bed." She peers into his eyes. "It's surrounded by vanishing window walls on two sides."

He slips his hands underneath her cardigan to pull her to him. "Come here," he whispers.

She flies her fingers through his hair, leaning forward to press their foreheads together. "Welcome to my home."

He curls his fingers around her hip bones. "I'm honored to be here."

"I hope so," she murmurs playfully. "I rarely bring people here."

He skims his nose along hers. "Really?"

"Mhmm." She trails her index finger down his sternum slowly. "Even Nathan never visited. He was supposed to, but we broke up before he—"

He shushes her. "I'll make you forget about him."

"Always so confident." She reaches the fastened buttons at the bottom of his shirt. "You know..." She deftly unbuttons one. "It was never an even game to begin with."

He glides his fingers up her spine. "How come?"

She loosens the other while kissing him softly. "You're the best I've ever had, Lucas."

He applies pressure on each of her vertebrae. "That works wonders for my ego."

"I know your ego doesn't need it, but it's true." She slides her palms under his shirt to make it slide down his shoulders. "There's no use trying to deny it."

He pulls back slightly to let it fall on the floor, locking eyes with her. "Wanna know a secret?"

As soon as it lays at their feet, she reaches to paint his trapezius with her fingertips. "Always," she murmurs.

He grabs her hips, bending to ghost his lips over hers. "You're also the best I've ever had." He half-smiles. "I wasn't kidding when I said so before."

She hums, scratching her nails along the stubble on his jaw. "We're a great match, then."

He angles his head to lay a gentle kiss on her wrist. "The best one."

The second he captures her bottom lip, she lets go of all her barriers.

There's clearly no use trying to resist this inexorable pull that Lucas exerts on her. Her whole skeleton is already alight from their tongues flawlessly tangling together for fuck's sake.

At this rate, she's certain that she's going to combust before the end of the night.

He is kissing her like it's his damn job, and fuck does it feel good.

As he smoothly defines her clavicle to then delicately push her cardigan off of her, she moans deep into his mouth.

No one ever touched her with such care and abandonment. The simplest touch from Lucas is electrifying.

Years ago she blamed this bliss on the fact that they were on vacations. That none of it mattered. That sex is potentially always better with no strings attached.

She can't use those excuses now.

They both know who they truly are; no matter what happens they won't remain strangers who once hooked up. They're definitely not on vacations this time around.

But since he waltzed back into her life, her body has been yearning for him, and her mind is a whole mess by sending her all those mixed signals about how well fitted they are together.

How phenomenal he always makes her feel, but how he could be her worst mistake.

She forces herself to push the unwarranted thought away. The only thing that matters is *him*.

And she still wants him as bad as she did back in his car coming back from Cambridge.

Back on that rooftop grinding with him on the dance floor at that fundraiser.

Back in front of her building when they made out in the middle of the night.

Not even an hour ago back on Black's Beach.

Lucas is part of her blood flow. He's literally coursing through her veins. She can't dissociate her desire for him from the rest of her life.

Once her cardigan hangs at her elbows on both sides, she leans back, taking hold of his hand to pull him along with her in a silent invitation.

He complies, never breaking eye contact. They walk through the living room and kitchen to reach the stairs that she begins to climb backward.

He's looking at her with the intensity of all the tenderness he harbors for her, and she only wants to drown in him.

She wants to fall in those beryl irises and never come back to the surface.

The moment they enter her room, she drops his hand to throw her cardi on the Barcelona armchair opposite to the bed before curling her hand into the waistband of his shorts to bring him to the bed.

The whole space is only lighted by the moon rays reflecting on the mirror pool of the ocean.

It creates an enticing glow. She loves the serenity it offers.

Lucas wastes no time wrapping his arms around her again, kissing her fervently.

She can feel the exact effect she has on him as he seeks friction while she pulls herself flush to him. It makes her moan low into the kiss.

When the back of her calves hit the foot of the gray structure, she sits on the mattress.

The second she starts unfastening his shorts, he places his hand on top of hers. "You don't have to."

She looks up at him. "I know." She smiles seductively. "I just really want to."

He leans forward, cradling her head, and forcing her to lay back on the charcoal comforter. "Not yet. Please let me bask in this moment right here."

He reaches behind her to slowly unknot the top of her bikini. She stops her movements, scanning his gaze.

As she grazes the pads of her fingers in the valley of his defined abs, she senses his muscles twitch as he hovers above her.

She barely audibly whimpers.

It's true that she wants to go down on him. She's been craving to pleasure him, and feel him lose control in her mouth for what feels like forever.

He's nothing other than magnificent when he does. She wants to experience that feeling again.

Preferably repeatedly.

She might say that she enjoys giving head. It's all about that mutual pleasure, and knowing that your partner is content in the best way, after all. The feeling of satisfaction is thrilling.

But Lucas is different. He used to make it good for her, too. She reveled in taking her time to lick down his chest and sense him react. She relished in hearing his ragged breathing as he progressively came undone on her tongue.

She whines.

The night is still young. She'll get her way with him soon enough.

She lets him remove her top, biting into her bottom lip as he discards it on the floor. The look of pure awe as his eyes travel down her body instantly sends her mind into a daze.

He circles her rib cage, brushing his thumbs on the underside of her breasts with that untamed wonder still shining in his gaze. "You're so damn gorgeous, Rae," he whispers as he skims his nose along hers.

She smiles as she grabs the back of his head to bring him down to her.

The minute she starts scooting up, he follows her lead. His frame envelops hers perfectly as he moves like a feline on top of her while making out. It's as if they have perfected this choreography for years.

The sync with which they always match each other is astounding.

Raven is progressively getting high on what's left of his woodsy cologne mixing with the refreshing scent of the ocean on his skin as he kisses her over and over again.

Having him in her own bed with her feels too good for words.

Their bodies are continuously demanding to mold together until there's no more space between them. She can feel a familiar heat rush through her as he swiftly unfastened her shorts.

She wants him even closer.

She grinds into him.

When her head hits the white cotton sheets of the pillows, he shifts his attention to her neck as she combs her fingers through his black locks.

She sighs.

He cups her breasts languidly, brushing his nose along the circumference, and letting his mouth follow suit.

He's driving her mad. She loves when he nuzzles into her cleavage. She wants him to—

He stops to define the mermaid tattoo on her rib cage with his index. "You have more ink than just on your spine," he murmurs in bewilderment.

"Yeah." She looks down at him. "This one I got not long after Mykonos." She scrapes her nails into the short hair at the nape of his neck soothingly. "I wanted a reminder of what I love. Your tattoo on the inside of your forearm inspired me to get this one."

He smirks. "I left my mark on you."

"You did. Both figuratively and..." She smiles shyly as she joins their hands to trace the drawing with him. "Kinda literally since I got this tattoo. My friends always told me I could've been a mermaid because they are one with the ocean. Quite like I'm in perfect harmony when in it. Water is my element."

He brings her hand to his lips to kiss her palm. "It's beautiful."

"And while sirens are usually the bad guys, mermaids help sailors and appease the sea." She paints idle patterns on his back. "They help people like I always strived to do. So here's to hoping that true justice always prevails, and that good conquers everything."

He resumes kissing his way down her abdomen. "Those were our ideals, huh?"

"Mhmm." She hums as he swirls his tongue inside her navel. "You think we forgot who we were?"

He tentatively starts sliding her shorts and bikini bottom down her legs. "If all my choices somehow led me to end up in your bed right now, I say I'm right where I'm supposed to be."

She bores her eyes into his as she shimmies out of her remaining pieces of clothing.

He looks dead serious.

He looks like he means every word he just said.

But if she believes him, it also signifies that his professional journey is—

She can't concentrate on all of that right now. Not when he is kissing and massaging his way up her quads, progressively rendering her mind thoroughly blank.

So she sets on caressing up his deltoid instead while he traces her adroitly.

He grunts. "You're more than ready."

"Don't be smug." She chases his fingers. "I know how *hard* it is for you right now to not constantly seek friction."

He massages her hip bones as he licks his way further up her leg. "Guilty as charged."

She caresses his scalp gently. "Want to do something about it?"

"Not yet." He sucks his fingers clean before laying a soft kiss on the inside of her thigh. "I've been dreaming of you for far too long to not do this first," he breathes out.

The instant he puts his tongue flat on her, she parts her legs a little more for him as she throws her head back.

Having Lucas bury his head between her thighs again feels like a dream.

A dream she doesn't want to ever wake up from.

He's wickedly talented with his mouth, there's no denying it.

Even after all those years, he feels like he knows her body by heart. He's also even more skilled than she remembered.

The fact that he welcomes each undulation of her pelvis with a small filthy groan into her core that reverberates through her bones makes her invariably moan.

He seems to take it all as an invitation to become increasingly solely dedicated to her pleasure.

Her grip in his hair tightens. She can feel the tendrils of an orgasm coiling low in her belly at each swipe of his tongue.

The second he darts it out past her folds while applying divine pressure with his nose on her bundle of nerves just above, she loses it.

His name gets laced within a whimpered curse as she falls off the edge.

A million tiny pieces of her psyche get scattered into the void as she is blinded by white hot nihility.

Her brain is absolutely unhinged trying to piece back together reality.

When she finally snaps back to the present, Lucas magnificently eased her through it, and he's not relenting. He even becomes more insistent.

He's steadily building her up again.

If someone would've asked her what would happen if she would ever cross paths with Lucas Blake again, she probably would've guessed that they would've been all about passion and urgency. They would've gone at it with a desperate fervor.

But this.

This is so much better.

He said he wanted to take his time with her. That's exactly what he's doing. He feels like he's worshiping her body with a reverence she thought was lost to humankind.

Fuck she would let him do it all night long.

But she also wants something else right about now.

She gently tugs on his hair to nudge him back up to her. He swiftly wipes his mouth on a corner of the quilt before facing her with the biggest grin she has ever seen him sport.

She curls her hand around his throat. "You look proud of yourself."

"Shouldn't I be?" He slides his hand across her cheek. "I just wanted you to remember what it feels like when I make you come." He brushes his fingers through her hair. "And I honestly wanted to keep at it all night. There's not a better feeling in the world than feeling you let go, Raven."

When he kisses her passionately, the taste of herself on his tongue mixed with something undoubtedly *him* makes her moan once more.

Every time she rakes through strands of his black locks, he purrs obscenely.

She could make out with him for hours like this. She could spend all night exploring every inch of his body.

But there's something she wants more at the moment. She shifts her attention to laying open mouthed kisses down his neck. "I want you inside me," she whispers into his skin.

He groans. "You still love it slow?"

She pokes him so that he rolls onto his back. "Mhmm." She hooks her thumbs in the waistband of his shorts. "And as deep as possible."

He props himself up to help her slide them completely off of him, breathing heavily. "You're driving me crazy, Rae."

She straddles him, running her fingertips down his chest unhurriedly. "Is that so?" She glances down to his crotch before locking eyes with him. "I must admit that you already look positively outstanding."

"That's honestly all because of you." He grabs her hips, smiling. "I don't respond to anyone else that strongly."

She pulls her bottom lip between her teeth. "If I didn't know better, I'd think this was the worst line I ever heard."

"Please excuse my poor wording." He smiles playfully. "I think most of my blood rushed south at the moment."

She chuckles as she reaches into her bedside table drawer to grab a box of condoms.

When she singles one out, and focuses her attention back on Lucas, a breath gets caught in her throat.

He already has bed hair thanks to her expert fingers, his touch is nothing but tender, and he stares at her with all the sweetness of the world. Her heart flutters of its own accord.

He's fucking stunning.

As she rips the foil package open with her teeth to then roll the rubber onto him, she is certainly set on letting the tension coiling inside both their bodies slowly, beautifully, snaps.

She intends to do it repetitively until morning comes.

Until they're both delightfully wrecked, and nothing else than the other's cry of ecstasy makes sense in the whole damned universe.

Lucas stirs in his sleep only to realize that he's currently gloriously naked laying on his stomach in Raven's bed. He distantly distinguishes that the sheets are crumpled at his waist, but he keeps his eyes shut; stuck in the rapturous limbo between awakeness and slumber.

As he progressively joins the land of the living, he smiles absent-mindedly.

He can remember how gushes of Raven's arousal coated his taste buds in the most exquisite fashion as he was lapping at her, and how his name falling from her lips sounded like hazy paradise.

How she divinely rode him into oblivion excruciatingly slowly a few minutes later.

How each undulation of her hips as he was nuzzling between her breasts was bringing him deeper to a point where he had no idea where she ended and where he began.

How her continuous moans as she was clenching around him propelled his mind into an exhilarating trance.

Her fingers combing into his hair while he caressed her spine through her movements rendered him peaceful and exalted at once.

He recalls having breathed her name like a prayer into her neck when he came apart a few seconds after her.

Please stay like this just a little while longer, Luke, she panted into his ear as he was finishing spasming.

He gladly complied, kissing her leisurely as they both ebbed through their respective climaxes.

When he finally went to the bathroom to clean himself, and came back to the bed with a damp washcloth to take care of Raven, he reveled in the way she caressed his forearm while he did so.

When she took the cloth from him to discard it, he couldn't stop himself from stretching on top of her to kiss her lazily.

They say one doesn't know what they're missing until they lose it. He guesses it's true.

He had been longing for Raven for years, constantly pushing the thought away because there was no possibility that meeting her again would ever materialize.

Now that he knows he wasn't hallucinating how perfect she feels in his life and his arms he'll be damned if he doesn't do everything in his power to keep her happy.

He inhales deeply, burying his head a little more into the pillow.

One of his favorite parts of the past few hours was when they got up to shower and grab a bite after round two.

He had fetched their luggages from downstairs, and took care of putting their respective wetsuits on a drying rack in her small gym away from any direct sunlight, before hopping in the roman cubicle with Raven. He then spent half an hour simply helping her wash her hair, and caressing her in silence under the water stream.

When they exited, he put on a pair of boxers and his old t-shirt.

The nicest surprise was Raven casually picking up another one he had left beside his bag to put it on top of her polka dot cheeksters.

She was stunning in it. He would honestly not mind seeing her in any of his vintage music bands t-shirts every night.

Working in concert with her who showed him the way around her kitchen, he quickly cooked some farfalle Alfredo with roasted mushrooms, and they ended up eating on the sofa to soft jazz in the background.

He had Raven's feet in his lap as she was stretched along the cushions.

He suddenly remembered something. *So let me get this straight.* He looked at her playfully. *You always have condoms in your bedroom, but you don't bring anyone here?*

I hooked up once or twice while being here. I like to be prepared. She took a bite. She waited for a beat before curving a corner of her mouth upward. *If I was to go check, I'm sure Heather put some more in the bathroom when she learned that you were tagging along.*

He snorted. *Remind me to thank her.*

Don't tell me you don't have any on you?

I do have some in my duffle bag. He hummed. *But in my defense I didn't put them there because I was so sure of myself that we would end up having sex.* He alternated pointing his fork between the both of them. *I always have a few on me when I travel. Better be safe.* He tilted his head toward her. *Now that we're talking about it, I also vaguely recall you always preferred using one.*

Mhmm. She nodded. *You remember well. Even if I'm on the pill it adds another layer of protection for STDs.*

We are in sync, and I just want to put it out there that I'm clean. He placed his empty bowl on the side table. *I know I tend to sleep around so I get tested regularly to make sure of it even if I never have unprotected sex.* He raises a suggestive eyebrow. *Unless I was to become exclusive with someone I really like...*

I appreciate you being open and honest about it. She ate some more before carrying on. *I do the same about testing. We never know, right?* He agreed. She continued as she smiled warmly. *And we've only just slept together.* She scanned his gaze. *You'd like for us to be exclusive?*

I don't see myself having sex with anyone else now. He was unflinching. *Do you?*

I don't either. She shook her head. *Let's see where this thing between us leads, yeah?*

Of course. I was just saying that I would never put you at risk, and you won't find me sleeping around like I used to as long as you want me in your bed. He smiled tenderly at her. *I'm not your average one-night stand.*

She smirked. *Oh, there's certainly nothing average about you.*

He smiled teasingly. *Glad you noticed.* He couldn't help himself from playing along. *Was it when you asked me to sit on the side of the bed, and you knelt before me or when—*

She cut him off. *Always so humble.* She snorted. *I knew it before all of that.* Her tone was amused. *Remember Mykonos, Lucas?*

We still both changed a little since then. He took hold of her foot, and dropped his tone to a whisper. *You feel even more exceptional.*

She bit into her bottom lip. *I seriously have to admit that you also feel even more spectacular.*

Her affectionate gaze made his heart swell in his chest.

He locked eyes with her as he smoothly applied pressure points along the arch of her foot. *Do you know just how phenomenal you are?*

Says the man who idly started massaging my foot so I could relax just because he felt like it. The one who wanted me to climax before him every single time without fail since the beginning of the night. She mixed her pasta as she smiled knowingly at him. *You're pretty amazing yourself, Lucas.*

He rubbed his knuckles on her metatarsals. *You better get used to the fact that I might very well never have enough of you.*

She grinned genuinely. *I can live with that.*

They stayed in comfortable silence while she finished eating. Soon enough, rhythmic R&B filled the space, and Raven crooned inattentively.

She put her bowl on the coastal coffee table. *This was delicious.* She gestured at her empty dish. *Thank you.*

It's my pleasure. He beamed. *I could cook for you more often if you allow me to.*

She hummed absentmindedly, seemingly ignoring the comment. *You know, Heather founded her own firm because of inequalities like the ones related in that song.* She wrung her hands in her lap. *Sometimes I wonder why I didn't do the same. It pairs well with my vision of the justice system. What she's doing is essential as you said back when I first told you about it.*

He used his thumbs on the ball of her foot to loosen some of the stiffness. *Maybe your drive was too strong to settle for something that wouldn't be as satisfying as what the big leagues could bring you.*

She frowned. *Are you saying that my ego got the best of me when I chose my path?*

Not your ego per se, but maybe your ambition? He kept his voice steady and comprehensive. *We all have multiple personality traits and ideals converging. One will always supersede the other depending on the situation.*

You're right. She slumped a little. *At that point in my life it made sense to go for the big firm, and the huge paycheck.* She smiled dejectedly. *I was young and naive. I like to think I have evolved since then.*

As if you're old now. He chuckled. *But for what it's worth, I think you did evolve. You might seem to feel a sure unease about your former work ethics, but you also feel very at peace with your decision to leave. I think that standing up for yourself is the most important thing.*

It took me years to reach the right level of awareness to have the guts to do it. One might say that I was blinded by power. She became reflective, toying with the hem of her t-shirt. *This rush you get when your name means something to the biggest people in the field gets dizzying.* She combed her fingers through her hair, smiling sadly. *It's as if I was stuck in a system that wouldn't let me go, and the worst part is that I was staying in it of my own accord.*

I totally get what you mean. He flashed her his best comforting smile. *Cognitive dissonance can be a mighty opponent.*

Deep down he knows that he's guilty of doing it himself. With the type of clients he has, he doesn't have any choice but to.

Or does he?

It's not as if he could just—

Raven's voice resounded in his ears as she tentatively asked, *You want to know why I resigned?*

He draped an arm on the back of the sofa, leaning toward her. He wanted her to know that she had his full attention. *There's nothing I'd like more.*

I had this big banking client... She took a pause, breathing in before disclosing a name. *Cameron Wallace.*

He perked up, gliding his hand up her calf. *I've heard of him. He was accused of—*

She interjected to finish that sentence. *Money laundering.* She nodded in confirmation. *The trial is still ongoing, and I honestly hope he gets condemned because he's guilty, and not only of what he's on the stand for right now.* Lucas stayed quiet to let her go at her desired pace for sharing what she wanted to. After a few minutes, she continued. *At some point, the district attorney decided to bring forward three women.* She swallowed audibly. *The D.A. wanted to use their testimonies to show which type of person Cameron Wallace is, and add another layer to his despicable persona: human trafficking.*

Lucas made a face. *Oh, fuck.*

You don't say. She exhaled deeply. *Now, I had heard rumors about him and his right hand Morgan Shaw, but I had never asked Wallace directly about any trafficking. A big part of me was probably already aware that if he was to say yes I would've ran for the hills way before the trial even started.* She let out a small disheartened laugh. *I know it was a blatant oversight on my part to not look into it. I usually do my job way better than that, and am prepared for any eventuality.* She frowned at herself. *I've been thinking about it since I quit, and I truly think doing so was also a way for my brain to shield itself. At that point of my career I just couldn't take all the bullshit anymore. I did turn a knowing blind eye on some shady shit through time. Just couldn't take it anymore.* She smiled shyly, analyzing Lucas' features as she talked. *My brain reached its limit before I became consciously aware of it.* She reached on the back of the sofa to slowly caress the top of his hand with the pad of her fingers. *Anyway, long story short, human trafficking often goes hand in hand with money laundering.* She shrugged. *Maybe I sabotaged this whole trial singlehandedly without even knowingly wanting to.*

He snorted. *Your subconscious is pretty damn stubborn too, I see.*

Very funny. She scooted closer. *You already admitted that you love how headstrong I am.*

I do. He welcomed her as she cuddled into his side with her legs still draped over his. He wrapped his arm around her, and curled his hand around her calf. *Always will.*

You should've heard those women speak, Luke. She put her head on his pec. *He destroyed them. His network ruined their lives because of his vision of business.* She trailed her fingers along the extensor muscle of his arm caressing her leg. *Because of what he put them through while promising a better life as a smokescreen.*

He painted aimless patterns on her hip bone. *So you just left the courthouse and never looked back that day?*

That's about it.

You did the right thing. He angled his head to kiss her forehead. *This man deserves to be harshly judged for what he submits people to. He's not only conning a system with his money schemes—which would be bad enough in itself—there are also people suffering because of his hunger for profit and power.*

Exactly. She nuzzled into the crook of his shoulder. *Thank you for listening to me. It still lingers in my brain most days.*

I'm proud of you for having stayed true to yourself. He slid his hand up her thigh. *And I'll always be more than happy to listen to everything you have to say.* He slid his hand up her side, holding her tighter. *Especially when you randomly start cuddling as you do so.*

She chuckled as the only answer while the last lines of the tune washed over them.

After a few minutes of just snuggling, Raven looked down at his fingers slipping underneath the hem of her shirt. *Do you like your sparkly nails?*

Do you?

You're always sexy, I already told you as such. She took his hand in hers. *You rock it.*

You know, my sister used to love painting my nails so you could say I've been used to it. He brushed through the hair at the back of her head soothingly. *I honestly think it's awesome. I don't get why so many guys in high school insulted me the next day for having black, purple or any color nails.*

Maybe it has something to do with being scared of not being masculine enough. Which is bullshit. She intertwined their fingers. *You should've gotten a french manicure just to show them. Let them talk, I say.*

It's all a state of mind, anyway. Everyone should accept all parts of themselves, and be open to possibilities. He softly pressed on each of her cervical vertebrae. *Screw stereotypes.*

She untangles their hands to sneak hers underneath his t-shirt. *The world would be vastly different if everyone was sharing your views on that.* She scratched his abs lightly. *For the best if you ask me.*

His muscles twitched under her touch as he resumed gliding his hand up her thigh. *I'm going to let you in on yet another secret of mine.* He rested his palm flat on her ass. *I love going to the barbershop to get a professional stubble shave whenever I have time.*

That's great. She arched into him. *It's like going to the hairdresser in some ways?*

I guess so. He hummed, bending down to trail his nose down her cheek. *Every time I go for my hair, I also take time for my beard. That's in part why I'm very particular about my traditional shaving brush, cream and oil at home. I brought them with me on this trip because I can't do without my ritual.*

Can't wait to see all of those displayed on my bathroom counter then. She skimmed her fingertips along the scruff on his jaw. *It's gotten a little longer now that I'm noticing it.*

He laid a kiss just below her earlobe. *Are you complaining?*

No. I love it. She bit into her bottom lip, flying her fingers into strands of his hair. *It drives me mad in the best way when you let your mouth roam all over me.*

Good. He continued his trail of kisses along her jaw. *It's due to be trimmed in about two days to keep my usual look so you'll experience slightly different lengths since then.*

I'm in for all of it. She angled her head to give him better access to her neck. *As long as it's only your beard's length that changes...*

Hilarious. He smiled into her skin. *But if you ever find my stubble unsatisfying let me know, I'll trim it sooner.*

Duly noted. By the way, the whole 'size matters' debate is also total bullshit to me. It only depends on what works for each body and person. You just happen to be the perfect type of 'big' for me. He groaned. She smirked. *Wanna go back to bed?*

He fakely pouted. *The couch is very comfy.*

True. She pressed her lips to his ear to whisper, *Plus, I never had sex on it.*

That's another blatant oversight. He slid his hand to support the small of her back, ready to support her if he was to flip her under him on the cushions. *Shall we fix it?*

We shall. She toyed with the waistband of his boxers. *But I'm craving you in my bed right now.*

He hummed as he kissed her softly. *Your wish is my command.*

As Lucas now opens his eyes only to be met by the moon at the peak of darkness reflecting through the room, he seeks Raven beside him.

He instantly sees her also laying on her stomach no more than a feet away. Her latin script tattoo is on display for him to see except for the last few words which are shielded from prying gazes by the sheet covering a little less than half her back.

He props himself up on an elbow to let his stare follow the letters along her spine.

'Eternity dwells in the fragile equi...'

He furrows his eyebrows.

He didn't ask her about it in the shower before, and didn't take time to read it in its entirety either. Someday he will inquire.

He already feels privileged that she shared how she feels about her resignation as well as why she took that step in her career with him. Other important subjects can be addressed in due time.

He's in no rush.

He only wants to be with her.

That's the only thing that matters.

The rest can wait. Everything flows naturally with her anyway.

At the moment, he only wishes to feel her against him.

He scoots closer, sliding her hair to the side to get better access to her neck. Trailing kisses up her shoulder blade, he then skims his nose up her jugular, to end up nuzzling into the crook of her neck.

She stirs as she yawns, blindly reaching to grab his hand, and brings it onto her abdomen.

He lets her do as she pleases while she turns onto her side, pressing her back to his front as he molds his body to hers.

She intertwines their fingers on top of her navel while he slides his other arm just under her head resting on the pillow.

When he curls it fully around her shoulders, pulling her flush to him, she angles her head to lay a soft kiss on his forearm. "Never hesitate to wake me up like this. You feel amazing, Luke," she breathes out drowsily.

He sighs in contentment.

Spooning like this with anyone never felt as good as with Raven right now.

With his nose buried in her hair, he knows that her warmth will smoothly lull him back to sleep.

FIFTEEN

Portal to Plenitude

"Really?" Raven snorts as she slides her phone in the back pocket of her denim shorts while looking at Lucas putting four packs of cookies in the cart. "Sandwich cookies?"

He smiles playfully, standing beside the cart in fake defiance. "What's wrong with them?"

She takes a minute to just take in the moment she's living through as some catchy beat resounds through the store speakers.

She inhales steadily.

Lucas looks beyond handsome with his charcoal baseball cap, mid-indigo washed jeans, white tee, and low top sneakers.

Plus, he is gazing at her as if they've done this a thousand times before.

Grocery shopping.

If there's *one* thing she didn't expect to be as fun during their week in San Diego, it was certainly that.

The ease with which they interact and navigate each situation continues to amaze her.

She saunters toward him, her black canvas street-style sneakers contrasting perfectly with the pale gray tiles of the aisles, and her messy ponytail swaying slightly at each step.

She had wanted to come here because the small neighborhood gourmet store is close to her place, and it offers a nice selection of products.

She stops a few feet in front of Lucas. "Nothing. I also love those cookies." She half-smiles, glancing at the selection on the shelf. "I just had no idea you did." She redirects her stare to him. "Are you sure we need that many packs though? We're only here for a week."

"You see, the problem is that..." He closes the gap between them, grabbing her hips once at her level. "Once I start eating them, I have trouble stopping." He bends down to murmur, "Just like when I go down on you." He smirks. "I wish I could do it forever."

She wraps her arms around his neck. "Did you just compare me to a dessert?"

"If I inadvertently did, would you excuse my poor wording? My mind might have trouble functioning correctly." He starts toying with the hem of her top. "You in that damn t-shirt you tucked in the front of your shorts today is making my brain short circuit every time my eyes land on you."

"What can I say?" She runs her fingers along his shoulder blades. "I have developed a fondness for your t-shirt since last night. It's very comfy."

She also remembers all too well how Lucas slowly undressed her when they climbed back into bed after their late lunch.

He barely lifted the tee at first to lick across her stomach before moving it up a little more to repeat the process on her chest to finally end up pulling the garment over her head, and letting it fall on the floor.

She left it there for the remainder of the night, but it was a no-brainer to put it on when she had to dress in the morning after their shower.

It's perfectly oversized, and it smells like Lucas.

What more could she—

His warm voice reaches her ears. "You're simply divine in it, and there's no comparison to be had with pleasuring you. That easily surpasses every other craving I could ever have."

She angles her head to kiss him softly. "You're excused." She smiles against his lips, whispering, "But only because you're too damn good with your mouth."

"Duly noted." He hooks his index and middle fingers into her back pockets. "I will try my best to keep this level of excellence."

"I'm sure you'll have no trouble." She pulls herself flush to him as she scratches the short hair at the nape of his neck. "I could get used to waking up like I did this morning every day."

He groans slightly. "Lazy morning sex is the best, huh?"

She recalls that when she woke up tangled in his limbs, she felt elated in ways she hasn't been in years.

She's certainly walking around with a very high level of oxytocin running through her veins right now, thanks to all their activities of the last few hours.

From the very moment they stepped into her house last night until they left it to run errands, she's been living in her own little bubble of happiness.

She brushes her nose along his. "Especially with you."

He brushes his scruff along her cheek to reach her ear. "You're alarmingly addicting, Rae."

As he lays a kiss just below her earlobe, she sighs.

If she's being honest, the bliss she's experiencing with him at the moment is also not only because of having slept together. Every conversation, interaction, and instant spent with him feels special.

Although, she definitely can't deny that the sex is nothing short of amazing every single time.

Sensing his arousal on the small of her back this morning, and having him softly caress her while she was waking up, made her instantly express her desire to feel him inside her.

In true Lucas fashion, he made her roll onto her back, and lazily kissed his way down her body first. He expertly edged her to the point where her mind was completely unhinged. She *desperately* needed release.

When he granted it to her, she's sure that a whole new galaxy formed under her closed eyelids from the strength of her orgasm.

It is truly the very best way to wake up.

A few minutes later, it also felt amazing kissing him sloppily while leaning her head back on his shoulder as he was slowly thrusting into her in the shower. The water rippling down their joined bodies as he was gently massaging her clit and palming her breast was amplifying every sensation to a rapturous degree.

She recalls her fingers grabbing fistfuls of his hair the closer she was getting to the edge.

She remembers the high-pitched sound of the slate tiles of the cubicle walls as her nails scraped them while trying to grip the surface when she came apart.

Lucas' husky tone in the crook of her neck when he groaned her name as he splintered a few seconds later is still living rent free in her mind at the moment.

When he delicately lathered her with soap to help her wash in the aftermath, a strange feeling took hold of her entire being.

She knows that he now has definitely ruined her for anybody else.

She doesn't want to even entertain the possibility of allowing someone else than Lucas in her bed ever again. No one could make her feel as good, that much is certain.

Lucas is unequaled, and dangerously feels like he could be the missing piece of—

She swallows in an attempt at focussing.

She can't let those thoughts take hold. It's a risky road to travel.

Her body has been deprived of Lucas' touch for years at this point. Experiencing it again, and being able to indulge in it anytime she wants is making her feel like she's living through a damn fantasy.

Can someone really feel that perfect?

It sounds like a rhetorical question. She knows the answer.

Lucas feels fucking perfect to her.

It's becoming clearer by the second since they fell in bed together.

But she's trying to not linger too much on the repercussions of what having hooked up with him will mean once back in NYC.

When he'll go back to his job, his way of life, and his view on the future.

She has to become better at living in the present because anything else threatens to destroy her if she lets it take hold of her psyche.

So she pats his pec, smiling as she decides to reorient the exchange. "Now let's gather those ingredients you desperately need, and get to Heather and Zoe's before they get home."

He crosses his arms in her back to hold her closer. "Can we stay like this instead?"

"Cooking this dinner was your idea." She pulls away, sounding amused. "Now you deal with the consequences."

He laughs lightly while letting her go. "Fine." He fixes his hat. "Did Heather reply?"

"She did." Raven hums. "She said that she was glad we were bringing dinner."

"Perfect." He seems excited and nervous at once. "They're not expecting it so I hope it'll be a nice surprise."

"Not a lot of people would offer to take care of dinner so casually after having known them for two days." She grabs a pack of limited edition cinnamon bun flavored cookies. "Trust me, they're gonna love it. Particularly after the day they're probably having."

He opens his mouth to reply, but his phone chimes. He instantly fishes it out of his pocket, checking the caller ID. "I have to take this." He gestures at his device while looking at her. She hums. "It won't be long."

As he walks a few feet away, Raven continues her quest to buy items to fill her pantry for the week.

Heather did a good job putting the essentials in there—including her beloved oatmeal—as well as in the refrigerator, but her friend was right when she said that she'd need to buy a few more things.

Raven doesn't mind. She didn't even expect Heather to take time to take care of any of it in the first place. Especially with the events of her life lately. It was insanely kind of Haddy to prepare things for when she would arrive.

Raven always considers herself lucky to have such incredible friends.

Her thoughts naturally circle back to the fact that having a nice meal with her friends will certainly be very enjoyable as she picks up some chickpeas.

Heather and Zoe both have packed work days.

Haddy has to be at the courthouse early for an all-day jury selection, while Zoe is presenting concepts at 3PM for her latest project: a whole rebranding for Moonstone Hotel—a new player in the San Diego area.

Their schedules apparently prompted Lucas to suggest that he could cook chicken shawarma for them when they get home. He said he would like to thank them for their hospitality, and hopefully help them spend a relaxing evening amidst all the uncertainty.

You're sure? she asked while seated on a charcoal Glass Coco stool at her kitchen counter.

Yeah. Lucas was facing her on the other side of the island, adding the soy milk to his pancake batter. *I'd love to cook for all of you. Everyone is okay with chicken?*

Yes. She nodded. *No one is vegetarian or vegan. Although if Jun would be there you would need to make tofu shawarma.*

Duly noted. I was wondering since we ate portobello mushroom burgers last time at their place.

That's very considerate of you. She looked at him taking his cup of coffee from under the espresso machine. *We're still eating meat, but we try to be more responsible about our consumption, eat less of it, and try to take it from local producers whenever possible.*

Gotcha. I highly respect the approach you guys have. I just want to make sure I buy the right ingredients. He grinned. *Plus, as I already told you it's my mom's recipe, and my comfort meal. I was planning to cook it just for you as a date or something, but I think your friends are so nice and welcoming that—*

She smiled playfully, taking a spoonful of her oatmeal. *Oh, so you'd like to bring me on a date?*

He raised a curious eyebrow under the visor of his baseball cap while whisking the preparation. *Isn't that what one must do when they want to give a shot at staying with someone for a while?*

She looked at him intently. *Didn't we just say that we would see where this goes between us?*

Mhmm. He casually put a pan on the stove. *We also both said that we don't want to have sex with anyone else. Unless you changed your mind, and you—*

She cut him off. *I didn't change my mind.* She curved a corner of her mouth upward. *I want only you in my bed for the week.*

That's music to my ears. He beamed. *If I'm not allowed to take you out on an official date, could I at least cook for you?*

She bit into her bottom lip at his sweetness. *You could.*

Marvelous. He started heating up the pan. *Is actually eating something off of you also acceptable?*

It shall be discussed. She frowned. *Sticky, and syrupy stuff is the worst as I already stated.*

He laid his elbows on the surface, peering into her eyes. *But you know I would make sure there's not a trace left.*

Mmm. Very tempting. She idly made a show of licking the inside of her spoon upside down, lingering on the tip before continuing. *The way your scruff pairs with your tongue on my skin drives me crazy.*

He grunts. *That's a happy coincidence because your whole body drives me mad.*

She felt playful. *I personally feel that covering your abs with whipped cream to lick across them wouldn't add much.* She was dead serious. *The experience is pretty fucking perfect with just you on my taste buds.*

She could see his pupils steadily dilate at the image her comment seemingly conjured in his brain.

She smirked.

He's always so fun to flirt with.

Maybe he—

He held her stare. *You know what? I'm not only attracted by your stunning physique.* He slid a hand on the side of her face gently. *It's also all about your fabulous wit.* He used his thumb to trace her jawline. *It's the softness contained in your gaze, and lighting up the sparks of aqua within the green of your irises when you look at me.*

He smiled shyly. *I could dive into your eyes and drown.* He defined her industrial piercing while combing his fingers into her hair. *It's your amazing kindness, and your big heart, Raven.* He dropped his tone to a whisper. It's *your drive, your beautiful mind, and your unparalleled spirit.* He smiled tenderly at her. *It's all of it that is drawing me to you.*

Her heart skipped a beat.

She thought he would continue with their signature banter. She definitely didn't expect that level of heartfelt confession.

Obviously she thinks the same. It's not only just about his body for her. It never has been.

His personality is beautiful. It shines bright, and blends with her own in ways she never thought would be possible.

Even with all her concerns about the path ahead, she wanted to let him know that he's her most beautiful moment of surrender.

But she must've waited a bit too long before wording a reply. He leaned back, smiled coyly, and changed the subject. *For tonight I'd like to go buy the ingredients so we can cook at their place.*

She blinked trying to readjust her train of thought. *Maybe Heather and Zoe already have what you need.*

Maybe, but I'd prefer to bring everything. He spread some batter at the bottom of the warm pan. *I'm seeing this as if I'm inviting all of you. I'll thus take charge of it all.*

She resumed eating. *That's really sweet of you.*

You all made me feel at home as soon as I got here. He took a sip of the lungo in his cup. *It's the least I can do.*

She had an idea. *I have a key to their house. What do you say we go there, and have the meal ready when they arrive?*

That's brilliant.

I think they should be home around 6PM factoring their schedules, the traffic and all. She unlocks her phone lying flat on the counter next to her bowl. *I can text Heather to ask her if she'd be cool with us taking care of dinner.*

Sounds good. He rubbed the back of his head. *But please be vague. I'd love for it to be a surprise.*

She typed a quick message. *No problem.*

You're sure you don't want some pancakes? He flipped the one in the pan. *I know you love your oats, but I assure you that I perfected this recipe. I think you'd love it.*

She felt like playing a little. *Last time I had pancakes, William made them.* She shrugged. *I'm doubtful yours can be better.*

Are you for real? He stared at her, a look of slight deception on his face. *William was the 'morning after pancakes' type of guy?*

She snorted. *As if that's not what you're doing yourself at the moment.*

That's vastly different. He sounded fakely offended. *I wanted to eat pancakes, and you wanted your oatmeal. We decided to each take care of our breakfast.* He turned around to stretch a little while opening a cupboard to grab a plate. *If I was to be the 'morning after meal' type of guy, I would certainly pick something else than pancakes.*

Her gaze lingered on his hip bones defined by the waistband of his boxer briefs that became on display when his t-shirt lifted a little.

She smiled absentmindedly. *Like what?*

I don't know... He reflected for a second. *Oatmeal?* He grinned teasingly. *That's the one thing the woman I'm crazy about right now craves in the morning. It limits my choices.*

She pulled her bottom lip between her teeth. *Oh, but that woman also craves other things in the morning.*

And she knows I'll always be more than happy to satisfy all of her morning cravings. He puts the cooked pancake on the plate. *No matter what they are.* He glances at her. *Because I might share most of the same.*

She's one lucky lady. She takes a sip of her cappuccino. *But seriously, William never cooked for me. He even only stayed once overnight. I just wanted to gauge your reaction.*

He tsk-ed her, pouring some more dough in the skillet. *Did I pass the test?*

With flying colors. She chuckled, but felt like she needed to clarify something while the occasion presented itself. *You know, that night when you saw Will at my apartment, I ended things with him. Even before you knocked I had realized that I couldn't keep sleeping with him when I actually wanted you.*

So we both didn't hook up with anyone that night, but we both assumed the other did? It was his turn to chuckle. *Boss moves on both our parts.*

You don't say. She put her cup back on the counter, examining Lucas' features as he cooked. *Missed opportunity, too. I really wanted to spend time with you that night.*

It would've done me some good. He smiled shyly. *You always manage to quiet my mind. It's one of the true wonders of you.*

You might have a similar effect on me... She tilted her head, half-smiling. *You know, not a lot of people actually offered to cook for me.*

He didn't skip a beat. *Not even Nathan?*

She was slightly taken aback, but stayed calm. *Mhmm. Nathan did.* She thought she could at least share a little of that part of her past with him. *I always loved cooking, but we were super busy, and ordered in a lot. It somehow became a tradition that he would cook on Thursdays, and sometimes he randomly did it through the other days, too.*

He flipped the second pancake to then scan Raven's gaze. *How long were you together?*

Nearly five years. She stayed unflinching. *We met at one of my firm's BBQs during the first year I was working for them. A colleague of mine was friends with him, and he had invited him. We got along well from the start.*

Lucas hummed. *He's also a lawyer?*

Yeah. She pulled her coffee toward her to hold it with both her hands. She felt that she would need the slight comforting warmth of it while talking about Nathan. *Criminal law, too. We were honestly sharing the same drive and passion for our jobs. That was until he got progressively more consumed by cases he was working on, and we also realized that we didn't want the exact same thing out of life.*

Lucas peered into her eyes. *He chose his job over you?*

You could say that. She inhaled deeply. *It's honestly more complicated than just that, but it can be encapsulated as it being the end game, yeah. I've been guilty of that myself. Of prioritizing work pretty much constantly. For a brief moment back then I thought that I could potentially change that, but alas...*

His features were painted with comprehension. *You truly loved him, huh?*

I did. She took a sip of her coffee to compose herself. It can be awkward to talk about important past relationships with a current lover, but Lucas always makes everything natural. She thought that being fully honest was the best course of action. *I wanted to build a future with him. I thought we had a real shot at doing that.*

You know you can't blame yourself for loving him, right? There was nothing but mellowness in Lucas' stare. *For having wanted a shot at it working.*

Yeah. We still had a great run. She hummed. *He's a good person. No hard feelings.* She smiled half-heartedly. *Just as you said about you and Stephanie, me and Nathan just weren't meant to be.*

She was a little tense.

He seemingly noticed her sudden stillness, and chose to bring back the discussion to more fun grounds. He made a show of flipping the pancake in the air. *But the question is: did Nathan ever wow you with pancakes?*

Okay, go ahead, give me one of those pancakes.

As the souvenir finishes washing over her while she takes a left to go back to the fruit and vegetables section, she notices that the music in the distance now shifted.

She frowns as she stops in front of the citruses.

The lyrics talking about how arguments can become ugly between couples are uncannily tied to her current thought process.

She usually doesn't talk a whole lot about Nathan, and what he meant in her life.

She can recall the heated arguments they had for weeks. How their respective neighbors probably indeed thought they were going to tear each other apart.

Which wasn't that far from the truth.

She remembers having slammed the door behind her in anger a time or two, and ended up sleeping at Jun's because she didn't feel like being alone. Those were the days of bad romcom vibes where they would both eat ice cream or sugary treats while watching TV, and discussing their failed relationships.

Raven has no idea why she tried to make it work with Nathan even when everything was clearly falling apart. She's a rational person. She was seeing the signs for fuck's sake. They were way past the breaking point. They were in a place from which you can't come back unharmed.

But she did love him.

That made her try way harder than she would've with anybody else. Lucas is also right: she can't blame herself for having loved him. Nathan is responsible for his own decisions. Even if the hurt gutted her.

Opening that Pandora box again is hitting differently this time around. She feels slightly more at peace with the events.

Water has run under the bridge for sure, but maybe letting it out there with Lucas is the first step toward truly leaving it all behind.

Her friends helped her deal with the conflicting feelings it awoke in her back then, but she's aware that she decided to build those walls around her heart by herself, and against everyone's advice.

It's been working pretty well so far.

Although maybe she wants more out of life moving forward. What she might steadily start feeling toward Lucas is—

She feels Lucas' hand slide onto the small of her back. She smiles as she automatically leans back into him. She'd recognized his touch anywhere.

He puts a couple of garlic bulbs in the cart as he bends down to whisper in her ear, "We might have a problem."

She makes a face, turning to face him. "Why's that?"

"It was Jun." He takes a step back. "They found no DNA on the new letter and envelope." Raven opens her mouth to speak, but he shakes his head before she has time to. "Not any pet DNA either."

"That's a shame." She exhales soundly. "It would've been nice to start making some links."

"But speaking of links, she looked into Gabriel Smith's financials and dealings."

She raised a curious eyebrow. "And?"

He puts his hands in his pockets. "Financials look semi-clean apparently, but—"

She interjects. "Semi-clean?" She furrows her eyebrows. "What does that even mean?"

He half-smiles. "He seems to not be directly dealing in illegality, but Jun found a couple of questionable business links and transactions."

"Again, not illegal on paper so nothing we can really do about it."

He hums inattentively. "I'd love for you to go through the document I'm supposed to sign to lock him in as a client. He sent it back with his lawyer's annotations, and our legal team will undoubtedly go through it, but I trust you." He searches her eyes for any kind of approval. "You'll tell me if there's anything in there that would put me in a bad position if he starts acting up."

"Sure." She smiles warmly. "I'll take a look."

He angles to look at the citruses. "Here's another thing Jun told me. Smith is clearly in business with Cameron Wallace." He glances at Raven. "Ring a bell?"

She breathes in. She has to come clean. "I had a hunch."

He looks surprised. "You had a..."

She cuts him off. "Don't hate me." She sounds determined. "I saw them talking to each other a while back. That's the main reason why I saw a big red flag at the fundraiser when I learned that he was becoming one of your clients."

"Why would I hate you?" He laughs lightly. "You still told me to be careful. You had your reasons for not wanting to share all the info. Doing so would've meant telling me why you quit your job, and I think you weren't ready to at the time. Which is totally fine by me." He picks up some lemons, smiling teasingly. "It just took me blowing your mind in bed for you to feel comfortable enough to share."

"You're truly hilarious." She summons her best fakely offended gaze. "Let's blame the insane amount of serotonin spiking through my body after each orgasm now."

"Oh?" He raised an interested eyebrow. "An insanely high level?"

"Don't be smug." She smirks. "You look radiantly wrecked after every climax, too."

He puts the lemons in their basket beside Raven, peering into her eyes. "I have no trouble admitting that."

She reaches to curl her index finger in the right front pocket of his jeans to bring him to her. "Same here."

He grabs her hips instinctively. "Why did we go out of the house again?"

She smiles amusedly. "You really want me to remind you why?"

"No." He lays a kiss on her forehead. "Before I lose my train of thought due to your proximity, I also wanted to tell you that I asked Jun to dig deeper into this odd bond between Smith and Wallace." He idly traces patterns on top of her shorts. "Kyan told me about some rumors that are spreading across the city. It hadn't gotten to my ears yet—probably because I was too busy with everything happening at work—but a big transaction that involves the transfer of important assets from a powerful individual is at play apparently. And word is that it needs to happen quickly." He breathes in steadily. "Big names like Smith and Wallace run the show more often than not. It wouldn't surprise me if they were somehow involved in that transaction. It would also at least explain the urgency Smith seems to have about signing the contract asap."

"Would make sense." She places her hands flat on his pec in an attempt at making him relax. His heart is thumping in his chest. She keeps her tone light and reassuring. "This thing is becoming a full blown investigation."

"It is." He half-smiles, sounding more cheerful. "But we're on vacation for now, yeah?" He pulls away to get another lemon from the display. "Let's enjoy ourselves, and not think about it too much. I quite like it here, far away from the chaos that is governing my life in New York."

She watches him choose some pomelos. "You really feel that way about your life?"

"I didn't used to think that, but I've been more in tune with my inner voice lately I think, which prompted me to analyze a few things." He grabs a few red grapefruit next. "You know, my sister told me my life was more tumultuous than I thought when she gave me this hat." He tilts his visor up, smiling coyly. "That to her the symbol on it was a great reading of me constantly trying to find balance both in life and when surfing. She said that the symbol of that open infinity loop laced within a wave was for me still being on the quest of finding said equilibrium."

"That's quite amazing, and a whole lot of great symbolism." Raven picks some mandarins. "I love it. I agree with your sister. You have this beautifully layered personality." She flashes him a soft smile. "You need to let every part shine, Lucas."

"I have a feeling that *you* are making me be more attentive to what I want, Rae." He goes back to the cart, turning to look at her. "You challenge me, and make me question things."

She faces him, scanning his eyes. He's very serious.

She has to admit that he always listens to what she has to say, and takes her suggestions into account. Even when he starts with an a-priori because he wants to protect his business and his lifestyle, he is still willing to dig further. He never dismisses anything she tells him.

However, she can't let that get to her head. They are arguably still on vastly different journeys, and—

She inhales to focus. As Lucas said, they are on pseudo vacations. Better enjoy it.

She gets closer to him. "Happy to be of assistance." As she puts the citrus next to the lemons in the basket, her eyes linger on another item. She half-smiles. "That's an awful lot of garlic." She looks at Lucas beside her. "Are we battling vampires?"

"How did you guess?" He slides a hand around her waist, bending down to murmur against her lips, "We can even use it as if we're true vampire hunters."

"So if we want to keep them away, we just have to hang some garlic, and stay in our bubble?" Lucas hums. Raven brushes her nose along his. "That's gonna be nice."

"Oh, yeah?" He kisses her briefly.

She reaches to trace the stubble along his mandible. "Mhmm. Because I want you as close as possible."

"Lucky I'm not a vampire, then." He curves a corner of his mouth upward. "I intend to stay as close to you as humanly possible."

She mirrors his expression, gently caressing the back of his neck. "We sound like freakin' teenagers sometimes."

"Do you really care?"

It's her turn to kiss him tenderly. "Nah."

"Good." He beams as she leans back. "The garlic is because I'm making toum." He watches her walk away toward the apple selection. "You'll see, you can't enjoy chicken shawarma without toum."

"Oh, I know what toum is." She turns around quickly to smile something soft at him. "I was playing around. I can't wait to test the actual traditional Lebanese recipe you have."

"I'm sure you won't be deceived. It's the best, you'll see."

She hums to herself.

She can still feel the coarseness of his beard, and his silky lips on hers.

The sensation is delightfully numbing.

She's never been one for overflows of PDA. A kiss here and there or holding hands can be fine. Although she hasn't done any of it in a very long time.

Because it never felt right.

Somehow, just like the rest, it comes naturally with Lucas.

She truly doesn't care about them sounding like they're in high school sometimes. She couldn't care less about what other people can think.

She's happy right now, and she doesn't give a damn about the whole world knowing it.

She's having the best sex of her life, and she wants to scream it from the rooftops.

She reflects as she grabs a mango.

This new rush at the beginning of any encounter is a normal thing, right? It usually goes away with time. Although, she never truly got it with any of the partners she had in the last few years since Nathan.

The thing is, she's not certain it's fleeting at all this time around.

Lucas is not a new encounter. He's even been inhabiting her mind for years. She feels like she knows him inside and out a little more each day.

And even through her doubts, she absolutely loves what she's seeing. She feels good with him to a point where everything makes sense for the transient moment when she's in his arms.

Looking out of the corner of her eye, she realizes that Lucas is staring back at her with an eggplant in his hand. He points at it, wiggling his eyebrows suggestively in silent questioning as to if they should buy it or not.

She laughs brightly.

It's for all small moments like this that she feels like she wouldn't want to be anywhere else than with Lucas Blake.

She feels that together they navigate through instants just like they surf waves. With an ease and abandonment she desperately needed before he came back into her life.

She can sense that this week is off to a great start.

Sixteen

Uncovering Layers

As Lucas finishes adding the oil to the toum he's making from scratch in Heather and Zoe's kitchen, he hums to the beat of Raven's playlist. She asked him if he wanted to listen to his own music because she'd love to, but he felt like being engulfed by hers.

So he told her as much, and the music is enveloping them as they've been cooking.

Raven might live in Brooklyn, she's definitely all about California. She is right at home here. He can sense it everywhere he looks, and in each of her gestures.

She blends seamlessly within the environment. Everything she does is bleeding from an ease he had yet to fully experience with her.

He felt right at home yesterday in her house, and he has to admit that he feels good every time he's surrounded by her—or anything that can be tied to her.

Coming to San Diego on a whim is possibly the best decision he ever took in his life since he decided to go to Mykonos all those years ago.

The common denominator of both those defining moments is Raven.

She's clearly in a league of her own.

No one ever made him feel as amazing as her, and he doubts anyone else ever will.

It's intoxicating.

Plus, they seem to only be growing closer and closer since they've been away from the whirlwind of New York.

The quietude he's living through is a perfect contrast to how his professional life seems to be slowly sliding into unpredictability.

He could deal with menaces toward himself, but ever since he got the second letter, only one thing is making rounds in his head. The fact that the people he cares about might be targeted is unacceptable to him.

In addition, now knowing that there's a high possibility that the whole thing is orchestrated by individuals dealing in big scale money laundering and human trafficking is making his head spin.

One step at a time, he muses.

He shakes his head as he takes out two bamboo cutting boards.

He is trying his best to not let the whole situation overwhelm him, and having Raven near greatly helps in that regard.

He wasn't kidding when he told her that she was able to quiet his mind.

Things make sense when he's with her. She always manages to soothe his psyche.

The feeling of plenitude that inhabits him is in all of their kisses, in each time they have sex, and at every single moment when their eyes meet.

When she smiles at him just before breaking out into laughter, he wants to melt on the spot.

She's bringing him pure peacefulness.

He wants to make it last.

He won't abandon just yet to bring her on a date. Maybe later this week they could have a nice evening together by the ocean, and—

"The table is all set," Raven's joyful voice reaches his ears as he puts the kalamata olives in a serving dish.

"It was a great idea to choose the balcony upstairs like last time." He opens the refrigerator to take the marinated chicken out. "I love the energy up there."

"Same." She takes a knife. "Heather and Zoe have a great view, and they arranged the space wonderfully."

He prepares a baking tray, focussing on the task at hand. "Chicken has not marinated for as long as the original recipe states, but it will still be great." He looks at the time on the microwave. "It's very nice of Heather to have messaged us to say that she was with Zoe, and that they were both on their way home together. It will be perfect timing for it to be cooked by the time they get here."

Raven starts dicing tomatoes. "And you're going to serve it with the Mediterranean salad we'll make now?"

"Exactly." He lays the chicken in the tray to then go wash his hands. "And I'll put the pieces of chicken in pita pockets. Pitas will be *loaded* with it." He smiles coyly as he slides the tray in the pre-heated oven. "Then you can put as much of the Toum I made as possible on top. That's the whole beauty of it."

"Can't wait to taste it." She beamed, quickly looking at him mirroring her actions by cutting cubes of cucumber. "You said that the chicken hasn't marinated as long as you usually do, but it's okay?"

"Yeah." He smiles knowingly at her. "Normally it would sit in the refrigerator overnight, but one hour will do." He puts the cubes in a bowl as soon as he chops them. "My mom was very particular about letting it marinate for as long as possible until that one time when she noticed that it didn't matter."

Raven perked up, sounding very interested. "What happened?"

He decides to share this little part of his past with her. "My sister unexpectedly came back from school in tears one day because her boyfriend had broken up with her." He lifts a corner of his mouth upward at the memory. "She said that the only thing she wanted to eat was our mom's chicken shawarma." He grabs a bunch of parsley next. "Now, my mother had prepared some for the next day, and so it was already in the fridge." He starts chopping it, smiling absentmindedly.

"The meat had only been an hour or so in there, but she couldn't refuse anything to my sister so we cooked it."

Raven adds the tomatoes to the cucumbers in the bowl. "And it was just as good as usual?"

"Yep. It was ultra tasteful." He puts the herbs in the salad bowl. "So one hour is enough."

"That's great." She leans her hip against the counter to face him. "You talk about your mom with a softness that is very endearing."

He's not one to usually open up and share things about his family or personal life easily.

He somehow feels safe in this moment right here to do so with Raven.

"I owe my mom a lot." He drizzles some olive oil on top of the salad, becoming reflective. "She stopped her nursing studies when she got pregnant with me. Different era back then, and it was all too much for her to deal with at the time." He breathes in. "She then became a waitress. We were a pretty normal family until my dad disappeared."

Raven frowns. "I'm so sorry that he—"

He doesn't let her finish. He wants to get this slice of his life out there while he has the courage to. "Then she did everything in her power to give us the life she said we deserved." He clenches his jaw a little at the recollection of what his father's behavior had meant for his mom. "She was working long hours. At some point, she even had three jobs at once to make ends meet."

Raven reaches to curl her hand around his forearm gently. "I can only imagine how hard it must've been for you back then."

"I took care of my sister as best as I could in the evenings when my mom wasn't home. Helped her with her homeworks and all school projects when she was older. We grew really close Lena and I." He inhales deeply. Raven's thumb soothingly rubbing his extensor muscle is the only comfort he needs. He puts his hand on top of hers. "I saw my mother struggle a whole lot, and be dead tired more often than not." He peered into Raven's eyes. "But whenever my sister or I would smile or we would have a nice dinner all together, she was the happiest I've ever seen her."

"I'm sure that having you with her was the best encouragement she could've had." She scoots closer, pressing her nose to his bicep. "When life throws us curveballs, being with the ones we love most is often what gives us the strength to keep going."

He relaxes as he slides an arm around her waist. "When I made enough money, the first thing I did was to buy my mom a proper house." He buries his nose into Raven's hair. "She also went back to nursing school, and finished her degree. Nowadays she works in a retirement home."

"That's amazing." She rubs the small of his back softly. "What's your mom's name?"

He smiles tenderly, turning to face Raven. "Yasmine."

"It's a beautiful name."

He feels good talking to Raven like this. He senses that she's not only listening, she's supporting him.

If he always used to think that opening up to people could just give them more ways to potentially hurt him in the future, he doesn't care right now.

He doesn't mind being more vulnerable in front of Raven.

She's genuinely *in* the moment with him. She's embracing it.

It spurs him on. "My father's name is James. James Blake. He was an engineering project manager." He presses his lips into a thin line. "I absolutely hate what he put my mom through. To this day, she still wonders what happened because we all haven't got a clue. He just left for work one morning, and never came back. I'm convinced that he probably even has a whole new family now." He lets out a disheartened breath. "I hope he treats them better than he treated us." He becomes reflective as he gets lost in Raven's presence as she presses herself closer to him. "Close friends of mine have asked me through the years why I never changed my last name despite the resentment." He toys with the hem of her t-shirt. "I think it's because a big part of me wanted to show that I could maybe be a different kind of 'Blake'."

"I say you're succeeding quite well." She traces idle patterns on his pecs with her fingertips. "You never had any desire to actually track James down at any point?"

"Strangely no." He shakes his head. "A big part of me doesn't even want to hear what he might have to say. If he would've liked to show a sign of life he could've. He didn't." He furrows his eyebrows. "I constructed my life without him in it so I say that I have nothing to tell him either."

"Fair enough. You're the one who knows what's best for you." She smiles warmly at him. "Sometimes it helps people to have proper closure, that's all I'm saying."

"I know you only have my best interests at heart." He slides a hand on the side of her face. "I blamed myself for the longest time that maybe I wasn't good enough for my dad to stay." He uses his thumb to trace her mandible. "That I wasn't a great enough son." There's sadness in his attempt at a smile. "Therapy helped, but then what if I have it in me to do the same?" He frowns. "To just not care about people I—"

She cuts him off. "You're not your dad."

He exhales soundly. "You don't know that."

"True. I don't." She stays unflinching. "I never knew him, and never will from the looks of it." She reaches to scratch her nails along his jawline. "But you're aware of the pattern, and that's a big step." She bores her eyes into his. "You're also one of the kindest and most considerate men I ever met." She leans forward. "Your dedication when you put your mind to something is staggering." She kisses him softly. "It's inspiring."

He lingers against her lips.

He never thought that he would ever talk about part of his family experiences with such ease casually in the middle of a mundane task such as cooking.

Raven has an uncanny way to sneak into every part of his brain to make him feel safe and accepted.

It's powerfully dizzying.

"Now my mind only wants one thing though."

She hums, skimming her nose along his. "What's that?"

"You," he whispers before kissing her lazily.

The make-out session becomes heated in no time.

He wants Raven to feel the extent to which he means what he just said, and she feels like she wants him to understand that she's not going anywhere.

He doesn't want her to. His life is tremendously better with her in it.

Now being able to hold her close or kiss her whenever he feels like it is exhilarating.

When she fully curls her hand around his throat to angle his head, he swiftly lifts her up on the empty island behind them.

The instant he presses himself flush to her between her parted legs, she moans deep into his mouth.

As he brushes his fingers through her hair, he can feel her grab the visor of his cap to remove the hat from his head. She places it on the counter next to her before flying her digits into his black locks.

He couldn't be more glad to not put any product in his hair lately. Having her caress his skull is terrific.

He instantly sighs against her tongue.

She shifts her attention to trailing her mouth along his jugular. "You feel so good, Luke," she murmurs into his skin.

He groans.

He's steadily getting lost in her. His thoughts are becoming blurrier by the second.

He massages her scalp, deftly removing her hairband to free her hair from her ponytail.

She leans back to flip it on one side, reaching between them to take hold of his belt buckle. He instinctively sets out to kiss her passionately as she pulls him even closer to her.

The second she lightly sucks on his tongue, his self-control falters dangerously.

He wants no clothes between them.

He wants to worship her for hours.

He wants to hear her panting his name.

He can feel himself responding in strides to her as he caresses up her thighs.

He slips his hands under her t-shirt, applying pressure on her lower vertebrae. "I want you so bad right now, Rae," he breathes out.

She moans as she arches into him. "I want you, too." She scrapes her nails across his abs under his top. "But we're not at my place, and—"

"I know." He sighs once more, pressing his forehead against hers in defeat. "I wouldn't want to be disrespectful of Heather and Zoe's space."

She bites into her bottom lip. "Later, yeah?"

"Mhmm." He inhales steadily. "All night."

"I can't wait." She flicks her stare down to his crotch to then peer into his eyes. "Will you be okay keeping this under control until we—"

He interjects, snorting. "I can summon a few images that will help me calm down, don't worry."

"My curiosity is piqued." She smiles amusedly while tracing his shoulder blades with the pads of her fingers. "What works to tone down your erec—"

The sound of a door closing in the distance startles them.

"What's for dinner, guys?" Heather's voice reaches their ears. "I saw your car outside, Raven. I know you're already here."

The call out instantly prompts Raven to get off the counter and onto her feet while Lucas puts his baseball cap back on.

As he adjusts it on his head, Heather turns the corner of the dining room in her black pantsuit, looking equally tired and solemn. "Zoe will arrive in a minute. She's on an important call about a potential new project." She fixes some loose strands of hair falling from her bun. "Have you thought about what to order for—" She trails off, smirking while looking directly at Raven. She raises an eyebrow as she approaches the kitchen. "New t-shirt, Raven?"

Raven finishes straightening, and tucking said shirt in the front of her shorts. "I'm sure you know it's not mine."

"Obviously." Haddy smiles knowingly. "I just wanted to tease you a little. You're glowing, my friend." She glances at Lucas briefly. "You're *both* glowing." She alternates her stare between Lucas and Raven. "So you two..."

"Yeah." Raven combs her fingers through her hair, smiling something mellow at her friend. "Yeah, we slept together."

"Well I, for one, am happy about it." Heather returns the coy smile, directing her attention to Lucas. "Raven doesn't get that smile on her face because of just anyone. You better keep her satisfied, mister."

He holds Haddy's stare. He wants her to know how serious he is about Raven. "Trust me, I have no intention to do any less than that."

"Good." Heather stops in front of them. "I hope I didn't interrupt anything just now."

"We know how to behave." Raven puts the cutting boards in the sink to wash them. "You don't have to sanitize your kitchen if that's what you're asking."

Her friend shrugs, a playful expression flickering through her eyes. "I was thinking more about the sofa in the living room, but—"

"Because of that one time after a party at your place in college?" Raven tilts her head in questioning while facing Heather. "You're aware that back then I was just making out with Steve, right? It didn't get very far."

"Oh, I know very well." Heather looks around at the plates and bowls on the counter. "You even let him know you weren't interested in it going any further the next day, and never had sex with the guy. I just like teasing you."

"How kind of you." Raven laughs lightly. "Anyway, your couch is safe. We were actually preparing dinner for you and Zoe." She gestures at the food in front of her. "Lucas wanted to cook one of his family recipes for you."

"That's so kind of you." Haddy gazes at Lucas with gratitude. "I can't wait to taste it. I'm sure Zoe will be equally delighted." She seems to analyze the situation. "Is there anything I can do to help?"

"No." The managing director shakes his head. "Your only job is to sit back and relax. Actually, you and Raven can go upstairs and wait, I'll bring everything up." He grins at them. "Go unwind."

As Haddy takes his suggestion, and exits the kitchen, Raven wraps her arms around his waist. "You sure there's nothing else I can help you with?"

"Well..." He purposely trails off, raising a suggestive eyebrow.

She snorts. "Except *that*, you obsessed man."

He puts his palm flat on the small of her back, pulling her to him. "I think you're equally obsessed."

She hums, trailing her index finger down his sternum. "Touché."

"But no." He lets his own fingers glide along her forearm. "There's not a lot left to do. You can go, I'll join you in a few."

"Sounds perfect."

He bends down to whisper playfully, "And you'll tell me all about Steve."

She chuckles while making a face. "Steve was a very bad kisser, and we never talked again." She tilts her head up. "I only had one boyfriend through college, and it lasted about a year. I highly preferred to be on my own, and not bother with useless relationship drama." She smiles amusedly. "There. Happy?"

"It's like you and I are sharing a brain. Why bother indeed." He gets lost in her eyes. "Although I feel that you're different from all the rest for me, Raven."

"Same." She breathes in soundly, and gives him a peck. "Come join us soon?"

He hums as he watches her stride to the second floor.

This all consuming feeling he has toward Raven is only growing the more time they spend together. It's not something he experienced a whole lot before, if ever.

He's unsure how to deal with it.

For the first time in more than a decade, he wants to give a shot at a real relationship with someone. Raven makes him feel mighty, and allows him to be unguarded at once. He can sense his whole being wanting to abandon itself to her.

She *is* different from everybody else.

Even if she just said that he was also unique, she looked a little preoccupied.

It's arguably because they still haven't chatted about those concerns she had before, but he's certain that it can't be a deal breaker. He's very ready to navigate anything and everything with her.

For now, he'll continue to go with the flow.

As the tangy fragrance of the shawarma fills the space, he checks on the chicken in the oven. It looks to be done.

He smiles.

He can already taste the satisfying spice in his mouth.

He can feel that the evening will be exactly what he needs: easy times with uncomplicated and great people.

And that's all he needs at the moment.

Seventeen

Immersive Convergence

"I swear you should've seen her dance to that song, Lucas." Heather takes a bite of her cheesecake. "You would've lost your mind."

Lucas beams, turning his head to look at Raven beside him. "I have no doubt about it. She already convinced me that she's in a class of her own."

Zoe snorts while fixing the collar of her black floral blouse. "Let me play it to get the right energy here."

The graphic designer swiftly takes her phone out of her jeans pockets to connect it to the outside sound system, choosing the right tune before gathering all the playing cards on the table into a deck to shuffle it anew.

Raven looks at her friend who just won the past two games of rummy while everyone hums to the beat.

The whole meal has been nothing but delightful. The food was beyond delicious, and the conversation, natural.

As Heather continues to reminisce about old memories of that time when she accepted a dare—and stripped down to her bikini in front of Nathan and her closest friends to a well known summer anthem composed of lyrics about women and beaches in California—Raven slowly feels the tiredness creeping through her skeleton.

So far, the slight jetlag hadn't taken its toll, but the limited amount of sleep she got during the last day is now definitely playing a part in her mental state.

Which is not a bad thing at all per se.

If she had trouble finding slumber in New York lately with everything that has been going on in her life, being here with Lucas is a soothing respite to all the outside noise. She'd have no trouble easily falling asleep next to him for the foreseeable future.

Preferably snuggling up against him.

This sudden love of intimacy is a little destabilizing. She hasn't desired gentle moments like that for the longest time. It took Lucas for her to want to live through them again.

He feels tremendous at every touch.

Even right in this instant, having his arm draped behind her on the chair while he aimlessly caresses the nape of her neck feels idyllic.

She sighs as she absentmindedly makes a small dance move to the tempo. "I blame Jun for the idea."

Haddy chuckles. "You definitely can't blame the alcohol, you were very far from being drunk."

"It makes it even better." She smiles warmly, idly reaching to curl her hand around Lucas' thigh under the table. "I was in total control."

Zoe places the deck beside her plate, signifying that they won't go for another gaming round just yet. She half-smiles teasingly. "Couldn't say the same thing about Nathan."

As the last line of the tune echoes in the space, Lucas presses his nose into Raven's hair. He makes up his own reference to the music. "Do you really not mind sand?" he whispers.

She bites into her bottom lip. "You know sand never bothered me in Mykonos."

He hums, laying a gentle kiss on her temple. "Same. You made it worth it every time."

She leans into him. "I could do it again."

"Don't tempt me," he murmurs into her ear.

She slides her hand up toward his crotch. "If I intend to follow up on it I don't see where the harm is."

He shifts in his seat. "Before we actually make it to the beach, I'd very much like to see you fall over the edge on your balcony."

"Mmm." She brushes over the bulge forming in the front of his pants. "Do you want to bend me over the railing or—"

He cuts her off. "No. I want to see you when you shatter." He combs his fingers into her hair at the back of her head, massaging gently. "I want to kneel in front of you before I—"

Heather's laughter snaps them back to the moment. "Poor Nathan didn't expect what hit him that night." She looks at the managing director. "You know about him, Lucas, yeah?"

"A little." He clears his throat while straightening on his chair. "Raven told me what happened between them."

Raven brushes her fingers through her hair, silently thanking Lucas for having stayed vague.

She knows that her friends wouldn't open that can of worms again, and hand out information she doesn't want to be out there for just anyone. Nathan has always been a sensitive subject to address.

The fact that Lucas is considerate to the point where he gave just enough away to answer, but not too much so someone could build from it, and potentially make for a more loaded exchange, is heart-warming. He doesn't fish for things she's not willing to share by herself.

In his smallest gestures and actions, he is thoughtful.

He is constantly showing that he has an utmost respect for her. That he navigates events alongside her, taking her feelings into account.

She considers herself lucky to be involved with someone that mind-ful.

She inhales deeply, removing her hand from Lucas' leg to grab her cup of coffee.

Can she truly consider that she's on her way to build something with Lucas?

It's only been a little more than a week since they reconnected, but they have gone through a lot together so far. Those powerful feelings toward him she had kept buried for years resurfaced progressively. She let them take over at one point or another. Just like all the rest with him, it felt natural to succumb to them.

Those feelings crept up on her without warning.

Actually, if she's being honest, the signs were very much there.

She furrows her eyebrows as she takes a sip.

She never liked putting labels on things.

A 'lover', a 'boyfriend', or a 'husband' can have the same ring to her. It can be as meaningful when the feelings are just as strong in either case. When the significance of that person in one's life is undeniable and unequaled.

She's always been a firm believer that when you know within your soul that it feels right, you know. It's embedded there for better or worse.

She places her mug back on the surface, her digits lingering along the handle.

So is this where she wants to go with Lucas? Does she want a real shot at constructing a future with him? Let him have access to her heart unlike anyone ever has since Nathan?

She knows he could crush it in a split second.

But there's no true happiness without the prospect of pain, they say.

Is she willing to put it all on the table?

Even if she tries to go with the flow, and not let anything get to her, the thought is making rounds in her head.

She is aware that there's a lot at play here. She'll have to confront Lucas sooner or later about their very different views of where they want their lives to lead.

She's unsure she can stay in New York. She certainly has no desire to continue dealing with the level of corruption she's been witnessing for years.

But he's been opening up to her more and more and he feels like he might want to—

As if Heather had read her mind, her steady voice reaches Raven's ears. "So you know that what went down with Nathan is in great parts why she built an armor around herself." Her friend is staring at the managing director. She points her index finger at him. "If you ever manage to pierce through it, don't hurt her. If you do, I'm gonna track you down myself."

"Isn't that a direct menace?" he teases. "Coming from a lawyer at that."

"I would take it very seriously." Zoe smiles knowingly. "Haddy is fierce when it comes down to protecting her loved ones."

He puts his free hand over his heart solemnly. "I have no intention of hurting Raven."

"Sometimes we have the best intentions, but things slip from us, right?" Heather locks eyes with him. "All I'm saying is that I've never seen Raven be so much at ease with someone in forever. So I'm keeping an eye on you, Lucas."

He nods seriously. "Duly noted."

"I can take care of myself, Haddy." Raven's tone is nothing but serious. "Thank you. We'll be fine."

"I know you're stubborn as fuck, and very capable of handling yourself." Her friend laughs lightly. "I'm just making it clear that I have your back."

Raven mirrors her expression, a playful smile dancing on her lips. "I think Lucas knew that even before you said anything."

"You guys are tightly knit, and it's something I highly admire." The managing director trails his fingers up Raven's shoulder blade. "It's essential to be able to have good people in our corner throughout life."

"Agreed." Zoe pushes her plate away from her, gazing at the lawyer in front of her. "At least Lucas knows how to cook, that's a definite plus, Raven. That dinner was fabulous."

Lucas bows his head. "Thank you. It makes me happy that you loved it."

The graphic designer looks at her wife beside her. "I think we hadn't eaten chicken shawarma since—"

Heather finishes the sentence. "Angie's funeral."

Silence falls upon them.

A slight tension buzzes through the air.

Raven furrows her eyebrows. "I wasn't there."

"No. It was after you and Ju had gone back to New York. We decided to honor her somehow." Haddy glances at Lucas to explain. "You see, she was a big fan of horror movies, Middle Eastern cuisine, thriller books, and a big believer of Day of the Dead."

As Heather trails off to take a sip of her coffee, Zoe finishes the story. "So we decided to watch a horror classic while eating chicken shawarma." She smiles sadly. "It became very emotional fast because a ton of souvenirs flooded over us, and it tainted the experience a little. So I think our subconscious purposely made us stay away from watching any horror flicks and eating shawarma since"

"I'm so sorry." Lucas frowns. "I had no idea. I—"

Heather cuts him off. "Hey, it's all good. You've rewritten over this difficult moment with a way better one now." She smiles warmly. "I want to eat this chicken shawarma every week."

Lucas grins. "If I was living closer it could be arranged."

"Just ship it to us." Zoe flashes him a soft expression. "Angie would've loved it, too."

"She was such a beautiful soul. Always there to help others in any way she could." Heather breathes in. "I remember how she was accomplishing such great things during the time when she was clean. But she was putting so much pressure on herself that it didn't help her addiction." She makes a face as she feels her wife gently caress her thigh in a comforting gesture. "It was fueling it."

"We truly lost one of the best." Raven sounds very reflective. "But I guess she is still amongst us in multiple ways."

"Mhmm." Heather hums while taking another sip of her coffee. "You have the most beautiful, and pretty permanent saying for that directly on you."

Lucas stares at Raven, dropping his tone to a whisper in sudden comprehension. "The tattoo along your spine."

"Yeah." She turns to lock eyes with him. "Did you read it?"

He shakes his head. "I was otherwise busy, and then the sheets were hiding part of it. I didn't want to risk waking you up so no, I didn't."

"As if it would've bothered me that you pushed the sheet away. You still started kissing down my neck and I—" She trails off. She can vividly recall how good he felt when she pulled him close, and she ended up as the little spoon to go back to sleep. "Anyway. That's not the point."

"Oh, but you can just admit that you liked it." He leans forward. "Because I certainly adore when you fall asleep in my arms."

"You know I loved it, too." She scans his eyes as she puts her palm flat on his stomach. "And if you would've read it all, the script says 'Eternity dwells in the fragile equilibrium between life and death'." She smiles something soft at him. "I always loved to think that as long as we remember the dead, we keep their memory alive, and they forever live with us. We can honor them with our lives. By talking about them, and striving to do better at every step."

He half-smiles. "It also circles back to Angie having those beliefs."

Raven scratches his abs lightly. "Exactly."

"That's amazing." It's his turn to reach for his cup of lungo. "I love how the ink on your body ties into the very core of who you are."

"Isn't that the whole point?" She yawns against her will. "If getting tattooed, better make it count, I say."

He frowns. "You're tired, huh?"

"Yeah, but I want to stay." She shifts her look to her friends in front of them. "I feel great being here with all of you."

"You can also sleep here." Heather looks at Zoe for approval. "We don't mind. Right, sweetie?"

"Obviously not." The graphic designer smiles brightly. "Something also tells me that Lucas won't have to sleep on the sofa this time around."

The managing director looks at the couple in front of him over the rim of his cup. "If Raven wants me to, I will go on the couch no problem."

Raven drops her hand in his lap. "Stop being silly."

Heather lights up at the prospect of them staying. "We could also all go have an early breakfast at 'The Mission Cafe' before I go to work."

"It's a great idea. I love that place." Raven suddenly knits an eyebrow remembering something. "But we don't have a change of clothes. We could go back to my house and—"

He interjects. "I left the ones we had put on the side of our luggage for the beach in the trunk. If you want to stay here tonight we can use those."

"See? Your boyf—" Zoe stops herself short to finish that word, swiftly reformulating. "Lucas is offering a nice solution. I know I personally would love for you two to stay. We could continue to play, eat, drink, and spew nonsense just like the old days."

Raven has to admit that spending another nice evening with them like old times would be fantastic.

But Lucas and her thought that—

She ignores the slight slip-up of her friend, directing her gaze to Lucas instead. "You're sure you don't mind if we don't go back to my place tonight?"

"No." He smiles tenderly at her. "This week was originally all about you spending time with your friends and being in San Diego. I have no trouble following your lead for anything you want to do."

His mindfulness never fails to impress Raven.

He knows very well that no matter how much she craves him, she arguably won't feel comfortable having sex in her friend's guest room with them just next door.

Even in the en-suite bathroom she'd have to try to be quiet, and it's something she has trouble doing with him. Although, he usually loves to drink her cries of ecstasy every chance he gets. Kissing him sloppily as she unravels is nothing short of glorious.

Maybe they could—

She inhales deeply.

She's exhausted, anyway. And he seems to be very on board with just living every and any moment with her.

She slumps into her seat. "Okay." She gestures at her friends. "Deal another round, Zoe."

She can feel Lucas rub her back soothingly upon hearing her say this. She smiles.

Those small instants are slowly and steadily growing on her. The more it goes on, the more she can imagine Lucas not only in her bed, but in her everyday life.

He is passionate and sweet in everything he does.

He blends incredibly well with her friends, and she felt right at home with some of his not long ago.

She can navigate any serious or silly conversation with him openly.

He makes her feel happy.

There's always this pleasant warmth spreading through her every time they're close, and this sublime overwhelming tingling rush along her nerve endings.

Could she be fall—

"Amazing." The graphic designer sets to shuffle the cards, locking eyes with Raven. "Want to switch things up and play a round of blackjack?"

She chuckles. "Feeling like pulling off a Jun?"

Lucas sounds curious. "What does Jun like to do when playing blackjack?"

"It's always a dare blackjack," Raven starts explaining. "Jun is the dealer, and if we lose we have to execute a dare. The fun is that she always comes up with some inventive shit. Part of the fun is to discover what she has in store for us."

Heather snorts. "That's how Raven ended up executing that half strip tease on the beach."

Zoe raises a playful eyebrow. "Want to dare another one now?"

Raven hums. "Bring it on."

The graphic designer looks surprised. "You're serious?"

"Sure." She shrugs. "I'm feeling lucky."

Zoe smiles coyly. "Game on, then."

As the song shifts to another cheerful one, Raven prepares herself for what should be an enjoyable night.

Hours later, as Raven climbs down the stairs to fetch a glass of water in a pair of shorties and a black tank top, she combs her fingers through her loose hair, and smiles absentmindedly.

Climbing into the platform ivory upholstered king bed next to Lucas after her quick shower earlier was everything she didn't know she needed.

Come here, he breathed out while extending an arm on the pillow beside him in invitation.

He had washed himself prior while she was still chatting with Heather about her friend's upcoming trial in the kitchen.

She couldn't resist his sleepy expression while he was laying stretched on the mattress in only his geometrically patterned boxer briefs. The dim lighting in the coastal decorated bedroom was painting his body in a perfectly warm hue.

He looked fucking bewitching.

She lifted the white bamboo flat sheet to snuggle into his side. *Thank you,* she murmured against his lips before kissing him tenderly.

He wrapped his arm around her, curling his hand around her hip bone. *For what?*

For everything. She nuzzled into his neck. *For making this evening even more enjoyable than I thought it could be. You've been nothing but adorable.*

I'm just being me.

She smiled into his skin. *Well, then, thank you for being you.*

He sneaked his hand under her tank top. *It's just a shame that you won at blackjack, and didn't have to honor that dare.*

You would've liked for me to strip, huh?

Is that even a question?

She skimmed her nose along the scruff on his jawline. *But you're aware that you can see me naked anytime you want now, right?*

He traced her curves lazily with his fingertips. *Apparently not right now.*

There's a few exceptions. She laid a kiss on the underside of his mandible. *Being in public is one of them.* She trailed her lips on his pulse point. *Being in the adjacent room as my friends who are going through a rough patch is another.*

I get it, don't worry. You know, just having you pressed against me is enough.

Oh, really? She smirked as she licked up his jugular. *So you wouldn't want me to go down on you right now?* She slid her hand down his abdomen. *With no barrier between my mouth and your cock this time. Build you up just enough so I can then straddle you, and—* She trailed off as she dipped the pads of her finger underneath the waistband of his underwear. *Oh, but I wouldn't even have to build you up, would I?* She propped herself up to face him. *I could just lazily gives you head, and swa—*

He cut her off, groaning. *Do you have any idea how hard you're making it for me to not roll you over, and go bury my head between your thighs right now?*

She kissed him lazily, palming the bulge at the front of his boxers. *I think I have a small idea.*

His breath became shorter, his muscles tensing in an attempt at not bucking into her touch. *Rae...*

She lingered against his lips. *Yes?*

He took hold of her wrist, his pupils steadily dilating. *We better stop that before it gets out of hand, huh?*

She shrugged. *If you say so.*

He pinned her hand beside her head, deftly propping himself up to hover above her. *Don't act like you don't want me, too.*

She furrowed her eyebrows. *Of course I...*

He interrupted her, gently massaging her inner thigh. *How?* He released her hand, pressing his forehead against hers. *How bad do you want me?*

She instantly brushed her fingers through his black locks, peering into his eyes. *You can check for yourself.* She took hold of his hand to guide it under her shorts and underwear. *I've been aching for you ever since we left my house.* He groaned as he traced her core. She grinded into his palm. *You should've joined me in the shower just now.* She moaned low as he circled her rib cage, letting his thumb caress the underside of her breast. *I wanted to feel the ceramic tiles on my back as you would've held me against the wall, your fingers digging into my ass while you—* She trailed off, biting into her bottom lip as he let two fingers tentatively part her folds.

He started pleasuring her. *I've been a fool.* He curved his digits *just* right. *You're soaked. Let me take care of it.*

The only sound that came out of her mouth was a whine as she chased his lips.

Having him play her perfectly as he was kissing and caressing her felt like an out of body experience. Her mind was leaving the material plane fast.

She couldn't help but constantly moan deep into his mouth under his ministrations. Her nails were gently scratching into the soft flesh of his neck and intensely gripped his back.

It didn't matter if anyone was to hear her at this point. Lucas was making it too good for her to care about anything else than him and how he felt as if he was dedicating his whole being to make her come apart.

His dexterity was dizzying.

His touch was galvanizing.

It took no more than a last flick of his thumb on her clit for her orgasm to sweep over her like a magnificent tidal wave.

The instant quietude that engulfed her was vertiginous as Lucas eased her through it.

Her brain was swimming through a pool of pure lavishness.

He seeked friction when he leaned back. *Feels good?*

She raked her fingers through his hair as she kissed him softly. *Mhmm.*

Great. He brought his fingers to his lips as he flipped onto his back. *I'm proud.*

She watched him lick his fingers clean, the most filthy sounds escaping him as he did so.

She reached to define his abs leisurely. *You have every right to brag.* She pressed her nose to his pectoral. *You feel fucking perfect, Luke.*

He instinctively wrapped his arm around her. *I'm only equally as good as my partner.* He slid his hand on the side of her face. *You bring me to new heights, Raven.*

She frowned as she looked down at his arousal. *But I didn't help you with that yet, and—*

He interjected. *You're tired. Get some rest.* He kissed the top of her head. *A rain check is fine. We weren't even supposed to do anything just now. The fact that I was able to help you release that tension coiling in your body is already an honor.*

She could feel her whole body slump against him. *You're really going to be okay?* She angled her head to lay a kiss on his wrist. *I'm sorry I'm too tired to enjoy pleasuring you right now, but if you want I don't mind if you go in the bathroom to—*

He shushed her. *It's fine. I prefer to stay in bed with you at the moment.* He rested his hand on her hip to bring her closer to him. *Don't worry about it.*

You're gonna summon those images that calm you down? she teased.

Something like that. He chuckled. *Picturing Flip vomiting on his computer over columns of numbers is usually very effective.*

It really happened?

Mhmm. He buried his nose into her hair. *At college after a hangover.*

She snorted as she draped herself half on top of him while nuzzling into the crook of his shoulder.

She had to admit that she was elated and relaxed in the best way. No other lover ever managed to render her brain that empty. Having Lucas' body against her own is easily one of the best sensations she ever experienced in her life.

Taking his hand into hers, she placed it on the other side of him, idly gliding her fingertips along the lines in his palm.

Without realizing it, next thing she knew she was tracing the outline of his tattoo on the interior of his forearm. She stared at it through heavy lidded eyes. *You said that my ink is meaningful, but something tells me that yours is, too.*

His gaze went to her face. *You didn't buy into the whole broad explanation I gave you back in Mykonos?*

I've always been convinced that there was something more to it. She half-smiled. *Quite like me on other subjects, you weren't ready to share it just yet.*

Now I feel like the very fabric of my soul is trying to converge with yours. He breathed in. *I think I can spare a few more details.*

Her heart swelled into her chest.

His words were uncannily profound, and always full of a softness she's been looking for without ever thinking she'd ever find it in her lifetime.

She delicately painted over the wiggly lines forming a crescent shape, down to dotted ones which led to an encompassing target encapsulating a wave. *From the sun to the waves, the sky to the sea,* he murmured. *The balance of the elements, what connects everything, and all that I love about the challenges I pursue in life as well as when I surf.* She kept going over a cedrus libani resting inside an upside down triangle. Lucas began drawing idle patterns next to her navel as he whispered, *That's for the roots I never felt I got, and the ones I want to remember. My mother sacrificed a lot for us. What she did in great parts made me the man I am today. Even with the little money we had, she always made sure all our needs were met. Plus, everytime we visited her side of the family, it was the closest thing I ever had to stability. Now, the symbolism of that inverted pyramid represented water and femininity for the Mayans and Egyptians.* He turned his head to kiss Raven's forehead. *I was raised amongst strong women. There's nothing more important to me than to honor the women in my life. And so this part of my tattoo also represents my undying love of water, and reminds me to always be in tune with all sides of myself.* He smiled shyly into her hair. *I might've forgotten about that part on occasions. You're slowly reminding me of the importance of it.*

She remembers she was in awe at the level of thought he put in that design. She finally glided over the arrow pointing down toward his wrist. *And what about this last part?*

That's for the path I'll make for myself through life. He closed his eyes. *It's a work in progress. Open-ended, but it ends at the tip of my fingers.*

She couldn't help herself. *The ones you just expertly pleasured me with, huh?*

Yeah. Those ones. He laughed lightly. *Honestly, I told you before, but if all this road led me to you, I'm very okay with it. I don't know what you're doing to me, Rae, but it's mind-bogglingly all-consuming.*

She hummed, intertwining their fingers. She wasn't sure she was still ready to address the potential implications of that statement he keeps repeating. She wanted to just bask in him for a while longer. So she breathed out, *You made the tattoo design yourself?*

Yes. It felt right to come up with it myself. He rubbed the side of her hand gently. *I used to draw often when hanging out with Sab and Brooke at LC. It was a way for me to unwind. I would listen to them, and sometimes create whole new worlds and characters to inhabit them through doodling. I guess it tapped into my more creative side quite like music does.*

That's so cool. You're really— She yawned. She could feel the steady thumping of his heart and his body heat guide her toward respite. *Sorry, I guess I'm too comfortable like this.*

I won't complain. I am, too. He rested his head as close as possible to hers. *You can sleep. I'm not going anywhere.*

She gathered some strength to lift her head and lay a kiss on the underside of his chin. *Good night, babe.*

As the memory washes over her while she grabs a glass from the cupboard, she becomes aware that she hasn't called anyone 'babe' in forever.

Last time she did it, it was back in university, and it somehow didn't even feel as natural as it did when she casually used it with Lucas just now.

She's certain that it won't fall from her lips that often, but the fact that it sounds as if it belongs to him in her life could be seen as another proof that—

The quiet voice of Zoe reaches her ears. "You weren't able to sleep or it's because you got some action and needed hydration?"

Raven turns around to see her friend wearing her light pink polka dotted nightgown sitting in the armchair in the corner of the living room a few feet away.

She fills her glass with tap water. "I woke up, and felt thirsty so I decided to get up." She closes the faucet, and starts striding toward Zoe. "You really think I would go for a sex marathon under your roof?"

"I wouldn't blame you. Lucas is the whole package from what I gathered so far." The graphic designer reaches for the remote on the side table. "Get some whenever you feel like it, I say." She brings down the volume of the stereo a few notches. "Life is too short to not indulge."

"To be honest, we might've fooled around a little." Raven pulls her bottom lip between her teeth. "But nothing too intense."

Zoe smiles knowingly. "It wouldn't bother me and Haddy if it was, you know."

She notices that calm music is playing in the background as she sits down in the middle of the sofa. "Isn't it weird to hear your friends moan while having sex next door?" She smiled amusedly. "It can be annoying beyond measure when it's strangers in a hotel room, when you actually know the person it brings it to a whole other dimension, no?"

"True." Her friend snorts. "But also, you're kinda glad because you know they're getting it good and that's what they deserve?"

"Also true." She takes a sip. "I still try to be respectful."

"And we all appreciate you for it." Zoe becomes reflective. "You know, Heather and I haven't had sex since I learned about my tumor. I fear that she thinks I am distancing myself, but it's just because I have trouble coping with everything going through my mind you know?"

"It must be a lot to deal with." Raven curls her legs under herself, angling toward her friend to give her her full attention. "I'm sure Heather understands. You're in this together. I know she worries, but you guys have always been champions at communicating."

"I know she respects whichever pace I set, but we haven't really talked about much of it." The graphic designer inhales deeply. "I get those throbbing headaches and lack of balance that are getting more frequent as time goes on. It's why I went to the doctor in the first place. It wasn't normal for me to get that level of pain over and over. It also prevents me from concentrating for even short periods of time. So putting thoughts into sentences can be a challenge. It all feels like a mountain I have to constantly climb."

"I'm so sorry, Zoe. That can't be easy." She rests her glass in her lap. "Haddy told me that you two talked on Saturday, and she was really happy about it." She flashes Zoe her best reassuring expression. "Maybe if you navigate things in small chunks it's gonna be easier? I already told your wife, but you two are the strongest couple I know. My gut tells me that you're gonna keep thriving. You'll make the most out of this scary situation."

"Yeah. Thank you for saying that. I try keeping the dialog open." Her friend toys with the hem of her pajamas. "At first I was too scared to talk about any of it. The second I set foot in the hospital to get some tests I was internally paralyzed. My feet were moving, but my head didn't want to. I still have no idea how I managed to make it to the scan room." She frowns. "The uncertainty is slowly killing me, Raven. I couldn't sleep tonight because I'm equally eager to get the results, and terrified at what they will mean."

Raven puts her glass on the coffee table. "I kept being unable to sleep just because of the uncertainty of my professional future, so I can only imagine what it would be like if I felt that my literal life was on the line like you right now."

"Trust me, it's a lot to process." Zoe wrings with her hands in her lap. "I hope you find a way to conjugate your views with any future work you'll tackle by the way."

"I hope so, too." She shakes her head. This is not about her. She wanted to share a small part of her own worries in hopes that her friend would feel her slight comprehension of sleepless nights because the brain won't shut up. She has to let Zoe know that she is the one who's important. "But my small doubts are not the focus here. Did they give you any hints of the type of tumor it could be or—"

She trails off as she sees Zoe look behind her while smiling softly. She follows her friend's stare only to see Lucas sauntering toward them.

As he brushes his fingers through his hair, she quickly takes note that he has put on a vintage t-shirt to complement his boxer briefs. There's a sure drowsiness in his movements, and it instantly makes her curve a corner of her mouth upward.

He plops down on the couch behind her. "What were you ladies talking about?"

"Just life stuff. I came downstairs to get some water, and Zoe was already up." She instinctively leans back into him. "I'm sorry I woke you."

He drapes an arm along the cushions behind her to then bury his nose into her hair. "I was missing your body warmth," he whispers.

She angles her head to gaze at him. "I was going to be back soon."

He hums. "I couldn't wait that long."

"You two are really, really sweet. It's nearly sickening to see." Zoe laughs at her own comment before staring at Lucas and Raven seriously. "Raven was asking me if doctors have any idea about which type of tumor I might've. And I was gonna answer that they used some very technical terms that my lovely wife noted somewhere, and I'm not sure I remember."

"Oh, yeah." The lawyer straightens in Lucas' embrace a little. "Haddy did mention something about meningiomas, schwannomas and oligodendrogliomas."

"Wow." The graphic designer raises a shocked eyebrow. "I'm impressed you retained the information."

"Part of my job has always been to remember lots of information and details, you remember?" Raven half-smiles as she absentmindedly caresses the top of Lucas' hand that he placed on her thigh. "Sometimes it's arguably useless, and sometimes it serves a purpose."

Lucas loosely wraps an arm around Raven's shoulders. "Honestly, meningiomas occur more often in women, and when they're benign they can easily be removed by surgery without much lasting sequels unless they are very close to vital structures. But even then, the prognostic is usually pretty hopeful. They can also be grade two and three, but let's not go there yet." He sounds solemn as he locks eyes with the graphic designer. "Schwannomas are mostly always benign, but can grow close to the spinal cord thus causing some pressure on it that can lead to some sensory loss and/or bladder and bowel problems. I didn't hear you mention any of that so I assume that it's not part of the troubles you're having?" Zoe confirms. The managing director continues. "Which is a good thing. Those can also be easily removed if they cause trouble. Now, oligodendrogliomas are another game. They are rarely benign and usually can't be removed only by surgery." He keeps his tone supportive. "But if it ends up being that one, they'll probably come up with an adapted plan to tackle it."

"How do you even know all this stuff?" Zoe looks astonished. "You're more reassuring than my own doctor and neurologist."

"My best friend Sabrina is a neurosurgeon in Boston." He smiles modestly. "I might've listened to her a whole lot through the years. She's one of the best at her job, and I always learned a great deal from her. I love to keep my mind active. There's so many interesting topics to grasp in life."

"Agreed. I do wish it's one of those easily removable tumors, then." The graphic designer's features become more relaxed. "It would offer an optimistic plan to get rid of it. You just gave me some hope, Lucas, thank you." She smiles coyly at him. "You know, for the first time in a while, I actually felt good today. Presenting that project for Moonstone hotels was invigorating. It was a good day where I could stay concentrated, and I love when my creativity shines. It was a blessing to get my designs accepted by them."

"I'm so happy for you." Raven beams. "I'm also glad that this new small hotel chain trusted you with it."

"It's so rewarding. I also like that they are expanding in California, and Hawaii, but keeping it familial." Zoe takes her glass to take a sip. "I now have to go and create a whole new web interface for them based on my approach to their branding."

Lucas perks up. "You also do that?"

Zoe nods. "Sometimes. Although I'm not the best at coding from scratch so I'm grateful for web interface facilitators."

Lucas carries on. "That's so fun. I do code a little if you need help." He gets lost in thought. "Back in uni I was often creating algorithms to help us study by formulating the most possibly challenging questions."

"Really?" The graphic designer grins. "That's so cool."

As the conversation unfolds, Raven leans back a little more into Lucas. His presence and his touch are getting alarmingly familiar.

He really does blend pretty flawlessly into every part of her life.

It's petrifying and exquisite all at once.

Projecting herself with him feels riskily effortless. Getting involved in something serious with Lucas is feeling more and more like a legitimate possibility.

But what about what he—

As she hears him laugh with Zoe, she sets on just enjoying the moments as they pass. Reality will catch up with them soon enough, anyway.

Eighteen

Drowning In Abstraction

As Lucas paces on the sidewalk in front of Raven's house while talking on the phone, he tries to keep his tone steady to get his point across. "Flip, you're drunk." He briefly looks down at his slides, putting his free hand in the pocket of his cargo bermudas. "Go sober up, and we'll talk tomorrow, okay?"

"You don't get it, man." Felipe sounds a little unhinged. "I made a huge mistake, and I don't think I can fix it." His tone is only getting slurrier as time goes on. "If Em finds out about it she'll file for divorce I'm sure."

"So you keep saying." Lucas deftly pulls down the sleeves of his LC hoodie. It's getting chilly near the ocean this evening. "But you've always been awfully vague since the beginning of this discussion about whatever you did." He frowns. "Did you cheat on Emma?"

"No." His friend's voice is sharp. "No no no no. I would never." He exhales soundly. "It's our condo. I messed up so bad, Lucas."

"Calm down." The managing director tries his best to be comforting. "Don't forget to breathe." He brushes his fingers through his hair. "Are you on your way home now?"

"Yes." Flip inhales deeply. "In a taxi."

"Good." Lucas thinks quickly. He has to help his friend any way he can even if he's on the other side of the country. Felipe sounds desperate and very alarmed. "Please give the driver my address."

"But I—"

"No 'buts'." He stays unflinching. "Em won't be pleased if she sees you like that. Plus, in the state you're in, you're definitely going to blurt out nonsense that you'll regret in the morning." He reaches the corner of the street. "The doorman knows you well, he'll open up my penthouse for you. Go crash down on my sofa, and take care of that hangover tomorrow morning."

"Thanks, buddy. I don't know how to—"

He interjects before Flip has any chance to start another rant. "No need to thank me. That's what friends are for, right?" He breathes in slowly. "I'll text Emma myself to tell her that I asked you to go look after something at my place, that you'll have to spend the night there, and that your phone died so you couldn't reach out to her just yet. You can then text her later. I'll also message you to remind you of what we just said in case you have only a partial recollection of it when the alcohol has been metabolized."

Lucas hears his friend give the new directions to the driver.

He half-smiles.

If Felipe is usually very impulsive, and energetic, he's even worse when inebriated. The managing director can't even count the total number of times he prevented his friend from making harsh decisions on a whim after having drank.

Emma is definitely better off not seeing her husband in the state he seems to be in right now.

Lucas is glad that Flip called him as soon as he left the bar he was at with some colleagues. He hopes that having a good night's sleep in his apartment will help his friend get his priorities straight, and relax a little.

Felipe's voice nearly falters as he goes back talking to the managing director. "Done."

"Awesome." Lucas looks up toward Raven's balcony. Through the glass and metal railing, he distinguishes a shadow on the gray sectional outdoor couch. He beams. Raven went upstairs while he answered Felipe's call when they got back from their shopping spree. She wanted to give him some privacy. He now has only one desire: go join her. He rapidly gets to the point. "I have to go. I still haven't had dinner yet. With Raven, we'll go grab something to eat, and—"

Flip interrupts him. "You're sleeping with her now, huh?"

Lucas becomes defensive. "What does this have to do with anything?"

"You've been crazy about her for a decade," his friend snarls. "Now that you're alone with her on the west coast in a great setting, I'm sure you're fucking her senseless." He cackles. "Good for you, man. I'm sure that she's a fre—"

Lucas cuts him off. This is sliding in dangerous territory. "I'll stop you right there. I have the utmost respect for Raven, and I would appreciate you not talking like that about her."

"Look at you getting all sensitive," his friend mutters. "Where's the Lucas who enjoys good sex for what it is?" Lucas can hear the frown in his friend's intonation. "Unless you now want to commit somehow? Oh, is this what it is? You—"

Lucas doesn't give him the opportunity to finish that sentence. "I'll be back in town in three days." He knows he needs to end that conversation now. Felipe is on a slippery slope. "We'll grab lunch then and discuss what's happening with you. In the meantime try to keep your head clear, and focus, buddy."

As Lucas hangs up without waiting for an answer from his friend, he looks at a distant point on the horizon. Past the moon high above the waves, he becomes reflective.

Even if drunk, Felipe had a fragmented good reading of the situation. Lucas would love to get a shot at a future with Raven.

The thought is making rounds in his head repeatedly as time goes on.

From the very moment when they made out after the fundraiser up to now, something inside of him unfurled. He has to admit to himself that he doesn't feel like wanting anyone other than her by his side moving forward.

The prospect of lowering down all his walls is daunting, but it might already be too late. Maybe the fortress he constructed is steadily crumbling down.

Because the thing is that Raven is acting like she might very well want the same thing he does.

She's accepting him in every part of her life, she's opening up to him more and more, and he only wishes to be worthy of her trust and affection.

He could easily see her in his existence, but he could also see himself be part of hers.

Every one of her friends is consistently feeling like his own people. He knows he'll be more than happy to be there for them just like he does for his closest buddies.

The exchange they shared in the middle of the night with Zoe is a good example of it. Having Raven curled into him as they all chatted was another very natural experience that instantly sent his mind into a perfectly relaxed state.

Her sweet chuckling every time they would joke throughout the conversation was constantly making his heart swell.

He wants to hear her be this carefree all the time.

He wants her steady breathing against him to fall asleep every night.

Flip was also right in alluding that Raven is constantly making it spectacular for Lucas in bed, but it's much more than that for the managing director.

He wants the intense and the soft instants with her. The mind-blowing sex, and the sweet aftermath. The easy as well as the challenging conversations. The tears and the laughter.

He wants to navigate life with Raven Collins for as long as she'll have him.

He might've even wanted it a decade ago when he let her go.

Maybe he's been a fool. Maybe he wasted too much time.

But Raven still hasn't expressed any of her concerns. They seem to have flown out the window the minute they got to San Diego, but he's certain that they still exist. She'll definitely talk about them when she judges that she has to.

He won't push.

Things are too gratifying for him to want to open that potential can of worms just yet.

It might be unhealthy to not address everything heads on, but he doesn't care. He has faith that they will overcome whatever this leads to.

Everything is natural with Raven.

Everything feels powerfully organic.

This connection they share feels like it could bring him to whole new heights. It's all-consuming. It inhabits him completely.

He never needed anyone in his life so far, but he might very well need Raven.

Juggling those feelings is something very new for him. He never had them with any of his past girlfriends, and certainly with none of his one-night conquests.

He inhales deeply.

The ocean breeze is peacefully inspiring. He can understand why Raven loves her spot so much. He feels like he could become accustomed to it.

There's something about this place that makes him feel at ease everywhere he goes. It's arguably because of how Raven inhabits each corner of that vast space for him.

He once told her that he got the most relaxing feeling visiting California a few years ago without her. But this time around there's not a single situation when he isn't enveloped by all her strength and kindness. Sharing her world is a privilege he hopes to be allowed to keep.

He feels utterly good in Raven's universe.

Arriving downstairs before her after their shower this morning was another perfect example of it.

He recalls how Heather and Zoe were making out heatedly in the kitchen when he walked in.

He grinned.

As he padded around the island, he noticed Haddy's hands roaming beneath Zoe's blue striped blouse while the graphic designer was tenderly making a mess out of her wife's hair. They looked amorous and unbothered and it filled him with untamed joy.

After what Zoe shared with Raven and him the night prior, seeing the couple melt into each other that beautifully was heartwarming.

As he grabbed the keys to Raven's car on the console, Zoe's voice startled him. *You slept well, Lucas? I mean for what was left of the night when we all went back to bed.*

He turned around to face them. *I had a great night, thank you.* He smiled coyly. *How about you two?*

Zoe tucked back her shirt into her jeans while her wife straightened her gold argyle notched-neck blouse in her black suit pants. *We also had a good rest of the night, right, baby?*

Heather hummed in confirmation. *Yeah. We chatted when Zoe came back to bed, and I guess that's also why we got a little carried away just now.* She slid an arm around Zoe's waist. *It's been nice to feel like we are on the same page again.*

The graphic designer leaned into her wife's embrace. *Thank you for sharing your knowledge, Lucas.*

It's all thanks to Sab. Without her I wouldn't have been that knowledgeable, and I wouldn't have been able to talk to you about any of it. He put the keys in his shorts pockets. *And I'm glad to see you both like this now.* He alternated his stare between the two women, smiling playfully. *There's something about your kitchen which somehow makes it great to get lost in each other.*

Haddy raised a fakely reprehensive eyebrow. *Are you saying that you and Raven—*

He shook his head as he cut her off. *No. We only made out. Nothing more.*

Good thing we arrived, huh? The lawyer teased. *I feel like it could've gotten out of hand.*

He frowned. *Raven told you. We know how to behave.*

I know. I just love teasing you. Heather kissed Zoe quickly before walking toward him. *I think I speak for Zoe and I when I say that we're happy that Raven brought you along.* She stopped in front of him on the other side of the island. *I wasn't kidding when I said that I've rarely seen her be this at ease. She looks at you like I've never seen her look at anyone, Lucas. She might not admit it to herself yet, but she is letting you in. She hasn't done that in forever.* Haddy locked eyes with him, sounding determined. *I would hate for her to be deceived so please make sure to know exactly what you want, and don't drag her along into something you're not ready for.*

So you've already warned me about last night, albeit more vaguely. He held her stare, trying to not become defensive. He highly respected Heather's honesty in that moment. He also wanted to share a truth with her. *I want Raven to be happy. My job has been my whole life for a long time, and I know Raven's been challenging me about my clients and how I'm conducting business. But it's also because of my work that I've been able to get the life I have now.*

Zoe joined Heather at the counter. *Which you love, right?*

He hesitated for a split second. The double guessing about his line of work has been sporadically coming back in his head lately. He keeps pushing the thought away. It wasn't any different this morning. *Of course.* He nodded assuredly. *I have everything I ever wanted.*

Heather tilted her head in questioning. *Everything?*

He inhaled soundly while thinking about his sister who tells him all the time that he used to be way more fun. That his job is taking too much space in his life. He started thinking out loud. *I do think it's possible for me to achieve a better balance between my personal and professional lives. It's still a work in progress, but I worked hard to get where I am now, and I would hate to lose everything I built. You must understand, right? You have your own firm, after all. That takes sacrifices, and a sure drive to overcome obstacles.*

I do have my own firm. The lawyer hummed while staying unwavering, *I personally founded it because I wanted to make a difference, and help people. The mission I gave myself back then hasn't changed, and it's the main reason I can still look at myself in the mirror every morning because I'm true to that vision. I would honestly recommend the endeavor to anyone who feels like they would love to control their destinies more.*

In my wildest dreams, I would appreciate founding my own company one day and simplify things to focus on financial planning, investments, and auditing. It would be on a much smaller scale than the investment bank I'm working in for sure, but it would also mean that I can maybe have a shot at balancing everything more successfully. The funniest thing is, that I've already saved enough money to do that now.

It felt good to admit this out loud. He had tucked away this ambition of his for the longest time. It suddenly resurfaced upon chatting with Heather.

I'm certain you would be very successful if you ever did. She smiled brightly. *If you have a great support circle it truly makes all the difference in the world.*

It can get lonely at the top, huh? Dreams come with a price, I guess. He half-smiled shyly. *I did a number of things for my clients through the years, and now with the threats I'm receiving I fear for my loved ones. I started questioning the basis of how I'm doing business as well. I always said that there's a line to not cross, and—*

Heather interjected before he could go dig any deeper into his soul-searching. *I think the most important part is to love what we're doing. To be able to justify every decision so we feel good about them.* She glances at Zoe tenderly. *It wasn't always easy starting from scratch, but loneliness is not something I felt. I'm also the luckiest woman in the world to have a supportive wife by my side.*

You know, you're a wonderfully inspiring couple. He pulled up the sleeves of his hoodie. *It's an honor to know you.*

Thank you. Haddy breathed in. *I couldn't have done anything without Zoe. She grounded me when I needed it the most.* She directed her attention to a distant point behind Lucas while becoming absorbed by her thoughts. *I only hope to be able to give her back a fraction of what she did for me during my lifetime.*

Don't be silly, baby. The graphic designer took her hand in hers, squeezing it gently. *You're already giving me the best of you on a daily basis. We're in this together.*

He smiled as the two pressed their foreheads together before kissing softly.

Throughout the uncertainty governing part of their journey for the time being, Heather and Zoe seem determined to overcome the hurdles as a united front. Raven had already told him about how strong and unique Heather and Zoe's bond was, but witnessing it first hand brings everything into perspective.

They are the very definition of a supporting couple. One in which love is the only true motivation behind each action they take toward one another to thrive.

A split second later, Raven came down the stairs in her ragged jeans, cropped knitted pink sweater, and with her hair up in a messy bun she realized with an ivory clip. She joined him on his side of the island, wrapping her arms around his waist. When he bent down to gently capture her lips, the whole world disappeared.

Thinking about it all now is reminding him once more of how he feels lucky himself for having Raven in his life.

How past the threats and the questioning he's experiencing, she makes him feel at home wherever they are.

During breakfast, he was clearly in the middle of another casual discussion between friends. Even when it became more profound, and strangely intense, he still felt right where he needed to be.

This just brought me back to that time when your cat hated hearing a particular style of music nearly as much as Nathan. Heather laughed brightly while finishing eating her omelet as a depressing tune started playing in the restaurant.

Raven snorted. *Don't remind me.*

Wait. He perked up, taking a sip of his espresso and draping an arm behind Raven's chair. *What's that story?*

Haddy smiled amusedly. *You see, Raven's ex-neighbor used to blast music in the middle of the night or very early in the morning for the whole floor to hear.*

Her boyfriend and her had splitted, and for weeks she couldn't stop listening to powerful breakup songs. Raven smiled fondly at the memory. *Tootsie would meow while pawing the door as if to tell me 'please let me out. I can't take it anymore', and Nathan would become grumpy in no time when he was there.*

I feel like I would've turned it into a big joke. Lucas smiled brightly. *Start singing off key and bust out my guitar to accompany the melody.*

Raven looked at him with joy sparkling in her eyes. *That would've been hilarious.*

He nodded. *Life is too short to be annoyed at those things, I say.*

Raven hummed. *That's what I kept telling Nathan, but he just couldn't bear it, and we ended up spending way more time at his place because of it.*

Lucas tilted his head in curiosity. *You guys never actually lived together?*

We never bought a place specifically for us, no. Raven let her fingers trail along the handle of her coffee mug, staring at the liquid inside as she got lost in thought. *It could've been a red flag, but back then we were both truly all about our work, and we thought we had all the time in the world to figure out what being committed meant.* She let out a snort. *Reflecting back on it, I guess it was totally our own way of keeping one foot out of the door. Nathan ended up really not wanting to commit at all, so it was a good thing in the end.*

Speaking of Nathan and his love of commitment... Heather cleared her throat, sounding sheepish. *Since we chatted about him last night, I got curious and went to check what he was up to.*

Raven shook her head vigorously at her friend. *You didn't.*

I did. Haddy locked eyes with her. *I know curiosity kills the cat and all, but I had an urge to.* She took a deep breath. *It looks like he's engaged. Tons of pictures with his girlfriend on his socials. I decided to tell you because I feel like you'd have learned about it one way or another.*

I appreciate you telling me. No worries. Raven sounded dismissive. *It's not like we owe each other anything anymore.*

Heather tried to dig a little deeper into the fellow lawyer's mind. *But you'd have every right to be pissed or annoyed after what you guys argued about, and how he was set in his ways back then.*

Yeah. Raven clenched her jaw a little. *It's kinda surprising, but it's been years so it was bound to happen, I guess. I just wasn't the right person for him. Just like he wasn't the right one for me.*

Everyone stayed quiet for a beat.

Raven was clearly cogitating about something, but was also definitely unwilling to talk about what it was.

Zoe seemingly took it as a cue to swiftly reorient the exchange while Heather was in a staring contest with Raven. *So you play guitar, Lucas?*

He took the occasion to participate actively in making the discussion less awkward. *I do.*

We really have to get Jun over here, and have one of her beach parties. The graphic designer was beaming. *We could gather old friends, colleagues, and family, and just let loose. I know my cousin's been telling me we should all get together like old days soon.*

That would be great. Raven leaned into Lucas' touch as he brushed his fingertips along her cervical vertebrae. *Next time I talk to her I'll let the idea slip. I'm certain she'll be on board. I might video call her soon, actually. I noticed she left me a message this morning that I haven't listened to yet.*

I would love to attend one of those gatherings with you all. Lucas grinned genuinely, raising a teasing eyebrow. *That is if I'm allowed to come back.*

You'll always be welcome here, Lucas. Heather stared at the managing director seriously. *It will be our pleasure to extend an invite.*

Zoe took a sip of her tea. *Be warned that you might get dared to play guitar though.*

Haddy instantly added, *And Raven could be dared to sing while you do so.*

We already joked that we could sing some jazz together at the next event we're invited to. Raven curled her hand around Lucas' thigh, angling toward him. *Right, Luke?*

As he was fascinated by her calling him 'Luke' in front of her friends, Zoe's cheerful tone echoed in his ears. *I'm so here for it.*

The souvenir of them laughing and having a good time following that conversation is bringing a smile to his lips right now.

He finishes typing the message to Emma, deciding to go back inside to ask Raven what she'd like to eat for dinner so they can pick a restaurant.

He'd love to take her out to dinner, and go for a quiet walk along the cliffs after.

They spent the day shopping with Zoe, and helping Raven's friend get her mind off of things for the span of a few hours. He did like the experience, and would do it all over again.

But now he's craving some alone time with his favorite lawyer.

He takes out the key Raven left him prior as he enters the building, choosing to go for the stairs instead of the elevator to get to her floor.

For the brief instant when he wonders what Felipe got himself into as he pockets his device, the whole anxiety from the blackmail he's receiving, and how Gabriel Smith could wreak havoc on his life comes back to haunt him.

The whirlwind of questioning threatens to take over his psyche with the anxiety it induces in him when his mind lingers too much on any of it. The emotions it triggers are overwhelming. His whole life might be on the line, and the people closest to him could pay a strong price for his chosen way of living.

However, he's also becoming increasingly better at pushing the thoughts away as soon as they creep up on him.

He said he would focus on his time with Raven this week, and that's exactly what he's still planning to do.

Once he closes the door behind him, he locks it, and wastes no time striding up the stairs to then make a beeline for Raven's bedroom.

As soon as he sees her in the distance, he removes his earphone only to distantly hear some faint music leaking through the outdoor speakers.

Lucas curves a corner of his mouth upward as he takes a few more steps, stopping to stand in the doorway, and away from Raven's gaze as she's absorbed by her book.

He fishes his phone out to subtly capture a picture of her. He smiles absentmindedly.

She's stretched on the sofa beside the fire burning in the outdoor gas fire table, her head slightly angled with her hair flipped mostly on one side as she reads. The flames are flickering on her golden skin, and reflecting in her reading glasses under the early moonlight.

She looks fucking stunning.

Her relaxed expression as she seems to be consumed by the story on those pages is adorable. It instantly sends a discharge of warmth rushing through his veins.

The moment she idly pulls her bottom lip between her teeth nervously, he sighs.

He gets to hold her anytime he wants to now.

He knows perfectly well how her body feels against his own.

He knows how she smiles into their kisses when he pulls her closer, and how she moans against his tongue when he combs his fingers through her hair to massage her scalp at the same time he grabs her ass.

How the sensation of her abandoning herself to him feels like—

She must've sensed his gaze on her. She drops the book down in her lap, turning to face him. She removes her glasses to place them on the side table, smiling softly while looking at his clothing. "You know, you and I could start a war over this *Liberty Cove Business School* hoodie you seem very fond of."

"What about it?" He mirrors her expression, sauntering across the teak flooring toward her. "It's highly comfy. It's my favorite hoodie." He sits beside her on the sectional. "Has been for years."

She puts her book away. "Because of the memories it brings or just a general feeling?"

He makes a show of thinking before answering. "Both."

She squints her eyes slightly. "It's like your baseball cap."

"Exactly."

"I have a *Harriers Law* sweater I adore, so I get it." She leans her head on the top of the cushions while peering into Lucas' eyes. "I was saying that earlier because we could get into a *Harriers* vs *Liberty Cove* fight."

He reaches to languidly brush his fingers through her hair. "I'll take that confrontation any time."

She inhales steadily, trailing her hand on the inside of his thigh. "I always wear that sweater during cozy evenings at home."

"Can't wait to see you in it, then." He puts his head on his bicep while his hand continues to toy with some of her ash brown strands. "You curl up on your sofa with it when you're reading quite like now?"

She sneaks her hand under his hoodie. "Yeah."

He flashes her a tender smile. She is perfectly relaxed at the moment. She's watching him with all the mellowness in the world.

He certainly doesn't feel like moving.

Looking around, he gestures at the book she put aside. "Is it any good?"

"It depends." She smiles amusedly. "Are you going to spoil the ending for me if I answer?"

"I haven't read it, so no. Not a chance." He shakes his head. "And I would never do that. I'd highly prefer to read over your shoulder anyway."

"As I snuggle up to you, huh?"

He smirks. "How did you guess?"

She softly scrapes her nails over his stomach, humming. "Had a hunch. I'd love to do that, too." She angles her head to lay a kiss on his forearm. "How is Felipe?"

"He kept blurting out nonsense about a mistake he made." Lucas frowns. "He was also very drunk. I told him to go to my place for the night."

"You're being a really great friend looking after him that way."

"Emma would not be pleased to see him like that." He furrows his eyebrows. "They're going through a rough patch, and he keeps making things worse. I can't believe him sometimes." He breathes in as if to get some composure. "The last time he went home in that state was last month. They got into a big fight, and he became very mean. I feel like I had to protect him from himself this time." He instinctively wraps a hand around Raven's hip as he scoots a little closer. "Flip should be better at handling the consequences of any decision he makes. He has to own his mistakes." He exhales in defeat. "But he's always been very impulsive."

"You're already doing everything you can to help him." She traces aimless patterns on his abs. "His first instinct was still to call you to ask for your help or advice or whatever it is he is after." She offers him a tentative smile. "Maybe it's a good sign?"

"You're right." He slumps a little on the couch at her words. "I still have no idea exactly what he did this time, but it sounded bad."

"I'm certain you'll learn about it soon enough when he calms down."

"You don't know Felipe. He won't calm down. He's just more intense when inebriated. He'll keep freaking out."

Raven seemingly decides to steer the conversation slightly away from the main topic to allow him to get his mind off of his friend's troubles. "And something tells me that you're not like that when drunk."

"I'm mostly very cuddly. I get emotional more often than not." He presses his nose into her hair, whispering, "I would just end up falling asleep nuzzling against your navel."

She runs her fingers through his black locks soothingly. "You already do that when sober."

He breathes her in. "Oh, but it would be different."

"Yeah?"

"Mhmm." He grazes his lips to her ear, murmuring as if he's sharing very confidential information, "I tend to snore a little when drunk."

She chuckles. "Such a happy prospect."

"I'm not drunk very often, so it shouldn't be a recurring problem." He lays a soft kiss on the underside of her jaw. "Don't tell me you don't do any weird shit when you drink too much."

She angles her head to give him more access. "Quite like you, it doesn't happen that often, especially nowadays, but yeah, I've been guilty of a few crazy moments."

"Do tell." He skims his nose up her neck. "Drunk Raven can't be anything other than fun I'm sure."

She smiles as she rakes her fingers into the shorter hair at the back of his head. "Back in college I've done the classics of dancing on tables, drunk texting, and online shopping to a point where I once ordered fifty-two bottles of salad dressing."

"Fifty-two?" He leans back to look her in the eyes, an amused glint shimmering in them. "Please tell me they were an assortment and not all the same flavor."

"Actually..." She cringes at herself. "All Ranch. It was very funny when it got delivered though. You should've seen Heather's face when she opened the package." She tries her best to imitate her friend's voice. "I think her exact words were 'you swear you didn't order this when drunk? Because you absolutely hate Ranch dressing'."

"That's hilarious."

"It was." She bites into her bottom lip nervously. "But the funniest thing was when I waxed James' arms."

Lucas gapes at her. "No way."

"Yeah." Her gaze gets lost following her index finger defining his jugular as she carries on her recollection. "We were all tipsy, and he kept complaining that he had too much hair on his arms." She shrugs. "I offered to help."

He chuckles. "How nice of you."

"The worst part is that I didn't do a good job." She half-smiles. "He had one arm done and just patches of the other. It took weeks for it to all grow back."

"Wow." He sees her stretch her legs before curling up into his side, draping one leg half on top of his. He also feels like sharing one of his best drunk stories. "I once fell asleep in a taxi, and when I woke up the counter was at a couple hundred dollars." He massages her thigh. "The driver had never stopped, my friend had left me, and I was hugging a traffic cone."

She snorts once more. "You must've been very cute."

"The orange cone was the best hugger ever." He sounds very solemn. "I kept it in our apartment for about a year. It was the proud center of attention of the living room."

Her amusement morphs into a full blown laugh. "You could've created a decorating trend."

"I tried." He smiles teasingly. "It sadly never took off."

She scans his facial features tenderly. "Shame."

He greatly enjoys those easy conversations. Trailing his hand up Raven's calf while she scoots closer to let her lips trail along his jawline feels marvelous.

"Your beard is getting a little longer now," she whispers. "Still love it."

He purrs. "I was going to trim it tomorrow."

He feels her leave an open-mouthed kiss on his jugular. "I know you said that you're very particular about your shaving ritual, but I can help you with it if you want."

He can't help himself. "You're gonna wax it like you did with your friend James?"

"Very funny." She pulls away, scraping her nails across the scruff on his cheek. "I won't be drunk."

He peers into her eyes. "If it involves you half-naked on your bathroom counter, I'm in."

She nuzzles into his neck. "Deal."

As he basks in the moment, the lines from the chorus of the song wash over him, and send his mind into a reflective space. He feels like asking. "Would you go swimming all clothed with me on New Year's Eve?"

"We could do better than that." She tentatively slides the pads of her fingers underneath the waistband of his boxer briefs. "We could go skinny dipping."

"I adore the sound of that." He sighs, his tone remaining playful. "Plus, you already did a strip tease on the beach so it wouldn't be that far off."

"I kept my bikini on." She sounds fakely offended. "I wasn't naked."

"Fair enough." He smiles coyly, remembering something else. "Earlier when you dismissed Heather about Nathan over breakfast, I couldn't help but feel curious." He senses her touch still. He continues. He wants to try to understand the whole situation she lived with her ex-boyfriend. "It's all good if you don't feel like sharing more, but—"

She cuts him off. "Nathan is free to do whatever he wants." She breathes in soundly. "I just cringed a little because of how he despised commitment with me, but seems to be very on board now." She begins toying with one of the strings of his hoodie. "I know people can change. It looks like he found the right person for him, and honestly I'm happy for him."

He kisses the top of her head. "It would also be okay if you were annoyed by it. All very valid feelings."

Her idle humming followed by a short silence doesn't startle Lucas.

He's determined to wait for as long as she needs. He'll be happy to listen to whatever she has to say.

If she doesn't even want to say more, it's fine. He won't—

She finally speaks again, her voice steady and reverent. "You see, what started it all is that I didn't want to follow him abroad so he could get a promotion." She turns the string around her index and middle fingers. "I know I said it before but we were both all about our jobs, and it was even more true at that moment. I didn't want to lose everything I had worked hard to build, and start anew somewhere else just for him." She inhales soundly. "I also thought I could make a difference within the system here back then. That turned out to be one hell of a lie, but I was younger and more ambitious, I guess."

"You're just as ambitious now. You can still make a difference. You will continue to change people's lives." He rubs her back smoothly. "That's what drives you, and it's who you are." He looks down at her. "I'll always believe in your capacity to fight the right battles. No matter how difficult they might be."

"Thank you," she breathes out.

He decides to circle back to Nathan. "So you two fought, and he decided to leave it all behind for this promotion?"

She leans her head back on his shoulder to stare at him. "If only it was that simple." She pauses for a beat, boring her eyes into his. "At some point during that time I thought I was pregnant. I was late, and—" She trails off, seemingly choosing to spare him the details. "Anyway, it wasn't the right moment to have kids. Not in my head anyway."

"You got an abortion?" He pulls her closer, resting his palm on her bare skin between her cropped top and pants. "It was probably for the best if—"

She interjects. "No. It was a false alarm." She glides her fingers up beneath his hoodie to caress his rib cage gently. "But the thing is that it forced me to reevaluate my priorities. What if I really had been pregnant?" She furrows her eyebrows, never averting her gaze from his. "Did I want children with him? Was I willing to balance my professional endeavors with a family life? That's when I realized that I loved Nathan, and was very willing to invest myself in something else than only my work." She smiles knowingly. "But he made it plain clear that he wasn't. He even said that work was, and would always be, his whole life."

"Hence you hinting at having different priorities when you talk about what happened between you two."

"Yeah. From that moment on, I felt like love wasn't worth the hassle, and I wanted to go back to how I was before him." She smiles nostalgically. "When things were uncomplicated. When feelings didn't hurt."

"You and I both know that it's sadly not how it works." He curls his hand around her thigh once again. "Sometimes you have no control over your feelings. It's not like you can pick when and how you fall for someone."

He's strangely feeling that profoundly into every fiber of his being. Although, he's not about to let it show. It can only lead to complications. He's sure of it.

Plus, he's not even sure that this sure affection he has toward Raven can be identified as—

She analyzes his expression, looking deep in thought. "Don't get me wrong, I got closure, and I clearly don't feel anything for Nathan anymore."

"Good to know," he teases. He presses their foreheads together. "I was already aware of that, but thanks for the precision."

"I'm actually not certain he even had my whole heart at any point because I—" She stops herself, and reorient to get her main conclusion across. "Anyway, I was surprised about his engagement."

"With reason." He slides a hand on the side of her face. "I'm sorry he was such a stubborn jerk, and that he didn't see what he was letting slip through his fingers."

"I'm pretty headstrong myself as you know." She leans into his touch. "It's not as if we didn't butt heads a whole lot."

He goes for the easy joke. "Was the make-up sex worth it?"

"There wasn't a lot of make-up sex involved." She laughs lightly. "Mostly heated arguments, and sleepless nights." She half-smiles before he has any time for a quip. "And not the good kind. Jun could vouch for how bad it was."

"I'm sorry you had to go through that." His thumb traces her jawline slowly. "Nathan made the worst mistake of his life," he murmurs.

She puts her palm flat on his pec. "I was the one who ultimately called it quits."

"He was still a fool for not fighting for what you guys had." Lucas' intonation is unhesitating. "You did the right thing. You stayed true to yourself like you always do. It's exactly the same as why you handed in your resignation. You're fierce, Raven. It's part of what makes you so unique."

"I just try to be able to live with myself and my ideals in harmony." She closes her eyes briefly. "Been aspiring to that more and more as I age."

He lifts a corner of his mouth upward. "As if you're getting old."

She bites into her bottom lip. "Well, I'm clearly entering the decade to start thinking about having children for example. As women, our biological clock is ticking in our thirties."

"Would you like a big family?"

"Nah. Not a big one. It's not in my immediate priorities either, but if I find the right partner, I could see myself founding a family with him." She curls her hand around his throat. "Even if I don't want to get attached, I could potentially be swept off my feet."

He hums. "Stay open to possibilities and all that." He inhales steadily, telling her a truth he usually keeps buried within himself. "Quite like you, if I ever fully commit, I could also see myself having a family of my own. Past the traumas, and my father's mistakes I don't want to reproduce, I'm ready to do everything in my power to see where life leads me if I'm with the right person." He trails his fingertips along her cervical vertebrae. "Love is always different every time we feel it, but I'm convinced that when you meet the one you want to build a real future with, you know. Then you have to decide to wholly commit, or accept that this connection might just never come back ever again."

"Mhmm." She ghosts her lips over his. "For the record, you'd make an amazing father down the line."

"And you an absolutely extraordinary mom," he whispers.

As he brushes his nose along hers, he wonders if they're both thinking the same thing without voicing it.

It's clear to him that she feels dangerously like the one he doesn't want to let get away. The one who he could realistically *commit* to.

When she eagerly captures his bottom lip to kiss him lazily, he groans at her passion.

She wastes no time to straddle him, flying her fingers through his hair, and whimpering against his tongue.

The first accords of a modern lecherous song faintly resound in his ears. He can't help but think that the tempo is a perfect pairing to their make out session.

It harmonizes flawlessly with how he's steadily melting into Raven, and how she grinds into him.

The instant he grabs her hips as he purrs, she leans away slightly. "I just realized that I hadn't welcomed you properly yet." She kisses him again. "We were all talk and no play."

He slides his hands to her ass. "If this is how you welcome me, I want to come back home to you every night. Previous talking part included."

She momentarily stops her movements. He internally curses at himself for having let slip such a loaded statement.

There's no way in hell she'd ever consider being with him every day. She hasn't lived with her ex-boyfriend of nearly five years for fuck's sake.

But does it mean that his subconscious is sending him yet another less than subtle clue that he would be willing to—

She resumes massaging his scalp while flashing him a coy smile. "Before I forget, While you were chatting with your friend, I read that Gabriel Smith contract you shared with me." She locks eyes with him. "It's very standard. Nothing out of the ordinary there. I still worded, and added, a small clause to exonerate you of any illegal dealings that may have happened before he joined your roster." It's her turn to skim her nose along his. "That way, if you somehow decided to get his business for whatever reason, you can plead plausible deniability on any of the dealings. He can't try to pin any of it on you, and say that you knew. I also placed it very subtly within a paragraph. They shouldn't pick up on it."

"You're also a master of loopholes, I see." He chases her lips. "You're the best."

"Just doing my job." She pulls away, smiling playfully. "I thought it was important. Especially if you see that Smith's truly not been clean before, but you still feel like signing with him to not infuriate your employers. I wouldn't want you to go to jail."

He circles her waist, his fingers gently caressing her spine. "Would you visit me?"

"Mmm." She kisses him tenderly, humming to the music under her breath. "My body would crave conjugal visits."

When he reaches her bra clasp, she arches into him. He smirks. "Good thing that New York is one of the few States allowing for them."

"Although I'm not sure I could go without you in the real world for so long." She takes hold of the hem of his hoodie and t-shirt underneath. "So please be careful, and just don't get arrested."

He puts his arms up in the air to help her pull his top over his head. "But I could hire the best lawyer out there." Once she discards it on the cushion beside them, he sets on removing her sweater. "Surely she could clear my name."

She happily complies, letting the garment join his beside them. She smiles softly as she glides her hands down his chest. "Right now there's something else she wants to do with your name."

He circles her rib cage. "What's that?"

She slides across the stubble on his cheek to reach his ear. "She wants to scream it in ecstasy," she murmurs.

He grunts, trailing kisses along the column of her neck. "What about dinner?"

She curls her hand around his belt buckle. "How about we order in?"

He smiles into her skin. "That's the best idea I've ever heard."

Nineteen

Sparkles Through the Darkness

The ocean breeze never felt so delightful to Raven.

The last rays of the sun are disappearing on the horizon before her eyes as she's sitting in her bohemian v-neck short sleeves dress with her back molded into Lucas' front. Her gaze lingers on his bare feet on either side of her, his toes digging a little in the sand at the end of the fouta.

She recalls that he removed his slides before plopping down on it after their small walk along the shore, and she had to inhale deeply at how handsome he looked in his knee-length cargo shorts with a hint of his marl gray t-shirt peeking from under his hoodie.

They decided to settle on the beach to eat dinner they got from the taco food truck, and just bask in each other.

Now her wide brim straw hat is sitting beside them with her pair of canvas high top sneakers and the small speaker faintly playing music, Lucas' arms are wrapped around her middle, he is nuzzling into her neck as she combs her fingers through his hair, and she can't get enough of the soft kisses he delicately trails down her throat sporadically. He feels like he wants to never let her go. She wants time to stand still.

She wants this moment to last forever.

Contrary to what she used to do the past few years, she knows that she could easily spend every night in Lucas' arms moving forward.

She remembers how he felt like he was venerating her at every swirl of his tongue when he gave her head on her balcony.

How every moan escaping him as she was pumping him before rolling a condom onto his length sent her mind spinning.

How he ardently caressed her curves as her body was steadily undulating along his while she was riding him under the starlit sky.

How he let her chase her pleasure exactly like she wanted, following her lead at every step, and looking at her as if she was the eighth wonder of the world.

How he groaned into her chest as she dug her nails into his shoulder blades and his skull when she came apart.

She loves sensing him let go. She revels in diving into his eyes as he does.

More than that, she adores the intimate cuddling that naturally occurs afterward. She could literally devote an eternity to mapping his body with her fingertips while they chat in the aftermath. Watch him react to her touch, and pull her closer.

Kissing him lazily in bed is slowly becoming her favorite activity.

She reminisces about how she could've climaxed just from how he palmed her breasts, and skillfully teased her into hard peaks at dawn.

She leans back into him as she idly hums to the song.

She's pretty much certain that this is exactly what it feels like to live through a dream. She used to laugh at people describing their relationship like that, but now she might just get it.

While she can totally get along fine on her own, being with Lucas is bringing her an inner serenity she didn't know could exist. She got a glimpse of it when she met him a decade ago, but now there's clearly no denying it. He feels perfect in her life.

She will soon need to address her concerns and expectations with him so they—

A slight shiver runs down her spine from the cool evening air constantly brushing her skin.

Lucas' tone is preoccupied. "You okay?"

"Yeah. It's a little chilly, but I'm used to it." She smiles softly. "It's fine."

"Nonsense." He swiftly removes his hoodie. "Here." He gives it to her. "If you feel like you need some extra warmth."

"How could I refuse?" She takes it from him, and slides it over her head. "I must admit that I love wearing your clothes."

"And I love seeing you in them." As soon as she sits back into him, he presses his lips to her ear. "Does that make me a Neanderthal?"

"Nah." She rolls the cuffs of the sleeves a little. "The gleam you get in your eyes when you look at me in them is highly sexy."

"You're the one who's sexy beyond measure." He slides his hands underneath the hoodie to rest them flat on her abdomen. "No matter what you wear," he whispers.

She leans her head onto his shoulder. "You'd be pretty partial to me not wearing anything at all given the choice, yeah?"

He hums. "Fabric is a burden."

"Mm." She absentmindedly reaches behind her to scratch her nails along his jaw. "And you could let your beard ignite a fiery trail on my skin at any hour of the day. Especially now that it's back to its usual bristliness."

He rubs it against her cheek. "Any complaints?"

"None." She angles her head to kiss the corner of his mouth. "It's perfect."

When she helped him trim it this morning, she remembers that she felt oddly privileged to share this ritual with him.

They had stumbled into the shower after having gone for an early jog together. She had foregone her usual yoga for hopping into the roman cubicle with Lucas, and hadn't regretted her decision.

So that's how Lucas Blake achieves his signature look, she teased.

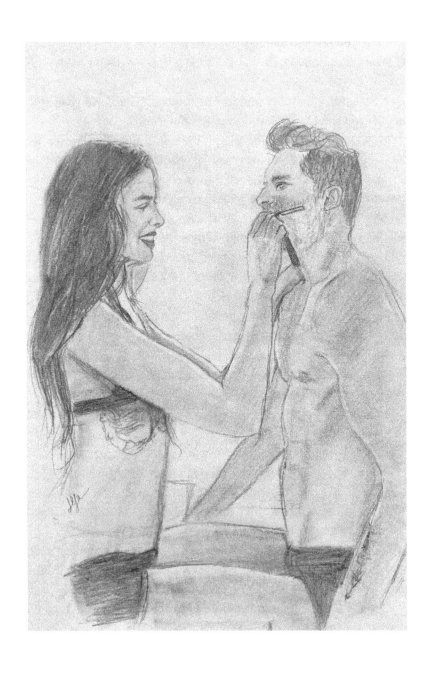

She was sitting on the counter wearing nothing else than a black bra with matching shorties as Lucas was standing between her parted legs in only his bermudas.

He let out a snort, opening up the tin of shaving cream. *He also used to put lots of gel in his hair to tame it.*

She wet the brush under the warm stream of water from the faucet. *He won't anymore?*

Maybe he doesn't feel like it as much. He shrugged, putting the cream on the counter. *He thought it was giving him a more professional look, but maybe he can do without.*

She shook off excess water. *You certainly won't hear me complain about it, and Sabrina would agree that it's beautiful when untamed.* She ran the bristles into the shaving cream in the tin. *Although the world might not be ready for the awesomeness of it.*

He stared at how she dexterously handled his shaving brush as she started rubbing it in circular motions along his mandible. *How come you seem to have that much experience?*

She furrowed her eyebrows, concentrating on the task at hand. *You don't want to know.*

Oh, but I do want to know very much. He smiled cockily. *I think no subject is off limits between us, right?* He raised an amused eyebrow. *Were you a bearded woman for the circus, and—*

She cut him off. *Nathan was also very particular about his beard.*

He hummed, looking equally pleased and playful. *You have a type.*

I wouldn't say I have a type, but I do like a man with facial hair. She focused her attention on his cheeks with the brush. *It's not news to you, I think I've always been very clear about that fact.*

Mhmm. Judging by how you react to me exploring every inch of your flesh with my mouth, I think I have a good idea. He slid his palms up her legs. *I adore how it prompts you to comb through my hair more forcefully to bring me exactly where you want when I'm kissing the inside of your thighs on my way to—*

She interjected quickly. *Gotcha. You picked up on the fact that I love it.* She smiled coyly. *Guilty as charged.*

He mirrored her expression, clearly basking in her attention. *This is one of the most relaxing parts of shaving.* He breathed in. *Creating the lather. You're doing it wonderfully.*

Thank you. I'm glad you're enjoying it. She took her time to transition from his upper lip to his chin, smiling softly. *I like the tiny spots of white through your beard. I guess that you blame them on stress?* He hummed in approbation, and the second he tilted his head up to allow her better access, she smiled playfully. *Well, they're very cute. Plus, I now know your secret for driving me crazy. Your cream smells so good.* She pulled her bottom lip between her teeth. *The lemon and sage mixed with the shea butter is inebriating.*

He sounded determined. *No more than you.*

I would beg to disagree.

He seemingly decided to challenge her a little. *My shaving cream is hopefully not the only thing about me that drives you crazy.*

Obviously not. She curved a corner of her mouth upward. *Your annoying stubbornness is also a great trait you nurture.* She morphed her tone to a sweet murmur. *Your tendency to be able to make me want to fall into your arms every time you look at me is another.* She noticed how he swallowed slowly at her words, his thumbs starting to rub soothing patterns on her thighs. *Have I ever told you that the way your hands caress me makes me lose contact with reality?* She breathed out, briefly using her index finger to spread some more cream at a small spot below his ear. *That nobody except you ever felt like my perfect complement both physically and emotionally.* She put the brush back in a dish on the counter, reaching to scrape her nails over his abs as he tilted his head down to look at her. She locked eyes with him. *All of you drives me crazy, Luke.*

He sounded dead serious. *The feeling might very well be mutual, Rae.*

She chose to reorient the exchange a little. *What was your ex-girlfriend like?* She picked up his safety razor equipped with a brand new blade. *The one you had back at Liberty Cove.* She grinned teasingly. *You know, before you became CasaNova.*

CasaNova was also an alchemist and a spy. He stood up straighter. *A very complex individual, but I'll let your assumption about him being nothing other than promiscuous slide.*

How generous of you. She half-smiled. *I know my references. He was also a church cleric at some point. The irony.*

Of course I'm aware that you know your references, and I was kidding. He softly caressed the underside of her knees. *If you must know, my ex was quite tall, brunette, and with blue eyes. She was studying engineering.*

She beamed proudly. *So you also have a type.*

I would beg to disagree, too. He stayed still while she applied practiced gentle short strokes along his facial hair. *Everyone is different, and she didn't have the same effect on me as you do.* He glided his hands up so his fingertips sneaked underneath the hem of her panties. *She didn't have that softness in her eyes when peering into my gaze. Nor the glint illuminating the dark aqua freckles within the azure of her irises each time she talks about something she's passionate about.* Raven did her best to concentrate on following the grain as she was shaving. His smooth touch mixed with the tenderness in his voice was slowly making her melt. *Her laugh wasn't the kind of sound I want to hear on a loop because it brings me a pure discharge of serotonin every time I do.* She bit into her bottom lip, restraining herself from just crashing her mouth to his while his beard was only half-trimmed. She couldn't believe the affection in his tone. He bent down to whisper, *She didn't drive me mad with desire with the slightest touch.* Raven swiftly changed the blade's angle to not cut through his skin, sighing low. *Her kisses were not sending my mind into the most beautiful daze.* He got even closer, his hands grabbing her hips to bring her to him. *And when I was having sex with her, I didn't feel this indescribable sensation of elation and absoluteness.*

She blinked as she stuttered. *Lucas, I—*

He cut her off. *I think I'm slowly realizing that you're the only partner I had who has such an effect on me.* He reached to take hold of her wrist. *All that happened outside of us is inconsequential.*

She scanned his gaze, lowering the blade and putting it next to the brush on the counter. *You can't mean that. It's not—*

When he closed the gap between them to kiss her with all the sensuality he harbors, she moaned.

His fingers traced her spine as she flew her hands into his hair.

The subtle taste of his toothpaste on her tongue was pairing with the shaving cream on her lips to lace beautifully with the feeling of pure surrender taking over her whole body.

She was being steadily engulfed by his whole tenderness.

They had just gotten out of the shower a few minutes prior, but she was yearning to shove him back into it.

She wanted to throw all of their plans for the day out the window to stay tangled up in bed with him instead.

More than that, she wanted to never get out of her house ever again.

When he deftly unclasped her bra, he shifted his attention to her neck.

A split second later as he was cupping and kissing her breasts, she curled her hand into his belt buckle, and lost grip with reality.

Now feeling him draw aimless patterns on her belly is having a similar effect.

But his statement from just before they stumbled back into bed this morning is currently making rounds in her head. The way he casually heartfully confesses deep feelings in the most mundane moments is dizzying.

He says that he means it every time, but they're far away from their lives in New York. Thousands of miles away from their usual routines. They've been living in a small bubble, and maybe it is bound to implode as soon as they go back on the east coast.

They haven't addressed any of the big concerns she was having. *Is* having.

They haven't made it plain clear where they stand, and—

"I'm glad to hear," he murmurs into her skin. "I had to be presentable for our Temecula Valley escapade."

She tries to get her attention on anything else than the whirlwind taking hold of her brain. "You're lucky I had finished trimming your scruff this morning when we unexpectedly abandoned the shaving for more fun activities then."

"Was it truly unexpected?" He snorts softly. "I have a hard time not wanting you closer every time you're with me. I'm glad you chose me over yoga."

She drops her tone to a whisper at the memory flooding her mind. "It was nearly a yoga session taking that shower with you."

He hums, husky and low. "You're exquisitely flexible."

She places her hands on top of his. "As are you."

It's his turn to sigh, putting his chin on her shoulder. "You know, I wouldn't even have minded having uneven spots in my beard from the potentially incomplete shaving."

"For the record, I personally also wouldn't mind you letting it be a little longer than a three-day stubble, you know." She turned her head to nuzzle into his neck. "You do whatever feels good to you."

"Mmm." He smiled nostalgically. "When I was young, I was making fun of my uncle's mustache because I thought that facial hair was ugly." He laughs lightly. "Look at me now. Not being able to go without."

She half-smiles. "You could rock a mustache."

He sounds surprised. "You think?"

"Absolutely." She lays a gentle kiss on his pulse point, relishing in the slight coarseness of the very scruff they're discussing on her lips. "I already told you that you can make anything work. You're naturally handsome."

He lets his fingertips travel down to go dip under the thigh-high slit of her dress and onto her bare skin. "And you think the man who flirted with me earlier would've found me equally handsome if I had one?"

She involuntarily arches back into him. "Definitely."

"I have to admit that he was very attractive. I was flattered. I could've left you there during your call, and escaped with him." Lucas leans his head against her. "There was only one small problem."

"What's that?"

"I only have eyes for you," he says without hesitation, his voice deep and steady.

As she decides to close her eyes as the only answer, and let his words sink in, she clearly remembers that moment when they were entering the diner for a later lunch after having toured some wineries, and before going to the farmer's market.

Raven recalled that the family-owned restaurant had sustainable seafood, and a seasonal menu from a past visit at their Catalina Island location, which prompted Lucas to want to try it.

Just after stepping out of her car, her phone rang. The caller ID showed that it was Jun. Since Raven had called her earlier while Lucas was pressing fresh grapefruit juice, and ended up leaving a short voicemail because her friend was unavailable, she thought answering would be a good idea.

Jun and herself had been having trouble getting hold of each other since San Diego. This was a great opportunity to quickly catch-up.

So when she stopped dead in her tracks, she showed Lucas her phone screen.

Go ahead. Answer. He beamed, disentangling their fingers. *I'll go wait at the bar counter to give you some privacy.*

Thanks, babe. She hooked her index and middle fingers into the front pocket of his shorts to bring him to her. *I won't be long.*

He grabbed her hips, pulling her flush to him. *Anything you want me to order you?*

Surprise me?

He slid his hands down to her ass. *That can be dangerous.*

She brushed her nose along his. *I'm willing to take the risk.*

She kissed him slowly, lingering a little longer than she should've against his lips. When he took a step back, he flashed her a mellow smile before putting his hands in his pockets. *Tell Jun I said 'hi'.*

Raven smiled as he sauntered away, putting the phone to her ear. *Hey, Ju. It's good to finally be able to talk to you.*

Raven. Jun's voice was joyful. *I wondered if we would ever have the chance before you come back to New York. I swear Lucas is easier to reach than you. Plus, he didn't even want to tell me anything more than 'she's doing great' when I asked him about you last time.* While Raven was internally smiling at Lucas' permanent boundless consideration of her, Jun sounded suddenly inquisitive. *Actually, is it still Lucas or does he have a different title these days?*

Raven smiled knowingly, combing her fingers through her hair. *You know, I think the downside of this friendship is that we both know each other too well at this point.*

There was a clear playfulness in Jun's tone. *I am merely inquiring about the fact that if I need to call Lucas any other title like 'boyfriend' or 'lover', as one of your best friends I should know.*

She tried to turn the tables on her friend as a diversion. *What about Gary? How was your date? We haven't talked since, and—*

The crisis manager cut her off. *Don't change topics. This is about you and Lucas Blake.* She was very solemn. *Did anything happen between you two? Did you finally come to—*

Raven interjected. *I did.* She hummed, biting into her bottom lip. *I have come multiple times since Sunday if you must know.*

Jun laughed soundly. *I love you, Raven.* There was a renewed twinge of amusement in her intonation. *Only you are able to announce that you're sleeping with a man you're probably falling for with an innuendo.*

It's been phenomenal, Ju. She inhaled steadily, quickly going back to her previous strategy to not address her potential emotions. *But really, what about Gary?*

You don't want to talk about how scared you are at the prospect of feeling something genuine for the first time in ages? Fine. But you're not off the hook, girl. It was Jun's turn to let out a breath, making Raven understand that they would definitely have that conversation later. Knowing them, it would probably take place as soon as they'd physically find each other in the same room. *It went well with Gary. We're going to take things slow, and I will hopefully meet his son very soon. I told him that I am all in. I want this relationship to work.* She pauses for a beat before mildly admitting, *He said that he loves me, Raven.*

That's amazing! She beamed. *I'm so happy for you.*

We'll see how everything goes from here, but it's certainly a big, and important step. I'm very happy, the manager stated smoothly. *But I wanted to talk to you about something else. Wow Gabriel Smith, huh?* She let out a disheartened laugh. *When I got confirmation that he was working with Cameron Wallace, I had to let Lucas know asap. I hope it didn't cause trouble between you two. I know you hadn't told him about all that went down at court, and—*

Raven interrupted her before she could blame herself for no reason. *It's all good. He knew by the time you broke the news to him.* She started walking away from her car. *We had chatted about the reason behind my resignation, and he even knows the whole Nathan story by now.*

Mm. Pillow talk is quite effective, I see.

You're hilarious. It wasn't just pillow talk. Raven smiled absent-mindedly. There was no escaping Jun digging deeper. *And it's not only because I'm having sex with him that I'm opening up. Talking with him about anything is so very natural under all circumstances, it's bewildering.*

So you've said. Ju hummed knowingly. *You're sure you don't want to have the feelings discussion now? I got time, you know.*

No. Raven stayed resolute. *With Lucas, we agreed that we were going to see where this leads between us. Being in San Diego is just making things probably more perfect than they would be under normal circumstances.*

You mean in New York? When he'll go back to his job that you despise, and you'll take up my offer?

Even through the joke about the job offer, Raven could hear her friend be extra serious. She knew that it's also a big part of her inner questioning that she can't escape.

She chose to be honest, and tell Jun a little more than she initially wanted to.

I don't despise his job per se. I just see the pattern because I've been there myself, I guess. Helping people who mostly profit from the system, and who are acting shadily.

Was this part of what made it into the pillow talk?

Partly. She shrugged, approaching the restaurant. *But I haven't told him about those concerns I have.* She bit nervously into her bottom lip. *Because he feels like everything I ever wanted, Ju. If we really try to build something together, construct some kind of future, I...*

She trailed off purposely, not wanting to go any further.

Jun picked up on it. *Here it is.*

You're good at this. She chuckled. *You would've been a marvelous lawyer. Interrogating people is your forte.* She stopped to look around, identifying the outside bar in the distance. *I saw you coming though,* she teased. *So don't flatter yourself too much. I decided to go there on my own.*

Oh, I'm aware. Jun laughed cooly. *Raven Collins would never give away information she doesn't want to.* She instantly carried on the conversation with other topics, knowing Raven enough to be aware that she wouldn't share more. *What about Haddy and Zoe? How are they? Do they like Lucas?*

They appreciate him very much. Raven smiled as she saw Lucas talking with a tall athletic golden-haired man at the counter. *They even said we needed to throw one of your signature beach parties with all of us.*

That would be fun! Jun was cheerful. *I should book some vacation and go back to San Diego soon. I'd love that. I could maybe even ask Gary if he wants to join.*

I'm sure he'd love to see that side of you.

Like Lucas is loving yours? her friend supplied merrily. *You're a California girl through and through, Raven. You shine brighter than every star up there when you're back home.*

Mmm. She dismissed the comment, answering one of the previous questions instead. *Other than that, Haddy and Zoe have been hanging in there, but it's not easy with the looming diagnosis, and all the uncertainty.* She half-smiled at Lucas patting the man's bicep while chatting with him. *But you know them; they look unbreakable despite the hurdles. I saw how difficult it was for them, but they are strong for each other. It's beautiful to see.*

I'm glad to hear it. A clear smile could be discerned through Jun's speech. *They've always been such a supportive couple. I hope they get some good or at least encouraging news soon.*

Me, too. She oriented herself toward the entrance. *So, what are you up to today? Any big plans? I'm going to go grab a bite as soon as I hang up our call. We've decided to spend some time in wine county today.*

That's awesome. Please drink some Chardonnay for me. Man, I really need to go to the west coast soon. The crisis manager exhaled steadily. *I just need to go check up Lucas' place later. I wanted to tell you guys that I dug deeper into Mister Smith's finances today. From what I saw from my quick look into it, he seems to be dealing with a bunch of high profile businesses, but also shell companies. Add a couple of offshore accounts and you get my conclusion: that can't be good.* She suddenly sounded more preoccupied. *Seeing that, I double-checked everything, and was able to trace some of those companies Smith is in business with to Wallace.*

Raven hummed inattentively while following her friend's rationale. *That strengthens the link between them. Those guys love to deal with big money, but also require for most of it to be untraceable in offshore accounts—the more of those, the better—for future business.*

Yeah. Jun's tone was steady. *Lucas wanted me to look into it because he said there's talks around the city about some big transaction needing to happen soon. He thinks Smith might be involved, but there's none of Wallace's assets that fit that bill. Plus, I went through a bunch of recordings from Smith's phone that Graham was able to give me access to, and he never discusses with Wallace about any deal.*

Maybe that huge deal investment bankers are talking about has nothing to do with either Wallace or Smith, but I would bet those two are involved somehow. Raven switched into work-mode effortlessly. *Smith sounds too eager to sign into Lucas' client list for it to not be linked. He also specifically told Luke he wanted to acquire some assets as soon as he could. I don't believe in coincidences during a perfect storm.* She paced around as the wheels in her head kept turning. *You know, they froze Wallace's bank accounts and assets as soon as he got arrested for money laundering. It's standard procedure.*

What are you trying to say?

That if something needs to be transferred to someone else, it won't be from Wallace himself. I'm sure of it. Raven kept her focus as too many past memories flooded her mind. *Check into his children and his wife.*

Why?

Wallace once told me that he knew he was going to get arrested. He got wind of it through some contacts in law enforcement. The lawyer furrowed her eyebrows. *It wouldn't surprise me that he transferred some of his assets to his family. Him and his wife are close from what I gathered. They are even business partners. I indulged in some cognitive dissonance to not think too much about it, but he clearly has a scheme going on with her. Run a thorough background check on Veronica Petrocceli. I have a feeling you'll find something.*

Jun sounded hesitant. *The biggest donor of the children's hospital downtown?*

Yeah. She clenched her jaw slightly. *You know what the worst part is? Veronica is someone who is involved in lots of charity work around town. She classed herself up from the young stereotypical local woman a long time ago. She always kept her maiden name to have a strong and independent public image for their business with Wallace. Girls and women alike often look up to her. They aspire to be like her, and how influential she is. Just thinking about the fact that she could actively participate in recruiting some of them for their trafficking makes me sick, I—*

Her friend interjected rapidly. *Woah. Don't blame yourself, Raven. There's nothing you could've done to stop this.* She sounded comforting. *Cameron Wallace was not an active client of yours before his trial, and you resigned as soon as he appeared as the monster he is. He lost the best defense attorney in New York, that's a big punishment in my book. He'll lose, I'm certain of it.*

Thanks for the vote of confidence. I feel like after those testimonies, he must know that his hours are counted. She pinched the bridge of her nose, unable to calm down her train of thought. *Maybe that's why he would like to transfer assets to Smith so Smith can manage them.*

Veronica couldn't?

She could. But from what I gathered she's not involved in the nitty gritty of the business. She is the front woman, and has a clean public image. She frowned. Plus, spousal privilege means that she can't be forced to testify against him. It's honestly brilliant if he gave her the assets he'd like to transfer.

I'll look into it. Jun became more relaxed. *I knew having you on board would come in handy.*

Mmm. Raven went back to striding in the direction of the front door. She suddenly got an idea. *You could also look into one Morgan Shaw. He is very close to Cameron Wallace. He often takes care of the dirty work from what I heard between the branches. If Smith and Wallace are doing business, Shaw could very well be involved, too. Maybe he could even be the one putting the blackmail into action.*

Brilliant. Thanks for the tips. I'll take a look.

Please keep me posted.

I will. Her friend sounded joyous. *I'll let you go have lunch now.*

Thank you. Don't hesitate to reach out. I'll be more responsive, I swear.

Before either of them had time to hang up, Jun added, *Oh, and don't forget to not bury what you're potentially feeling for too long. You know it's going to come back to bite you if you do.*

Raven snaps her eyes back open, her mind reeling at the souvenir.

She rapidly realizes that she's still in Lucas' embrace on the beach, but the last words of her friend during their conversation are coming back to haunt her.

Is she really falling for Lucas? It's not as if she never entertained the questioning by herself. She just usually pushes it very far in the back of her head before it has any time to take hold.

Before she has any occasion to come to a conclusion.

She knows the signs. She knows that wanting all the intimacy, deep conversations, and soft moments alongside the physical craving is a recipe for disaster.

If she doesn't want feelings to be involved in whatever is going on between Lucas and herself, all those things shouldn't even be part of the equation.

She curls her hand around his knee, tracing aimless patterns on his skin with her thumb. Whatever she's drawing, it's as chaotic as what's going on inside her psyche.

His unvarying breathing is still working wonders to calm her down. She concentrates on it.

On him.

She has to reply something to his latest statement.

Maybe addressing some of it could work. Everything is indeed natural with Lucas. Those topics shouldn't be any different.

Should they?

One thing is for sure, she'll never know if she doesn't—

She's clearly been silent a bit too long. Lucas seemingly chose to pick a new topic of conversation. "It's Connor's birthday soon. Would you like to accompany me to the festivities?"

"Really?" She swallows slowly, doing her best to keep her recent thought process in check. "You want me to meet your best friend's son?"

"Yeah." He tightens his hold around her middle a little. "You went along well with Sab and Brooke, and I know we said we would see where this thing between us goes one step at a time, but I don't intend to go anywhere." He turns his head to press a kiss to her forehead. "I feel good with you, Raven. You bring me balance through the chaos. Having you with me for this celebration would mean a lot."

She rolls her bottom lip between her teeth. "I'm enough for balancing entropy?"

He hums low. "You are."

She scans his gaze. He also effortlessly has that effect on her. She feels in harmony with the world when she's with him.

There's no use arguing with him any further. Truth is, she'd love to accompany him to Connor's birthday. "Okay." She smiles shyly. "It'll be my honor to go."

"You have no idea how happy you just made me." He goes back to looking at the horizon in front of them, reflecting. "Since he loves to play football with me, and is a big fan, I was thinking of offering him tickets to the next big game."

"Really? How would you even..." She leans back to stare at him in slight disbelief. "Tickets are mostly distributed by the league, and the teams themselves. They even got rid of the lottery for fans not long ago. It's ultra difficult to—"

He cuts her off to explain. "I have a client who is very close to the league. I know he could get me tickets."

"At which cost though?" She frowns. "Surely this client of yours will want something in return."

"I'm already managing his wallet." He stiffens a little. "A bunch of my clients are powerful people, and they sometimes like to treat me with the same consideration their families have."

Raven thinks it's of no use to confront him head on about his way of life that is making a comeback full force at the moment. It's an essential subject they'll definitely need to tackle, but not right now. Right now something else is more important. She steers the exchange back to Connor. "You don't necessarily have to go for a grand gesture, no?" She scans his gaze. "What's his favorite team?"

Lucas smiles defiantly. "What's your guess?"

"The local team?"

"Spot on."

"Who knows, maybe they won't even make it to the finale!" She idly trails her fingers up his leg. "Maybe just regular tickets for one of their games would be a great gift for him? I'm sure he would love it."

"True." His expression morphs to a more profound one. "I used to want to bring him to a game in New York at some point, but I got too busy."

"Maybe you could try getting tickets for a NY-Boston game in the Big Apple?" She raises an inquisitive eyebrow. "Connor could stay with you for a few days if time permits, and—"

He lights up. "That's brilliant."

"Oh, you're not against having a kid in your penthouse?" she supplies teasingly.

"I've never been against it ever." He peers into her eyes, green reflecting on sparkly emerald in the pale moonlight. "You know, you just made me notice that ever since I'm making good money, and have made a name for myself, I want to make the ones closest to me benefit from it."

"Which is all in your honor. It speaks tons about the person you are." She smiles coyly at him. "But I think people also love you for who you are deep down. Not your money or what it can buy them. Connor will love you no matter what."

"You're right. I should probably remind myself of that more often." He takes a deep breath. "I feel like it might be because I didn't have much when I was young. When we were going to visit my mom's family abroad it was because her cousins from Miami were paying for the plane tickets, and coming with us." He sounds sheepish. "Every little thing we were able to buy that wasn't the bare essentials we had to save for months to get it." He reaches up to slide a hand on the side of her face, starting toying with a loose strand of her hair as he keeps recollecting. "I am well aware of the value of things. I remember that one Christmas after I had gotten my first job when I was in high school. I was helping my mom pay the rent and the groceries while I was only working fifteen hours per week. But I was somehow convinced I would be able to save enough money to get my sister the first item on her wish list."

Raven leans into his touch. "What was it?"

"She wanted one of those portable gaming consoles." He smiles something mellow at her. "By the time December came around, I didn't have enough to buy her one. I ended up buying her a plush of her favorite gaming character instead." His expression changes to being more shy. "I thought that if she couldn't play the game, she could at least have a tiny part of it. You should've seen her smile when she opened the box, Raven. It was as if I had given her the moon. She still has that plush to this day."

"That's incredibly thoughtful of you." Raven angles her head to lay a kiss on his wrist. "Not that it surprises me." She curls her hand around his forearm, leaning forward to brush her nose along his. "You have the biggest heart, Luke. It's beautiful to witness. I consider myself lucky that you allow me to see that side of you."

He lets out a small laugh. "I usually hide it a little, huh?"

"I think you do. Just a tiny bit." She half-smiles. "I get it though. It's part of the work persona. We often build fortresses around ourselves for protection." She combs her fingers through his hair. "But all those sides of you are beautiful. They make you who you are." She massages his scalp gently. "The passionate, resilient, kind, and tender man you are." She brushes her lips on his. "Let it all shine, babe."

She feels his whole body relax at her words, and under her touch.

Not wanting to linger on the implications of her casually calling him 'babe' more and more, she kisses him sensually.

By the time she's completely drowning into him, the music distantly skips to a familiar pop beat.

Raven kneels between his parted legs, cradling his head, and becoming more insistent.

The instant she senses his hands slide down to her ass, she moans deep into his mouth.

He instantly groans in response.

She also doesn't want to linger on the fact that every time he kisses her it feels as if he's dedicating his whole being to her, and her only. He kisses her like he truly doesn't care about the whole world outside their bubble when she's pressed against him like this.

It's fucking staggering.

Actions speak louder than words, they say, and for all the heartfelt confessions he made lately, Lucas brings them to life. He makes them transcend the heedlessness of literacy.

Each time she finds herself in his presence, he makes her feel the truthfulness of them through all his reverence, and consideration. All his softness, and his intensity.

Air is sucked out of her lungs as the revelation dawns on her.

This.

This is re—

Lucas leans back, curling a hand around her throat smoothly, and sounding very solemn all of a sudden. "Rae, I think I'm—"

She can't help the snort that escapes her and interrupts his train of thought, upon identifying the song. "Sorry. It's just this tune. It's as if this specific pop singer is making a comeback in my life."

He listens for a second before joining her in chuckling. "Although it's not the tune to which you did a strip-tease, and you have no dare from Jun to honor, so no undressing this time."

She puts her forehead against his, listening to the first verse while raking her fingers through strands of his hair.

His fingertips slowly caress her jawline. "It's true, you know."

She scratches her nails into the short hair at the nape of his neck. "What's that?"

He defines her bottom lip with his thumb as he echoes the lyrics. "You're gorgeous without makeup."

She kisses the pad of his finger. "Yeah?"

His hum is husky and low. "Mhmm."

"You know that we put makeup on because it makes us feel good, right?" She smiles coyly. "Sometimes some give in to too much societal pressure that makes them overdo some plastic surgery and that's too bad, but, to me, at its core anything of the kind just spawns from the fact that everyone wants to feel good about themselves. It's not a straightforward equation. Women don't necessarily do it to attract people. They do it because they like how it makes them feel. I started putting on makeup when I was in high school because I loved how I looked with it. To me, the important thing is no matter what you do, do it for yourself. Not others."

"You're right. I had a conversation about it with my sister once. She thinks exactly like you, and I totally get your point. I was saying because to me you're gorgeous no matter what, and part of it comes from the self-confidence you exude that I adore so much. The fact that you're doing things like you want to, and that it makes you happy. You radiate well-being, and that's highly attractive paired with your personality." Lucas thinks further on what she just said. "You ever wondered what would've become of us if we had met back in college in another life? Or even while in high school?"

She rolls her bottom lip between her teeth. "Something tells me that I still wouldn't have been able to resist you."

He peers into her eyes. "Same."

She goes for blunt honesty. "I don't know what would've happened to our respective career paths, but what we have now..." She pulls away to flick her index finger between them to make her point. "This? I would've wanted more of this."

He kisses her softly. "I already told you; I'm right where I'm supposed to be."

She smiles into the kiss.

Lucas sneaks his hands underneath her top to rest on the small of her back.

As she arches into him, she deliberately ignores how the last lines sound uncannily close to reality. "You know, even if it's not the right song..." She pulls away, and gets up. "Or I don't have to honor any of Jun's dares..." She takes a few steps back. "I still feel like removing my clothes very slowly for you right now..." She takes hold of the hem of the hoodie. "And you want to know what the best part is?"

As she pulls it over her head, he stays put, gazing at her in awe. When she's done, she flips her hair on one side, smiling coyly at him as she starts dancing.

He keeps his eyes on her face. "Please enlighten me."

She sways lasciviously to the beat as she pulls on the waist string of her dress. "We're alone on the beach."

"We are," he breathes out, mesmerized.

As soon as her dress hangs open, she lets it slide down her arms while she performs her best baladi moves. The garment rapidly joins his hoodie in a puddle on the sand.

Lucas begins to get up, but she stops him by holding her hand in a stop motion between them. "Don't." He complies, inhaling deeply as she continues to bellydance lecherously. "We're alone, and I want you."

She reaches behind her as she makes her way back to him, her eyes never leaving his face. The minute she kneels in front of him once more, she deftly unclasps her bra as he instantly grabs her hips. She smirks as his stare gets lost in her cleavage, his pupils unmistakably dilating.

The effect he has on her is mystifying.

The way he looks at her will never fail to make a gentle heat pool low in her belly.

She dexterously removes her bra, and throws it away. "Which means that..." She brushes past the stubble on his cheek to go whisper in his ear, "I don't have to keep anything on this time." She slides her hands along his shoulders, sucking on his earlobe softly. "You always make me feel so good."

"You always do, too," he murmurs. "I wanted to join you just to feel you against me." He circles her rib cage, his thumbs grazing the underside of her breasts. "Feel you grind in sync with me. In my arms." He angles his head to nuzzle into the crook of her neck. The second she slightly shivers at a cool draft of wind, he pulls her closer to his chest. "It's cold out here tonight."

He's right, but she thinks it's invigorating.

She loves the pairing of his body heat quenching the chilliness of the breeze. She can feel herself responding to him in strides already as he trails kisses along her clavicle. She wants him to redefine every past souvenir she has of this beach so that he inhabits each corner of it every time she finds herself walking on its shores.

She toys with the hem of his t-shirt, placing an open mouthed kiss on his pulse point. "You can keep me warm, yeah?"

She hears him barely audibly *growl* in the small space between them as he puts his arms up in an invitation for her to remove his shirt.

She beams into his skin.

TWENTY

Thunderbolt

As Jun is riding the elevator up to Lucas' penthouse, she pockets her phone in her purple suit pants, nervously stomps her heel onto the tiles of the cabin, and straightens her matching jacket.

Her day has been hectic managing a couple of internal crises at her office, and she hasn't had time to check more into Gabriel Smith, Veronica Petrocceli and Morgan Shaw.

She still just took time to send a message to Gary to let him know that she would be home right after checking up on one of her client's apartments. She can't wait to be back home in SoHo to go change before spending the rest of the evening with him.

His son is with his grandparents, and when the driver texted her not long after she had talked to Raven, they agreed to get a nice dinner as well as go catch a movie afterwards.

She is hopeful that it will be a relaxing night in his company.

They hadn't had a lot of chances to do any of those mundane things before. Mostly because of Gary's constant fear of not wanting to get too involved. Now that their feelings are out in the open, she wishes to live more of those casual moments.

She also can't wait to finally meet his son.

Once I'm fully ready, and judge that it's the right time, Gary said.

Jun is very okay with that approach. She truly wants things to work out with Gary.

Her latest serious boyfriend dates back from when she had just moved to New York. She was certain going into that relationship that it was nothing for the long haul at the time, but one thing led to another, they still lasted for more than seven years.

Until he left her for one of his colleagues.

They sold the condo they had bought together, and went their separate ways. They tried to do it with as much respect and kindness they could both muster after having spent nearly a decade together.

She remembers she had some trouble getting over her ex at the time, but Gary appeared in her office one day for an interview, and her mind was overridden by how handsome he was. She figured that if her new driver was willing, they could have a little fun.

And that's exactly what they did for the past year and a half.

Through the amazing sex in various hotel rooms all over the east coast when visiting clients, and long hours spent traveling together, she learned to know Gary.

Really know him.

She didn't expect to end up feeling anything, but she did. And she has to admit that it's one of the most beautiful things that happened to her in her life so far.

She definitely never felt something as strong as she does for Gary with any of her past partners. The driver feels like he is the one she wants to spend the decades with. She's very down to Earth while he tends to daydream more often than not. He brings her some sense of relativity on every event they live through.

He's her perfect escape as well as her anchor.

Loving him was unexpected, but feelings have a way to sneak up on you when you least anticipate it.

She snorts quietly at her musings.

She's pretty certain that the exact same thing is happening to Raven at the moment. That is if it wasn't already in motion before. Lucas always sounded special from the very first instant her friend told her about him.

The acoustic version of a familiar song soon fills her ears, making her curve a corner of her mouth upward at the memories this brings her.

Raven and her used to sing off-key on it more than once—tipsy or not—when going through a rough patch. The lyrics recollecting about what one does or not in life, and how it can translate to stories shared when older always hit deep.

Jun hums the verse, letting her thoughts drift fully toward her friend in San Diego.

It was a nice surprise to finally be able to chat with Raven today. Jun has to be honest: she misses having her friend around in New York with her. She is very used to interacting with her mostly every day, and being able to message her any time she wants to go grab a bite at the end of the day.

As the lift stops, and the doors open at Lucas' floor, Jun steps out of it while she reflects on the fact that she'd really love to work with Raven.

Their previous exchange once again showed her that the lawyer would be an amazing addition to her team.

Plus, they work well together.

For the few times they unofficially collaborated before by exchanging ideas, their minds usually end up converging in beautiful ways.

They complement each other's thinking flawlessly. It's stimulating.

Through the years, Raven helped her multiple times to unstuck herself from a professional tricky situation she had to deal with regarding legal advice, and brainstorming sessions.

Likewise, the lawyer also used her company's services more than once to gather evidence or run background checks when her firm's investigator was otherwise occupied—or when she just didn't trust him with the task at hand.

Even if it won't be an easy path forward, she's happy that Raven quit her job, and is set on living by her ideals. Her friend deserves better than getting swallowed whole by an unforgiving system.

Jun recalls how Raven was excited to finally get into the big leagues when she started at her old firm. She thought she could make a real difference in the world.

What Jun noticed through the years was the opposite. Raven was more and more consumed by her work, trying to untangle herself from a treacherous web that was slowly taking over her personality, and dimming her spirits a little more each day.

Through it all, Raven remained combative.

The crisis manager thinks that it's probably this fierceness that always resided in her friend that allowed her to say 'enough is enough', slam the door, and not look back.

It's the same strength that Lucas, and everyone in her life, loves in her.

Lucas.

Raven seems to *live* since he walked back into her life. Jun was serious when she told her friend to not bury what she's feeling for the managing director.

Jun knows Raven. She knows she is falling hard for the man. It's honestly incredible to see.

She has never seen her friend be this affected by someone. The fact that she seems to not want to address the elephant in the room—also known as her concerns about his career and future path—is quite on brand though.

As a teenager, Raven was always very pragmatic, and determined. When her boyfriend in high school ghosted her without any explanations to the point where they ended up breaking up, she first tried to understand. However, as soon as she noticed that he wouldn't talk to anyone about his problems, she rapidly moved on.

There was a clear shortage of dialog from his side back then. Raven said she had no time to waste dealing with someone who didn't want to be helped. She was sad about the fact that her ex-boyfriend had pushed mostly everyone in his life away by closing himself off, but she didn't love him enough to fight for what they had.

At least that's how Jun filed it.

Then, years later, the opposite happened. The minute Raven realized she was ready to commit to Nathan, it was the closest to deep emotions that Jun ever saw her friend harbor. She confronted everything heads on with him, but she's the one who ultimately walked away because of the irreconcilable differences they were experiencing.

Raven was ready to fight for her couple that time. He wasn't. That's always terrifying. It crushed her. She indubitably doesn't want a repeat of that.

All in all, Jun is aware that Raven is not one for lack of communication. She dealt with that enough with her own parents that she clearly doesn't want to repeat the pattern. But she also knows that her friend can postpone the inevitable in an attempt at shielding herself from harm.

That's why she keeps pushing back the inevitable talk she needs to have with Lucas.

As she approaches Lucas' front door, she takes out the key he gave her from her ivory tote bag, still crooning.

Oh, the things Raven and herself went through individually and together during the course of this friendship so far.

Some of it will certainly make for great bedtime stories for their grandchildren one day.

Jun gets that her friend is scared, but Lucas sounds like he is equally as smitten by her than she is by him. Every time he talks to Jun about Raven, he has this undeniable softness in his tone that would make anyone swoon.

Raven has never been one to be easily swept off her feet. Jun is unsure she ever was to begin with. It doesn't mean that she's not falling for Lucas Blake. Jun is quite sure that, on the contrary, she very much is.

The crisis manager only wishes that they manage to have a heart to heart discussion about it sooner rather than later. Raven merits the very best this world has to offer, and if she thinks she can find it with Lucas, she shouldn't deny herself the happiness.

For now, Jun is set on checking up on her friend later. By tomorrow she should've had some time to dig more into everyone's business, and give Raven and Lucas some kind of update.

This whole case potentially involving powerful individuals dealing in human trafficking, money laundering, and highly illegal activities is making her head spin.

The more information she uncovers, the less she feels totally safe about all of it. Which is a first for her. Her usual cases don't implicate criminals. The stakes are definitely higher this time around.

Maybe Raven is more used than her to—

The second Jun finds herself in front of Lucas' home, she frowns.

The door is partly open.

That can't be right.

She pockets the key, and takes hold of the pepper spray in her bag. It looks to be exquisitely quiet on the other side, but she wants to account for any eventualities.

If someone is inside, pepper spray might not be enough. She better remember her kung-fu moves from when her Raven took some classes a year ago.

She mentally prepares herself as she slowly slides the door open with her foot, rapidly analyzing the lock which seems to have been dented.

She takes a step forward only to stop dead in her tracks at the sight in front of her upon setting foot in the entrance.

"Fuck," she curses under her breath, stiffening in the doorway.

A quick glance to take stock makes it undeniable: there's no one around, and Lucas' place has been ransacked.

His personal items are spread out everywhere.

Furniture has been moved, things have been toppled onto the floor, and even some frames are tilted on the walls.

It's a complete mess.

Someone was definitely looking for something here.

Jun never believed in coincidences. Especially not one such as this.

Maybe she'll need to reach out to Raven and Lucas sooner than planned, after all.

TO BE CONTINUED...

Breaking Patterns

Book Two of the Entropy Series
Excerpt

I f there's one thing Veronica Petrocelli is proud of, it's certainly her social status. She worked hard to get where she is today, and being in high spheres comes with a slew of advantages she is happy to bask in.

Sitting at a dinner table in her bright colored designer strapless dress and freshly cut asymmetric hair, she assesses her surroundings. The gala venue is classic. There's a sure art deco energy emanating from the decor, and the few hundreds of people currently listening to a speech about new treatment options for rare illnesses are dressed to the nines.

It's always been funny to her to witness how society is. It works in such a way that it's arguably too easy to look like a good person by performing well calculated gestures, and acting in accordance with some general conventions.

As she sips her porto slowly, she lets the rings she proudly wears on each of her right hand fingers catch the luminescence of the lighting in the ballroom. She quickly gets lost in thought at the prismatic dance they elicit while she slides her digits along the stem of her glass.

When she joined Gabriel at that fundraiser for orphan diseases a few weeks ago, she instantly saw an opportunity to solidify her reputation in a time of need. She quickly made the necessary arrangements to make a big contribution to the main institution in charge, and couldn't have been more pleased with the results.

She can remember her decision process clear as day.

She had to divert attention away from her husband's trial, and the shit show it had become. This was a perfect way to achieve that goal. No one can be against helping children and research, after all.

Contributing to good causes through otherwise questionable dealings, and nurturing a clean public image is definitely one of the most effective approaches to pull wool over someone's eyes.

The welcome she got since she arrived a few hours ago, and the conversations she entertained with potential new investors, are telling her that she succeeded well in her plan so far.

Despite the fact that her husband is currently facing money laundering charges, she is still able to flock around their investors, and raise money. It comes from the fact that she always dissociated herself from him and constructed her own image.

She smirks.

That's how the game is played.

Because to Veronica Petrocceli, life is a game where one makes its own rules to succeed, and only the most skilled can win.

Mostly everything is based on first impressions when the time comes to negotiate deals or expand business. One has to have multiple cards up its sleeves, and play them strategically to achieve their goals. Veronica always strived to take well calculated risks to make it happen.

She recalls that back when Cameron and her were in their early twenties, they were openly dreaming about making it into the big leagues. More than thirty years later, the road has been challenging, but they made it.

Somewhat.

The fact that he got caught because of a technicality still pisses her off way more than she allows herself to show. They triumphed in building a thriving empire, but it took decades to get where they are. He should've been more careful to protect what they worked hard to construct from the ground up. He's getting lazy. They sacrificed a lot to stand where they are now. He should remember it at every step he takes.

All their achievements are now shadowed slightly by his failure.

Maybe she should step up, and be more proactive in the transition.

She frowns. She has to repeat to herself that Cameron was doing a great job managing all of the complexity of their operations before that overlook, and she was more than happy to let him do so. She still has no desire to put her nose into that side of their business. The only thing that was essential to her was basking in the glamor while her husband relished in managing the nitty-gritty. It still is.

They grew into having separate, but extremely fulfilling lives, and one thing is for sure: they definitely both enjoyed their fortune to the max.

However, she can't shake off the thought that young Cameron Wallace would've never made such a rookie mistake.

He was way too charismatic, and focused on the task at hand to ever be swallowed whole by the system. He used to unwaveringly play to his strengths. Her husband was not one of the top dealers of the city for nothing. People naturally flocked to him because of his nonchalant attitude, and enticing physique. He could've sold sand to people living in the desert. That's how skilled he's always been at cutting deals.

When one of her friends introduced her to him to buy some recreational drugs, she didn't expect the instant connection they shared. What started out as a fun one-night stand with a guy she met in a nightclub led to them fleshing out a literal conglomerate. By morning, they had redone the world ten times over, and realized that they ultimately shared the same ideals. They might've even had a way to make them become reality.

Her stern expression morphs into a smile.

Her husband has always been highly charming, and driven. He's even become more so as the years went by. His piercing blue gaze pairs with his thick lush mid-length silver hair and shaved beard to communicate sure poise nowadays. She likes it a lot.

His assurance and stance are definitely what drew her to him back then. His unforgiving personality made her stay and crave more.

She can't dismiss the fact that coming from two dysfunctional families might have also helped them recognize themselves in each other.

Her parents wanted to put her in a box so she fled her home as soon as she finished high school.

His folks didn't give a damn about his existence.

She wanted to emancipate from them. He had to find a way to thrive on his own.

No wonder they both ended up chasing their dreams in odd places. It could've led them anywhere, but everything turned out for the best. It all went down according to plan.

Or close enough to.

She breathes in.

It has been far from easy to navigate their existences during those years. Although, every time her brain brings her back to where they both come from, she forces herself to put things into perspective.

They acted like true professionals to get to the top. They went through a lot of hurdles, but they are stronger for it.

It has been a long way up from being a street dealer and a barmaid with limitless ambition. The city streets saw Cameron and herself morph into one of the most powerful couples of the country out of sheer will.

They could've climbed the ladder of the criminal organization he was working for, but chose otherwise. Cameron wanted to end up like his wealthiest clients, and she yearned for the spotlight. She wanted for her name to mean something. To show the world that she succeeded by doing things her own way. Plus, they both didn't want to spend their lives watching their backs because of shady allegiances, and unpredictable competitors out for blood. Being respected in the streets can mean very little. Climbing to the top of that pyramid would've come with a slew of dangers they had no intention of facing. Through multiple coups and mutinies they saw some of Cameron's toughest adversaries fall before having any chance to make it.

They could do better. They were convinced there was a way to blend with high society. That pairing both worlds would be the best way to get an irreproachable reputation, make big bucks as well as elicit respect and fear into the hearts of their competitors.

She can distinctly recall how she carved out a whole strategy with her now husband to start a real estate empire. They had a perfect grasp of the underworld. They needed to blend in with the financial spheres. So she researched, observed, and developed a whole blueprint. Through well calculated savings, a solid proposal, and budding connections with some traders willing to take risks, they made their first acquisition. Their business only grew from there.

They easily agreed on the general terms: she was the good face of the operation, and he was the uncompromising tycoon.

The more prosperous they became, the more attention they got. The media, the industry, and financial markets were at their feet. People love second chances stories, and self-made entrepreneurs. They love to root for the underdogs. They made it their branding.

Everyone fell for it effortlessly.

And if they stayed on the lawful side of things at first to establish themselves as a legit venture, they expanded their operations to maximize profit soon enough. That's where Cameron's old contacts came in handy. Her husband took care of that side of the operations, and it suits her well. She found her niche taking care of their philanthropic ventures.

She never had any intention to manage all of her husband's assets herself. She has no time for that. She greatly enjoys being the polite front image of their business. She learned a lot from Cameron through the years about how to be her most enticing self, and is putting this charisma to good use.

That's where true power is to her.

Supporting worthy causes is a great smoke screen. It's also because of it that people end up eating in the palm of her hand, and swear their allegiance to her down the line. Without her activities, they wouldn't have recruited that many sponsors.

She is proud of the road traveled.

Although she is aware of what is going on behind the scenes, it's of no importance. If people are unable to elevate themselves above the rest, they don't deserve her attention.

She cackles to herself.

She's heard it all before. The whole discourse about being cruel to people and exploiting them for profit. Of acting like monsters for putting such an operation in place.

Truth is, she doesn't give a damn.

If people weren't smart enough to chase their dreams like Cameron and her did, it's not her problem. The world is a jungle. Only the strongest survive, and the smartest thrive. She's proud of every achievement, and wears a reminder at each of her digits.

Her rings are eternal trophies of her ascendancy.

The gold band on her index is the one that started it all.

As part of their trafficking scheme, people are forced to remove all personal belongings so as to not keep any visible ties from their former lives on them. She can recall how Cameron told her that the instant he saw that specific hammered band in the pile, he thought she'd like it. The fact that it belonged to one of the women who were part of the first batch of individuals that were recruited made her want to instantly put it on. To her, it was a tangible symbol of her success, and of others failures.

Veronica has no compassion for the weak.

If she battled her way up, anyone with enough guts can do it. Since then, three other small bands all different in sizes and shapes made their way onto her index to pair with the gold one. All come from different people that were either recruited or brought into the country on a deceptive promise that they would be awarded a fresh start.

People are gullible.

A fresh start doesn't necessarily mean freedom. Especially when owing the ones who arranged everything to make the move happen.

She toys with the signet ring on her middle finger inattentively.

That one belonged to an agent who wrongly thought she could make their drug dealings crumble down. The spy had nearly managed to infiltrate part of Cameron's reception team at the docks, but Veronica smelled something sketchy. As soon as she learned about the woman's true intentions, she had her mysteriously disappear, but asked Morgan to keep the ring. She wanted it as a reminder of her superiority over her enemies.

They're not clever enough to outsmart her. They never will be.

She grins maniacally as her eyes skim over the small simple blown glass one on her ring finger to land on the latest addition on her pinky finger.

That one is recent. The snake ring is embedded with hundreds of tiny diamonds glittering along the tongue of the reptile. Their latest investor is producing and trafficking those magnificent rocks. Some will call them blood diamonds, but who cares? They are incredibly profitable, and now make for an everlasting statement to her power.

It was a no-brainer to have this shape custom-made for her.

Snakes are cold-blooded, just like her. They can take their time to encircle their enemies, and revel in slowly absorbing their life essence. She recognizes herself a lot in those vipers.

She puts her glass back on the table, straightening in her seat, and nodding politely at the server putting her dessert in front of her. Her stare ends up lingering on her wedding band as soon as the waiter leaves.

Cameron and herself will forever have an undying respect between them, but love isn't there anymore. It hasn't been for years.

They are business partners, and they agreed to keep the front so that everything doesn't crumble down. She can't deny that they still connect sexually, and she is delighted every time they fuck, but she mostly lets him have his fun with others while he also accepts that she has her own adventures.

In that context, maybe she shouldn't be that frustrated about the opportunity of carrying their scheme herself with a new partner like Gabriel Smith.

Even if she worked with Cameron all these years, he got arrested.

Collaborators are meant to be interchangeable, right?

She picks up her dessert spoon as she squints her eyes in reflection.

Her relationship with her husband is odd, but it works. It should be all that matters. They depend on each other. They are two sides of the same coin. They know how the other functions, and they use their individual strengths to make their company advance. She wouldn't want to do this with anyone else than him.

When he's not around, a part of her is missing.

As she glares in front of her plate, she realizes that it's exactly the reason why she's enraged.

When Cameron transferred his most important assets to her, she dismissed it thinking that it was simply a failsafe they wouldn't have to use. He would be fine, and he would get out of his trial unscathed. He had one of the best lawyers in the city to take care of his case, after all. Their usual firm recommended her specifically because she was the best of the best for money laundering charges, they said. She was notorious for acquitting big names of such chargers in the past, and Cameron's go-to legal advisor affirmed that, out of all the attorneys out there, Raven Collins was his best chance to walk free.

What a mistake this was.

The prosecution unveiled the human trafficking part of their scheme, and Miss Collins abandoned Cameron.

To be fair, she also quit her firm in the process. She probably had enough of the pressure.

Veronica tightens her jaw. Raven Collins is just another weak link in the equation.

Following this, her husband refused to change lawyers in the middle of his trial, and stated that no one could outdo the damage that had been already done at the tribunal. He resigned himself to be convicted by the jury, and told her to speed things up with Gabriel so their business could continue to grow while he would be behind bars.

She grits her teeth.

This transaction should've already happened by now. The fact that it hasn't is a definite rock in her shoe.

She's always been satisfied with her investment bank for their stellar service in the past. This time it seems that Lucas Blake decided to be a gigantic pain in her ass.

She picked that bank for very specific reasons all those years ago. Keeping a distant eye on Mister Blake's career while dealing as a client within the same firm sounded like a great idea back then. Lucas was only an analyst, but climbed the ladder quickly enough to get where he stands today. It's a true feat.

{...}

Spring 2024.
Stay Tuned.

Printed in the USA
CPSIA information can be obtained
at www.ICGtesting.com
JSHW022106021223
52984JS00005B/114